# BRONC

## WOLVES OF IRON VALOR MC BOOK 1

DEX HAVEN

UNDER A TEXAS SKY PRESS

# DEDICATION

**Mean Man,**

*Thank you for being the Alpha who takes such good care of me. You've made this magical life more than I've ever hoped it could be. I wouldn't want to run with anyone else.*

# QUOTE

"A harmless man is not a good man. A good man is a very, very, dangerous man who has that under voluntary control.
-Peterson

# CONTENTS

# TRIGGER WARNINGS

All of my books contain graphic intimacy, and likely some kind of violence (sometimes sexual)—but always with a triumph-centered resolution. Guaranteed HEA. I don't believe in giving away the journey before it begins, but I believe in honoring your peace. If you know certain topics are hard for you, I encourage you to trust your instincts and read with care.

That being said, I thought it was important to note that there are a couple of scenes in Bronc that include non-consensual sex at the worst and dubious consent at best (most in terms of a twisted Alpha/omega dynamic). If this is painful or triggering for you in any context, I do not recommend you continue.

A complete list of warnings can be found on my website: www.dexhavenauthor.com

# Chapter 1

## Juliet

The leather strap of the large tote bit into my collarbone as I swept through the penthouse one final time. My ballet flats made no sound against the Carrara marble, a habit cultivated through years of learning how to disappear in plain sight. The scent of his cologne still lingered near the wet bar—Dior and cruelty masquerading as deliciousness.

Three white buttons glared up at me from the dressing room floor. My fingers twitched toward them before curling into fists. Let him find those. Let him wonder which of his thirty-seven custom shirts had flipped custom studs across his precious Italian tile.

The walk-in closet exhaled chilled air when I yanked open the door. Rows of silk whispered as I reached past them, my forearm brushing against a gown worth more than most people's cars. The twill blend of my practical gray slacks rubbed against my thighs as I knelt, safety pin pricking my hip where I'd altered the waistband myself last night.

"Passport," I muttered, fingertips finding the false back of the shoe rack. The embossed gold letters of my new name felt like braille under my thumb. "Julia Marie Harris." A bland American name, close enough to my own for me to remember, perfect for a woman who needed to disappear.

The kitchen timer I'd set dinged from the counter. Fourteen minutes until the doorman's shift change. My reflection in the Sub-Zero refrigerator showed a stranger. Dark hair pulled into a ball cap, honey blonde roots betraying my natural color beneath the black dye. I'd practiced the Texas accent for months between murmuring "y'all" into bathroom mirrors. I knew they'd never buy that, so I'd settled on a Chicago background. Midwest kids go to Columbia too.

Eight thousand dollars in twenties formed a brick inside the Ziploc bag taped behind the ice maker. My thumbnail split the Scotch tape cleanly, a skill honed by removing price tags from thrift store blouses before smuggling them with department store perfume. The bills smelled of mint and paranoia.

Fourteen months. Twenty-eight monthly transfers from grocery funds to a secret local bank account. Month in and month out of watching him sign corporate checks with his Montblanc, learning which oversight gaps even sharp accountants might miss. Today, that stolen knowledge would carry me halfway across the country in a bus seat sticky with other people's escape attempts.

The Louis Vuitton tote at the foot of our bed yawned open. His mother's wedding gift, now holding my beautiful lingerie, the only current clothing I truly feel comfortable taking. Nobody would see it. I also packed a few sweaters to wear against Amarillo's chilly August nights. I grabbed my sketchbooks as well. One that had blank pages waiting to be filled and the last two I'd finished. He'd broken all my charcoal pencils and chalks so that was fewer things to pack. I'd find an art store when I settled.

A strand of pearls slithered from its velvet coffin as I slammed the jewelry armoire shut. They pooled on the floor like a broken smile. My left earlobe throbbed with the memory of when he'd torn out a diamond stud last Christmas. "You want to look cheap?" he'd hissed, blood blooming on my collar. "I'll let you explain the hospital bill to your father." As though he'd take me to the hospital.

The burner phone vibrated against my sternum, tucked in the sports bra compressing breasts he'd called too large for my slight frame. One new email from Baucaum Iron Valor Custom Cycles verifying my arrival.

Seventeen hundred miles southwest, and thirty-nine long hours until I'll be free. A grease-stained office would become my sanctuary. I'd balance ledgers for men who reeked of motor oil instead of ambition, track parts inventories instead of lies. When they asked why a Chicago number cruncher wanted to hide in the Texas panhandle, I'd tell them I'd recently lost my fiancé and wanted a new start. Not entirely a lie.

The wall safe behind the Rothko painting sighed open at my third attempt. His birthday, our anniversary, his golf handicap—all combinations I'd tried over the years. Turned out the bastard used his first yacht's length: 62.37. The stack of hundreds left a paper cut on my index finger. I licked iron from my skin as pulled it free from its once secure hiding place. So many ill-gotten dollars, now in my hands.

My palms flattened against the cool glass of the living room windows. Forty-three floors below, yellow cabs swarm like angry hornets. In just under two days, I'd be squinting at prairie grass through Greyhound windows, the horizon stretched taut as a drumhead. Texas wouldn't care about my trust fund pedigree or the way Park Avenue hostesses used to compliment my "exotic" bone structure.

The thermostat read 68°F—always 68°, because he liked seeing goosebumps rise on bare flesh. I cranked it to 80° before leaving, a petty rebellion that would cost him $378 in excess utilities. Small victories.

Three burner phones lay disassembled on the Carrara countertop. My thumbnail pried open the fourth's battery compartment, the plastic casing still warm from four hours tucked between my thighs during final packing. Messages blinked in green text bubbles—code phrases assembled over fourteen months of grocery store messages hiding behind produce stands and workout room Wi-Fi.

*Margarita mix recipe?*

*Confirmed. Package arrives Thursday.*

*Don't forget to salt the rim of the glass!*

I deleted each thread with surgical precision. The SIM card snapped between my molars, bitter silicone coating my tongue. When the last device joined its siblings in the trash chute, I scrubbed my hands raw under scalding water. Steamed mirrors couldn't fog away the paranoia itching beneath my collarbones. I didn't want Harrison finding out my source of new ID anymore than I wanted her strange Bratva father knowing she helped me. Erase every trace of our friendship. Every trail of our interactions.

I stared at the leather duffel at the foot of the bed for the eighteenth time that hour, my stomach twisting like one of Harrison's cursed neckties. Early afternoon sun bled through floor-to-ceiling windows, painting our penthouse in guilty pinks. Our penthouse. Not for much longer.

The burner phone in my back pocket buzzed—three short bursts, our old college code.

"Lucia," I breathed, thumb hovering over accept. Letting her in might crack this fragile resolve.

I answered anyway.

"Kotyonok," came the smoky laugh I'd missed like oxygen, syllables rounder than Midwestern vowels ought to be after twelve years stateside. "Tell me you burned that hideous cashmere scarf he bought you."

My knuckle flew to my mouth, stifling something between a sob and a snort. "You're checking on scarves? Not say... whether Interpol's raiding JFK?"

"Pfah! Passport's cleaner than my cousin's vodka still—Julia Marie Harris now has six Whole Foods coupons and two parking tickets in Amarillo." A lighter clicked on her end. "But you'll still dress like someone who owns art galleries, da? Terrible camouflage."

The sound of her exhale curled warm in my ear despite the miles between New York and whatever Bratva-owned warehouse she was holed up in this week. I traced the forged birth certificate peeking from my bag—thick cardstock that smelled faintly of her father's cigars and promises kept in blood oaths rather than ink.

"Promise me something," she said suddenly serious, those four words laced with steel wool grit that scrubbed away college sisterhood. "When he comes looking—and moy dorogoy, that man doesn't like to lose. You vanish like smoke through his fingers." Paper rustled; maps unfolding perhaps, or money changing hands nearby. "Use every drop I taught you."

It was time I got to the station according to plan B-7b scribbled in her blocky Cyrillic handwriting last June over whiskey sours with expiry dates tattooed across contingency plans...

"Lucia—"

"Go," she cut me off gently as brakes squealed seventeen floors below us both hearing sirens where there were none yet. "Be ordinary woman who picks ugly ceramic roosters at thrift stores now, yes?" Her smile traveled through satellites. "And text when you reach Amarillo so I know which fools not kill if you don't"

The line died first like she always did, leaving me with static worse than silence.

Marble floors leached warmth through my socks as I made the final sweep. Crystal decanters threw prismatic daggers across the breakfast nook where he'd shattered a Waterford tumbler last Thanksgiving. My hip still carried the faint mark from where he'd shoved me into the Sub-Zero, punishment for suggesting we donate to a food bank instead of pretending to host another "fundraiser" where I knew the money would go directly into his bank account.

The foyer clock ticked through its Westminster chimes. 12:00 p.m. Flight risk window closing. My tote slumped against the Biedermeier console, pocket gaping where I'd torn out the GPS-tracked luggage tag. Through arched windows, Manhattan sprawled like a circuit board—every blinking light a potential witness.

I touched the wall where his fist had left a hairline crack in the Venetian plaster. Two years of learning which textures muffled footsteps (Persian rugs), which surfaces hid fingerprints (brushed nickel), which silences meant he was counting pills in the study. The click of my keycard against the sensor pierced the stillness like a pistol cocking.

At the threshold, I pressed my forehead against the door-frame we'd brought back from Versailles. The carved oak left indentations in my skin. Two years of memorizing which floor-boards creaked, which wine glasses rang at specific frequencies, which silences meant danger. My keycard hovered above the sensor.

"Good afternoon, Ms. Bettencourt," the elevator AI chimed. I stared at my distorted reflection in the brass doors—a raven haired ghost in last season's trench coat and ball cap. When the car hit the lobby, I walked past the concierge without meeting his eyes, my large tote pulling at the collar bone he'd broken last Christmas.

"Heading out, Ms. Bettencourt?"

The concierge's voice slithered up my spine as the elevator doors parted. My gloved hand tightened around tote's strap.

"Just returning some library books." The lie flowed smoother than the South African syrah he'd force-fed me at our engagement party. "Harrison prefers physical copies."

Mario's gaze lingered on my ball cap. I *never* wore a ball cap. His nostrils flared. Whether at my drugstore perfume or the sweat blooming beneath my polyester blend turtleneck, I couldn't tell.

"Shall I schedule the Escalade?"

"He's sending a private driver."

The lobby's black lacquer doors swung open on a gust of diesel-tainted air. I stepped into the concrete canyon, my shadow stretching gaunt across Fifth Avenue. Somewhere beyond the sulfur-yellow haze, a Greyhound idled at Port Authority—its plastic seats and rattling windows my chariot to oblivion.

The trench coat's belt dug into my ribs as I merged with the afternoon crowd. Every man's shoulder bump became his hand on my neck. Every shouted cellphone conversation his slurred threats. By the time the subway grate blew hot garbage breath through my makeshift bangs, I was running.

Chipped sapphire tiles announced the E train's approach. A teenager in Air Jordans eyed my tote. I clutched the burner phone's corpse in my pocket, plastic shards biting into my palm's flesh. When the downtown local screeched into the station, I let three cars pass before boarding.

Between 42nd and 34th Streets, I transformed from Upper East Side trophy wife to middle-aged tourist to whatever feral creature would emerge in Amarillo.

The bus terminal's fluorescent lights exposed more than the Penn Station mob. I kept my chin tilted at precisely fifteen degrees—the angle security cameras rarely captured. Ticket machines whirred objections to crumpled twenties fed sideways. Behind bulletproof glass, a clerk with spiderweb eyelashes snorted.

"One-way to Amarillo?"

Her acrylic nails clacked the keyboard. "Got family out there?"

"Something like that."

The Port Authority's flickering fluorescents turned every face into a suspect. I wove through bodies smelling of stale pretzels and desperation, my heavy tote bumping against hip bones still slightly bruised from last month's "lesson." A toddler's ice cream cone smeared across my white sneakers, a vanilla bloodstain on synthetic leather. Good. More camouflage.

"Amarillo, 3:15," barked a voice through crackling speakers. My new name tasted sour on my tongue when the ticket clerk demanded identification. Julia Harris from Newark smiled up from a library card.

"Transfer in St. Louis?" The clerk's nicotine thumb dented my precious ticket.

I nodded, throat tight. Every syllable risked exposure. "Final destination's Amarillo." Lie nesting within lie—Dairyville didn't merit printed destinations.

Two men in Rangers caps lingered near Gate 22. Not his build, not his walk, but the way they scanned the crowd tightened my bladder. I bought burnt coffee from a kiosk, watching their reflections in the stainless steel napkin dispenser. Three sugars stirred clockwise—counting seconds until boarding.

I shouldn't be worried. He wouldn't have missed me yet. It's his mistress night. He'd take her to whatever sex club they went to on Tuesdays. His discovery wouldn't happen 'til he got home after two in the morning.

A janitor's cart blocked the women's restroom. Strategic accident or surveillance tactic? I veered toward the family bathroom, lock clicking like a cocked pistol behind me.

The mirror confirmed what security cameras would see: thrift store pants, Walmart turtleneck swallowing my neck, harsh dye job erasing the woman who once lunched at Per Se. My fingers trembled applying lipstick—Maybelline's "Toast of New York" replaced by "Barely Blushing." The color of forgettability.

Boarding calls echoed. I timed my emergence to blend behind a church group hauling Bibles and bassinets. Their rendition of "Blessed Assurance" drowned fear.

"Ma'am?" A bus driver's flashlight raked my face. "Ticket stub."

The paper stuck to my palm sweat. He squinted at fresh ink. No smudges, no hesitations. Clean escape requires clean documentation.

"Window or aisle?"

"Window." Always window. Only one side available to grab.

The vinyl seat groaned beneath me, cracked leather breathing out decades of dead skin cells. I wedged my tote on my lap between me and the side of the bus. To the right, a grandmother shelled peanuts into plastic bags, salt crystals spraying my forearm.

Engines coughed to life. Across the aisle, a teenager's Air Pods leaked tinny trap music. I counted exits—two front, one rear, windows rated for emergency egress. Plan A: stay vigilant. Plan B: ballpoint pen to the jugular.

As we merged onto the Lincoln Tunnel helix, Manhattan's skyline pierced the fog like accusatory fingers. My last glimpse of our penthouse, forty-two floors of electrochromic glass where, by morning, he'd likely smash the Baccarat decanters. Let him choke on shattered crystal.

Darkness swallowed us whole. The tunnel's tiled throat vibrated with secrets. Someone's phone played a TikTok dance tutorial. Peanut shells crunched. A trucker guy in front of me ordered a pepperoni Hot Pocket from the onboard microwave.

I unzipped my duffel's secret compartment, fingertips brushing laminated certificates. CPA license issued to Julia Harris. Notarized transcripts from Columbia where I'd graduated before I'd been sold to Harrison Hastings. I took extension courses to stay on top of changing laws during chemo rounds—his sister's chemo, my alibi days.

Mr. Liam Baucaum's email burned behind my eyelids: *Need someone discreet for ledger work. Cash basis.* Discreet meant possibly criminal. Criminal meant untraceable. Perfect.

Trucker guy belched meat-scented fog. Grandma offered peanuts. I declined with a headshake, mouthing *allergy* while calculating how far my remaining money will go in Texas. Protein bars were tossed into my tote, eighteen day's rations if things went sideways.

Newark's industrial wastelands streamed by. Factories pumping carcinogens into the rain-slick air. I practiced smiling in the greasy window reflection. Not too eager, not too sharp. Just hungry enough to take shit, competent enough to balance books for bikers.

The woman behind me argued with Medicaid. "...yes, the lesions are back..." Her resignation tasted like my mother's words when she informed me of my engagement to Harrison.

At 11:47 p.m., when we'd made St. Louis, the driver announced this was our transfer. I followed Grandma to the to the terminal. There, I bought a Lotto ticket, then counted and recounted the change. Clearly, the look on my face told my story.

"Running from something?" She gestured to my wrinkled Benjamins.

"Toward," I answered with a shrug, blowing my bangs.

The parking lot's lights turned everyone jaundiced. Truckers compared CB radios. A meth-eyed teenager hawked bootleg Jordans from a garbage bag. We'd be getting on another bus after what was the equivalent of a layover. An hour later, we were back on the road.

The Greyhound's diesel growl vibrated through my molars as we merged onto I-76. My thumbnail picked at the vinyl seat's split seam, counting each exposed spring coil like rosary beads. The shiny white St. Louis arch loomed in the distance.

I'd taken my seat by the window, my mind drifting as the scenery flew by. I tore a page from my sketchbook and took out a pen. Before I realized it, I'd sketched a black wolf standing along a ridge, full moon in the sky. Odd. He was looking right at me. Through me. I did that sometimes. Just started sketching. Let the pencil take me where it wanted to go. A handsome wolf wanted to say hello today.

We made different stops here and there, Tulsa, I think, maybe Oklahoma City. Sleep finally took me and when I awoke, the bus engine hummed like a nervous heartbeat beneath my thighs as Amarillo's city limits sign blurred past. I pressed my forehead to the cool glass. New York's ghosts dissolved in the rearview—cracked crystal decanters, his monogrammed cufflinks glinting like fangs in low light, all shrinking beneath Texas dust. My new driver's license burned in my sweater pocket. *Julia Harris.*

A toddler kicked my seatback in rhythm with my pulse. His mother mouthed *sorry* through the headrest crack, unaware my smile was rehearsed through years of charity galas. I'd groomed that smile for shareholders and ER nurses alike—once when he dislocated my shoulder, shoving me into an Italian marble staircase railing. "Clumsy," he'd sighed to the patrons attending the art exhibition, thumb rubbing circles over my wrist bone. Always so tender in public. My parents promised me to him when I turned 23, shortly after I'd graduated from Columbia. His family, Wall Street royalty, of course. Things were fine for the first few months. Then his temper would flare. I tried to tell my mother. She told me he was in a high pressure business. I needed to exercise patience. His family and my family owned each other. So *he* owned *me.*

Outside, oil rigs nodded like iron stallions guarding the plains. The Greyhound smelled of diesel and microwaved burritos instead of his Acqua di Parma cologne. No pearls strangled my throat today—just sweat and the brush of my new bangs touching my lashes.

The Iron Valor's crumpled job offer crinkled in my fist beneath my tote, emailed through three VPNs from a burner account after six months cleaning crypto ledgers for biker forums during his golf weekends. "Accountant needed," their president had written below a signature quoting Sun Tzu. *Not what I expected*, I almost replied, before remembering Harrison once hissed that *expectations were shackles.*

Rubber screeched as we pulled into Amarillo Station. My legs were stiff as I stood—new Hey Dudes instead of Louboutins gripping the aisle floor. I stepped into air thick with diesel and cricket's song. An older man built like a house with graying black hair leaned against a pickup sporting an Iron Valor cut. He was the handsomest man I'd ever seen. And the roughest. Damn.

"Harris?" he drawled, eyeing my ball cap and mom jeans holding every cent I'd could scrabble together from money that Harrison thought were his alone.

"Depends," I said, tasting freedom on parched lips. "You bring coffee?"

His laugh echoed across cracked pavement. "Oh yeah. You'll fit."

I didn't think I could make it into the enormous truck. He literally almost had to lift me up. The engine roared to life after I'd managed. Then we went barreling toward whatever came next.

# CHAPTER 2

## BRONC

The wind carried grit from the cattle pens two blocks over, sharpening the diesel fumes into something that stung the back of my throat. I leaned against the chipped concrete pillar, thumb hooked in my belt loop as the Greyhound wheezed to a stop. Travelers spilled out—tired salesmen clutching briefcases, college kids hauling overstuffed duffels, a grandmother herding three sticky-faced children. None of them matched the woman from the grainy driver's license photo Wrecker had dug up.

Then she stepped down.

The black dye job was worse in person—roots bleeding gold along her neckline, a fringe of bangs brushing her eyelashes actually were damn cute. That thrift store cardigan hung loose around narrow shoulders, swallowing her whole until the wind pressed the fabric against her torso. My gaze caught on the way her jeans pooled around new looking Hey Dudes, the hem frayed where she'd cut off the original length. Every inch screamed a struggling woman chasing work in a podunk Texas town.

Except for the hands.

She gripped the bus's handrail like it might dissolve beneath her fingers, knuckles pale under a fading July tan. Hands that had never hauled bales or scrubbed floors, the nails bitten ragged but still shaped with the ghost of a French manicure. I pushed off my truck just as she stumbled into a teenager barreling toward the vending machines. Her apology came out too crisp, vowels rounded with an accent she couldn't quite flatten into something midwestern.

"Julia Harris."

Her spine snapped straight at the name, chin lifting as she turned. She made a joke about coffee. Damn cute. Up close, the dye looked even worse—store-brand box color, applied in haste. But beneath it lurked something richer, like sun-baked wheat stalks caught mid-sway. Her eyes widened, lashes sweeping up to reveal irises that couldn't decide between brown and midnight except for the amber flecks. A shiver raced through her before she locked it down, full lips curving into a smile that didn't touch those watchful eyes. And a pert nose dusted with the most appealing tiny fucking freckles. I shook my head. I needed to get my shit together.

"Mr. Baucaum." She adjusted the strap of her rather large Louis Vuitton tote, the movement pulling her sweater tight across collarbones sharp enough to draw blood. I notice the wince she gave against the pressure. "I'd shake hands, but mine are currently auditioning for an earthquake simulator."

The joke landed with a self-deprecating twist, her voice lower than I'd expected—smoke and honey where I'd prepared for something brighter. Behind us, a toddler wailed as his mother dragged him toward the restrooms. Julia flinched at the sound, shoulders creeping toward her ears.

"Bronc's fine." I reached for her bag, noting the fresh scrape along its leather exterior. "Welcome to the friendly side of nowhere."

Her laugh came out with half a cough. "If by friendly you mean determined to sandblast my retinas..."

A gust whipped her bangs sideways, revealing a thin scar along her hairline—old, poorly stitched. My fingers twitched toward it before I caught myself. "Wait till the tumbleweeds roll through. They'll steal your left shoe just to watch you hop."

"Charming." She fell into step beside me, her strides two to my one. The bag banged against her hip as we walked. She hadn't let me take it from her. Her ankle twisted slightly in a parking lot crack and she almost lost her footing. My hand found her elbow before she face planted into a parking meter.

She hesitated, staring at the passenger door handle like it might bite. When I moved to open it for her, she jerked back, boot heel catching on the curb.

"I've got it," she blurted, hauling herself up with a white-knuckled grip on the 'oh-shit' handle. The seat creaked as she settled in, knees knocking together until she forced them still. Her gaze swept the dashboard—clean, no club insignias, GPS disabled—before landing on the dented thermos in the cupholder.

"Coffee's fresh," I said, sliding behind the wheel.

She eyed the thermos like it contained hemlock. "Only if you have cream and sugar."

"Noted."

The engine roared to life, drowning out whatever she muttered next. As I pulled onto Main Street, her reflection flickered in the side mirror—chin ducked, fingers worrying a loose thread on her sweater cuff. Waiting. Assessing. Cataloging exits.

"How was Chicago when you left?"

"Damp." Her thumbnail picked at the thread's knot. "Though after eight hours sitting next to a man who believed Axe Body Spray counted as bathing, I'd take a monsoon."

The barb held an unexpected bite. I glanced over to find her studying the feed store we passed, gaze tracking a cluster of ranch hands loading hay bales. Her tongue darted out to wet chapped lips.

"You ride?"

"Horses?" A beat too late, her shoulders lifted. "Only if they're attached to carousels."

Bullshit. That hitch in her breath when the geldings nickered? Pure muscle memory. I drummed my fingers on the wheel, letting silence pool between us. The tactic worked better than interrogation—innocents rushed to fill voids, liars clammed up tight.

She lasted three traffic lights.

"Any decent barbecue joints around here?"

"A few." I thought of my mother's bar and grill, she'd likely frequent when she settled in. "Now for gourmet food? You consider Fritos in chili 'gourmet'?"

Her nose crinkled, the first unguarded expression she'd shown. "That's depends on the chili. Where I'm from, we put beans in ours."

"Careful." I slowed for a jaywalking calico. "Talk like that'll get you drawn and quartered in most circles where you're heading."

The corner of her mouth twitched. Not quite a smile, but the shadow of one.

"So, how was the ride down here?"

"Two buses." She picked at her cuticle. "Seat cushions smelled like regret and corn nuts."

"And Texas called because...?"

Her fingers stilled. "Fiancé's funeral." The words came too quick, rehearsed. "Car accident. Six months back."

Liar. Grief has a sound—wet earth over raw pine. This was porcelain shards in my molars.

"Condolences." I downshifted past a tractor, tastebuds flooding with the saccharine rot of deception. Beneath it... something feral. Musk buried under layers of human stink. Not quite wolf. Not quite not.

"Was the wedding..." I inhaled subtly through parted lips, "... close?"

Her laugh shattered like safety glass. "Too close. He preferred brunettes. Hence..." A brittle gesture toward her dye job.

The steering wheel creaked under my grip. Every instinct snarled—she smelled of wrongness wrapped in softness. Trapped rabbits and attic dust. But when the wind whipped through her hair, I caught the ghost of pack bonds. Frayed threads of belonging.

A pickup hauling horses passed on the right. Her eyes held a distant longing as she following it until it was out of sight.

"Are you sure you don't ride?" I gave her an incredulous look.

Her smirk was telling. "Pretty positive." The dashboard clock ticked off seven seconds before she unspooled the truth. "Charlie hated horses." Her thumb rubbed circles over the tote's strap. "Allergic."

Another lie coated in fact. My canines ached.

The truck tires crunched over gravel as we turned onto Magnolia Street. "Pearl's does decent chicken-fried steak," I said, nodding toward the neon-lit bar. "But avoid the coleslaw unless you enjoy yours tangy and sweet."

Julia's chuckle sounded hoarse and deep. I don't think she laughed much in her world. "Noted." Her fingers danced along the edge of the seatbelt, tracing the stitching with military precision.

I cataloged the motion—too controlled for casual fidgeting, too rhythmic for nerves. Ballet training? Combat drills? The torn cuticle on her index finger suggested habitual picking. "Library's two blocks east," I continued. "Park committee keeps flower boxes looking like Martha Stewart's personal hell."

"Chrysanthemums?" she guessed, leaning toward the passenger window.

"Marigolds. Blood orange ones that reek of fertilizer and misplaced ambition."

Her shoulders relaxed a quarter-inch. Good.

The apartment over the garage behind Ma's house loomed ahead, just inside pack territory. We drove through the gates and I gave a wave to one of the new prospects. I'll have to give instructions to leave well enough alone. Ma's house sat about a block past the front entrance. Its new cedar shakes glowed amber in the late afternoon glare. I killed the engine, watching her eyes track the security features—steel-reinforced door, double-pane windows, motion lights disguised as garage sconces.

"Fire escape's out back," I said, rounding the truck. "Leads to roof access. Not that you'll need it."

She paused mid-step, head tilting toward the neighboring oak. "Is that—?"

"Wisteria. Should bloom purple come spring." I jingled the keys louder than necessary, letting their metallic song announce our approach. "Ma had the floors redone in hickory. Claims it's scratch-resistant."

The lie tasted like nickel on my tongue. I'd overseen every renovation myself—chosen the wood for its warmth under bare feet, installed the Shaker-style pegs so she'd have somewhere to hang that damn scarf.

Julia trudged up the outside stairs lugging that bag that was almost as big as she was. Then she crossed the threshold with the reverence of someone entering a cathedral. Her knuckles went white around the strap of that damn bag as she took in the open living space. Early evening sunlight fractured through the lead-ed glass transom, painting her black-dyed hair with unexpected cobalt highlights.

"Refrigerator's propane," I said, trailing a finger along the butcher block counter. "Stove too. Power goes out most win-ters—you won't starve."

She set her bag down with excessive care, as though disarm-ing explosives. When her fingers brushed the satin finish on the cabinets, I caught a slight bruise on her wrist.

"Closet space might disappoint." I leaned against the arched doorway to the bedroom, tracking her micro-expressions. "But the mattress..."

Her breath hitched.

"...is memory foam. Doesn't sag."

The bed frame's iron scrollwork threw barred shadows across her face. She blinked rapidly, throat working around unspoken words. Most women would comment on the quilt—hand-stitched by the Widow Granger last Christmas. They'd sigh over the farmhouse sink or coo at the subway tile.

Julia strode to the east-facing window instead, palms flattening against the sill. "Screen's removable?"

"Twist latch at the top. Why?"

She didn't answer, but her spine straightened as she counted the steps from bed to back exit. Twelve paces. Solid footing. No rugs to trip on.

Smart girl.

I moved to the kitchenette, deliberately turning my back. Glass clinked as I filled two mason jars from the tap. "Water pressure's better than the Hilton. Showerhead's got six settings—including 'hurricane' and 'monsoon.'"

When I turned, she stood frozen between the sofa and coffee table, shoulders hunched like a spooked mustang. The fading light caught the uneven dye job—jet black at the roots, bleeding to blueberry near the ends. Chemical burn marks along her hairline told of bathroom sink disasters and hurried cover-ups.

"Keys." I tossed the ring. She snatched them mid-air, reflexes honed by necessity rather than sport. "Silver one's for the deadbolt. Gold does the handle. The key fob will arm the alarm system."

Her eyes went wide. "Alarm system?"

"You are safe here, Julia. The alarm system is just an added element to be sure you feel as safe as possible." Truth wrapped in practicality. Let her think me a pedant about her feelings. But something tells me she might be running from something or someone. This is the quickest way for us to be notified if a bad guy has breached her residence. I explained the very simple instructions for arming and disarming the system and the importance of her always having it armed whenever she's at home.

She drifted toward the bookshelves flanking the fireplace—empty except for my sister's hideous porcelain spaniel collection. I should've cleared them out.

"Storage ottoman doubles as a safe." I nudged the tufted leather cube with my boot. "Combination's your birthday."

Her head whipped around. "How did you—"

"Your application. It included little vitals like that. This job may pay on a cash basis, but I needed to know a few things about the person I was opening up my books to. Like if you were old enough to be a CPA." I gave her a wink. "Seems you are."

The pink flush creeping up her neck said she didn't believe me. Good. Let her wonder what else I knew.

I checked my Rolex—18:47. Church convened in twenty-three minutes. "Groceries get delivered Tuesdays. Cash envelope under the fruit bowl."

"You don't have to—"

"Yes." The word came out sharper than intended. I softened it with a shrug. "Corporate account. Tax thing."

She opened her mouth, no doubt to argue, when the wind shifted. Through the screen door came the distant howl of the 6:15 freight train—two long, one short, echoing across the plains. Julia's pupils dilated. Her pulse jumped in that delicate throat.

Wolf instinct. Had to be.

"Schedules posted on the fridge." I moved toward the door, leather cut flapping against my chest. "My number's there too. In red."

She hovered near the breakfast bar, arms crossed protectively. "What if I need something after hours?"

The challenge hung between us—a gauntlet thrown in honeyed tones. I let my gaze drop to her chipped nail polish, the raw spot where she'd worried a hangnail into an open wound.

"Then you call." I palmed the doorknob, brass biting into my scarred palm. "Day or night."

The screen door slammed behind me like a gunshot report. Wind whipped dust devils across the driveway, carrying the metallic tang of approaching rain. Through the apartment's warped glass, I watched Julia trace fingertips along the butcher-block counter—a moth testing forbidden heat. Her reflection fractured in the windowpanes as she took a coffee mug from the cabinet. Testing weight. Checking for defects.

"Prez?" JT's voice crackled through my cut's comms patch. "Church in ten."

I thumbed the mic hidden under my collar. "En route."

She drifted into view again, clutching the yellow gingham curtains around her shoulders like a child's security blanket. The fabric strained against her collarbones. Too thin. Too damn thin. My knuckles ached where they gripped the truck's door handle.

Raindrops pocked the windshield as I keyed the ignition. Through the garage apartment's window, Julia pressed both palms to the glass. Streetlight haloed her thick and wispy bangs, turning black dye blue. For three heartbeats, we stared across the electric-dark space between vehicle and refuge.

Then she stepped back, swallowed by shadows.

I took a ride through town on my way back to the compound. Gravel crunched beneath my tires. At the Stop-N-Go's amber glow, I caught my own eyes in the rearview—wolf gold bleeding through human blue. Her scent lingered. Not just fear-sweat and drug store perfume. Underneath... jasmine. Southern jasmine, like the vines strangling my mother's porch back in the summer.

Pearl's neon crucifix bled crimson across the truck hood as I rolled past. Muted bass throbbed through the bar's shuttered windows. Old habits made me note the fresh motorcycle treads in the mud—two Harleys, one Indian Scout. All pack-registered.

The compound's outer fence materialized from the storm. I licked diesel rain off my lips, tasting Julia's lie again. *Dead fiance.* Bullshit. But trauma? That sharpened bone-deep.

Roadside cattails bowed as I passed, their feathered heads brushing the truck's flanks. In the ditches, field mice fled prowling shadows. Every instinct said turn around. Post guards. Chain her doors.

Instead, I parked in front of the compound. Through the downpour, prospects scrambled to cover bike seats with tarp. Their laughter died when I strode past.

"President." Doc emerged from the fog, medical bag dripping. "Heard you found our stray accountant."

Lightning fork-lit the canyon. Somewhere beyond the ridge, thunder rumbled an answer.

"Not stray," I said, shaking rain from my cut. "Hired."

Doc's nostrils flared. We both knew what that twitch meant—his wolf had caught the same thread of wildness in her scent that I carried. He adjusted his wireframes, rainwater beading on the lenses, as he peered toward Pearl's cottage across the compound. "Smells like someone dipped a tea bag in moon water."

I shouldered open the lodge door, wood groaning against iron hinges. The church room's low lights cast long-jawed shadows over Wrecker's scarred knuckles, where he dealt poker cards across the map table. Four faces lifted—pack elders and enforcers—their animal scents clotting the air beneath tobacco smoke.

JT rose first, prayer beads clicking against his belt buckle. "She clean?"

I straddled my chair at the table's head, leather creaking with a warning. "Cleaner than your conscience."

Chuckles rolled through the room like tumbleweeds before dying beneath another thunderclap. Wrecker dealt me in without asking—ace of spades face up. Omen or joke, I let it lie burning against oak wood stained with old bloodstains.

That scent you're carrying... "Hybrid?" Mama Pearl materialized from the kitchen archway, flour still dusting her black dress.

She set a pecan pie between bullet hole clusters pocking the wall behind me—sugar weaponized as an interrogation tactic.

"Don't know yet." My thumb worried the card's edge. "Human enough to bleed slow when cut."

Mama's spatula cracked against the pie server. "But not human enough to leave be."

The truth hung heavier than August humidity as I laid out facts like tarot cards. "I don't know. But she's a tiny thing, not even as tall as my shoulders. Smells like fuckin' ginger and burnt sugar. She heard the damn subsonic train whistle and responded to it."

Wrecker leaned back until his chair groaned apocalyptic protest. "Did you bring an *omega* into our den?"

Gasps rippled through church elders—old superstitions flaring like struck matches. JT's crucifix glinted as he crossed himself twice—once for man, once for beast.

I stood slow, palms flat on wood veined with generations of claw marks. "It's clear she doesn't even know *what* she is, what *we* are." Power bled into my words—alpha compulsion thickening the air until breathing felt like swallowing wet wool. "But *someone* might."

Mama set a slice of pie before me, pecans glistening like amber traps in syrup. "Now *that* sound like trouble."

I imagined Julia's fear flashing under her bathroom light as she box-dyed evidence away—black rinses circling the drain in a porcelain bowl while bruises ripened beneath whatever she wore at the time. Not thrift store sweaters, I'd wager.

"Probably whoever she's running from," I said softly into my coffee steam rising like sacrificial smoke between us all.

The storm chose that moment to shatter cracked windows we'd yet to replace from the last big storm—glass teeth raining down as emergency lights bathed us red.

# Chapter 3

## Juliet

The screwdriver slipped from my grip again, clattering against concrete as wind whipped rainwater sideways into my eyes. My fourth attempt to unscrew the floodlight casing became a battle against the storm itself—fingers numb beneath dripping sleeves, soggy sweater suctioned to my skin like a second layer of regret. Lightning cracked the sky open three miles west, the delayed rumble vibrating through my molars. These damn lights had to be turned off. I'd never get to sleep with them shining in my windows, plus they draw too much attention. I had to turn them off. Also, he could find me any minute. Had to make it harder for him.

"Almost...there..." I wedged the flathead against stripped screws, my makeshift ladder—an overturned feed bucket—wobbling beneath wet socks. Every flicker of illumination from the remaining security lights felt like a homing beacon. *They'll see. He'll see.* The mantra coiled tighter with each gust, snapping the oak branches overhead. This paranoia had only gotten worse in the past few months. I didn't enjoy living in fear, shouldn't have had to. If I had parents who cared more about me than their bottom line, I wouldn't have had to.

Metal screeched as the bulb housing finally gave. Darkness swallowed the eastern corner of the garage apartment just as hail began pelting the corrugated roof. Triumph burned acidic in my throat. Finally, this was working. Hope Mr. Baucaum wouldn't be pissed that I undid these, but why should he? Not his apartment. I didn't hurt anything.

A sizzle-pop overhead. The world dropped into black. Dammit.

I froze mid-reach for the next light, arm outstretched toward nothingness. No amber glow from the coach lights. No humming streetlamp at the property's edge. Just the keening wind and the sudden, suffocating awareness of being silhouetted against a dead apartment.

"No. *No*." The screwdriver slipped from trembling fingers. Hail stung my scalp as I scrambled off the bucket, socks slopping through wet grass. Three stumbling steps toward the exterior stairs when thunder detonated directly overhead—a cannon crack splitting the night.

I ran.

Rain needled my face as I took the steps two at a time, cardigan snagging on the wood rail. The deadbolt resisted twice before surrendering, my shoulder slamming the swollen doorframe hard enough to leave tomorrow's bruise.

"Three locks." Breath sawed between chattering teeth as I twisted each deadbolt. "Three windows." Palm slapped every sash handle—bedroom, bathroom, living room. "Solid metal door." Forehead pressed against it as another lightning burst illuminated the room in strobe-flashes.

*Alarm system. Right. The alarm system.*

I fumbled toward the breaker box beside the fridge. Dripping sleeves left dark Rorschach patterns on the wood floors as I flipped switches with numb fingers. Nothing. Not even the faint digital chirp of resetting electronics. There's a storm. Transformers blow. It happens.

"Okay. Okay, think." My reflection in the microwave door showed a drowned alley cat—black dyed hair looking darker than ever, bangs plastered to furrowed brows. "Candles in jars around the rooms. Lighter, kitchen drawer."

A matte black lighter from Pearl's Bar caught on the first strike. Flame sputtered as I touched it to wicks—vanilla-scented from the Dollar General. Shadows reared up along the walls like restless phantoms.

Living room first. Then bedroom. The flame trembled as I passed the double-pane window overlooking the driveway. Something moved in the periphery. Is that a shadow detaching itself from the swaying pecan trees?

I spun, lighter raised like a talisman.

Nothing but my own warped reflection in the rain-lashed glass.

"Stop." The command bounced off beadboard walls, too thin to convince. "You checked the windows. You—"

The candle in my hand dripped hot wax onto my thumb. I hissed, nearly dropping it. Shadows deepened in the corners where feeble light couldn't reach. Every creak of the apartment became footsteps. Every moan of wind through the eaves whispered, *found you.*

I'd barely been here a day. Spoke to Mr. Baucaum a couple of times. I should call him. Desperation fueled the next three candles until the bedroom glowed like a séance circle. Still, the dark pressed in—thick and liquid at the edges of the rug, pooling beneath the dresser.

I backed toward the living room, sopping sock feet soaking floorboards. Twenty-seven steps to make the circuit. Front door handle jiggled. Windows rattled. Three locks held.

Held. Wandering back around. *"Calm down, Juliet."*

The bathroom mirror showed a stranger's face—smudged mascara bleeding into hollows beneath eyes that darted like spooked livestock. I peeled wet fabric from shuddering skin, each layer hitting the tile with the weight of discarded identities. My last silk camisole from Neiman Marcus clung stubbornly to wet skin.

A Sponge Bob sweatshirt bought at a Dollar General waited on the bathroom counter. It was surprisingly soft as I slipped it over my towel turbaned hair. A complete mismatch for the beautiful silk panties I'd wear after drying myself off. It didn't matter. I'd cover those panties with a baggy pair of flannel pajama pants.

I finished blotting my dripping hair with a fluffy towel and pulled it into a messy bun atop my head. My heart stopped when I swore I saw the vinyl shower curtain sway ever so much. Five seconds staring at floral vinyl until logic overrode instinct. *No movement—just my imagination.*

Bronc had mentioned the fridge was powered by propane, so it still worked. I wasn't really hungry but I knew I had to eat something and I found the perfect thing—an individual yogurt cup, strawberry swirl. That actually sounded yummy.

Candlelight carved hollows in the living room walls as I settled on the couch. The first spoonful burst tart-sweet across my tongue. Somewhere between strawberry and third bite, memory ambushed me—Bronc's hand brushing my elbow when he kept me from falling at the bus terminal. His touch felt electric against my skin, even through my sweater. I wondered how much older he was than me.

Rain lashed the roof as I curled finally dry socked feet beneath me, still thinking about him. Everything about him was different. It's ridiculous. I'm a child compared to him. But being next to him had felt safe. Why? The way he looks? He is beautiful. His scent? Yes—scent? Like deserts and earth and leather. Ok, that's weird. But it's true. I'm going insane, clearly.

The spoon clattered against the empty plastic container. Wind howled through eaves carrying phantom engine growls. Every muscle tensed. Waiting for headlights that never came.

*Keys.*

I bolted upright, the yogurt container rolling under the coffee table.

"No. Nononono—"

Pillows flew. Candle flames danced wildly as I overturned a couch cushion. Three years ago, losing a phone meant sending staff to the Apple Store. Tonight, it meant no connection to help if I needed it. Where is my damn phone?

My bedroom? I tried to stay low as I crawled along baseboards, hunting metallic glints. Behind me, floorboards groaned.

"Not now," I hissed to the empty room. To myself. To ghosts wearing Armani suits.

I finally rushed to the kitchen and rummaged through the drawers. Steak knives and takeout menus. No phone. Was that knocking on the front door? I ran to the bathroom, under the towel on the counter. No phone. Where is it? The bedroom search turned feral. The comforter flew, pillows turned over, to no avail. Pure panic had set in. My sobs blurred my vision.

A blue glow pulsed beneath the dresser. I lunged, cracking elbows on the hardwood. Fourteen percent battery. Three bars of service. Three unanswered texts from Bronc time-stamped 7:03 PM:

*How 'bout I pick you up tomorrow at 5:45 am sharp?*

I walked to the kitchen, reading.

The last message arrived eight minutes ago:

*Power's out at your place. You good?*

I stopped. I typed. *Lost my phone earlier, just found it. All good here.* Deleted. Rewrote *No lights but I've got candles. See you at 5:45.* Backspaced again. What is wrong with me?

The window above the kitchen sink rattled. Not wind this time—something solid tapping the glass.

The lighter clattered to the floor when the floodlights blazed across the yard. My spine hit the refrigerator door, cold condensation bleeding through the Sponge Bob sweatshirt. Three violent thumps shook the window above the sink, the same cadence as knuckles rapping on a limo's privacy glass.

*He found you.*

Candle flames bent sideways as I sprinted past. Fingers numb, I tore open the deadbolt. Metal shrieked against weather stripping. Night air slapped my face, carrying diesel fumes and something darker—vetiver cologne clinging to memory.

"Julia."

Thunder cracked as lightning arced across the plains. Silverback silhouette resolved into Bronc's waterlogged form, black denim plastered to tree-trunk thighs. Rain sluiced off his stubble, caught the flicker of candles behind me. His shadow stretched monstrously across the porch wall, wind whipped his hair wild.

I swayed in the doorway, torn between slamming the metal against his chest and clawing him inside. "You...the texts said..."

"Didn't answer." He shouldered past, bringing the storm with him. Wet boots left wet prints on the entry rug. "Left six goddamn voicemails. You think this—" A calloused hand swept toward the gutted light fixtures, the scattered steak knives gleaming dully near the baseboards. "—is the best way to keep yourself safe?"

The door slammed itself. Bronc didn't touch me, didn't need to. His presence compressed the room like the atmosphere before a tornado. I backed into the kitchen counter, hip bone striking the drawer handle where steak knives still waited.

"Lost my phone," I lied.

His nostrils flared. "Bullshit."

"Found it later—"

"Later than what?" Leather creaked as he stepped closer, rainwater pooling around his boots. "Than when I drove past at eight and saw every security bulb unscrewed? Than when the power grid failed in the storm and you sat here playing pioneer with dollar store candles?"

The lightbulbs hummed to life as electricity surged back. The light of the pendant lights exposed my shaking hands, the damp patches spreading under Bronc's arms where his thermal shirt clung to battle-scarred musculature. He smelled like soaked leather and wet sand.

I gripped the counter's edge. "Not your problem."

"Made it mine." He stormed toward the bedroom when he saw the overturned bedding and the dresser drawer hanging open where I'd ransacked it for my phone. "You think I can't smell adrenaline souring your sweat? That I don't recognize combat breathing patterns?"

Lightning flashed again. For one fractured second, his eyes seemed to glow gold.

My knees buckled. The counter dug into my spine as I slid downward. "Please. Just go."

Bronc crouched, a controlled predator's descent that brought us eye level. Rain dripped from his hair onto my crossed ankles. "Tell me who you're running from."

The look of genuine concern brought me up short. His heat reached me first, radiating through the chilled air like a banked forge. Then fingertips brushed my cheekbone, rough as saddle leather and just as capable of holding fast.

"Don't." My throat closed around the plea.

His palm cradled my jaw. "Who hurt you, little one?"

Three years of frozen screams thawed in my windpipe. Tears scalded worse than the hot candle's wax that still slightly stung my hand. "I can't—"

The kiss shocked us both.

Not gentle—a collision of desperation. His growl vibrated against my lips as I clutched his soaked shirt. His tongue mapped the seam of my mouth, not asking. Taking. Claiming.

And God help me, I opened and let him in.

He broke first, forehead pressed to mine as we gasped the same oxygen. "You're coming home with me."

It wasn't a request.

Bronc's thumb brushed the tear track I hadn't realized escaped. The calloused sweep ignited fresh tremors, my ribs cracking open beneath the weight of three years spent building armor from just to survive. He helped me stand.

"Little Wolf." His exhale warmed the hollow beneath my ear. The pet name unstitched me.

I braced for mockery, for cruelty masquerading as concern. Instead, his hands framed my face—a sculptor steadying fractured marble. Rainwater seeped through my sweatshirt where his chest pressed mine against the kitchen cabinet. Each breath dragged his scent deeper into my lungs—desert and leather. But there was something else, something wilder, earthier. Something animal.

His nose grazed my temple. "Should've known a skittish thing like you might bite."

The low rasp unraveled another knot between my shoulder blades. My fingers curled reflexively in his soaked Henley. Brushed cotton rasped as he shifted, trapping my shuddering exhale between our bodies. Distant thunder rolled across the plains, answering the growl vibrating his sternum.

"Look at me."

I didn't want to. Couldn't bear seeing pity reflected in his eyes. But his thumb pressed gently beneath my chin, insistent as sunrise.

Gold still bled through his irises, but softer now, embers rather than wildfire. His gaze tracked the scars peeking above my collar. I tensed, waiting for questions. Instead, callused palms slid down to bracket my throat, not squeezing. Testing pulse points.

"Christ." His forehead dropped to mine. "Who let this happen?"

The raw ache in his voice broke me.

My knees never made it to the hardwoods. His arms banded around my back, hauling me against his chest. I eyed the faded Army insignia tattoo on his arm. His heartbeat thundered through wet cotton—an artillery barrage syncing with mine.

"Easy." A rumble more felt than heard. "Got you."

Fingernails dug half-moons into his biceps. The storm's wrath faded beneath labored breathing and the creak of leather as he rocked us slightly. His scruff tangled in my hair when he turned to glare at the windows.

"Should've had guards here tonight." The admission roughened his voice. "My fault."

I shook my head, nose brushing his collarbone. "Don't want babysitters."

A huff warmed my crown. "Not prison guards, Julia. Sentries." His palm swept up my spine, blunt nails scraping just hard enough to quiet my shivers. "Club looks after its own."

The possessive pronoun lingered between lightning strikes. His hand stilled between my shoulder blades. Waiting.

Outside, the tempest hurled mesquite branches against tin roofing. Inside, his silence asked every question I'd dodged since crossing state lines.

When my nod came, it barely shifted the air between us. Bronc's arms tightened fractionally. Get what you'll need for work tomorrow.

# CHAPTER 4

## BRONC

The truck's heater roared against the last gasps of thunder, shaking the cab windows. My knuckles stayed white around the steering wheel long after the rain stopped, every bump on the ranch road sending Julia swaying against the console. She kept her face turned toward the passenger window, black hair clinging to the glass where she'd rested her temple. The memory of her mouth, warm and startled against mine, thrummed louder than the engine.

"Almost there," I said to the silence between us. It was just a couple of miles to my house from my ma's. I lived deeper in pack territory.

She nodded without turning, running her palms up and down her baggy pajama pants. The fleece smelled like a dollar store. All wrong on someone who moved like she'd been born in silk. Every instinct screamed she didn't belong in this pickup truck, no matter how nice it was. Or in this town, in the crosshairs of whatever trouble clung to her like perfume. But when lightning had split the sky an hour ago, revealing the tremor in her hands as she'd packed her soggy ledger books... Christ. I'd have taken in a feral wolf pup looking at me like that.

Gravel spat under the tires as we rounded the final curve. My log cabin materialized through the scrub oaks—two stories of hand-hewn pine glowing amber against the bruised sky. Julia sat forward, palms braced on the dashboard. "You live alone?"

"Depends if you count the mice in the walls." The joke fell flat. Her exhale fogged the windshield as I killed the engine. "Back door's reinforced steel. All windows have security film. Motion lights cover three hundred sixty degrees."

Her door creaked open before I could come around. "How many exits?"

"Two. Both alarmed." I watched her catalog the property—lingering gaze on the detached garage, the treeline beyond the pasture. What kind of woman knows how to track trouble like this? "Inside's warmer."

She hovered on the porch while I disarmed the system, shoulders hunched under the sweatshirt's too big size. The entryway light caught amber flecks in her espresso eyes when she finally stepped over the threshold. Not human. Not entirely. My wolf stirred at the scent I'd been trying to place since I picked her up at the bus terminal. Wild ginger and burnt sugar, like something left to caramelize too long.

"Half bathroom's down the hall," I said, toeing off muddy boots. "Guest room's got its own lock."

Her choked laugh bounced off the exposed beams. "You think I'm scared of you?"

"Should be. You don't know me, Julia. Not really. You oughta be scared of any man you meet until you get to know him. But, I'm gonna reassure you. I'd never hurt you." The words came out rougher than intended. I busied myself relocking the deadbolt, brass clicking like a gun cocking. "Anyone brings trouble to my door ends up fertilizer in the rose beds."

She drifted toward the stone fireplace, trailing fingers across the leather sofa back. Her elegant hands and nails had seen better days.. "Do you make all your employees sleep over after they scare themselves half to death?"

"Just the ones who taste like desperation." The second it left my mouth, I wanted to yank it back. Her spine stiffened, hand frozen on the mantelpiece. "Julia—"

"Where's the guest room?"

I led her upstairs, each step groaning under our weight. The spare bedroom smelled like lemon oil and gunpowder—Maddie's doing the last time she'd cleaned my rifles. Julia paused in the doorway, gaze snagging on the hunting knife display above the dresser.

"It's decorative," I lied.

She set her waterlogged purse on the quilt's bright pink flowers. "Do you always prepare for Armageddon?"

"Only since Tuesday." The attempt at levity died as she turned, moonlight catching the bruise-like shadows under her eyes. My fingers itched to smooth them away. Instead, I nudged the bathroom door wider. "Towels are under the sink. Toothbrushes still sealed."

Her throat worked. "You keep spares?"

"For unexpected guests."

"Do you get many?"

"A few. None that stay." The confession hung between us, sharp as barbed wire. I retreated to the hall, palm sweating on the doorknob. What this tiny woman did to me. "Alarm code's 1029."

Her voice stopped me at the landing. "1029?"

October 29th. The date we'd pulled a bullet-riddled prospect from a collapsing barn. The night I'd learned some men scream for their mothers when dying. "Birthday," I lied, and stomped downstairs.

Dawn found me scrubbing engine grease from under my nails when floorboards creaked overhead. Julia descended with her hair twisted into a severe bun. She wore a loose black tank top under a baggy short sleeve floral cardigan and a simple pair of black pants. Every piece looked like it came from a discount store. The outfit screamed accountant, but the way she held herself—chin lifted, shoulders squared—belonged to a woman who'd fit in any boardrooms, if you discounted her blonde roots showing under the black. Fuck, she was stunning. Tiny, too damn thin, but beautiful, and her scent was seeping into my bones. My wolf was pacing, growling, "Mine."

"Coffee's fresh." I nodded toward the percolator.

She bypassed the mug I'd set out, opting for a chipped tumbler from the drainboard. "What time does the shop open?"

"When I get there." My gaze caught on her wrists as she poured—pale skin mottled with faint crescents. Old scars shaped like fingerprints. "You eat breakfast?"

"I'll grab something in town."

She didn't want to take anything from me. I scraped a fried egg onto toast, sliding the plate across the island. "Eat. There's not a restaurant within walking distance from the shop. You'll need steady hands balancing my books."

She stared at the food like it might bite. "I don't take charity."

"Eat, Julia." I leaned against the fridge, tracking the pulse fluttering in her throat.

The fork clattered from her hand. "I'm fine."

"Your choice." I grabbed my keys, leather cut sliding heavy over cotton. "Truck leaves in five."

As soon as I turned my back, I heard the crunch of the toast as she took a bite. She ate standing up, shoulders angled away from me as if guarding the plate. Each bite precise, me-chanical—the table manners of someone who'd survived state dinners, fancy brunches. When I turned to see her lick yolk from her thumb, my wolf growled low in my chest, satisfied we'd provided food for her.

The engine hadn't finished warming up when she slid into the passenger seat, laptop bag clutched like a shield. Her per-fume today was crisp. Forgettable. But beneath the drugstore floral notes, that wild ginger scent lingered.

I cranked the defroster. "Seatbelt."

Her fingers fumbled the clasp. "Do you always follow traffic laws?"

"Only the fun ones." Gravel pinged the undercarriage as we reversed. In the rearview, a tumbleweed swirled across the pasture where the pack's sentries would be patrolling. Julia's reflection watched them too, lips moving silently—counting? Calculating?

Halfway to town, she spoke to the window. "The kiss was a mistake."

My grip tightened on the gearshift. "Noted."

"It won't happen again."

"Planning to muzzle yourself?"

She turned, cheeks flushing beneath cheap foundation. "I'm trying to be professional."

"So file a complaint." The stop sign loomed too suddenly. Brakes squealed as we lurched forward. Her hand shot out, bracing against the dashboard.

Silence pooled thicker than the mud splattering the windshield. At the shop's back entrance, I killed the engine but left the keys dangling.

The slam echoed through the parking lot. I got her set up in the office space directly across from my office. Through the grimy office window, I watched her attack the ledger books like they'd personally offended her, spine rigid, pen slashing margins. Whatever ghosts she was running from, they'd better pray I found them first.

The scent of burnt coffee and gun oil followed Wrecker into my office. He leaned against the doorframe holding two mugs, steam curling around fingers tattooed with kill counts. "Your stray's got teeth. Bought her breakfast yet?"

I didn't look up from the parts manifest.

"I fed her. Don't you worry about it." I growled.

Through the grease-smeared window, Julia hunched over the office desk inside the main shop. That thrift-store blouse gaped at the collar when she reached for the calculator, revealing twin scars along her clavicle—those bones had been broken and more than once. My wolf stirred the way she winced when she moved certain ways.

"Find info on her. Dig deep," I said.

Wrecker's eyebrow twitched. "Even if she's clean?"

"She's runnin' from someone. I wanna know who it is and why. She's not the dirty one.

The neon cowboy boot above Pearl's Bar & Grill sign buzzed like an angry hornet colony, casting fractured pink light across gravel. Julia hovered at the truck's passenger door, fingers whitening on the handle.

"Chicken-fried steak's better here than your overpriced Chicago bistros," I said, coming around the hood. My shadow swallowed three parking spaces whole.

"I wouldn't know." Her voice came out sharp, irritated. She smoothed the thrifted cardigan hanging off one shoulder, its pilled wool looking out of place on her delicate frame.

Inside, sawdust and cayenne bit the air. A pedal steel guitar's mournful wail tangled with laughter from pool players. Behind the scarred mahogany counter, a silver-haired woman wielded a cocktail shaker like a conductor's baton.

"There's my boy!" Ma's smile could light up a room. She emanated class standing in a biker bar—pink dress and a triple strand of pearls. "And you brought a stray."

My palm pressed low on Julia's back, warmth bleeding through thin cotton. "Ma, this is—"

"Julia Harris." She reached out to pull her into a hug. Left hand glittering with a single diamond wedding ring she still wore.

"Aren't you the prettiest little thing? And those freckles across your nose! Adorable." I noticed Julia's shoulders tightened fractionally. "Except someone needs to help you out with that fringe of bangs, honey. And if I could say so, your color. You need to let your true color shine darlin' black is way too harsh for an angel like you."

Color crawled up Julia's throat. "DIY disaster."

"Mm." Pearl's gaze dropped to the half-moon scars peeking beneath Julia's sleeve. "We serve mistakes here nightly. Sit." She nodded toward a corner booth upholstered in split leather.

I slid in first, my thigh brushing Julia's when she joined me. Every touch set me on fire a little more.

Pearl materialized with sweet tea in mason jars. "Number four special, extra gravy?"

I grunted assent.

"And for the angel girl?" Ma's pen tapped her order book.

"The smallest salad—"

"Cornbread," I interrupted. "With honey butter."

Julia stiffened. "I can order—"

"You're all bones." It irritated me she seemed to worry about her weight. She was clearly underfed. "Eat."

Pearl snorted. "He gets that from me. Ran the PTA bake sales like boot camp." She vanished behind swinging doors that hissed with grease-fire breath.

Julia traced a knife scar on the table. "Why am I here?"

I spun my fork, tines catching the low light. "You looked..." Metal screeched against wood. "... hungry."

Across the room, Ma laughed at something the bartender said, but I didn't miss her gaze darting back like a hawk circling prey. When the food came, I grabbed the pepper mill, grinding black snow across Julia's greens.

"Tell me about Chicago."

Her lettuce wilted under the dressing. "Museums, shopping. You know."

"Don't." My knee pressed hers under the table. "Why'd you really take this job?"

A glob of gravy plopped onto my shirt. I made no move to wipe it.

"Money's good." She crumbled cornbread, golden crumbs falling on her plate, eyes glancing through her uneven bangs. "Steady."

She studied her plate like it held the secrets of the universe.

"It's a long way to Texas. We established you're hidin' here. I'd like to know from who, and why?"

"Maybe I'd like to know why you hired me?" Her whisper cut through George Jones's drunken crooning.

My thumb swiped honey butter from her lip. "Wanted somebody who knew what they were doin.' Then when I saw you. Felt right."

Ma's sudden reappearance made us jump. "Dessert? We got peach cobbler that'll make you slap your grandma."

It was time to go. "Check."

Outside, cicadas screamed in the parking lot's lone mesquite tree. Julia hugged herself against the cool summer evening. "I need to go home."

"Fine. I'd prefer you'd stay in my guest room so you can relax. But Ma's house is on club grounds too, so you'll be safe. I still say you'd be more comfortable at my place."

She'd moved away from me and instinct had me grab her wrist.

Her pulse fluttered against my grip like a scared sparrow. "No more cages."

I released her so fast she stumbled. "Alright, as long as I have keys, I can get to you quickly if you need me. But until we get you a car, you ride with me."

The glare she gave me said she didn't like it. But she also had no choice. I could arrange a car for her in a heartbeat. Wasn't going to.

I opened the passenger door of my F250 for her and waited for her to haul herself inside, offering no help. Couldn't keep the smart ass smirk off my face as her short legs struggled with the height. At least she had running boards and the 'oh shit' handle for leverage. Her breath caught when I leaned in and pulled the seatbelt across her chest and fastened the clasp. My mouth was mere inches from hers.

"Fun traffic laws." I breathed, my lips almost touching hers.

The night sky whispered promises I wanted to make but wouldn't as we rode in silence, pack land only a few miles away. She asked if I could stop at Walmart so she could grab some art supplies. This woman. Apparently she sketches. An artist. What I wouldn't give to see her work. I went in with her and loaded her up with every kind of charcoal pencil, ink, paint, and brush I could find to fill the cart. She stood with her mouth hanging open when we checked out.

"I told you I don't like charity." She huffed when we were back in the truck.

"Maybe I'm simply a patron of the arts." I told her with a grin, never taking my eyes from the road. Her tiny huff in response was precious.

From the corner of my eye, I could see how she watched my hands. Calculated their movement. I'd barely put the truck in park and she was out, standing by the door, waiting for me to bring her supplies. I trailed her up the stairs and into her apartment where I carefully set everything on the kitchen counter.

"I hope you enjoy creating beautiful things with your supplies. Maybe they can bring you some peace in your down time." I told her as I headed for the door.

Just as my hand touched the handle, she called out to me.

"Bronc. Thank you so much for your kindness. That was honestly about the nicest thing anyone has ever done for me."

I didn't even turn around. How could anyone not cherish this woman? If I turned to her at this moment, I'd have her wrapped in my arms and I might never let her go.

"It was my pleasure, Julia." I said as I walked out the door.

The fragrance of her shampoo lingered in my truck cab. Not flowers. Green apples mixed with uncertainty. I'd clocked the mismatch when she climbed in earlier—badly dyed black waves framing a face too adorable to belong to a soon married suburban wife, ankle boots paired with dime-store cardigans. Every contradiction screamed mine from my wolf.

My comm squelched, cutting through the silence. "Yo, Prez?" Bridgers's voice came through. "We still got church in ten?"

I thumbed the key fob's jagged edges. Ran my tongue over the tiny chip in my front tooth from that bar fight in Lubbock. Habits died harder than men in these parts. "Reschedule."

Static crackled. "You sure, we got—"

"Tell 'em not tonight." I squeezed the comms button 'til I thought it'd bust through. Several feet away, a lit window in the garage apartment behind my mother's house told me she was pacing. Prospect's shadow passed the garage door—gangly kid better not scare her pissing in bushes all night.

Leather creaked as I leaned against the truck's seat. Memory served up today's crime scene. Julia bent over ledgers in the shop office, pencil behind her ear, muttering depreciation schedules like battle plans. She'd caught me staring. Those espresso eyes held steady while her fingers worried that scar along her collarbone. Those old wounds. Broken bones? Stitches?

My wolf also paced behind my ribs.

The intercom buzzed again.

Cicadas ratcheted up their dying symphony. Somewhere beyond the fence line, a steer lowed. I catalogued each sound, each tremor in the dark. Julia's apartment light winked out.

Truth was a greased pig in these parts—slippery, messy, best cornered with allies. But the way she'd said no more cages earlier, voice splintering like cheap plywood… Let Wrecker do his job. Let him turn over every stone.

The first fat raindrops smacked my windshield as I headed toward the clubhouse. I grinned into the gathering storm. Tonight, the wolves would run.

# Chapter 5

## Juliet

It had been a few weeks since the Walmart run where Bronc had loaded me up with art supplies. On the nights when I heard the mysterious songs of wolves, my hands would almost automatically sketch the beautiful black and silver wolf of my dreams. I liked to pretend he was one of the wolves somewhere outside my window. I'd started drawing when I was a little girl. It was one pastime my mother indulged. Probably because it was a quiet activity that kept me out of her hair. She kept me supplied with sketchbooks, colored pencils, and crayons. Then, as I got older, I had her buy charcoal pencils and chalks, even watercolors. YouTube was the best teacher. These days, when I wasn't sketching the wolf, I'd sketch Bronc. My bottom dresser drawer was filled with countless sketches of him. I'd be so embarrassed if he ever knew of my obsession with his beautiful face.

I'd grown accustomed to his rhythms—the gravel-dust scent of his leather cut filling the truck cab each morning. We'd fallen in to a natural routine of him picking me up each morning for work. Right on time, I heard his truck rumble up the street and that gave me the signal it was time to meet him downstairs.

His truck crunched over gravel and came to a stop, and I waited at the foot of the stairs as he came around to help me up into the cab. His hand still lingered on my lower back every time he helped me, though today seemed longer than yesterday, and I still counted those seconds. August heat clung to my Walmart tank top as I slid into the comfortable leather seat.

"Morning trouble." His breath was close to my lips as he fastened my seat belt for me, as always.

I grinned despite myself. "Still not tired of chauffeur duty?" My new steel-toed boots knocked together beneath the dash.

He caught my gaze straight on. "Not when it's chaufferin' you." He put the truck in gear and pulled out of the drive, as I smiled to myself.

Bronc's presence in the truck was as solid as the early morning light pooling across the dash, catching in the creases around his eyes and hinting at his own years. It mixed with the heavy heat of the air and created a new, intoxicating blend I struggled to understand. I was so attracted to this man. Wanted him like I'd never wanted a man before.

He drove with ease, and I let my gaze drift out the window, clinging to the endless plains instead of to the man next to me. My new jeans felt tight against the seat. The white tank clung to me in a way that would've gotten me banned from my Harrison's dinner parties. I kept my eyes on the road. "It's been busy in the shop. I wouldn't think so many people around here besides your club rode motorcycles." I tried to sound casual to mask my worry over the growing concerns that I'd found in his books.

Bronc's voice carried a rough edge as his laugh settled around us. "Be amazed at the weekend warriors that live in and around Amarillo. Folks everywhere want the freedom that a bike signifies. Doesn't freedom sound good?"

I flinched a little, wondering how much of me he saw. If he knew that my entire life was a disguise. The empty road stretched on like a promise, long and unwavering.

"Yeah, guess it does." My hand brushed against my bangs, trying to smooth them down. His knowing glance took in more than I was ready to offer.

His truck eased onto the highway, and he shot me a sidelong look that carried the heat of his hand against my back. "So, you found a smoking gun yet?"

I wanted to matter. To prove my worth, to him, to them. Let him know I could be useful. "I'm still getting things organized. I'll hopefully know more today." The early light reflected a steady glow of his calm, solid presence. I turned the air vent toward me, let the air blow around me.

"You're doin' a good job, Julia." I felt him next to me, sure and certain as the rising sun. My breath caught like I'd been expecting a storm and found life giving rain instead. Trusted the feel of it, if only for a moment.

His words settled in, burrowed deep inside me. Words I wasn't used to, words that built instead of broke. I sank into the seat, let the thrum of the truck fill every part of me as we moved further from the life I left behind.

When we stepped out of the truck, the wind whipped and tangled my hair, but I didn't care. For once, I didn't worry about who might be watching. The solid sound of Bronc's laugh moved over me, unfamiliar but warm. I let myself sink into the assurance of it, knowing it could pull away without warning, just like everything else.

The shop hummed with the electric sound of tools and grit. Like I'd dropped into the heart of a machine that pumped noise and heat instead of blood. The clamor of voices met me, and I cut through the bustle and ordered my thoughts while everything in the shop moved around me. I set my bag down on a bench scarred by years of hard use and let the steady lines of numbers steady me in return.

Their precision quieted the chaos around me, offered a kind of comfort I'd been missing since I left New York. Mechanics shouted and joked as they moved from bike to bike. Wasp wore a bandana, Radar had piercings like some kind of sideshow act, both were friendly and easygoing.

I focused on the tidy columns instead of them. Tapped into the part of myself that used to balance every aspect of my life with the same careful, controlled arrangement of numbers and rows. That used to think everything in life could be quantified, given order.

The sun cut through dusty windows and across the shop, and I slipped into the books like into another world. The small desk was in a corner away from the worst of the noise. Far enough from the open garage doors that the heat didn't drown me, but close enough that I still felt the tightness in the air.

I rolled my sleeves of my plaid overshirt to my elbows and refused to let anything else matter. The gentle smudge of graphite and the crisp marks of ink against yellowed pages pulled me away from the clatter and chaos and pulled me into the familiarity of my own skill.

Skeeter's glances cut through my concentration. I could feel his eyes on me even when I couldn't see him. He watched from behind the register, like he was waiting for me to fail. He was older than the others, looked as though he'd been there since the shop first opened. As if it was part of him, and I was the interloper.

Some books were as full of dust and disorganization as the shop. Skeeter's suspicion made it clear that he didn't want me involved with either. I saw numbers that should've matched but didn't. Items unaccounted for. I sighed as I shifted pages around, not used to seeing this kind of disorder. Not used to seeing any disorder.

I noted minor discrepancies on the ledger. I could fix the mess if they gave me a chance. Bronc would, but Skeeter didn't want to. His looks told me as much. And I wondered why. What was he afraid that I would uncover? The same tightness coiled in my chest that had when I discovered Harrison's offshore accounts. It was a familiar, unwelcome sensation.

Sunlight filtered through the room, but I felt the tension like a shadow. Like someone was watching and waiting for me to pull the curtain back. A bike roared to life, and my head snapped up at the sound, too used to the silence of my penthouse back in the city. One I couldn't leave without someone noticing.

The subtle inconsistency in the numbers matched the unease I'd been feeling. The closer I got, the more I saw the way they might jostle numbers—hide dollars here and there. I had to look for more patterns and inconsistencies.

Bronc stepped out from the shop floor, and I felt his presence cut through the haze of work and doubt. He motioned for me to follow. Led me into the cramped office where he'd cleared a space for me to join him. "Let's look at some invoices." The deep, steady current of his voice settled some of my earlier concerns, and I found myself drawn toward it, toward him. I took my place beside him and felt the strength and heat of his arm next to mine.

He led me past neon signs and machinery that lined the walls. I could feel Skeeter's glances like he was physically in the office with us. They pierced my concentration the same way as out on the floor, but Bronc's presence was something I couldn't ignore. Something I didn't want to ignore.

The space he'd cleared for me was an invitation. And I took it as a promise. The way he looked at me as I sat made my pulse rise, made me wonder what it would be like to be wanted by him. "These are the invoices I wanted to look at." His deep, steady voice settled the turmoil of doubt that seemed to follow me, and I drew toward it, toward him.

He pulled a worn notepad toward him. "Let me know if you find something." His words gave me a confidence I wasn't used to. The doubt I had that morning cracked around the edges. I picked up a pencil and started a list, leaned in to show him. The rough page seemed at odds with the way he took it. Carefully, gently, almost tender.

We bent over the desk, and Bronc's hand brushed against mine. It was steady, deliberate, unlike anything I'd known before. He wasn't Harrison. Wasn't even like any of my father's associates.

They never cared about more than their next business acquisition. They never had more than one face.

A promise wrapped in callouses. I moved a little closer. Felt like he was opening himself, opening a door. One I couldn't believe was mine. The sharp, contained ticks of numbers and totals filled the room like the heat from his arm, like a physical thing I couldn't help but breathe in. This shop mattered to him and the fact that he trusted me enough to let me in made my stomach do a little flip.

My heart sounded louder than the hum of the shop. The powerful line of his body made me dizzy. I pointed at a column that seemed off. He nodded once, like he already knew. It was no more than I expected. It was almost like he needed confirmation. No less than what I hoped for.

I was ready to question him, to challenge him about the things I'd seen. His voice met mine before I could.

"Trust me?" My entire life had been meant for others, and now I had a choice. His voice was a promise. One I might break if I answered. But I did trust him. More than I'd trusted anyone in my life.

"I trust you, Bronc."

His hand brushed mine again. "S'good. Cuz I trust you too, Julia. You see something's happening here. Now, go on back out to your desk and continue to do the job you're best at. Start at the beginning and find all that you can find. Don't worry 'bout anything else."

I felt like a weight had been lifted. Bronc trusted me to do this job, and I was going to do it.

I stabbed the adding machine's equal button hard enough to crack plastic. Numbers blinked red—$872 missing from last month's carburetor orders. Across the shop floor, Skeeter laughed with a customer while wiping engine grease onto cash register buttons.

My nail traced the carbon-copy invoice. Same part numbers, same vendor code, different totals. Three months of receipts revealed the pattern—minor discrepancies timed with inventory deliveries. I pulled the safe's combination from memory, fingers trembling.

The tally book's spine cracked open to reveal the former Club Treasurer notes in Axel's blocky handwriting. My eyes caught on a faded whiskey stain, smearing the March balance. Six grand unaccounted for between muffler sales and...

"Problem, Miss Harris?"

Skeeter's shadow loomed across the ledger. Pine-scented chewing tobacco wafted from his overalls as he leaned over my shoulder. I kept my palm flat on the incriminating page.

"Just cross-checking vendor codes," I said. "Seems we paid twice for January's piston rings."

His calloused finger jabbed at a random entry. "Axel always paid cash for bulk orders."

"How enterprising." I smiled the way Mother taught—lips closed, eyes sharp. "Perhaps you could show me where we store purchase agreements? To streamline next quarter's taxes."

The lie flowed smoother than expected. Let him think I'm another pencil-pusher. When Skeeter lumbered toward the filing cabinet, I slipped the tally book into my oversized plaid shirt.

# CHAPTER 6

## BRONC

The next day, Julia was back in my office, seated next to me. Her deep smoky voice mingled with the rhythmic shuffle of papers in the cluttered office, her pen tapping against the desk with quiet insistence hummed through my veins. She shot me a glance from beneath the jagged fringe of her hair, her eyes a flurry of caution and embarrassment as she realized she was talking to herself.

I needed to have a conversation with her about the other part of our business. She was keeping secrets. I had no doubt about that. But I was sure they weren't the kind of secrets that would hurt Iron Valor. They were secrets that posed a danger to *her.*

She had her hands in Iron Valor business now, though. And she'd soon see that wasn't all motorcycle shop money that wound up in bank accounts or our safes. "Do you trust me, Julia?" My sudden words cut through her calculator key clicks. Those espresso eyes slowly crept up to mine.

"I told you yesterday that I did, Bronc. Why would you ask me again?"

This was the easiest of the secrets I've kept from her, but dangerous nonetheless. I might be making a mistake because I know she still hadn't been honest with me about something, but my gut told me to trust her. And I've learned to trust my gut. The other secret, the one about the supernatural world she is a part of, would have to wait.

"The finances of the Iron Valor MC, the shop, etcetera, are private, and I know as a professional, you understand discretion. I've tasked you with taking a much deeper dive into our business and the club. This has put you in territory few people are allowed to enter. Some of Iron Valor's finances are more well guarded than others. The messy books of the motorcycle shop have put me in a situation I'm not happy about. You've proven to have the skills to pull back the curtain on what the hell's going on here, so it's likely you're going to notice other monies in Iron Valor accounts that you won't be able to account for. I'm about to give you the short version of where those deposits originated. I'm about to share with you the other side of Iron Valor. Not a word of this is ever to leave this office. Clear?"

She swallowed hard. "Clear."

"Shut the door, Julia."

Her eyes widened as she quickly obeyed me without question. Which had my dick hardening in my damn jeans, an entirely different issue. I moved the invoices out of the way and unpacked the lunch I'd picked up from Ma's. I figured that delivering this news over a meal might make it easier to hear.

Julia eased back down in her chair, sharp eyes narrowing like she was picking apart every word I hadn't said yet. I wiped my palms on my jeans. Damn, even now, after firefights and interrogations, this felt like walking into a kill zone without intel.

"You're not just mechanics," she said finally. Not a question. A verdict.

I snorted. "Didn't take you long to figure that out."

She pinged me with her balled-up straw wrapper, then gave a little giggle. She was nervous. "So, what do you do? You all move like... like some kind of precision military squad on the daily."

There it was—the opening I'd been dodging since she walked into the shop weeks ago. The shop hid plenty: false walls thick enough to muffle gunfire, vaults of gear, ready to go at a moment's notice. But hiding it from her? Felt wrong now.

I leaned forward, elbows on my desk. "You know what Delta Force does?"

Her brow furrowed. "Elite military stuff?" She shrugged. "Like secret, dangerous stuff."

"Menace and I were Delta," I said simply. Her breath hitched, good. She understood weight when she heard it. "Retired? Sure. On paper." I nodded toward the garage bay outside, where Wrecker's laugh boomed over engine noise. "Eli and Jess? Army Rangers—same unit back in the day. Ryder and JT? SEALs."

She blinked hard once—processing. Tactical precision down to her eyelashes. Almost cute if she weren't so terrifyingly smart. "So Iron Valor's not just bikes."

"Shop pays taxes," I said flatly. "The rest... governments hire us when they can't get caught holding the leash." The words came easier now, like briefing a teammate before insertion. "Extract hostages off-grid... recover stolen intel... dismantle shit that'd start wars if it went public."

Her fingers tightened around her cup, white-knuckle grip on reality unraveling in real time, but her voice stayed steady as hell. "And you trust each other because you grew up together? Your fathers were already Iron Valor?"

"Brothers before blood," I said—too raw for someone who didn't know what frostbite felt like at 20 thousand feet or how desert sand clung to fresh bullet wounds. But she flinched like she did, anyway. "We don't talk about it outside our circle," I added softly. "Not 'cause we're ashamed... but because trust is armor. Get sloppy with secrets? People die."

She didn't ask if we'd lost anyone, smart girl. Just stared at my hands—scarred knuckles cradling lukewarm coffee. Then she said, "You fix more than bikes, huh?"

I grinned. Savage. Pride flaring hot enough to burn through the dread. "Yeah. We fix problems. Quietly."

I leaned back in my chair, studying Julia's face as she drummed her fingers on her files. Precise, methodical, always one step ahead.

"Used to be we'd hit a dozen ops a year," I said, the words rough but deliberate. "Now? Maybe three or four." Her fingers touched a document, eyes flicking up to mine. I held her gaze. "Don't mistake quiet for safe, though. The MC world's still got teeth."

A beat of silence. She chewed her lip as if she were weighing risks versus regrets. I pushed on before doubt could settle. "But you're here. That means you're covered. Keep working like you have been—sharp, thorough." My boot tapped the concrete for emphasis. "You notice shit others miss. That's not luck; that's instinct."

She flushed, gaze dropping like praise was a grenade lobbed at her feet. Christ. How many people had let her think she was anything less than remarkable? My jaw tightened. "You should hear it more," I muttered, louder than I meant to. "That you're goddamn amazing at this."

Her laugh came out brittle. "Clicking keys on a calculator and balancing columns isn't exactly genius level or top tier work."

"Bullshit." The word snapped between us. I leaned forward, elbows on knees. "You could run a kingdom, Julia. You just haven't been handed the damn crown yet."

She cast her eyes down. Quiet, but I caught it. For a heartbeat, she looked... unguarded. Like part of her might actually believe me. Good. She deserved to.

I stood, chair scraping against concrete. "Next mission? You're lead analyst." No room for argument—not that she'd need it. "And when it goes smooth as hell?" I shot her a half grin over my shoulder. "Don't act surprised. But for now, we've got the mess that you're dealing with here. And from the look on your face, it just keeps getting worse."

She shuffled a few stacks of invoices and shook her head. "I just can't figure out how Axel? That was the person who kept all this together before me, right?"

I nodded.

"Well, I can't see how these kinds of errors were made by accident. Or are what I'd consider errors at all. It's almost like every single entry has a few dollars missing compared to the purchase orders. It will take me a good while to go through at least the past two years of orders and entries to see just how off everything is."

"Well, it's lucky you're not going anywhere, huh?" I gave her a wink, and her face turned the prettiest color pink I ever saw. Fuck if I knew what I'm doing with this 25-year-old woman when I'm almost 20 years older than her. But I've never wanted anyone more.

"It *is* a good thing." Her rare genuine smile made her beautiful smile even more so.

"So, you can manage this?" I asked, keeping my voice level while I leaned in over the desk. "The kind of chaos that comes with it?"

Her dark eyes fixed on mine. I felt her considering how many ways it could go wrong to believe in me. There was no paper trail for this kind of decision.

"I think so," she said, words so soft I almost didn't catch them.

I nodded, pushing the open manila envelope across the desk. Her fingers brushed mine as she reached for it, a shock of heat that ran from her hand to mine and back again, sparking our first night together like a live wire. She didn't flinch away this time.

"Good, 'cause I found this envelope full of invoices hiding under a box of parts. I don't want you worrying about rushing to get done. We're not on a timeline. There's more to life than the job. Right now, you don't really know people, but you will, and you'll want to have some fun someday. Take time for yourself to relax." I was playing it off like I didn't know she'd always choose to push herself to the edge of collapse.

She was gathering up things to take them from my desk. "Just let me collect everything from in here. And I know. I'm just not used to being able to come and go as I please." She quickly stopped herself like she hadn't meant to say something so honest. "I mean, I'm not used to having time on my hands. I always had so much work to do."

"Uh huh," I said. Knowing that's not at all what she meant. Sounded like somebody kept her under their thumb.

"Well, you've got some free time tonight. I've got church, so I can't take you to dinner. It's quittin' time. Gather up what you think you should take home, and we can lock up the rest."

I flicked off the neon "OPEN" sign with my elbow, watching its pink glow die against the cracked window glass. All the guys had already cleared out for the evening. Julia stood hunched by the register like a wilting sunflower, shop ledgers clutched to her chest like body armor. Her knuckles matched the white of the receipt paper stuck to her sleeve.

"Let's go," I said, nudging the door wider with my boot. The August air hit like a sauna when she didn't move. Christ, when had she last blinked? Her thousand-yard stare could've bored holes in the Pepsi cooler.

I gripped her elbow softer than I'd handle wounded livestock. She stumbled over nothing, climbing into my King Ranch, boot catching on running board chrome, but she didn't drop those damn books. Ledger pages fluttered under rubber bands as I slammed her door shut like closing a casket.

The cab smelled of leather and the fir tree hanging from the rearview. At every red light between Main Street and Ma's property line, I watched Julia trace column numbers on the cover of the top ledger book with one finger.

Her apartment stairwell light buzzed when we pulled up behind Ma's propane tank. One flight of painted white steps took us to the shelter of her little apartment.

"Hold still." My palm settled between her shoulder blades as she missed the third step entirely. A carpet nail snagged my sleeve while we shuffled upward. The butcher block countertop where I'd set her groceries the other day looked tidy and neat—ripening tomatoes sat on the windowsill.

She looked comfortable and at home, and I'd never seen a more beautiful sight.

"Chicken lasagna or stir-fry kit," I said louder than needed against those damn ledgers stacked on her kitchen table. "Not Pop-Tarts." My keys jangled gunshot-loud in cupped hands. "You hear me?"

Julia's eyes sparkled under the pendant lights, a look of mischief on her face. "No, Pop-Tarts," she repeated back to me with a half-grin. Fuck. She was beautiful.

I waited until tires crunched gravel down Mom's driveway before letting out a deep sigh—hot air fogging the windshield as a fingernail moon rose over fields sleeping under dew blankets where nothing good ever dies quietly.

The truck door rattled as I slammed it shut and made my way into the compound tech office, the dust of the late-summer night kicking up behind me. The room glowed with the light of LED displays, computers humming with a low and constant buzz as Wrecker's silhouette cut against their screens. I flopped in the chair across from him and crossed my arms over my chest. "I need to know every piece of information you've found on Julia—her background, her family, everything." The letters clicked into place as his fingers moved. My world growing more complicated with every keystroke.

"Well, you're gonna be disappointed. I've been checking and don't have much, because Julia Harris ain't your girl."

I froze. "What do you mean?"

"NYC DMV records show a Julia Marie Harris died seven months ago. Hit-and-run on Park Avenue."

I sat up straighter in my chair. The whirring of hard drives and the window unit's hum buzzed in the room. "Glitch in their system?"

"Funeral home receipts say otherwise."

Wrecker looked back at his screens. They filled with maps and background data. "You want me to hack facial recognition systems, boss?"

"Anywhere you can." I leaned forward. "There's somethin' in her past, somethin' we can't see yet."

I thought about the ledgers in her arms as I'd left her at her apartment. I now knew I was right about the fact that she was hiding something about herself. Something big.

"Is she in trouble?" Wrecker's voice was steady as he asked. I couldn't be sure if he was wondering about her or about what the hell I was doing falling in this fast and this deep.

"She's something." I met his eyes, the dim glow from the monitors flashing across his face. "Definitely hiding something or *from* someone."

Wrecker knew better than anyone how to disappear from sight, how to erase yourself and everything about you. If he didn't, there was a good chance he wouldn't still be alive and on our side of the law. It was imperative that we had the ability to become ghosts when we took certain covert missions. Unlocking others trying to do the same was his specialty.

We talked for a couple of hours. I told him about some of the things she'd said that led me to believe she was hiding from someone. I told him about the signs of abuse I'd seen. We're all particularly sensitive about men who abuse women. Three years ago a rival pack's Alpha had seen Bridger's sister Emma at a regional pack gathering. He decided he wanted her as his mate. I presented his offer to Emma. This alpha's reputation for cruelty was well known, and thankfully, Emma refused the offer. A week later. Emma went missing. We knew the Greenbriar Pack had taken her, but we had no direct proof. They are a large and powerful pack, so we had to tread carefully. We went through channels with the Supreme Supernatural Council, but after an investigation they denied having her, and the council found no proof that she was on their pack lands. So, we did what we do best, found her and extracted her. The Greenbriar Alpha was killed in the rescue. The Council reprimanded us for the way the rescue went down, but based on her condition, the council ruled we were justified in acting quickly. Greenbriar was sanctioned, which just meant they lost voting privileges for five years. They carry a vendetta to this day. Emma never recovered from her injuries. They'd bound her in silver so often her injuries couldn't heal properly. She passed away two weeks after we'd recovered her. Menace never got over it.

We take abuse of women damn fucking seriously around here. Julia, or whoever she was, had the hallmarks of an abuse victim. I would not let that stand.

The rest of the compound was quiet as we continued to discuss my little bookkeeper.

"I thought I was just hiring some uptown numbers expert," I said, more to myself than to him.

"Looks like you're in deep." He tilted his head, a shadow of amusement behind the words.

"Get used to it," I said, crossing my arms over my chest as the computer started filling with files. "I think she's stayin' awhile."

"Gonna introduce her to the pack, then?" Wrecker's expression was unreadable, but he'd been around long enough to know the signs. He could probably smell the change on me before I could myself.

"I am. I don't fucking care who she is. She's wolf, and she's called me."

"Well, boss, at least we know Julia Harris is dead."

I just shook my head. That beautiful little liar. "Definitely sure there's no mix-up?"

"Unless the Andrews Funeral Home in Cortland, New York buried the wrong person. This Julia Harris has the same date of birth, eye and hair color. She definitely passed in that car wreck on January 1, 2024."

"I'll be damned. Her paperwork looked fucking professional. I want you to pull out all the stops. Go ahead with facial recognition, the works. And when you find out who she is, I want to know who her parents are. Her grandparents. Everyone. The girl has wolf blood, and I want to know where it came from. I want to know yesterday."

"I'll have it for you by the party at the clubhouse."

"See that you do."

# CHAPTER 7

## JULIET

The first conscious breath tasted like fresh cotton and freedom. Not the perfumed jasmine of my usual morning haze back in New York, but oil-stained desert blooming plants and dry prairie air seeping through the barely opened window. My fingers curled into cotton sheets still holding the chill of desert nights as the dream residue slipped away—something about running through sagebrush, earth crunching deliciously beneath...

I jerked upright, palm pressed to my racing heart. The movement sent my hair tumbling down from the loose hair tie that had held the messy bun I'd slept in last night. A recent conversation with Pearl looped behind my eyelids when I blinked, her sweet voice slicing through the bar's whiskey haze. "Black doesn't suit an angel like you, darlin'."

The mirror above the apartment's sink showed the damage. Midnight dye job bleeding violet at the roots, bangs hacked just short enough to graze my lashes. A thrift store disguise stitched together with drugstore recklessness. My reflection wavered like a heat mirage over pavement, part runaway debutante, part scavenged roadkill.

Coffee grounds hissed as I dumped them into the filter, the sound syncopating with gravel popping under tires out on County Road 14. A few weeks since I'd traded marble foyers for this cute little one-bedroom filled with hopes, fear, and ambition. My pinky finger tapped the arrhythmic Morse code against the butcher block countertop—not going back, not going back, not—

A wolf's howl split the predawn stillness.

Or maybe just the wind through the canyon. I gripped my mug tighter, lukewarm liquid sloshing onto my skin. The memory arrived unbidden. Last night's moon hanging low and heavy as a bullet hole in the sky, that chorus of animal cries reverberating in my marrow. Something had answered deep in my gut, a primal string plucked hard enough to make my molars ache.

I made my way to my sweet little bathroom to wash my face and get my teeth brushed.

Bronc's knuckles rapped twice on the metal door. "You decent?"

I spat toothpaste froth into the sink and rinsed then headed to the door. "Define decent."

Put some pants on; we're heading to breakfast before work.

A small smile split my face as I yelled through the door, "Down in a minute!"

The smell of burnt coffee grounds and sourdough toast followed me into Dairyville's only twenty-four-hour diner. I stopped off in the restroom to fix my hair that had fallen out of my hair tie. God, what a mess. Bronc already occupied the corner booth; two mugs already sat steaming between placemats stained with decades of pancake syrup when I returned. His leather cut lay draped over the vinyl seatback like a second skin shed for my benefit.

"They're out of oat milk." He didn't look up from dismantling a sugar packet, calloused fingers precise as a bomb technician's. "Got you the cinnamon swirl French toast special."

I slid into the booth, knees brushing denim under the table. "How'd you know?"

"Noticed you doctoring your coffee with enough sugar to put a diabetic in a coma." His boot tapped mine—accidental?

Deliberate? The laminated menu trembled in my grip. "Figured French toast fell in the same category."

Three truckers at the counter swiveled on their stools when my laugh came out unbidden. Bronc's gaze tracked their reflection in the dust-specked mirror behind me. Something feral glinted beneath his civility, there and gone like the flick of a switch.

"Those wolves were at it again last night." I stirred creamer into my coffee, watching the liquid spiral into caramel depths. "Closer this time."

His teaspoon stilled mid-stir. Silver glinted at his temples where the diner's fluorescents caught threads of gray. "Probably coyotes. Sound carries funny over the plains at—"

"I know what I heard." The words emerged steadier than I felt. My left palm itched; strange sensations suddenly flaring. "Five distinct voices. One deeper than the others. Lower register, almost..."

*Almost human.* The unspoken words vibrated between us. Bronc's knuckles whitened around his mug. Across the diner, the waitress's voice carried through the service window as she berated a line cook about over-easy yolks.

He leaned back; the booth creaking under his weight. Sunlight through greasy windows caught the amber flecks in his eyes. "You always this obsessed with local wildlife?"

"Only the ones that sound like they're harmonizing." My smile felt stretched too tight. "Funny thing—whenever they start up, my... Never mind."

Bronc's eyebrow quirked. Heat flooded my cheeks as last night's dream resurged—hot and vivid as the Texas sun.

**Four hours earlier**

Calloused palms skimmed my ribs. The scent of motor oil and sagebrush. Warmth pooled low in my belly as teeth grazed the juncture of throat and shoulder. Not pain—*promise.* Bronc's voice rougher than denim wash, whispered things that made my toes curl in cotton sheets. *"Knew you'd taste like trouble..."* Then his face was between my legs, lapping at me like a dog drinking after being on a long run. All the way up from center to my clit. God, it was so real.

I'd woken gasping, thighs clenched around nothing, every nerve ending shrieking. The AC unit's hum had done nothing to cool the furnace under my skin. Through my apartment's thin walls, the distant howl of wolves had threaded through my panting breaths. Aching. Beckoning.

Now, across this small table, Bronc cleared his throat. "You okay? You're doing that starey thing."

"Hmm?" I nearly dropped my fork. "Just... thinking about something. Sorry."

His smirk said he knew exactly where my mind had wandered. Bastard.

The motorcycle shop's bell jangled like a drunk's laugh when I pushed through the glass door two hours later. It seemed like everything lately came down to scent. Bronc's office smelled of WD-40 and questions—the lingering ghosts of cigarettes smoked by previous accountants. I traced a finger along the ledger's cracked spine, the numbers inside whispering secrets in binary code.

I had quickly found four thousand dollars unaccounted for in spare parts orders. Invoices for Harley-Davidson tires dated six months after the company switched suppliers. A separate bank account with transactions timed to club runs. My finger split the calculator tape clean down the middle.

"Problem?" Maddie leaned against the doorframe, polishing a chrome fender with her grease-stained apron. I'd met Bronc's sister a week ago and instantly fell in love. Her resemblance to Bronc tightened my throat—same stubborn jaw, same predator's grace.

"Just cross-checking inventory." I flipped the ledger closed. The lie tasted like pennies. "Your brother keeps messy books."

She choked out a laugh. "Sounds about right. Or at least his past bookkeepers did. I'm bettin' you don't though." She gave me a Hollywood smile before she walked back into the shop.

The ancient wall clock ticked off three minutes after she left. I reopened the ledger, red flags blooming across spreadsheets like bloodstains. Three vendors listed under PO boxes near Amarillo. Two with phone numbers disconnected. One registered to a defunct LLC dissolved in 2019.

My pen hovered over the damning figures. Bronc's laughter rumbled through the shop walls as he haggled with a customer over exhaust pipe modifications. He put a premium on trust. And it looked like someone he should have been able to put his faith in was ripping him off. Trust warred with self-preservation—a familiar tango. What did $4,000 buy in Dairyville? Silence? Complicity? A shallow grave out by the canyon? I was new to the whole equation.

I promised Bronc I'd find out who was doing what. And I would. But I'd wait until I'd mapped it all out..

I tucked the evidence between innocent columns of numbers, a razor blade hidden in cotton candy. Bronc's shadow fell across the desk as evening painted the shop in oil-slick rainbows.

"Ready for your ride home, Miss Daisy?"

His thumb brushed mine, reaching for the ledger. Electricity arced between us—the same charge as in my dream. His nostrils flared like he could smell the memory on me.

"Everything balanced?" He asked for the benefit of anyone who could hear.

"Like a house of cards." I smiled sweetly, shutting the ledger with finality. "You should really consider QuickBooks."

His laughter followed me to the door, warm and dangerous. Outside, the first stars pricked through bruised purple skies. Somewhere beyond the town limits, wolves began to sing.

Receipts, purchase orders, and work orders going back months and into the previous year started to reveal a pattern. An overcharge here, a back order not received but paid there. It added up. I needed to tell Bronc. And I would, once I knew what was really happening.

The shop's overhead bell jangled like prison keys. I didn't look up from the ledger until cherry-red stilettos clicked into my peripheral vision.

"Christ on a bender. You weren't kidding about the Morticia vibe."

Maddie stood there, arms crossed beneath a leather corset that looked weaponized. Her dark hair slicked back into a high ponytail. "We're stripping that box dye tonight, yeah? Got Tina mixing the bleach cocktail over at Shear Ecstasy."

My fingers crept to the brittle ends of my hair. "Oh, yeah?"

"My big bro's never asked me to play fairy godmother before. But he arranged this little intervention." Her love and admiration for Bronc shone on her face. "Figured you must be really special." My heart might have skipped a beat.

The drive to the salon was short and revealing. Maddy slapped the steering wheel along to mewithoutyou. "So. You screwing my brother yet?"

I choked on the seatbelt.

"Relax, city mouse. All our prospects get vetted. I had to ask." Laughter followed. "But Bronc? Man hasn't brought a woman to the compound since... hell, since Bush was president. Which one? That would be W, but still a long damn time, girlfriend."

"Honestly, will anyone think it's weird? Won't they think I'm too young? I mean, I don't care. He's amazing in every way. What am I even talking about? Look, Maddie, there is no way your brother would have the slightest interest in a girl like me. He's so...

and I'm just..." I looked down at myself. All the shortcomings my mother had ever pointed out came to my mind. "He's just being nice. Trying to help me make friends."

"Uh huh. Keep thinkin' that little mouse. You're a sweetheart. Girl with a light around you like you got, you don't need help makin' friends."

The stylist, Tina, winced when she examined my roots. "Honey, who hurt you?"

Layers of black rinsed away in a sink stained coral from decades of rinse cycles. She massaged my temples, calluses catching on baby hairs. "Your natural gold's gorgeous. Like honey on toast."

Foils were folded across my scalp by the dozens. Maddie sprawled on the pedicure throne, scrolling through Grindr. "Blue eyes, six-two, tribal tats—swipe left. Ooh, bearded bear in the wife-beater..."

Mirrors told pretty lies here. The woman staring back at me wore borrowed confidence—golden balayage framing cheekbones I'd forgotten existed. Maddy wolf-whistled. "Fuck me sideways. Bronc's gonna swallow his tongue."

He was leaning against his King Ranch when we emerged. The dying sun caught silver strands in his close-trimmed beard as his gaze traveled from my restored highlights to the artfully torn jeans and a black tank top Maddy had produced from her backseat.

"Well?" I twirled, heart jackhammering. "Still look like I rob graves?"

Bronc's fingers ran through my golden beach waves that thank goodness didn't need more than a trim, bangs and all. His voice was just above a whisper. "Ma was right. An angel in the flesh." His hand traced over my neck as he turned to open the door for me.

The clubhouse throbbed with bass notes and body heat. Neon beer signs baptized strangers in cerulean and crimson light. A redhead with neck tattoos handed me a mason jar of something that smelled like rocket fuel and good times. "Prospect special. Drink three and you'll let Doc here pierce anything." I looked over at the handsome giant with wire-framed glasses who gave me a small head nod.

Bronc's hand settled between my shoulder blades as names and faces blurred. Some guy named Jester showed off his new nipple rings; Chainsaw debated barbecue techniques with a woman breastfeeding twins; Gator arm-wrestled a teenager by the pool table. My laugh sounded foreign, buoyant. Every man was brawny, tatted, and had muscles for days. It was a far cry from every gala and charity ball I'd attended in New York. But it was honest.

Maddie materialized with tequila shots. "To fresh starts!"

The burn down my throat kindled something reckless. I licked salt from my knuckles as Bronc's ringed fingers tightened around his own glass. His gaze lingered where citrus juice glistened on my lower lip.

"Easy, boss." Maddie elbowed him. "She's gotta work tomorrow."

"Tomorrow's Sunday."

"True story! I forgot. Drink up, Julia!"

The room tilted just enough to make me clutch Bronc's forearm. Muscled. Strong. Heat radiating through cotton. My hand slid to his wrist. His pulse jumped beneath my fingertips—a wild thing caged.

Somewhere beyond the compound walls, wolves began singing. My skin prickled like static before lightning strikes.

Bronc leaned close, whiskey and mint washing over me. "Still think they're scary?"

I watched his throat work as he swallowed. "I'm starting to like dangerous things."

Across the crowded room, a woman with electric-blue braids balanced twin toddlers on her hips while arguing with Chainsaw about the merits of mesquite versus hickory wood chips. Her laugh boomed through the chatter. "Sugar, if you can't smoke a brisket proper, just admit you're better at changing diapers."

Maddie pressed another drink into my hand—something fruity this time, condensation bleeding through the napkin. "That's T-Bone's old lady, Roxy. Don't let the mom act fool you. She once stabbed a guy through the hand with a meat thermometer."

"Overcooked steak?"

"Improper use of dry rub."

A snort escaped me before I could swallow it down. Bronc's low chuckle vibrated against my shoulder blade where he stood guard behind me. His pinky brushed the nape of neck, just once. Static crackled in the wake of his touch.

Jester sauntered over, silver hoops glinting beneath his open cut. "President's pet projects always get the good shampoo, huh?" He sniffed loudly near my hair. "Cherry blossoms and bullshit."

Bronc's growl shook the floorboards. "Eyes. Hands. Teeth. Keep 'em to yourself."

"Relax, Grandpa. Just welcoming committee business." Jester winked at me, all smiles and mischief. "Word of advice, princess? Never play poker with Gator. Dude's got a tell involving his—"

A teenage girl vaulted over the couch, combat boots spraying sawdust. "Tell Jester he owes me twenty bucks!"

Jester's laughter carried over the noise. "Now, Scar, I beat you fair and square!"

I blinked at the jagged line bisecting her left eyebrow. "Your name's Scar?"

"Birth certificate says Charlotte. Life says otherwise." She jerked her chin toward the pool table where Gator was teaching a preteen to chalk a cue. "Bet him I could outrun his Harley in wolf form. Short circuit took out his ignition coil at mile three."

Maddie's eyes got big and she shook her head at the gorgeous teen, then cut her eyes toward me. "We talked about that, Charlotte." She told her in a low voice.

"Sorry, Auntie."

I must have misunderstood what they were saying. Wolf form must be some kind of motorcycle talk. The room went a little sideways as someone cranked the stereo. A Lynyrd Skynyrd riff collided with the clack of billiard balls. Scar dragged me into a chaotic lesson on Texas Hold 'em, her friends dealing cards onto a grease-stained toolbox by the bar. My third whiskey sour burned through residual nerves, leaving flushed cheeks and loosened syllables in its wake.

"Pair of queens!" I announced, fanning my cards with mock solemnity.

Scar's friend slammed his fist on the makeshift table. "Bullshit! She's bluffing!"

Bronc's shadow fell across our circle. "Wouldn't bet on it. Lady's got a forensic accounting degree."

Eighteen eyes swiveled toward me. Scar whistled. "You keeping books for the club now?"

"I'm working on the shop's ledgers right now. Trying to make heads or tails of the inventory and all.." The words slipped out smoother than I'd intended, edged with a smirk I didn't recognize.

Laughter erupted like gunfire. Someone tossed a pretzel at my head. Bronc caught it midair, his smirk mirroring mine. For a heartbeat, the world narrowed to the flecks of gold in his irises—molten, primal, approving.

Maddie materialized with a platter of smoked ribs, sauce smeared across her leather vest. "Move your felony-in-training ass, Scar. Grown folk talking." She hip-checked her niece aside, lowering her voice as she handed me a napkin. "Heard you spotted some discrepancies."

The rib grease turned acrid on my tongue. "Minor ledger issues. Probably input errors."

"Uh-huh." She licked sauce off her thumb. "Bronc, tell you we had three bookkeepers quit this year?"

Ice slid down my spine despite the room's feverish warmth. "That happens sometimes. People move around until they find the right fit."

I noticed Skeeter hovering in the shadows, listening to our conversation.

"Let's call it creative differences." Her gaze drifted to where Jester was arm-wrestling a prospect. "Thing about motorcycle clubs? We prefer problems that can be solved with torque wrenches or tire irons. Spreadsheets..." She shrugged. "Tend to combust."

Fireworks of pain exploded behind my eyes—memory fragments of shattered laptops, shredded bank statements, Harrison's polished loafers grinding glass into carpet. My fingers found the small scar on the inside of my arm, raised tissue mapping old punishments.

Bronc's boot nudged mine under the table. When I glanced up, his gaze locked on me. *Safe*, his eyes promised. *Protected*.

The back door crashed open, wind hauling in the scent of rain and distant musk. Wolves harmonized beyond the tree line—a sound that no longer sparked fear, but recognition. My pulse answered in double-time, blood singing with secrets I couldn't name.

A woman named Roxy appeared at my elbow, one baby gnawing a teething ring shaped like a skull. "They're calling you, honey."

"The wolves?"

"Nah. The parts of yourself you've been starving." She adjusted the sleeping toddler on her shoulder. "They ain't ever wrong."

Bronc's hand closed over mine beneath the table. Calluses snagged on my knuckles, anchor and spark combined. Around us, the pack laughed and brawled and lived in Technicolor chaos. For the first time since fleeing New York, I craved rather than cowered.

The realization tasted like freedom and folly. Like tequila and terminal velocity.

Somewhere beyond the compound lights, another wolf howled—longing given sound. Strangely, my throat ached to answer. I took another drink.

Wrecker appeared to my left and tapped Bronc on the shoulder. "Hey boss. Can you meet me in the office for just a minute?"

Hesitation colored his movements. "Only a minute." He rubbed the back of my neck. "You ok for me to step away?"

Won't lie. I didn't want him to. But I'd put on my big-girl panties today. "No worries. Go ahead." I put on my best 'I got this' smile.

# CHAPTER 8

## BRONC

The bass from the jukebox vibrated through my boot soles as I followed Wrecker toward the office. Laughter and the sharp clack of pool balls followed us down the hallway lined with framed photos of old club runs. My fingers grazed the cool brass doorknob, the metal tasting like static against my palm before we stepped into the windowless room.

Wrecker didn't bother with the desk lamp. The glow from the multiple computer screens carved shadows under his cheekbones as he tapped the spacebar. "Ran her through every system I could access."

Three surveillance stills filled the monitor—Julia's profile caught mid-laugh behind Pearl's counter, her head tilted at that angle that made her neck look breakably delicate. Red text scrolled across the bottom: ***MATCH: 98.7% JULIET BETTEN-COURT***, daughter of Jules Bettencourt, B&A Financial, hedge funds.

My knuckles popped before I realized I'd clenched my fists. "More?"

"So much more." Wrecker's thumbnail clicked against the trackpad, pulling up a society page photo that stole the oxygen from the room. There she stood in ivory silk and diamonds cold enough to frost the screen, arm linked with a man whose smile had more edges than his Armani suit. "Harrison Hastings IV. Old New York money, pharmaceuticals. With a side of assault charges that never stuck."

The AC unit kicked on, blowing dust across the keyboard. I watched it settle in the crevice between the R and T keys. "That who she's running from?"

"Court records are sealed tighter than a virgin's cunt."

"Damn it," my mind was racing, worry thickening my voice. Through the thin wall, Julia's laughter spilled into the room—warm honey laced with tequila. My wolf stirred beneath my ribs, phantom claws scoring bone.

Wrecker leaned back in the creaking office chair, the leather sighing under his weight. "I'm thinking runaway bride. Look at this."

My eyes read over a New York Times Page Six engagement announcement. "Their wedding was supposed to happen last week." I palmed the stress ball from his desk, some neon-green monstrosity shaped like a brain. The squelch of silicone filled the silence between drumbeats seeping through the walls. "She got out in the nick of time."

"Yep." He gestured at the screen where the engagement ring glinted like a sniper's scope. "That's only part of it, Bronc."

I tossed the stress ball onto the desk, and it rolled towards him. "Tell me."

He handed me a thick folder. Filled with copies of birth certificates, marriage licenses, and black and white photos, Juliet's lineage laid before me.

"Fuck me."

"It's a lot to take in." Wrecker's voice was quiet.

"I don't feel so bad about wanting her now. She's still 18 years younger than me." I ran my hand through my hair.

"Dude. Once she hits 40, y'all will be about even," he said, laughing.

He wasn't wrong. The wolves in our pack lived a couple hundred years. Once we hit our forties, our aging slowed down to a crawl. She would eventually catch me. Didn't mean I wouldn't get more than a few dirty looks from the human population. Not that I had a single fuck to give about it.

I pulled the door open before I could respond, releasing a wave of Lynyrd Skynyrd and the tang of spilled beer. Through the crack, I saw her—perched on a barstool with two cards in her grip. Maddie's arm slung around her shoulders, Scar dealt another round. Julia or Juliet threw her head back laughing, throat exposed, and every muscle in my body went wire-tight.

"Christ, she's glowing," Wrecker muttered, not unkindly. "Like someone plugged her into a socket."

She was. The cheap club lights haloed her wild waves as she laid cards down, completing a winning hand, the table erupting in groans and tossed poker chips.

My back molars ground together. "She's drunk."

"Multiple alcoholic drinks will do that." Wrecker snapped the laptop closed. "You want me to—"

"I'll handle it." The words came out sharper than intended. Through the haze of lust, contemplation, and neon, I tracked the swing of Julia's hips as she slid off the stool. Her black tank top clung to her danger zones as her hips swayed to the music. She was no longer the malnourished woman who'd stepped off that bus weeks ago. She now had curves that were undeniably sexy, and every wolf in the room had taken notice.

Somewhere behind my sternum, my wolf bared his teeth. Not at her. Never at her. At the hungry eyes following the motion—prospects and hang-arounds alike, tongues hanging out like dogs at a steakhouse. My thumb found the scar bisecting my palm, an old knife wound from a mission in Slovenia. The ache grounded me. Barely.

"Need me to—"

"Stand down, Wreck." I was already moving, boots eating up the scarred hardwood. The club's heartbeat thrummed in my veins; pool balls cracking like gunshots, ice cubes screaming in glasses, the creak of leather vests breathing with each rise and fall of chests.

Her scent hit me first. Ginger, burned sugar, and fear buried so deep only a shifter would catch it. She turned as I approached, cards fluttering from her grip. Five of hearts landed face-up on my boot tip as she passed.

The card stuck like a paper cutout of bad luck. Through the haze of tequila fumes and Lynyrd Skynyrd wailing through blown speakers, I counted seven sets of eyes tracking her sway toward the makeshift dance floor. Seven fucking prospects specifically, who'd forgotten whose territory they were sniffing around. My knuckles popped in time with the bass line.

"Prez." A hang-around named Rook materialized at my left elbow, reeking of Drakkar Noir and eagerness. "Can I get you anything?"

"Air." The word came out half-growl. Wolf saliva pooled under my tongue, coppery and hot. Across the room, Juliet threw her head back, laughing at something Snake's latest fling whispered in her ear. The sound punched through my solar plexus. "*Mine.*" The beast gnawed at my ribs, all primal hunger and single-minded possession.

Rook scrambled backward, colliding with a waitress carrying a tray of Jäger bombs. Glass shattered. No one looked.

Juliet's hips found the rhythm of "Sweet Home Alabama," her movements liquid grace underscored by tequila courage. Three guitar chords later, Gunner's newest prospect—kid couldn't be older than twenty-two with his baby-faced swagger—slid up behind her. His palms settled on her waist.

My vision tunneled.

The song warped into a distorted whine. Every follicle on my arms stood rigid. The prospect's fingers flexed, thumbs brushing the underside of her ribs. Juliet stiffened, a fractional hitch in her breathing that would've been imperceptible to human ears.

I was moving before conscious thought kicked in. Bodies parted like wheat before a combine. Somewhere to my right, Maddie's whiskey-cured laugh cut off mid-cackle. The prospect's grip tightened as he leaned in, lips grazing the shell of Juliet's ear.

Her hands came up to push at his wrists. Too slow. Too polite. Mine weren't.

"Hands." I locked the kid's thumb in a pressure hold, peeling him off her like a sweaty t-shirt. His yelp harmonized with the static of the speakers. "You're fond of these?"

"Bronc, Jesus—" Juliet stumbled sideways, pupils blown wide. Tequila and adrenaline soured her sweat.

The prospect wheezed, knees buckling. "Didn't mean no—"

"Disrespect?" I completed his sentence through gritted teeth. "You're fluent in it."

Scar materialized from the mob, silver earrings catching the strobe lights. "Got him, Prez." Her hand closed around the kid's collar.

I didn't wait to see the fallout. Juliet's pulse thrummed against my palm where I'd grabbed her wrist—rabbit-quick and fluttering. She tried to dig in her heels near the women's bathroom, but I shouldered through the fire exit into the service corridor. Fluorescent lights buzzed overhead, bleaching the scuffed linoleum.

"Let go." She twisted, nails scoring my forearm. "You don't get to—"

I caged her against cinderblock walls painted industrial green. Her chest heaved, blonde bangs sticking to damp temples. My wolf preened at having her trapped, at the way her pupils dilated despite the anger tightening her mouth.

"You want to play at being brave?" My voice came out gravel-rough. "Fine. But you don't get to dance with danger in my house."

Her chin jerked up. "Your house? Last I checked—"

"My rules." I crowded closer, knee slotting between her thighs. She caught her breath. "You stroll in here smelling like sunshine after a decade of thunderstorms and expect—"

"Sunshine doesn't have a scent."

"It does on you." My nose skimmed her hairline. Vanilla. Salt. Faintest hint of jasmine shampoo. "Like crushed ginger and sugar."

She trembled. Or I did. The distinction blurred.

"Why does it matter?" Her whisper ghosted over my lips. "I'm just another—"

"Lie." My thumb found the frantic leap of her carotid. "You're champagne in a beer can, Juliet."

She froze. The name hung between us—an indictment and a plea.

I watched the realization crash through her, shoulders tensing, throat working, right hand twitching toward the exit sign. Her tells were textbook; upper-class training warring with feral survival instincts.

"Don't." I bracketed her hips. "Running's what got you here."

Her laugh cracked like thin ice. "And where's here exactly? Some backwoods purgatory where bikers play white knight?"

"Purgatory's got a pool table and bottomless pretzels." I traced the shell of her ear, delighting in her shiver. "Stay. Fight."

"For what?"

The challenge hung in the air, ripe and trembling. Behind us, the exit sign's red glow threw her face into sharp relief—flushed cheeks, parted lips, eyes gone midnight-dark.

I answered without words.

Our collision echoed off concrete walls—a cacophony of desperate hands and shattered restraint. Her mouth burned hotter than August asphalt, tasting of lime and recklessness. When she bit my lower lip, my wolf nearly shredded my skin from the inside.

"Bronc." My name spilled from her like a curse and a prayer.

I hauled her up, her legs locking around my waist. Her jeans just loose enough to give her room to squeeze me exactly right. The beast purred approval.

"Oh, God." She gasped.

I had to stop this. She was too drunk to consent. And I wouldn't do this until she understood what I was and that I knew who she really was.

"No."

Her face. All beauty and confusion. "No?"

"No Juliet. We can't do this. First of all, you're in no condition."

Her legs let go and slowly slid down my massive frame and hit the ground. If it were possible, I'd swear she was getting drunker by the minute.

"Fine. I get it."

I took her face in my hands. Those espresso orbs filled with tears were killing me.

"No, I don't think you do. But you will. Let me take you home."

She stomped her foot and almost fell over. "I will *not* let you take me home!"

"Ok Juliet. If that's how you want it."

I bent down and threw her over my shoulder. The parade through the clubhouse was not my finest moment, but I had zero fucks to give. I snatched her purse from the coatroom, and we were gone.

By the time I buckled her into the truck's passenger seat, she'd retreated into that glassy-eyed stillness rich girls perfect in finishing school.

The dashboard clock glowed 1:47 AM as we made the short trek to her apartment. She didn't speak until I killed the engine.

"Don't." She slapped my hand, reaching for her seatbelt. "I'm not some broken—"

Her heel caught on the running board. I caught her centimeters from the asphalt, tequila fumes blooming between us. "Easy, hellcat."

"Don't touch me!" She writhed, elbow connecting with my solar plexus. "I don't need your... your..."

The first dry heave doubled her over. I barely got out of the way before my boots were baptized in the remains of the barbecue she'd eaten earlier.

Bent over her on the driveway, I gathered her freshly colored hair while her body purged poison. Each convulsion mapped her vertebrae through thin cotton. My fault. Should've cut her off after the third tequila.

"M'fine," she slurred, swatting weakly as I carried her inside. "Put me down, you... you..."

"Neanderthal?" I got her door unlocked and got her into the quaint apartment that I'd only recently remodeled. "Original."

Her fist connected with my jaw. "Asshole."

"Consistent." I deposited her on the wedding ring quilt that adorned the wrought iron bed, ignoring how the moonlight caught the tears slipping past clenched lashes. "Boots off. Now."

She fumbled with the laces. I turned to the bathroom faucet to grab water, but the whimper froze me mid-step.

"Damn... fucking..."

The switchblade snicked open before I registered reaching for it. Juliet recoiled, arms crossed over her chest.

"For the laces." I knelt, slicing leather cords with surgical precision. Her breathing quickened when my fingers brushed an ankle bone sharper as I slid a boot from her foot.

The second boot thudded somewhere in the dark. She collapsed backward, one arm flung over her eyes. "Just go."

I should've. Would've. If not for the quarter-moon marks peeking below her forearm.

When I returned with the glass of water, she'd twisted herself in the sheets—tank top rucked to reveal that damned scar.

"Drink."

She turned her face away.

I gripped her chin, gentler than my wolf wanted. "Don't make me pour it down your—"

Her teeth sank into my thumb.

"Christ, woman!" The glass shattered against the hardwoods. She lunged for the biggest shard.

We hit the floor in a tangle of limbs and ragged breaths. Her back arched under me, wildcat fury burning through the liquor haze. "Get... off!"

"Stop. Fighting. Juliet!" I pinned her wrists, horror dawning as her struggles grew more frantic. Not anger—terror.

Submission came sudden and violent. Her body went slack, face turning aside to expose the unmarked cheek. Waiting.

Ice flooded my veins. Slowly—hands raised—I rolled off. "Juliet..."

"Don't call me that!" She scrambled backward until she was sitting against the wall. "He... when I wouldn't..."

The confession hung in sour air. I ground my molars until enamel threatened to crack. "Never laid hands on a woman. Never will."

Her laugh shredded what remained of my control. "No? What do you call tonight?"

"Tonight..." I stood, towering over her cowered form. "I was just trying to keep you from harming yourself and failing spectacularly."

The bathroom light revealed what I'd expect. A neat basket of toothpaste and face wash and other toiletries sat on the counter. Another with rolled towels and washcloths expertly placed in a row sat next to the tub. I soaked a fluffy hand towel in cool water.

She didn't resist when I cleaned the puke from her chin. Didn't react when I pried the glass shard from her bloodied palm. Just stared through me with those, now I knew were Bettencourt eyes—amber flecks set in espresso.

"Bed," I ordered when the clock ticked past three. She crawled atop the mess of covers without argument. Robotically, she lifted her arms as I peeled off the sweat-stained tank. I averted my eyes from the lace bralette. The hints of scars showed across her ribs. Failed.

Covering her felt like burying a Stradivarius in mud. I slipped an oversized tee over her head then helped her out of her jeans. I lingered to ensure she didn't choke on her own vomit, counting each shallow breath. Her hair fanned across the pillowcase—a golden halo.

"Stay." Her whisper stopped me as I stood.

I looked back at her. "Can't."

"Why?"

The truth perched on my tongue, feathered and lethal. *Because if I touch you now, I'll break my oath. Because you taste like forever, and I stopped believing in that twenty years ago.*

"Sleep it off, Juliet."

Her fingers caught my belt loop as I turned to leave. The contact burned through denim. "Not done talking."

The mattress creaked. I didn't look. Couldn't. Not when her voice had gone liquid and sharp all at once—vodka sincerity laced with lemon truth.

"You smell like...like leather and..." Her nose wrinkled against the stench of bile still clinging to us both. "And desert and engine oil."

"Perfume of the damned." I tried prying her hand loose. Mistake. Her palm pressed flat against my stomach, branding through cotton.

She laughed—a wet, broken sound. "You're warm. Harrison always felt..." Teeth sunk into chapped lips. A shudder ran through her slight frame. "Cold. Like money."

My wolf thrashed against its chains. *Kill him. Bury him. Make her ours.*

Her touch wandered higher. "Bronc..."

Every cell screamed to cover her body with mine. To lick tequila off her collarbone. To bite until she understood ownership. Instead, I gripped her wrist almost hard enough to bruise. "Sleep."

"Don't want to." She rolled onto her knees, sheets pooling at her waist. Moonlight through cracked blinds painted stripes across her delicate features. "Want you. Even if..." Her throat worked. "Even if it's just tonight."

The dresser mirror reflected our tableau—her trembling against the headboard wrought iron, me standing like a fucking monument to restraint. My knuckles whitened around her bones. "You're pickled, Little Wolf."

"So?" Defiance warped into something jagged. "Afraid I'll regret it? Newsflash—every damn choice I've made since turning eighteen tastes like battery acid. At least this..." Her free hand traced my jaw. "... would burn less."

I released her like scalding metal. Six steps to the door. Five more would take me through drywall and into blessed nothingness.

Her whisper hooked between my ribs. "Please. I need to know what it's like...to be with someone I want."

The floorboards groaned as I leaned in. Her breath hitched when I caged her face in my hands. Our foreheads touched—whiskey and tequila still lingered on her breath in the scant space between lips.

"Listen good." My thumb brushed the racing pulse in her neck. "When I fuck you? You'll be sober. Begging. Certain."

Her lashes fluttered. "Arrogant ass."

"Realist." I forced myself backward, muscles screaming. "We got rules. Codes."

"For mechanics?"

*For wolves.* "For men who don't prey on wounded things."

I reached the doorway as her laughter fractured, sharp edges cutting the dark. "Wounded, right." The mattress springs wailed as she collapsed. "Run along then. Leave this broken thing where it is."

The living room was neat as a pin. As I'd expect from the meticulous Juliet Bettencourt. Control what you can control. For her, it seemed wasn't goddamn much. What in fuck's name was I going to do with a 25-year-old girl? I laughed to myself. Claim her. That's what.

At 4:17 AM, she whimpered.

At 5:02, another glass shattered.

By 6:45, dawn threatened sunny lace curtains. I lay staring at the ceiling, rehearsing truths that could make or break us.

*Your real name's Juliet.*

*I know some of what he did.*

*You're one of us.*

I left to get fresh coffee. I needed to be awake for the conversation to come.

# Chapter 9

## Juliet

The alarm clock's red numbers burned through my eyelids before I remembered I hadn't set one. My tongue clung to the roof of my mouth, cotton-dry and tasting of stale tequila. I rolled onto my side, quilt bunching beneath me, the wrought iron bed frame creaking as my stomach lurched. Through the haze of nausea came the memory of large hands slipping the shirt over my head, calloused fingertips brushing my collarbone.

"Shit."

I bolted upright, vision swimming. Bronc's aftershave lingered on my pillowcase, cedar and leather. The living room couch sat empty behind the half-open bedroom door, indented leather cushions still holding the shape of him.

I stumbled into the bathroom, knees cracking against hexagonal tiles as I gripped the marble sink. The mirror showed a stranger—even though the hair color was now correct. Kohl smeared beneath eyes that looked too young in my gaunt face. I turned the faucet hard left, cupping cold water to scrub away the remnants of mascara and poor decisions.

The shower handle squealed when I twisted it, copper pipes shuddering behind butter-yellow walls. Steam rose around the clawfoot tub as I stepped in, the handheld spray nozzle trembling in my grip. Too-hot water needled my shoulders where Harrison had once dug his fingers deep enough to bruise. Except those bruises faded, but the memory lingered. Now they were just phantom pains that lasted longer than any mark had a right to.

I soaped up a sea sponge, the jasmine scent of shampoo mixing with my lilac body wash. My gaze drifted across the bathroom's crown molding, following hairline cracks in the plaster that formed constellations only I could see. This apartment, with its wedding ring quilts and butcher block counters felt more like home than the Bettencourt estate ever had. Here, the locks were brass and new;Okay the windows double-paned against the high plains wind. No one shouted through these walls.

By the time I toweled off, the digital clock on the microwave read 9:37 AM. I stared into my walk-in closet, fingertips trailing over the row of new Walmart clothes. Harrison's voice slithered through my mind like smoke under a door. *You need to lose several pounds to get into that dress, Jules. Why bother trying?* My hands closed around an oversized chambray shirt, the familiar armor of hiding.

The bedroom's hardwood floors creaked as I dressed. Through the window overlooking Pearl's herb garden, I watched two club members lead horses toward the stables, their laughter muffled by glass. Bronc would be at the shop by now, probably elbow-deep in some Harley's engine compartment. I imagined grease under his fingernails, the way his forearms flexed when he tightened a bolt.

"Stop it," I muttered, buttoning my jeans. The waistband gaped—even though I'd put on a few pounds and felt healthier since coming to Dairyville, I knew I was still too thin. At twenty-five, I shouldn't feel this brittle. Shouldn't have to press both palms against the dresser mirror to quiet its accusations.

My reflection wavered as I leaned closer. I was at least happy with my hair. Last night's memories rushed in. Bronc's kisses had been manic. Wild and almost felt forbidden. It was like he couldn't get enough of me. Until he did.

I yanked open the top drawer, hunting for socks. My pinky caught on a silk camisole I'd packed during the escape—its lace trim still smelled faintly of New York air conditioning and pretty perfume. I crushed the fabric to my face, inhaling until my lungs burned. I didn't even hear Bronc come in. There he stood, coffee cups in hand.

He filled my bedroom doorway wearing a charcoal crew-neck that made his eyes look like storm clouds over Lake Michigan—not that I'd ever seen Lake Michigan, but Harrison had vacation homes there and I'd stared at enough stock photos in his real estate portfolios to imagine.

"Figured you'd need this." He extended the second mug, steam curling around fingers still calloused from decades of wrench work. The scent of French roast cut through my lingering tequila regrets. "Kitchen table," I blurted, gesturing toward the small dinette where morning light shone on the pretty placemats. "For talking. Better... better lighting."

He followed silently, combat boots scuffing hardwood in a rhythm that matched the pulse behind my left eye. By the time I sat, he'd already produced a Moleskine notebook from his back pocket and laid it flat beside his untouched coffee. Military precision in the pen's angle against paper margins, spine straight as the canyon cottonwoods outside.

"Start with Harrison Hastings." Okay, then, right to it. Not a question. Bronc's thumb rubbed absentmindedly over the note-book's leather corner, wearing the hide smoother with each pass. "How'd the engagement happen?"

I traced the cardboard holder of my coffee cup. "My father brokered it during intermission at the Met." My laugh tasted bitter. "Third tier box seats, Puccini's Tosca. Mother said Harrison's family owned half the Upper East Side." The memory crystallized sharp—Harrison's cufflinks glinting when he reached for my program, mother's talon-grip on my wrist under the velvet curtain.

Bronc's pen scratched across paper. "Age?"

"He was thirty-two when we met. I was twenty-two." I watched him note the numbers, his jaw working like he was chewing through steel cable. "Daddy thought..." The words stuck behind my molars. I tried again. "Hastings needed the merger. They hadn't had a breakthrough for a few years. My parents thought my prospects for an advantageous marriage were less than stellar. Seeing as I was flawed. No self-respecting man wants to be seen with a chubby woman, after all. So, apparently, my father bargained for me. He'd invest heavily in Hastings Pharma, but Harrison would have to be saddled with me."

A horse whinnied outside, followed by Pearl's muffled curse about hooves needing trimming. Bronc waited, stillness radiating from him like heat off August pavement. When I finally looked up, his face was a raging storm. Tempests and hurricanes wanting to be unleashed. But he refused to unleash his rage as he listened intently. I knew it was safe to continue.

"He proposed at Le Bernardin." My thumb ran back and forth across the smooth wood of the dining table. "Seven courses, fourteen carats. The maître d' filmed the whole thing for Page Six." I remembered the weight of the ring, how the emerald-cut diamond pressed cold against my knuckle like a manacle. "I asked for a year to finish my degree."

Bronc's pen paused. "Which they gave?"

"In exchange for weekly brunches with Harrison's mother." The phantom taste of smoked salmon canapés rose in my throat. "She'd critique my weight between mimosas. Said debutantes shouldn't weigh so much, but I had plenty of time to get down to the right size before the wedding."

He made a noise low in his throat—not quite a growl, but close enough that the hairs on my arms stood at attention. "Your parents approve of this treatment?"

"Why would they disapprove?" My voice climbed half an octave. "They got their hedge fund merger with a promise of some new drug on the horizon. Mother stopped getting snubbed at the Greenwich Club." The confession twisted something loose behind my ribs. "When I told her about the first time, Harrison..." I swallowed. "He threw a Lalique vase. Missed my head by three inches."

Bronc's knuckles went white around his pen. "What did she say?"

I studied the soapstone pendant lights above us, each glowing orb a perfect sphere of containment. "That all relationships require sacrifice." My finger circled the cup's rim. "That I should be grateful he wanted me despite..." The words died as Bronc's chair legs screeched against the floorboards as I set the cup down.

He took my hands. "Look at me." His command left no room for refusal. Up close, the silver in his stubble caught the light like chain-mail. "Not your fault. Not then, not now."

I tried to swallow down my tears. Somewhere between the cinnamon notes of his aftershave and the warmth radiating through his sweater, the dam broke. "They sold me for a business partnership," I whispered. "And when they learned the person to whom I had been promised was abusing me, it was like I deserved it because I was defective."

Bronc's hand covered mine, rough skin snagging on my chipped nail polish. "You listen good, Juliet Bettencourt." His thumb brushed my inner wrist where the pulse fluttered wildly. "Only defective thing here's their inability to see a treasure when it's staring them right in the face. And as far as your weight. When you arrived here, you looked like you'd been starved. You look more beautiful and healthy with each passing day."

I looked at my hands, so small compared to Bronc's. He leaned back against his chair. His stillness reminded me of canyon rocks weathering storms—quiet endurance written in the fold of arms across his leather vest, the deliberate blink as I spoke.

"The first time he broke skin," I traced the slightly scarred web between thumb and forefinger, "was our engagement party. Tripped carrying champagne flutes." My laugh tasted bitter. "Mother told the staff to switch to plastic cups."

Bronc's pen hovered over his notebook. "What'd he break?"

"My collarbone." I unbuttoned the top of my blouse, revealing only slight scarring but mostly unmarked skin where silk met shoulder. "Took four weeks in a sling. Harrison insisted I learn to..." The words clogged my throat.

"Say it." Bronc's voice dropped to gravel-road rasp.

"To fall correctly." My fingers spasmed around the coffee cup. "He'd push me during charity galas when no one was looking. Said if I couldn't be graceful, I should at least be quiet when breaking."

Bronc's jaw muscle jumped. "Scars?"

"I have plenty of those." I pressed two fingers beneath my clavicle. "When he broke the skin or made deep enough cuts that demanded stitches, I have scars. Broken bones, they healed, depending on the type of fracture. A compound fracture took four to six weeks. Hairlines a couple..." I shrugged. "Mother said all thoroughbreds have strong bones. I have some permanent discoloration in some places."

His pen tip snapped against paper. I flinched at the sound, decades of training keeping me still as he circled the table. Bronc's calloused palm engulfed my shoulder, thumb pressing where fracture lines should've mapped the abuse.

"Shit," he breathed.

My pulse thumped beneath his touch. "What?"

"Look at me." Bronc crouched until our eyes leveled, his free hand anchoring mine against the table. "Normal humans don't heal that fast, darlin'."

"I don't know what that means, Bronc."

He held my eyes. "Ever see your parents, your mother specifically, take more than aspirin? Family doc ever ask questions?"

I shook my head, strands of honey-blonde hair catching on his belt buckle. "We had private physicians. I just figured that's what rich people do."

Bronc's thumb stroked the barely scarred skin once before retreating. When he stood, his shadow swallowed me whole. "Keep talking."

"I decided I'd had enough. There was no way I'd marry that monster. I refined my plan during a Met performance of Swan Lake. Third balcony seat bought with cash, program notes filled with code only my girl, a Bratva princess—Lucia would recognize."

"Lucia Kozlov?" Bronc interrupted, pen poised. "As in—"

"Philadelphia Kozlov Bratva." I finished for him.

Bronc's pen hovered over the notepad, ink bleeding through the paused 'K' of Kozlov. "Your college roommate's running counterfeiting operations now. Makes sense you got decent papers. We'll get back to the Kozlovs."

I abandoned my coffee to put a teakettle on the stove. "You believe me?"

"Question is..." He flipped to a fresh page, the motion too sharp for casual conversation. "Why my shop? Out of every garage from New York to Houston?"

I traced the whorls in the butcher block, morning light catching the faded scar along my knuckle. "The listing specified words like 'discreet, housing option,' stuff like that." My throat worked around unspoken words. "And...it said, 'safe environment for those seeking fresh starts.' Like you knew I needed help."

His jaw flinched at my explanation as though pondering why he'd written that ad. He studied my face—my spine straight as a ballerina's, but I know my shoulders curled forward like a kicked pup. When I lifted my chin, the ghost of Harrison's fingers clutched my neck beneath my jawline.

"You think it's stupid?" I busied my hands stacking napkins into a messy tower. "Some pampered princess playing businesswoman. Except I'm damn good at what I do."

"You're incredible. Seen how meticulous you are." He waited until my gaze snapped up. "Nothing gets past you. I knew you'd found stuff. Shady shit. That's why I brought you to my office. Trust me, Little Wolf. We're gonna get to the bottom of it. But first, we need to go back a few steps."

My foot was tapping on the floor... "I have questions. As I'm sure you surmised. But first, I need some tea." I grabbed a teacup and saucer from the cabinet and dropped in a tea bag before taking the kettle off the stove.

"Funny use of words you used earlier. I deepened my voice, mocking his tone. 'Normal humans don't heal that fast, darlin.' The words 'normal humans' make it sound like you are implying there is something out there other than normal humans." I used finger quotes when I said normal humans to drive the point home.

Bronc's tone was completely serious when he asked. "Would you truly be surprised to hear that yes, there is something *other* than normal humans out there?"

The tea bag danced in my cup while I rolled that question over in my mind.

"Your parents ever talk about family history? You ever had strange dreams? Urges to—"

I slowly sat back down and hesitated a moment before I spoke again. "When I was a little girl, I'd dream about wolves. But when I told my mother about my dreams, she told me never to talk about them. They were nonsense. And if I ever had another dream about wolves, I was never to speak of it, and if I did, she'd beat some sense into me. So I worked really hard at making myself not dream about the pretty tan wolf with dark eyes. I've not thought about her once in twenty years. Until I heard all the wolves singing to me here. Then, the night before last, I saw her in my dreams again. Only she wasn't alone. She was running with a big black and silver wolf with blue eyes. And I have found myself sketching the same wolf, over and over."

# Chapter 10

## Bronc

The coffee between us had gone cold, just like the eggs Ma brought up an hour ago. I watched Juliet's fingernails dig crescents into the palms of her hands. She hadn't touched the file folder I'd laid on her table either—the one holding birth certificates going back three generations, each marked with the Iron Valor MC's wolf-head seal next to DEPARTMENT OF HEALTH stamps.

"Your mother kept secrets," I started, then immediately hated myself for sounding like a damn Lifetime movie. My ring clinked against the ceramic mug as I turned it slowly. Noticed the chip on the handle from when Bridger dropped it last summer. Anything to avoid watching her face when I said the next part. "Some bloodlines would rather forget what they carry. This is going to sound incredible, Juliet. But there are some things in this world that defy belief. There are supernatural beings among us. Witches, animal shifters, and even vampires exist and have for thousands of years. Just hidden from human eyes."

Juliet's knuckles went bone-white around her teaspoon. She gave a skeptical laugh. "The next thing you're going to tell me is that I'm part werewolf."

"Shifter," I corrected. Her kitchen smelled like lemons and the cedar sachets Pearl tucks in every drawer. Normal things.

Safe things. "Difference matters. We don't lose control under full moons. Don't need silver bullets to die. But yeah, darlin'. You've got Ashbourne blood running through those veins. And that's an ancient shifter bloodline."

"*We?*"

I slid the folder closer, flipping to the 1940s pack records. "Iris Ashbourne Barrett—your great-grandma—helped lead the Ashbourne pack out of the depression in Nebraska. Kept that part of the county fed when banks failed. But she went on to marry a human male. That made her daughter Amina, your grandmother carry only half-shifter blood."

Juliet continued to shuffle papers as she listened. She stopped when I paused. Her face turned to mine, eyebrows up. "Please don't leave me hanging, Bronc. I'm dying to get to my part in this twisted fairytale." She sipped her probably now cooled tea.

Deep breath taken, I continued. "So, Amenia Barrett, your grandmother, who is only 50 percent wolf shifter blood married your grandfather, William Farris—a fully human male. Have doubts as to whether or not these males are oblivious to your grandmothers' wolfs' traits, however. Amina wanted nothing to do with pack life and culture. She left Nebraska and the pack. Normally when a wolf cuts itself off from its pack, it goes rogue—feral. But since she was just half-blood, this did not happen to her. She lived a life as a human, as you know."

The folder slammed shut and brushed her bangs out of her eyes. "Finally, *now* we're getting to the pertinent part. Dear sweet Mother."

"Your mother was born with quarter-shifter blood. Again, she put her shifter heritage in the rearview by marrying your completely human father. But by you telling me about private doctors and how discreet things were, I wonder how much she kept quiet to your father about it."

She scoffed a laugh that cracked halfway. "My mom? Quarter-shifter? What's that even mean—she turns into a chihuahua every third Thursday?"

A shadow of concern passed across her face when I spoke. "It's likely she can sense storms before they hit. Heal faster than most, like you. She probably has keener hearing than most. Her sense of smell and taste are likely heightened. Not things you could physically notice, but are there, nonetheless. Keeping things from your father would have been difficult. And I can't say for certain whether she knew about you. Your traits presenting as..."

Her spoon clattered onto the cup's saucer. "I'm what, some throwback?"

"Omega." The word hung between us, heavier than it had any right to be. "Rarest of our females. Not alpha or beta—you're the glue. The calm in the storm. And always paired with an alpha." My thumb found the scar under my jaw from Fallujah. Old habit. "Together, we're more than the sum. You've felt it."

She stood so fast the wrought-iron chair screeched against hardwood. "Felt what? Wolf traits? That I hear wolves singing from miles away? That I know what Pearl is cooking when her doors and windows are closed? And I'm attracted to you? D'uh, have you looked in a mirror? Every single woman within a 10-mile radius wants you in her bed. It has nothing to do with wolf genes." Her laugh tasted bitter, just like the coffee I finally choked down. "And even if it was. You've found yourself an incredible bookkeeper with stellar DNA. And so what? Sounds like what I'd guess a typical shifter could do. What's so Omega about any of that?"

I caught her wrist as she moved past. Not hard. Just enough to feel the racing pulse under her skin. "Your size is the first clue. You maybe didn't notice, but all the other women in the pack dwarf you. And not by a little. You are tiny in every way compared to them. Gunshots from the rifle range don't faze you in the least. You blaze through all of those numbers and calculations in a snap.

Can calm a customer's temper with just a word, I'm sure you could calm pack members even easier given the opportunity? And last week—"

"Leave it."

"When that pallet of oil cans slipped in the shop," I pushed anyway, rising to meet her glare, "you moved Menace out of the way five seconds before they would have crushed him."

Her free hand gripped the fridge handle. White-knuckled, shaking. "I've always had good instincts."

"Not like that."

We stood there breathing each other's air for six heartbeats. Seven. Her scent hit me first—the lilac soap from her shower, then her unmistakable ginger and burned sugar. Underneath, the crisp ozone crackle that made my wolf stir. I watched her throat work as she swallowed.

"If I'm this... omega thing," she whispered, "why don't I have..." A vague gesture at her own body. "Fangs? Fur? Whatever."

The relief almost buckled my knees. *Asking means she's considering it's possible.* I kept my hold light, thumb brushing her inner wrist. "Same reason some hybrids only get claws. Mixed blood needs a catalyst. For one of your ancestors, it was nearly bleeding out after childbirth. For you?"

Her pulse kicked. "You."

"Our bond," I corrected. I let go before I did something stupid like pull her closer. "Alphas and omegas... it's deep. Beyond biological. Once claimed—"

"Claimed?" She backed up until the fridge handle dug into her spine. "Like property?"

"Like partners." I spread my hands—nonthreatening, open. Military training kicking in. "It's consent, Juliet. Always. But once bonded, your latent traits awaken. Strength sharpens. Senses heighten. And with time..."

"Shifting." She breathed the word like a prayer. Or a curse.

I nodded toward the canyon visible through her kitchen window. "Imagine running those ridges without getting winded. Tracking game by scent alone. Protecting everything you love with more than just gritted teeth."

Her gaze stayed fixed on the horizon where earth met sky in a jagged line. "And if I say no? To all of it?"

The question I'd dreaded since meeting her and bringing her to pack territory.

"It will be a problem. Alphas are naturally drawn to omegas, darlin'. And since you've been around a pack..." Hated to have to break this to her. "Your body will go through a change, whether or not you want it to. And maybe sooner than later."

Spine rigid, she shot a look at me. "What kind of change, Bronc?"

"Called going into heat. And it's exactly what you're thinking. I'm not gonna sugarcoat this for you, sweetheart. Your body will produce supercharged pheromones and prepare itself to receive your alpha's knot. It will call to every alpha in every pack around here. They will kill to get to you. And I will kill to keep them away. Unless you are claimed. They will do everything they can to take you for themselves."

The tears started again. She was on information overload. "I didn't ask for this. And now it seems like my choices have been removed just like when I was in New York."

I wrapped her tiny body in my arms.

"Even if you rejected me, I couldn't stay away from you. That's the damn truth of it. I chose you. My wolf chose you. Your scent's in my lungs. Your name's etched in every beat of this blackened heart. I'll sleep on your front porch if you ask. Guard your back door from coyotes. Whatever you need. Wherever you'll have me. That's where I want to be."

Silence stretched. A pickup rumbled by on the county road below. Downstairs, Pearl started singing along to Patsy Cline drifting from her kitchen radio.

Juliet looked up. Slow. Deliberate. She turned and re-opened the folder. Those canyon-dark eyes locked on mine. Flipped past pack records and land deeds until she found the photo I'd tucked in back—Iris Ashbourne astride a massive gray wolf, head thrown back mid-laugh.

"You're sure?" she asked, tracing her great-grandmother's face.

"DNA tested twice. Doc verified the records."

"Not that." She slapped the photo down. "About us. This... bond."

I stepped into her space. Let her see the truth on my face. "Never been surer of anything. Not when I enlisted. Not when I took the club presidency. You're it for me, Juliet. Wolf or not."

Her palm hit my chest. Right over the patch. Right over the scar from a bullet meant for my VP I didn't move.

"I need to see."

Her palm burned through cotton and leather straight to bone marrow. "I need to see" wasn't a request—it was a dare carved from twenty-five years of mistrust and several weeks of stolen glances across Pearl's diner counter, through a greasy office window, and any number of other places. I caught her wrist before she could pull back, pressing those slender fingers harder against my cut. Let her feel the thunder behind cotton and bone..

"Need space," I growled, kicking chairs aside with more force than necessary. Kitchen light caught the tremble in her throat when I ripped my shirt off, then everything else. Not fear—anticipation. The kind that makes saints sin and soldiers desert.

My skeleton cracked first. Collarbones snapping outward like rifle reports. Hips realigning sent white fire up my spine that'd make grown alphas weep. Didn't flinch. Couldn't. Juliet stood frozen as cartilage reshaped my face, her reflection warping in my widening pupils—a funhouse mirror version of the woman who'd haunted my dreams since the first whiff of ginger and vulnerability. What seemed to take minutes in reality only took seconds.

Fur erupted in black waves. Should've hurt. But the magic of transformation made it painless after the first shift. Her gasp hitched halfway between wonder and recognition, sweet as Sunday hymns, and suddenly I was the goddamn phoenix.

When the last claw unsheathed, she crept closer. Bare toes curling on cold hardwood. "You... I've seen you. In the canyon shadows when I couldn't sleep. Under the mesquites during the hailstorm. I've drawn you. And in my dreams, I run with you."

My wolf preened. Tail sweeping. She didn't jump. Brave little omega. My wolf was head high to her.

Elegant fingertips grazed my muzzle. "Same scar." She traced the notch above my left eye—shrapnel souvenir from Fallujah. "Same stupid blue eyes."

A rumble built in my chest. Not a growl. Never at her. The sound she'd heard echoing through dream canyons, distorted by sleep and longing. Her nails dug into scruff when Mcnace's F-250 roared into the drive.

"Boss?" My VP's boots pounded upstairs. "Tyler's home early. Breezed past the gate guards."

Juliet jerked back. Pupils swallowing whiskey irises whole. "Your son?"

The shift ripped back faster than a bandage. Ribs stabbed lungs. Knees hit hardwood.

"Bronc!"

"Don't." I caught her reaching hands. Skin still fever-hot from the change. "He's infantry. Sees threats in shadows."

She yanked free. "I'm not—"

"You're everything." Jeans bit hot flesh as I stood. "Let me handle this."

Tyler's truck door slammed below. Combat boots took the stairs two at a time.

"Pop?" Tyler's voice hadn't cracked since sixteen, but the kid still said 'sir' like it owed him money. "Guard said you're up here with some..."

The door flew open. My boy filled the frame like a younger clone—same stubborn jaw, same tactical stance. Until his gaze landed on Juliet.

Green cotton pooled at her feet where she'd grabbed my shirt. My scent was all over her. Tyler's nostrils flared.

"Christ." His rucksack hit the floor. "She's half your age."

"Twenty-five," Juliet snapped.

"Exactly." Tyler turned that sniper's stare on me. "Mom was thirty when you split. This one's barely legal?"

I stepped between them. "Stand down."

"She human?"

"Enough."

"Enough what? Enough shifter to smell your rut? Or enough trouble when her family comes sniffing?" Tyler edged closer. Bronze Star gleaming. "You told me never to mix business and pussy."

Juliet moved fast. Too fast. Beyond human-fast. She snatched the photo of Iris Ashbourne off the table and slapped it against Tyler's chest. "Business? That's my great-grandma on the back of her pack's alpha. Is she shifter enough for you? I was pack before you swam in your daddy's balls."

Silence.

Tyler studied the picture. The grin spreading across his face chilled worse than any insurgent's glare. "Oh, this is rich. Pop finally gets his dick wet, and it's with the kin of a ghost."

I had him against the fridge before the last syllable. Crushed apple magnets raining down. "Apologize."

"Make me."

His knee came up. I twisted. Sheet metal dented under his skull. Juliet's protest died when Tyler laughed.

"Still quick for an old man." He didn't struggle. Smart kid. "She know you blacked out three states hunting my mom's trail? That you nearly torched the club over some cheating woman's choices?"

Juliet went rigid. Right on cue.

Tyler's smile died. "How many years you gonna outlive her? She'll wither while your supernatural body ages at a rate less than half the speed of hers. You gonna just set her aside when she's old and gray?"

"Out." I pointed downstairs. "We'll talk after patrols."

He saluted Juliet, mocking. "Welcome to the freak show, sweetheart. Try not to drown in the Kool-Aid."

The door slammed. Water dripped. Juliet stared at the dented fridge.

"I should..." she gestured weakly. "The mess..."

"Leave it."

"But—"

My hands framed her face. Still damp. Still human-warm. "You okay?"

Her laugh shook. "He's right. I don't know what I'm getting into."

"Tyler doesn't hate you. He hates anyone who makes me weak."

"Do I?"

I kissed her forehead. Let lips linger. "He has no idea. You're the one who makes me invincible."

# Chapter 11

## Juliet

After the revelation about my family, Bronc, wolf blood, I tried to make sense of everything. I wanted to call my mother. That was out of the question. The information I'd learned just had to sit with me. Mine to ponder. For the next several days, Bronc and I kept our routine. We ate breakfast and lunch together. The books were showing a pattern of a larger extortion plot that had been happening over the course of a couple of years. And something had his club officers meeting more frequently. I missed him. Honestly, I was falling in love with him. Craving him was a daily occurrence.

I encountered Tyler several more times. He seemed to pop into the shop randomly. I don't know if he wanted to see if I planned on staying or what. But on those visits, I found him to be bright and funny. So much like his dad. It was a slow acceptance, but anything that made Bronc happy made me happy.

One morning I woke with the wedding ring quilt bunched between my fingers as I stared at the ceiling fan's lazy rotation. Bronze light from the bedside lamp caught dust motes drifting above Bronc's abandoned sweatshirt—the one I'd stolen last week that still carried hints of leather and gun oil. My thighs pressed together beneath the quilt's geometric patterns. I thought back to how his calloused palms had gripped my hips the night he'd brought me home when I was so drunk at the compound. Before everything shattered.

*Alpha.*

The word ricocheted behind my ribs. I knew he was meant for me. Knew it when I stepped off that damn bus and saw him standing there like some kind of god. It didn't matter that his hair had silver mixed in with the raven strands. I still wondered what his closely shaved silver and black beard would feel like against the inside of my thighs. His massive biceps covered in tattoos should have been a turnoff. But I wanted to trace them with my tongue. I rolled onto my side, pressing a pillow over my face until the cotton pillowcase stuck to my damp cheeks.

Presidents led motorcycle clubs. Generals led armies. But Bronc—Bronc with his quiet laugh lines and patient hands guiding me through Texas Hold 'em, and cracking black pepper on my chicken fried steak—commanded wolves. Actual wolves who tore out throats under darkened skies. Who hunted. Who *changed*.

The sudden memory of his transformation punched through me. A crackle of tendons rearranging beneath tanned skin during last night's nightmare. Only it hadn't been a nightmare at all. Sunlight had gilded the silver streaking of his lupine fur as he changed right in the middle of my kitchen floor just days ago, those same blue eyes burning with streaks of gold through his beast's skull. My palm itched where I'd buried fingers in his pelt, equal parts terror and recognition thrumming in my veins. I'd dreamed of that exact shade of midnight-black fur since childhood. He was magnificent.

"Bullshit," I whispered to the empty apartment. The clawfoot tub's porcelain gleam winked from the adjacent bathroom, mocking me. Normal girls didn't fantasize about mythical creatures. My stomach churned. But this man was so much more. The way he'd stormed into my apartment that first night when I hadn't answered his texts or calls. His worried face told me he cared, even though we'd just met. Then, when his searing lips had touched mine. They set my soul on fire.

He had also been so kind when taking me to his house. His only concern had been my safety. I knew he wanted more, as much as I did. But he gentled me into a guest room. I never once feared that he'd violate my privacy. Never take what wasn't offered like it was owed to him. Not like Harrison. I shook those memories quickly away. Bronc was all man. And apparently, all wolf.

My memory went to how Tyler's lip had curled when came through my front door, a perfect sneer inherited from his father. "Another stray?" Is what he'd seemed to ask, boot heels digging into my living room's hardwoods. Disapproval filled his accusation.

I kicked off the quilt, bare feet slapping against hardwood still warm from the morning sun. Several steps took me to the kitchen's butcher block counter. Condensation fogged the window above the sink, outdoor heat warring with the A/C's aggressive hum. I traced a finger through the mist, revealing slivers of the pasture beyond Pearl's main house. Distant cattle lowed.

A hot blade twisted beneath my navel.

I gripped the counter's edge, knuckles bleaching white. Cramps weren't due for another seven days. Not that my cycle had ever been precise, not since the stress of living with Harrison. But this felt different. Sharper. Meaner. The wood floor rushed up to meet my knees as I folded over, forehead pressed to the cabinet door.

"Just breathe," I ordered myself, the mantra I'd used during the nights I tried to hide from my fiancé's tirades. But the invisible knife kept twisting, carving runes of fire along my uterus. Sweat slithered between my shoulder blades. I fumbled for my side pocket—no phone. Left charging by the bed.

Another spasm ripped through me. I gagged, acid burning my throat. The calendar above the toilet flickered in my mind's eye. Red Xs marched toward October. Wrong timing. All wrong.

The next cramp hit like a cattle prod to the spine. I crawled toward the bathroom, knees skidding on tile that now felt scalding against my skin. My vision tunneled—clawfoot tub emerging from the haze like some porcelain life raft.

Fumbling to tear off my leggings, I nearly ripped the Lycra getting them down. Brightness flashed behind my eyes at the sight of slickness staining my underwear. Not the rusty brown of old blood, but something clear and viscous, glistening under the vanity lights. The scent hit me first, honeyed earth and something feral that made my teeth ache.

"What, what, is this?" I chanted, scrambling backward until my shoulders hit the cold tub. Cotton wadded in my fist as I scrubbed at my thighs, but the moisture kept coming. Heat radiated from my core like I'd swallowed a coal, sweat pooling in the hollow of my throat. My reflection in the mirrored cabinet showed flushed cheeks, pupils blown wide and dark.

Another wave crested, muscles clenching in ways that had nothing to do with cramps. A whimper escaped before I could clamp my lips shut. The sound felt foreign, needy in a way that scraped raw against my nerves. My phone buzzed from the bedroom, muffled through the wall.

I lurched upright, catching myself on the marble sink. Cool stone bit into my palms as another contraction rolled through me. Liquid trickled down my inner thigh. The animal part of my brain screamed *danger* while some deeper instinct purred, *right, this is right*.

Staggering into the bedroom, I nearly tripped over the quilt pooled on the floor. Phone charger yanked free with a spark. Bronc's contact photo filled the screen, a candid Pearl had taken of him laughing by the shop's air compressor. Thumb hovering over the call button, I tasted copper where I'd bitten my cheek.

His son's sneer flickered behind my eyelids. *You don't belong here.* The phone slipped from my damp grip. What if this was... normal? For them? Some shifter puberty I hadn't been briefed on? Another cramp bent me double, nails scoring the wedding ring quilt.

The first ring trilled in my ear.

He answered before the second. "Juliet?"

Something in his voice, that Alpha gravel layered over genuine concern, unlocked the floodgates. "I don't... I can't..." My free hand clutched at my tank top, fabric sticking to sweat-slicked skin. "There's this... hurts... I'm... it's so hot."

"Stay put. Do not open the door for anyone." A motorcycle engine roared to life, drowning his next words. "Ten minutes. Less. Are you bleeding?"

"Not blood." I pressed the phone tighter to my ear, as if proximity could pull him through the cellular waves. "It's like... like when you... you know... pouring."

A growl vibrated through the speaker. "Fuck. Knew we should've... never mind. Get in the bathtub. Now."

"Bronc—"

"Now, Juliet." The command wrapped around my spine, steering me, stumbling back to the bathroom. "Cold water. Not ice, just cool. I need you to stay conscious."

Porcelain chilled my bare legs as I climbed in. The showerhead swung wildly when I grabbed it, spraying arcs across the black-and-white hex tiles. "What's happening to me?"

His engine downshifted hard. "Your body's choosing. Faster than I... shit, should've prepared..." Metal screeched in the background. "Don't fight it. Let the water run over your wrists. Pulse points."

Steel nozzles clattered when I dropped the showerhead. Rivulets snaked down my arms, doing nothing to quell the furnace beneath my skin. Through the window came the faint howl of an engine pushed past the redline.

"Still with me, darlin'?"

The endearment unraveled something in my chest. "Please, Bronc. Hurry."

Then, he was gone.

The next moments blurred. Cotton ripped at the seams as I tore off my top—too restrictive, too much. I got out of the tub and barely dried off. Cool air against the water droplets on my skin chilled my body. Bronc's t-shirt from yesterday lay draped over the dresser, smelled like him. I pulled it over my head, the hem brushing mid-thigh. Fabric against sensitized skin made me gasp.

Bedsprings squealed when I yanked the mattress askew. Every pillow in the apartment went flying. Couch cushions, decorative shams from the armchair tumbled across the floor. The quilt tangled around my legs as I dragged it onto the living room floor with the mattress in a makeshift circle. Something primal purred approval when I added Bronc's sweatshirt from the bedroom floor, the one he'd left "just in case."

Heels of my hands dug into eyelet lace sheets as another contraction hit. The shirt rode up, cool air ghosting over damp flesh. My back arched of its own accord, a sound escaping my throat that should've embarrassed me.

Tires crunched gravel outside.

Boots pounded up the exterior stairs two at a time. "Juliet!"

His roar shook the windows. I lunged for the door handle, fumbling with the lock. The doorknob slipped in my sweaty palm. Metal screeched when I finally wrenched it open, Bronc's massive frame filling the doorway. His chest heaved like he'd run across the compound, club cut straining over shoulders still twitching with residual shift energy. Blue eyes hinting at bronze in the early evening light, wild and needy.

I didn't think. Didn't breathe. Just launched myself at him, knees clamping around his hips as he caught me midair. His growl vibrated against my sternum when I buried my face in his throat, teeth scraping stubble.

"Christ, you're burning up." Calloused palms slid up my thighs, fingertips digging into bare flesh below the t-shirt's hem. The realization of what I wasn't wearing should've sent me scrambling for modesty. Instead, I ground against his waist, whimpering at the friction.

Bronc's nostrils flared. "Heat," he rasped, kicking the door shut with a boot heel. "Shouldn't be possible for…"

His words dissolved into a groan as I sucked the pulse point beneath his jaw. Every cell screamed for skin contact—my nails shredded his t-shirt before I registered him moving. Cotton tore like tissue paper under my frenzied yanking at his belt.

"Easy, Little Wolf." He carried me toward the nest, steps faltering when I ripped his fly open. "Need to call Doc first, get supplies—"

The last thread of control snapped. I sank teeth into his collarbone, copper blooming on my tongue. His roar shook the room, our bodies crashing onto the quilt-covered mattress.

He pinned my wrists above my head, blue eyes fully lupine now. "You sure?" The words came out guttural, more snarl than speech. "Once I start… can't stop. Won't stop."

My back arched, desperate for contact. "Need your knot. Don't know how I know… but I need it."

A sound ripped from his chest that wasn't human. He hopped on one foot, then the other as he pulled his boots off his feet. Fabric shredded, his heated skin searing against mine, his jeans and boxer briefs now on the floor. His cock was a thing of beauty. Long, thick and with throbbing veins. He stroked it as he fell to his knees and looked at me, a writhing mess of wetness on the nest I'd made. How dare he tease me when I'm dying here?

I growled and sat up, placing my hands on him. He was hot in my grasp. "I will rip this thing off if it's not inside my pussy in two seconds, ALPHA!"

He had the audacity to grin a feral grin! When he surged forward, there was no gentle preparation, only perfect, devastating alignment as we slammed together. As soon as his massive cock filled me, he made a guttural sound from his chest, less of a growl, almost a purr. It went through me and heightened every sense. My hips flew up to meet his. Slick running down my rear.

Fireworks behind my eyelids. The nest's mingled scents of sweat, musk, and leather wrapped around us as we moved. No rhythm beyond desperation, no grace in the animalistic snapping of hips. His teeth worried my earlobe.

"Gonna claim you." A promise and threat rolled into gravel-rough words. "Make everyone know you're mine."

"Yes." I scraped at his back, legs locking around his waist. "Now, Bronc, please now—"

His canines pierced the juncture of neck and shoulder as my climax detonated. White-hot pleasure fused with the sharp sting of canine teeth, branding me to the marrow. Bronc's roar echoed my scream, his release triggering something deeper, a click of cosmic tumblers slotting into place.

The base of his cock started to enlarge and tighten at the opening of my pussy.

"Bronc?"

He licked where he had left the claiming mark. "You were made to take my knot Little Wolf. Relax." He moved slightly, and another orgasm started to climb. He consumed my whimper with his lips.

His slow movements were driving me insane as his dick slowly continued to fill me until I swear he reached my cervix.

"You are beautiful, Juliet. You squeeze my cock so perfectly. Made for me," he reiterated.

My heat rose, and I had the inexplicable urge to bite him. Claim him. Still locked inside me, I sat up slightly.

"Bronc, I need. Need to bite you. Now."

I couldn't believe it when he bared his neck to me. Grabbing around his head, I pulled him to me and bit him between his neck and shoulder. Even with my flatter teeth, his blood filled my mouth like some kind of ambrosia. Another orgasm exploded through me as I felt his body shudder and felt him spray hot cum until it seeped out around his knot. Something suddenly shifted inside of me. I felt him everywhere. Through every vein. Muscle. My soul.

"I feel you. Inside me."

"Our bond makes less two and more one, darlin'.'"

Still locked inside me, more awed than afraid, I snuggled deeper into his arms.

Distantly, I felt him fishing his phone from ruined jeans.

"Bridger." Bronc's voice rasped worse than ever, free hand absently stroking my hip. "Need three days' provisions delivered to Juliet's. Doc handles the drop-off." A pause. "No, you dumb fuck, I don't care if Papa is on latrine duty—tell Arsenal to guard the southern perimeter."

I nuzzled his chest, licking the bite marks I'd left. His heartbeat stuttered under my tongue.

"Pearl's bringing electrolyte bottles," he murmured after ending the call, rolling us sideways. Calloused fingers traced my mating mark, the newly swollen flesh throbbing under his touch. "We'll hydrate between rounds."

"Rounds?" My laugh came out hoarse.

Bronc gave a satisfied smile. "Heat lasts seventy-two hours, my love." His palm slid between my thighs as his knot loosened and released. He rubbed his cum all over my thighs and stomach. "And I aim to spend every minute buried in my mate."

His words were the best aphrodisiac. I wrapped my legs around him and kissed him madly, moving my hips in a rhythm that would become all too familiar. I gave a yelp when he lifted me until I was on my hands and knees and he tucked pillows under my stomach to help prop my ass in the air..

"Now, Little Wolf, I'm going to take you as nature intended it."

The scent of sweat and sex clung to the sheets as I traced the raised edges of Bronc's claiming bite. His chest rose and fell beneath my cheek in a steady rhythm, calloused fingers idly twisting a strand of my hair. Three days of frantic coupling had left my thighs trembling, but the fire between us banked to embers rather than extinguishing.

"Still alive over there?" Bronc's gravel voice vibrated through me. His thumb brushed the fresh scar on my neck, making me shiver. His purr helped ease the more difficult parts of my heat ordeal. And honestly, I loved him for it. That realization hit me between the eyes. I loved him.

"Barely." My laugh came out raspy from screaming. "Do all your matings require triage teams?"

He nipped my earlobe. "Only the worthwhile ones."

Through the bedroom window, I heard Menace arguing with someone about perimeter checks. The rustle of plastic bags near the door signaled Doc's latest supply drop—protein bars and Pedialyte stacked next to Pearl's homemade tamales. Realization settled heavier than Bronc's arm across my waist. This wasn't a fling. These people weren't just neighbors.

Bronc had started gathering up trash and dishes.

"Where do we go from here?" I asked, nervousness in my voice.

"You are my mate, Juliet. Where you go, I go. Where you are, I am. But I am also the President of the Iron Valor MC, and the Alpha of this pack. Need to live in my house because it's more central to the activity of both pack and club. I want very much for you to live there with me. Everything has happened in a whirlwind, I get that. By the world's standards, it's too much too fast. But, I love you Juliet Bettencourt. Not just the physical parts of you. It's deeper than that. You are a part of me. I need you. You are mine, and I am yours."

Running to him, I jumped into his arms and kissed all over his face. "I love you too!"

Bronc's sudden grin crinkled the corners of his eyes. "Hellion." He kissed me hard enough to bruise. "Let's get to work on putting this place back together and get you packed up. Take only the things you love. We're buying you all new things. No more thrift store items for the Luna of this pack."

"Wait, what?" I gave him a stunned look.

"By you being my mate, you are also Luna of the Iron Valor pack. You are the perfect woman for the job. I feel your fear and doubt pulsing through our bond. Stop. The best part of the Omega/Alpha bond is we make each other better, stronger. This is just the beginning of what you will become my mate. We'll need to prepare for your first shift. Which I'd guess will be on the next full moon. That's only a week away."

# Chapter 12

## Harrison

The twelfth step into my father's office always required lifting my left heel slightly higher to clear the warped floorboard he'd refused to fix for decades. A test, like everything in this mausoleum of a mansion. I counted the amber light patches thrown by leaded windows—seven across the Persian rug, each precisely avoiding the path to his desk. His Montblanc scratched across bond paper like a scalpel, cutting flesh as I waited the required seven breaths before he acknowledged me.

The pen didn't pause. I noted the new vein map on his temple, tributaries of mortality undermining his marble complexion.

I settled in the Chesterfield chair, its burgundy leather sighing like a wounded animal. Then, I placed a vial of blood on his desk. "We've deployed three additional teams. Facial recognition hits in Denver required... reassessment." My thumb found the ridge under the armrest where Grandfather had chipped the wood during the '78 market crash.

The silence stretched into its eighteenth second when he finally looked up. His eyes mirrored mine, polished gunmetal assessing the kill radius picking up the vial. "Reassessment or failure?"

The air conditioner hummed. I adjusted my cuffs to display 1.5 cm of shirt sleeve. "The shifter gene can complicate tracking.

Thermal imaging becomes unreliable when their core temp can drop twenty degrees."

Her laugh suddenly echoed in my skull, that throaty vibration she'd made when I'd presented the Cartier necklace on her twenty-fourth birthday. I'd recorded the decibel level. 67.3 dB, well within human parameters.

Father's signet ring clacked against the humidor. "The team reports promising results with the new transfusions."

I saw the lab then, white coats moving through steam rising from jungle floor grates, the way Subject 14's claws had torn stainless steel restraints. "We've accelerated Phase Three. The longevity serum shows an eighty-three percent viability rate in primate trials."

His eyebrow twitched - the equivalent of a standing ovation. "And the other seventeen percent?"

"Neurological degeneration. Fascinating, really. The cerebral cortex liquefies within..."

Charles set down the vial with surgical precision. "The Bettencourt girl. It was quite fortunate for us you discovered this DNA phenomenon after Jules made her a part of his infusion of money into the company."

"It was a very fortuitous stroke of luck," I said, sliding my Montblanc folio across the table. Lab reports stamped with the Hastings Industries logo fanned out between us. "I knew there was something special within her DNA after several months of her recovering quicky to minor injuries that seemed to," I cleared my throat so my father understood my meaning, "befall her with frequency."

His greasy smile told me he understood my meaning fully.

Charles grunted approval. "Clever girl never suspected?"

"Her accelerated healing is something she never questioned. It's apparently always been a part of her physiological makeup, and so her assumption is that it's normal for her. Her parents have a private physician who must have knowledge of her special circumstances." A lifted eyebrow and nod from my father told me to continue.

"And that's what prompted my closer look at her family tree, finding the wolf shifters we now have in our possession in our underground lab in Costa Rica. The deal Jules Bettencourt made for his daughter will be the thing that will win me the Nobel Prize."

My father seemed to ponder my actions where Juliet was concerned. "I don't understand why you didn't just use the girl as your specimen as soon as you realized she had this healing gene. Could have saved you the trouble you're having currently."

He was such a damn fool. He did not understand what we were accomplishing here.

"There are a few reasons we are proceeding as we have. Finding the source of Juliet's DNA was paramount. We needed a baseline. Then, almost as important, our labs were not built when I discovered Juliet's abilities. There was nowhere for her to be placed where she could thrive in good physical health until we were ready to start working on the serum. She needed to be in an environment that was more conducive to a healthy lifestyle. Her being in good physical condition was paramount in getting the best results for our testing. Keeping her locked up in a cell for two years would not be conducive to that outcome. Married, living in a penthouse in Manhattan with a highly successful man whom her parents approved of seemed like a much better alternative."

The confession tasted of Scotch and betrayal. I remembered forcefully taking Juliet in our penthouse bathroom; her frightened eyes staring at me as my fingers wrapped around her delicate neck, her breath coming out in small gasps. I'd yanked the skirt of her dress up and ripped off the lace panties she wore. I'd managed to undo my belt and get my pants and boxers off with one hand and spread her legs with my knees. That same free hand reached between us and found her bare pussy dripping wet, despite her fear and loathing.

*"Look at you, little slut. You pretend you don't want me, but your body knows its master."* Deep down, I knew it was only physiology. But I pretended it was more as I slammed my impossibly hard dick into her tight wet heat until she screamed out her pleasure, my hand squeezing her throat hard enough to bruise. I pulled out of her and spilled my cum all over her stomach and dress, rubbing it in with my softening cock. When I released her neck, I noticed the bruises that had started dark black and blue had already started to fade. It made her the perfect canvas for my sadistic torture. I vaguely remembered how she'd stared past me immediately after, looking at the at the heated towel rack, whispering numbers in French, her childhood trick for dissociating from trauma.

The truth burned tart behind my teeth: how her body betrayed her during those forced couplings under crystal chandeliers—how I told myself *this was dominance*, not some deplorable assault even greed couldn't purge from my veins.

Shaking off the memory and calming my hardening dick, I continued. "Phase three trials can't proceed without viable mitochondrial donors." I clicked open my pen; the sound sharp. "I have her within my grasp."

Charles pressed; cold calculation steadied me again, numbers slotting into place like bank vault tumblers: extraction costs contingency plans... His shadow bisected Juliet's file photo when he stood smiling approval sharp as a scalpel slide but when he mentioned mother crying over our failed wedding it took everything not to snap.

"Your mother cried when she heard there would be no wedding, you know. *Actual* tears."

(Only thing Catherine Hastings mourned was losing access to belittling Juliet on a weekly basis). "She cried harder when you sold her Matisse." He laughed his first genuine laugh. I wondered if she'd cry when the old fuck has a stroke. Because one was coming.

My driver materialized curbside with an umbrella raised against nonexistent rain. The ride to the private airfield was quiet. Two and a half hours later, we landed on the private airstrip in Costa Rica where the lab was located. Changing into a lab coat, I entered an observation chamber where our principal scientist was about to try a new protocol on her latest subject. I watched. My mind imagined it was Juliet on the receiving end of the torture.

I leaned against the cold observation glass, my breath fogging a small circle as Lab 7's sterile white lights glared below. My team moved like specters around Subject 23—strapped to a reinforced table this time, after what happened with 19.

"Administer Protocol Kappa," I said into the intercom, my voice flat.

Dr. Chen's gloved hands trembled as she pressed the injector to 23's neck. The subject, a wiry ex-Marine named Coleson—jolted against restraints as neon-blue serum flooded his veins. *Good.* Pain meant his cells weren't rejecting it outright.

Monitors screamed to life.

"Cardiac output doubling."

"Adrenaline off the charts."

*"Muscle mass increasing—"*

Coleson roared, tendons writhing like cables beneath sudden slabs of muscle. The steel cuffs snapped with a sound like gunshots. My pulse quickened as he staggered upright, heaving the 500-kilogram bench press rack overhead like it was Styrofoam. Laughter bubbled in my throat—after nine months of corpses and combustions—

Then, his head snapped toward the observation deck.

Blood streaked from his nostrils first, black and viscous. His eyes met mine—pupils blown wide, sclera webbed with ruptured capillaries—as he hurled the weight straight at us. Safety glass spider-webbed under impact; scientists dove under consoles as shards rained down on me like diamond hail.

*"Get out,"* I barked into my comm, as Chen was uselessly pounding the lockdown button she'd already overridden. The subject lunged for her, eyes black-dilated and spittle flying. She backpedaled, tripping over a toppled crash cart as he loomed. Seven feet of engineered muscle twitched under synthetic adrenaline. His hand closed around her throat.

Then he froze.

A wet, guttural gasp echoed through the lab speakers. The subject's grip slackened; Chen scrambled free as he crumpled like a puppet cut from its strings. The cardiac monitor flatlined into a single merciless tone.

Silence pooled in the observation deck. I realized I'd stopped breathing.

"V-fib induced," came a clipped voice from behind me, Ellis, sounding almost bored. "As requested."

*Requested.* My jaw clenched. They'd waited until his bio-data crossed the fail-safe threshold. Let Chen dangle in those final seconds because regulations demanded certainty.

Below, she knelt beside the corpse, fingers pressed to its still-warm neck as if she could will back a pulse she'd fought so hard to stop minutes earlier. Her hands shook.

So did mine.

The alarms kept blaring long after the system crashed. I stared at the screens, now flickering with error codes, my hands numb on the keyboard. We'd been *right there.* A three-second delay in the stabilizers—*three goddamn seconds*—and the entire sequence unraveled like cheap thread. Jenna slammed her fist against the console behind me, cursing in that sharp, clipped way she does when she's trying not to yell. For once, I didn't blame her.

I replayed it in my head: Vargas shouting coordinates over comms, Johnson's hands shaking as he rerouted power cells, the readouts glowing green-green-green until everything flared red. We'd followed protocol to the letter. Done everything by the book this time. And still—still, it wasn't enough.

"We underestimated the variables," I muttered later in debriefing, pacing the dimmed lab as the others glared at holograms of failed equations like they owed us answers. "The feedback loop—it wasn't just about timing sensitivity. We need redundancies inside redundancies." I paused while I swallowed bile, thinking of how violently close we'd come before it burned out: 89% convergence rate glimmering for half a heartbeat before it disintegrated our sample core into stardust and ash.

Kiran leaned back in his chair, arms crossed tight over his chest like he was holding himself together. "So what? Another layer of safeguards? Double-check every output manually?"

"If that's what it takes," I said flatly. "Or we scrap phase three entirely and rebuild from waveform algebra instead of particle models."

They groaned in unison—another month down, another untested rabbit hole—but nobody fought me on it this time. Not after tonight's spectacular clusterfuck of wasted data and near-meltdown protocols humming under our feet like a threat even now.

Later, alone in my quarters with synthetic coffee and metrics spiraling behind my eyelids every time I blinked, I forced myself to think past frustration's iron chokehold. *So close.* Close enough that when I closed my eyes, I still saw that flicker of almost-success—a jagged crack in some unreachable door we hadn't even known existed two weeks ago. *But almost doesn't stabilize reactors or move investors*, Lila had snapped earlier today before storming out. Today, it almost got people killed.

She wasn't wrong. We'll fix this; I swore silently. Or next time we won't walk away with just scorched pride. Until now, we'd been using 100 percent shifter DNA to synthesize the serum. I knew Juliet was going to be the key. She's a hybrid, both human and shifter. My mind raced. Until I could get my hands on Juliet, I needed someone like her. I knew what I had to do. I picked up my phone.

"Dane. I've got a job I can trust only you to do."

# CHAPTER 13

## BRONC

The griddle hissed like a cornered snake when the batter hit for the first pancake, butter screaming into smoke. I counted twelve bubbles forming before flipping, military precision surviving another night of her teeth in my shoulder. Through the lace curtain's bullet-hole patterns, morning light caught the raised skin around Juliet's fresh claiming mark. The bite on her shoulder, a molten ridge of demarcation warning every male that she belongs to me.

She sat cross-legged in last night's oversized shirt, cotton stretched thin where my hands had roughly pulled it from her body. Golden waves framed her angelic face, such a contrast from the harsh dyed black disguise that she'd worn weeks ago when I'd picked her up at the bus station. When she reached for the syrup, the shirt sleeve fell back to reveal four fading fingerprint bruises flowering along her wrist. My left hand twitched in remembered barely constrained passion.

"Still takin' your eggs fried?" I asked, sliding the plate across the quartz countertops. Our breakfast ritual: me playing short-order cook, her playing civilized. The lie lasted three seconds before her pinky finger hooked mine under the plate's edge, nail digging crescent moons into my calluses.

Her coffee sent up smoke signals between us, steam curling around the almost glowing bite on her neck. I watched moisture bead along the scar I'd given her, resisting the urge to lick it clean. Her accountant's voice cut through the breakfast ritual.

"Section 6A of the parts invoices." A syrup-sticky finger tapped last week's ledger. "Someone's double-charging brake fluid."

I'd turned to tend the pancakes. The spatula froze mid-flip. Three drops of batter hit the floor like warning shots. I made my eyes stay on the perfect golden circle cooking instead of the V of tanned skin disappearing into her shirt. "How much?"

"Enough to buy a Harley carburetor monthly." Her mug clicked against the quartz, brown eyes tracking my reaction in the stainless steel fridge door. "Cash transactions from the Thursday rallies don't match garage receipts."

I killed the burner, knuckles white around the skillet handle. The kitchen's familiar sounds took on a new edge—the ice maker's rattle becoming ammunition belts feeding, wall clock's tick transforming into a countdown timer. Her bare foot brushed my calf beside the counter. That someone was actively betraying me tasted bitter on my tongue. It was a constant fight to control my wolf.

"You slept through the coyotes' 3 AM serenade," I deflected, pouring creamer in her freshened cup of coffee to cover my frustration. The spoon made slow circles—two clockwise, one counter, a suppressed memory of clearing Fallujah houses.

Her snort held more wolf than she knew, taking the cup from me in one hand. "You mean after you wore me out?" Claw-sharp fingernails of the other dragged across the invoice. "This skimming's been happening since Skeeter took over parts inventory I think. But there were other things prior."

Coffee boiled acid in my gut. I catalogued her tells: left eyelid twitch, right thumb pressing hard against the mug's crack, the way her new hair color made her cheekbones look dangerous. My fork sketched battle lines in congealing egg yolks.

When she rose to refill my coffee, the shirt rode up to reveal twin bruises from my thumbs. The ledger fell open to pages marked with oil smears and what might've been blood. I caught her wrist mid-pour, coffee cascading over our joined hands.

"Shit, sorry, darlin'," I murmured, licking bitter droplets from her knuckles. Her pulse jumped like a live wire under my tongue. The ledger numbers blurred into insignificance against her scent: ginger, burned sugar, and jasmine shampoo. Last night's sweat still clung between her breasts.

Her free hand found the fresh scar under my shirt collar where she gave a lick. "You taste like panic and pancakes."

The admission cost us both. I bit her thumb in retaliation, tasting copper and financial fraud. Somewhere beyond the kitchen's false calm, at least one person in my pack was betraying me. But here in the syrup-smeared dawn, amidst greasy ledgers, I held a treasure in my arms.

Noisy dishes clattered into the sink as I lifted her onto the cool quartz counter. Her arms automatically circled my neck. At this height, her eyes could almost meet mine.

"What are we doing, Alpha? Thought the shop needed to open."

I spoke against her lips. "Shop opens when I say it opens." My tongue plunged in, meeting hers. "Fuck if you don't taste like the sweetest honey, Luna." Her tiny growl went straight to my cock. "Want to eat you. Lap up every drop of you."

Juliet's hips rocked back and forth on the countertop.

"Lie back, Juliet." The words were a command.

"Are you really going to do this?" The rhetorical question dropped from her lips.

"What a fucking little actress you are, Juliet. Pretending you don't want me to." As she lay back, I ripped off the tiny panties she was wearing, finding her wet and wanting.

"Now, I need your legs spread as wide as you can get them. I can already see how your pussy glistens, beautiful. And, wetness, fuck if it's not the most gorgeous thing I've ever seen, apart from your face, that is." My fingers ran through her wetness, and her ass jolted up as much as it could.

"Bronc, please don't tease me."

Our bond hummed with our desire. I'd never felt such a heightened sense of carnal lust mixed with genuine emotion for anyone. I only wanted to please her, to make her happy.

Lifting her thighs under my forearms, I pulled her to me, raising her ass up in the air. Her pussy rose to meet my mouth. Fucking God, if ever there was ambrosia, this was it. Tongue stabbing at her opening I dove in. My lips working in harmony, touching every inch of her. Kissing, sucking, licking.

The sounds she made were like the sweetest song. They sang through our bond as well.

Teasing her clit with my tongue was my new favorite thing. "Fuck Juliet. I could eat you morning, noon, and night and still not be satisfied." I flattened my tongue and moved my head back and forth. Juliet's hands were in my hair, pulling enough to sting.

"Please, Bronc. I'm so close."

I eased her down so I could add my fingers to the mix.

"Sit up, Juliet." She was on the edge of the counter, so I scooted her ever so slightly back as she raised up. "I want you to watch me as I make you come. Watch me eat your beautiful pussy. See me take every drop you have to give me." Her eyes followed me as I lapped at her. She started to throw her head back in ecstasy. "Don't you do it, Juliet. Eyes on me." I plunged my tongue inside her sopping pussy as her hands reached into my hair, pulling me closer. Then I flattened my tongue and swirled it around her swollen clit until she exploded into a beautiful release all over my mouth. Her body writhed with as much control as she could muster.

The way she shouted my name is something I'll never tire of hearing. As she came down from her climax, I gently sucked and cleaned her and lifted her into my arms. A heart filled with profound satisfaction at pleasing my mate was my reward.

A quick shower and we were ready for work.

The Road King ate gravel like it owed us money. Juliet's thighs vise-gripped the saddlebags. Oh yeah, we'd fuck on this bike the first chance we got. I throttled past Pearl's neon sign. I knew everyone would smell her on me before we hit the shop doors. Her fingers walked up my ribs under my cut, accountant nails finding the scab from where she'd clawed through my shoulder blades.

The shop exhaled burnt rubber and betrayal as we rolled in. The lights glowed bright enough to find whatever was hiding. Menace's doing. He'd retrofitted the old airplane hangar with prison-grade lighting that made everyone look guilty. Juliet's heel caught in floor grating meant for oil runoff. Her stumble transformed into a predatory crouch that showed off the knife she'd stolen from my boot.

"Get to work on those ledgers." I growled, throwing her the office keys that jingled like Marine dog tags. She moved through the partition of wrenches hanging in size order, past the bulletin board papered with local takeout menus. Skeeter's shadow detached from the parts cage, all nicotine fingers and guilty shoulders.

Her office area reeked of Windex and motor oil. I watched through the greasy window as she spread invoices like tarot cards, lips moving over part numbers like she was committing them to memory. When the air compressor kicked on, she startled, momentary vulnerability before the calculator's click-click-click lulled her back into familiar territory.

Skeeter materialized with a camshaft that didn't need fixing. "She's workin' hard." His chuckle sprayed chewing tobacco on my boot.

"Yep." I palmed a ball-peen hammer, testing its heft. "She's going through a couple of bookkeeper's worth of files. She'll be feeding discrepancies to my wolf."

The lie curdled as Juliet's red pen circled something fatal. She'd pinned her hair with a pencil, tendrils framing her beautiful face. When our eyes met through the glass, she mouthed "love you" with scarlet lips that still shone from my mouth's attention.

I gave her a wink, knowing I was the luckiest bastard in Texas. Toolbox drawers screeched warnings as I stalked the shop floor. Every grease smear told a story. Skeeter's boot print on invoice #4421, the fresh grind marks on a supposedly defective cylinder head. I trailed fingers across a motorcycle seat indention from her thighs; the leather remembering what my hands couldn't forget.

Her scream was a piston misfire. I took the stairs three at a time, wolf eyes catching the blood first—crimson polka dots across freight manifests. Not hers. The ledger showed a Rorschach test in red transmission fluid blooming around part number C-442.

"Mouse got nervous," she deadpanned as she set aside the dented can, wiping hands on overalls that hung too temptingly low. "Sorry, didn't mean to scare you." She was embarrassed because she thought she looked clumsy.

I wrapped her in my arms. "Not your fault. Too much clutter." I had to slow my heart rate down. Her frightened scream was not a sound I wanted to hear again. "Only scream I wanna hear out of your mouth is my name when you come around my cock or on my tongue." I told her in a low whisper.

"Bronc. Don't be giving me talk like that when you can't immediately back it up." Her smoky laughter was as sexy as any dirty talk.

I tilted her chin and gave her a quick kiss, knowing she wanted to get back to work. Through the floor grates, Skeeter's shadow stretched long and shameless across crates of "lost" spark plugs. I kept my eyes on him as I headed back down the stairs.

The sharp tang of motor oil clung to everything in my office—stained blueprints, the cracked leather chair behind me, even my coffee mug from this morning. I was elbow-deep in inventory spreadsheets when boots thudded hard against the shop's concrete floor outside. Two pairs. Heavy, purposeful. The hair on my forearms lifted before the door even creaked open.

Menace filled the doorway first, shoulders nearly brushing both sides of the frame. His scarred knuckles rapped once against the steel doorjamb—a courtesy knock swallowed by the grind of overhead fans. His short-cropped blond hair always perfect. Wrecker slipped in behind him like smoke, shutting the door with a click that sounded too final for midday Wednesday, scrubbing a hand over his usually cleanly shaved head.

"Got trouble," Menace growled by way of greeting. He tossed a crumpled map onto my desk; state lines crawled across it like spiderwebs—Nebraska and Missouri, bleeding together under red marker circles.

Wrecker leaned against my filing cabinet, arms crossed over his grease-streaked Henley. "Seven shifters gone in three weeks," he said quietly. "Scent trails just... stop." His thumb tapped restlessly against his bicep—once, twice—before he caught himself stilling it with visible effort.

The spreadsheet numbers blurred as I leaned back in my chair. "Rogues?"

"No, they are from different packs. They're just now putting pieces together." Menace's jaw worked like he was gnawing on something foul. "Once word started getting out that shifters had gone missing, packs started comparing notes. If you check your email, you've likely gotten something from the Council. They'll be meeting soon. I'm sure to compare notes with all the packs."

Outside, an impact wrench screamed through metal somewhere in the shop bay.

"Damn, you think it's hunters?" I kept my voice steady even as adrenaline prickled under my collar.

Wrecker exchanged a glance with Menace before answering. "Maybe, but why are they only taking one here and one there? If it were hunters, they'd be wiping out packs." He pushed off the cabinet to tap a circled area near St. Louis. "But here's what keeps me up—disappearances started almost a year before Juliet got here. Might be completely unrelated. But that fiancé of hers. He owns the largest pharmaceutical outfit in the country. Think it's possible?"

"Fuck."

Wrecker repeated my sentiment. "Right. Fuck."

The A/C unit rattled in the window briefly before choking off into silence.

"I think it's best if we keep that speculation under our hats for right now. I still need to explain all of the Council business to Juliet. I don't want to overwhelm her too much. Finding out that shifters aren't the only supernaturals there are in the world could really knock her for a loop. Especially when she learns that her best friend from college is a vampire."

Menace jabbed a finger at my calendar still flipped to June's photo of some snow-capped mountain. "Full moon's what, four nights out? Your girl—"

"Juliet, your Luna." I corrected automatically, though we all knew her name, her position in the pack.

"—she'll be primed for her first shift." Menace didn't soften his tone. "Her scent'll rip through five counties if she bolts scared."

My coffee turned to acid in my gut. The pack's celebration bonfire already felt less like tradition and more like a beacon.

Wrecker cleared his throat. "We double perimeter watches starting tonight." His eyes met mine. Drought-yellow but sharp. "Ride rotations every two hours instead of four."

I stared at the blood-red circles until they burned behind my eyelids. My office suddenly felt too small, too full of engine parts and fading pack photos pinned haphazardly to the corkboard. Juliet's graduation picture that I got from her background file smiled at me from beneath a reminder sticky note: *Trans fluid order*, Nov 17th. She wore her mortarboard crooked, laughing mid-stride like she couldn't wait to leap somewhere new. Somewhere unguarded.

"She's tougher than you know. But with everything else happening, call everyone back from runs," I said finally, reaching for my keys with hands that didn't shake. Good. Strong leader hands, steady. "Every patroller runs at dusk."

Menace grunted approval as they turned to go, but Wrecker paused at the threshold. For half a breath, his posture softened into something that might've been pity if I didn't know better. Then he was gone, leaving only gasoline-scented air and ghost words hanging where maybe, maybe I imagined them:

"She's strong, boss... Like her old man."

The door clicked shut again, trapping me with ghosts of red circles and one truth clawing at my ribs: Whatever was hunting beyond our territory were hunting shifters for something specific. Hunters don't do random.

The golden light of dusk pooled over Juliet's desk as she straightened her final stack of receipts, her meticulous hands stilling at my voice. "Time to call it a day," I said, lingering in the doorway of her office. Pride surged hot beneath my ribs as I watched her glance up, strands of hair slipping loose from the pencil she'd used to twist it in a knot. Damn, she'd been buried in those ledgers all day.

"Gather every ledger," I added, stepping closer. My thumb grazed her shoulder, these quiet touches that anchored us both. "Can't risk leaving anything here."

She nodded once, pragmatic as ever, and followed me into the hall after tucking each binder into her arms like secrets we couldn't afford to lose. Outside, summer clung thick to the air as we walked arm-in-arm toward my bike parked beneath the mesquites. Our shoulders pressed snug together, no space left between us now unless duty carved it out.

I strapped the ledgers into both saddlebags with care while Juliet traced patterns across my back absently through my shirt. Her feelings of what I could only call contentment flowed to me through our bond.

Pearl's Diner hummed with twilight regulars when we arrived, its neon sign flickering pink against bruised skies. We claimed our booth by habit, the one farthest from chatter and closest to exits. Sliding into our corner booth, Ma greeted us with our usual cups of coffee. Black for me and Juliet's sweetened with so much cream and sugar it was basically a coffee milkshake.

Ma's triple strand of pearls glinted in the dim light of the diner, a smile as big as Texas on her face. "Well, if it isn't my two favorite people gracing me with their presence finally."

"Ma, we've been kinda busy. Work, and things."

"Uh huh. I bet you have." Her eyes went to both of our mate marks. "Well, I'm sure you're starving. Ya need some calories to keep you goin' after all of that... work."

I gave her a big sigh. "Ma, just bring us a couple of chicken-fried steaks and mashed potatoes, would you?"

"Thank you, Pearl!" Juliet hollered as Ma wandered back to the kitchen. Then she gave me one of her big, beautiful laughs.

"Full moon celebration's in four nights," I said finally...and felt her freeze mid-reach for a napkin like she'd been waiting all week for this knife to drop. Steadying myself took an effort. "We need t'talk 'bout what you'll face during your first shift."

Her lashes lifted slowly. That wildfire gaze locked on mine. I felt her wolf stir through the bond for the first time.

# CHAPTER 14

## JULIET

Our forks scraped against white china, the tension of Bronc's words clinging like summer to my skin. Flu-like symptoms. Fever. Body aches. His voice, slow and careful, unraveled all that my first shift might bring, laying each revelation between us like tender stones. I watched him push a notepad towards me, ink bleeding blue instructions. My eyes tracked his as I took in every letter of this new language we were learning together. He couldn't hide how seriously he took this, the gravity of what was coming. It was as if we were planning a battle rather than what was to me the exciting opportunity of a lifetime. The low rumble of the diner seeped around the edges of our booth while my mind stilled on this moment with him, on the edges of certainty that were already beginning to blur.

"It will start to feel a bit like the way you feel me through our bond." Bronc's eyes cut across to mine, steady as he spoke about my wolf. "But closer, because she's an extension of yourself." I nodded, turning the thought over in my head.

A tendril of doubt tugged at me as I considered what that would feel like. Was it what I'd already sensed, the tug of a distinct presence nearby? An awareness unlike anything I'd experienced before? The possibility was thrilling. It would mean I wasn't imagining things after all, and the news burst open inside me like fireworks.

I reached for my coffee and took a sip, too distracted to care that it burned my tongue. Bronc's attention was now on the paper again, his measured hand tracing notes, each word holding weight between us. Fever, aches. His voice grew softer, a stark contrast to the booming announcement he had made just days earlier when he told the pack he'd found his true mate. I felt it more than heard it, that crackling power of his as it spread through the room. My shock at being the center of his life and attention, the sense of belonging that eclipsed everything I'd ever known.

"I think I've felt her," I said finally. "I thought maybe it was you, but different."

His brows lifted. "Tell me."

"You're so loud, Bronc." I couldn't help laughing, this playful warmth spreading to him, though I knew the sound of it had a pained edge. Even though his protectiveness became stifling at times, I hoped he knew how much it meant to me. "I thought I was going crazy."

"Never." He was all seriousness. "Not about this."

I shifted my focus to the battered tabletop between us, the fine hair on my arms prickling at the thought of what lay ahead. His attention to detail both steadied and overwhelmed me, a firm hand at the small of my back guiding me through unknown terrain. My pulse thrummed, blood-rush in my ears loud enough to block out the restaurant noise until it was just the two of us at that table, our world defined by these written-down promises.

"I've never seen anyone write notes for this sort of thing before," I said. A fond grin stretched my lips. "It's cute."

He gave me one of those dry chuckles. "Well, I'm known for cute."

"Bronc! I'm serious." I reached across the table to tap his fingers where they rested near the notepad. That felt better—any excuse to close the gap and touch him, connect with more than words and worry.

His hand turned, palm catching mine and squeezing once, tight. "Juliet, I want you to be prepared. To understand everything you're facing." He hesitated, the protective instinct coursing through him in waves. "There's nothing more important."

I should've expected that response, but still it brought a sting of feeling to my eyes, settling as a knot in my throat. There was so much I wanted to say. Like how every day with him was like being slowly rewired into something stronger and more certain than I ever thought I could be. How he had already given me more than I'd ever dreamed of.

The clink of glasses came through the ambient din as a waitress refilled our waters, her motions efficient and practiced. I looked at Bronc's composed features, reading in the tightness of his mouth what he hadn't said aloud: that this might break me instead. That I was a fragile human woman entering a world where flesh split, where bones twisted and reformed.

"Is it strange?" I asked, watching a drop of condensation snake its way down my water glass, "that I'm not scared?"

"Yes." A small, genuine smile slipped across his features. "But that's just you."

His conviction had weight, settling into my chest like something solid and real. I knew I could hold on to it even when his voice was miles away and it came time to face this shift. The thought lit my nerves on fire. I'd never been one to stand on my own, always a careful extension of someone else, their desires carving out my path. First my parents, then the sorry excuse of a man I'd almost married because it was what was expected of me. Being here, on the edge of everything and on the brink of knowing myself, was a dream I didn't know how to hold.

"Your wolf is getting restless already," Bronc said, tapping his temple like he could feel her, too. His grin was still lingering at the corners of his mouth, blue eyes sparking with a hint of pride. "That's a good sign."

The quiet certainty in his words sank in deep, and I let myself relax against the leather of the booth, the smell of greasy food enveloping me in a strange sense of comfort. This was Dairyville, a place I would've mocked years ago but now embraced with every part of my being. And this was Bronc, larger than life, full of wisdom that only age could give, brimming with hope and hesitancy as he guided me into a reality neither of us could fully predict.

I exhaled, letting go of everything except this moment and the electric anticipation of what was coming. "I'm glad you're doing this with me," I said, a soft admittance of the fear that coiled beneath all my bravado.

"Not doing it any other way," he replied, and I knew he meant it.

The reflection of Pearl's neon sign flickered through the window, adding a strange glow to his determined features. All my life I'd been afraid of uncertainty, but now I reveled in it, my heart running wild even before my wolf got the chance.

"I must be the luckiest girl in Texas." I half-teased, my voice breaking with breathless emotion as I leaned closer to him, my chin resting in my hands.

"You're definitely something."

"Excited?"

"Crazy."

The sudden lightness in his tone lifted my spirits even further, and I let out a laugh that felt loud and raw against the evening's muted backdrop. I couldn't be sure if this feeling would last, if it would survive the first sharp edge of pain or uncertainty, but for now, it was everything. The presence I'd sensed stirred more insistently, and it filled me with hope.

I tapped my fingers on the worn wood, watching as Bronc gathered himself and settled more comfortably into the moment, the way he always did when my excitement was too infectious to deny. Our future hung thick in the air, our unfinished plates as forgotten as the past we were leaving behind.

He tapped the notepad again, drawing my attention back to his notes. He hadn't finished with my lesson on how my shift would go.

"You'll be naked under your robe, joining the pack for a ritual of transformation." Bronc's voice was calm, too calm, for the storm these words summoned. I swallowed hard and looked out the window as he continued, soft flares of color licking at the horizon like an echo of my pounding heart. The night of the full moon. Highest peak. His instructions were delicate and sure as a surgeon's knife, the stakes high and edged with worry. I held on, listening to how my bones would shift, how my wolf would rise. He leaned forward, a hand brushing my wrist, and the touch sparked through me like wildfire. This would test us both. My breath caught, the enormity of what lay ahead barreling in with dizzying force.

"We don't think of nudity the way humans do." His reassurance unfurled like the smoke from my father's cigars, a familiar comfort.

A knot of tension tangled its way through me. The thought of being so vulnerable, so exposed, hit hard, but I knew that to the pack, I would be just another wolf. And Bronc would be there. That single fact settled like a balm on raw nerves. Still, my voice wavered as I responded.

"I'm not sure about the robe, Bronc."

He reached for his coffee, wrapping a strong hand around the white mug, and smiled in a way that was both wicked and soft. "Your modesty is safe with me, darlin'. My eyes will be the only eyes on your perfect body that night."

My lips twitched at the corners, and the tension eased its grip just enough to let his confidence bleed through. It didn't take long for this assurance to take hold, this stark contrast to the shadows I'd lived in before. Already I was getting used to it.

"I still don't know how you all do it," I said, marveling at the freedom these shifters lived with, the shamelessness.

His smile turned fond, a proud glint lighting his eyes. "It's who we are."

Those words, simple as they were, tugged at something deep and long-buried in me. My thoughts drifted back to a pale and gleaming future that had been laid out since birth, one I'd quietly defied when Bronc stormed into my world. I still couldn't believe the forces that had brought me here. How I went from hiding bruises and swallowing down desperation to claiming my place in this fierce new life.

"When the time comes," Bronc said, his voice a low rumble like distant thunder, "you need to relax as much as you can. It's vital that you don't fight it. Talk to your wolf. Welcome her." His hands lifted to reinforce his words, laying down the foundations of this alien ritual. "She'll help you through."

I'd never seen him like this. Intensity poured from him.

"What if it doesn't work?" The words slipped out, bare and raw and unguarded. "What if I can't do this?"

He looked up sharply, brows drawing together. "Juliet."

I ached at the urgency in his voice. "You can't be sure."

His gaze softened but didn't waver. A promise shot through with steel. "I know my mate."

"Mate." I whispered it, still in awe that this was real, that he would be so sure.

I ran my fingers along the edge of the table, grounding myself in the mundane and familiar. It should have been easier by now to take him at his word, to let it settle in the hollow places, but doubt was still my most faithful companion.

"When you fight the shift, it hurts like hell." His mouth pulled tight with the memory of pain. "You've got to let go, baby."

I felt his words crash through me, relentless. Let go. I'd fought against everything, my nature most of all. But this time, for the first time, I wanted to surrender.

His hand moved across the table, finding mine. "I'll be with you," he said, a quiet assurance. "Every second. I'm not letting you face this alone. I'll lend you every ounce of strength I have."

My breath caught, heart twisting in my chest. He'd been saying the same kinds of things since I stepped off that bus. But the promise felt new every time, shattering the pieces of me that still believed I was unworthy. My eyes stayed fixed on our joined hands as if to memorize this moment and its impossible truth.

"I know you will," I said softly, swallowing against the thick emotions rising in my throat.

He held my gaze, the determination there a lifeline as the weight of what was to come pressed down. "When the moon rises to its highest peak, your bones will shift, stretching and reshaping. It's a lot to go through, even for someone with more wolf blood."

There it was again, the unspoken doubt of what I truly was. Even Bronc couldn't be sure.

"I'm tougher than I look."

"Always said you were." The hint of humor in his eyes quickly turned to seriousness again. "I won't shift until you do. Then we'll run together. Just like in your dreams."

I could feel my heart thumping, a feral beat keeping time with my racing thoughts. Every detail he laid out came with the potential to change everything, to either fulfill or shatter the life we were building.

Pearl's form came into focus at the periphery of my vision, and she approached with the kind of authority that suggested she knew what was best, just like her son.

"Don't you fret," she said, her warm smile fixing on me as if I were one of her own, and maybe I was. "It's gonna be a beautiful thing, darlin'."

My nod was half grateful, and I glanced to Bronc who wore a patient look that said he agreed with her but wouldn't push too hard.

"Thank you." My voice barely rose above a whisper as I tucked loose strands of hair behind my ears. The comforting weight of Bronc's hand stayed on mine.

Pearl refilled our coffee, her presence as steadying as the caffeine she poured, before she made her way back to the counter where she settled an old timer's bill and added some local flair to his drink by topping it off with a slug of whiskey.

The conversation at the tables around us barely registered as background noise, to the urgency of Bronc's instructions cutting through everything else like static. I tuned back into the quiet power of his voice, trying to commit every word to memory.

"I must be insane," I said, shaking my head in wonder, "to be so excited about something that sounds so awful."

Bronc's grin almost softened his features, if a man like him could ever be that. "Not like you've ever done things the easy way."

The way he looked at me, with unwavering faith, was almost too much to bear. It filled me to the breaking point, where fear couldn't find a foothold because there wasn't room for anything but him.

I watched as he closed his notepad with a decisive thud, and the last of my doubts scattered like shadows. How did I get here? How did a sheltered, mousy girl from the east coast land in Dairyville, Texas, at the center of this man's universe and on the brink of becoming something more than anyone ever thought I could be?

"I'm going to shift," I said, letting the certainty bloom between us.

"Damn right you are."

His approval crackled through the air, catching fire in the most reckless parts of me. The dark roads ahead glowed neon bright, daring us to follow. This was what it felt like to be alive, to breathe raw, unfiltered promises into blood and bone.

"Feels like you're counting down to Christmas," Bronc teased, but the spark in his eyes told me he shared the thrill.

"That's exactly what it feels like." I was breathless, giddy.

He pushed back from the table, an amused shake of his head, saying more than words ever could. I felt like we were the only ones left in the diner as he reached for my hand, his touch a warm brand of possession and hope.

We stepped outside into the waiting night. The neon sign flickered above, a witness to this strange and savage joy that built higher than uncertainty ever dared to climb.

# Chapter 15

## Harrison

I sat in my New York office, a hunter surrounded by prey. Reports, fluorescent graphs, multiple screens detailing my data. Their clamor nearly drowned out the photograph of her on the back monitor. Almost. My gaze slid across neatly arranged files and halted on the one variable I'd yet to solve: the small bandage, stained dark with the last thing I needed from her. I ran a caliper over it with mechanical precision, calculating what a twelve-and-a-half percent taint would require.

Outside my wall of windows, the city crawled with distraction. Below, finance bros in ill-fitting suits scurried along Fifth Avenue. I watched them dodge cabs and hustle toward trains, their oblivion stretching toward Westchester County.

With a controlled exhale, I pushed off the view and settled back at the mahogany desk. Every detail I could ever need sat arranged before me in regimented stacks. Computer screens flashing failed analysis. Thumb drives cataloging lineage and dilution. Pages of genealogies extracted from archives that stretched as far back as I needed. Results. None of them good enough yet.

I tapped a series of keys, the fluorescent desk lamp illuminating the latest serum failure in brutal clarity.

Her. That was the key. The problem and solution.

I shuffled papers, graphs, and results until I reached a screen displaying perfectly ordered bars and numbers. A lab analysis conducted just last week. I remembered those hours like they were minutes ago—monitoring each process, ensuring the transfer went as planned. Taking more samples than required because I refused to come up short.

Not when everything was this close.

The images in front of me narrowed to exactly what I needed to focus on, and I pushed the rest aside with a cool, clinical movement. My fingers flipped through another set of results, arranging them into a coherent sequence. Nothing missing, yet one step shy of perfect. This set would serve to correct that error. But the damn taint—thicker and more insidious than I had anticipated—continued to defy me.

I typed more entries, each key a hammer of calculation as I wove through graphs. Bloodlines and inheritances. Mixed strains that contaminated and confounded. None of them—none of them—could lead back to the first family of shifters unless I cracked this variable.

As I input new variables, the bandage with her sample demanded my attention again. I glared at it, defying its stubborn mutation to elude me much longer. It was hers, all right. Her entire family's, for that matter. A mess of squandered opportunities. Decades of that man's negligence had left me with far too much interference to isolate and analyze, but she could put it right again. This set would prove it.

If she thought running would keep her safe from me, she underestimated me. That had to be why she left, some insipid notion of breaking free. It would only be a matter of time before she realized that her obligations—and my tenacity—ran deeper than that. But time was one thing I refused to waste.

That photo of her—running on a constant loop across the back screen—insisted my patience with her wouldn't go unrewarded. The other screens, showing nothing but failure, had the opposite message. The one nearest me blinked more serum analyzes, a relentless inventory of faults. I couldn't let the dissatisfaction cloud my focus, but it had been months since the results showed a single spike worth pursuing. I tapped a sequence of commands to magnify the results, the last thing I needed taunting me from the precise center of every report. Hybrid. Undiluted.

Unwilling to lose ground, I shuffled the findings into the foreground. Lab entries chronicled the serum from its first conception to this unsatisfactory stage. Each step dated, documented, tracked down to its smallest error. I printed out new reports, intending to scrutinize them against my own projections before the next batch entered testing.

The file transfers completed, I stared at the single variable that defied resolution, knowing exactly how to solve it. I hadn't obtained the results I needed because they hadn't provided me with a sample from her yet.

The dissatisfaction pushed me back from the desk, my focus tunneling toward one thing only. But before I abandoned the chase for the night, I retrieved the stained bandage again. Dark. Disappointing. Not for much longer. I returned to the computer, keying the latest lab notes into memory. Every word and graph remained burned into me like her last reckless look.

As I placed the newly printed sheets into their precise order, the stacked files taunted me, imprecise and disobedient. This failure, like the damn stain, was as temporary as she imagined her defection to be. But with the new information, everything would fall into place. And then, in ways she couldn't yet conceive, so would she.

I remembered when I'd put that engagement ring on Juliet's finger her father's money was infused into my company and we began new research into what would hopefully be a groundbreaking drug that would bring Harrison Pharma back into the upper echelon of drug companies once again. It had been too long since we'd made a splash in the medical community. We had the top research scientists, so it would be just a matter of time before we'd hit on the next big thing; I was certain.

Juliet moved into the penthouse a few weeks after the engagement. She didn't seem any happier about the arrangement than I was. She didn't know me, and I didn't know her. She certainly wasn't aware of the rot that festered beneath my polished exterior. It started with a vase—some gaudy thing she'd brought from her old apartment. She knocked it over during an argument, porcelain shattering like the last thread of my control. My hand struck her face before I could leash the heat in my veins.

She stumbled, a gasp trapped in her throat, blood blooming on her split lip. Guilt curdled in my gut, sharp and sour. "I'm sorry," I murmured, thumb brushing the wound, my pulse racing not from remorse but fascination as I watched crimson bead and drip from the gash. "It won't happen again."

By morning, her mouth was smooth, unmarred. No bruise. No scab. Just pink flesh mocking my understanding of biology. I was stunned. There should have been swelling, scabbing, some sign of the violence I'd doled out to her. But there was nothing.

"Juliet, wasn't your lip cut from my unfortunate loss of control last night?" I'd inquired over breakfast.

She looked almost surprised at the mention, as though she'd forgotten all about the incident. She reached up to her lip. "Oh, um, yes, I think it was. It must have healed up overnight, thankfully."

She'd said it like that was normal.

"Well, I'm glad it wasn't worse than it was then. Again, I'm so sorry I lost my temper like that." I told her as I reached out and brushed my thumb over her lip. Her small flinch was the only thing that told me she even remembered what I had done.

I had to see if this was just an anomaly, so I rigged up one of the knives in our cutting block to slip the handle while she used it to cut vegetables for dinner, hoping it would slice open her hand. Much to my sadistic glee, while cutting a bell pepper, the knife slipped and sliced her hand across her palm. I was in my office when I heard her scream. I ran into the kitchen to see a good amount of blood dripping across the counter into the sink. This cut was deeper, so it took two days to heal. Still, much faster than any normal human healing.

When I'd asked Juliet about this, she had just told me she must be one of those lucky people who healed faster than others. She was naïve enough to believe that was possible.

Over the course of the next few months, I didn't have to do any type of setup to see her healing abilities, as Juliet had a way of pushing my buttons. I'm not necessarily proud of my behavior. She simply had a way of causing my anger to spike. Sometimes it was simply a hip check into the staircase. A slight elbow to the ribs was always a good way to get her back in line. Squeezing her fingers kept her from telling anyone about our dynamic. And her collarbone was a victim on more than one occasion. At first I was careful about breaking bones. Those required a doctor's intervention. Once I'd hired my own personal physician, things went more smoothly.

I catalogued each injury and how it healed. I realized her DNA had to have inherent qualities and that we could tap into those. I got my investigator involved in researching her family tree. We started with her maternal side. That led them to Nebraska. It took several months, but it turned out Juliet came from a line of people who were not human at all. They are as much animal as human. And I determined I would find a way to tap into their DNA and create a serum to make humans better without turning them into dirty animals in the process.

This was a dangerous proposition. We had to be incredibly careful and methodical. It was a long game, and one I was willing to play. I built a secret, well-hidden lab outside of the country. Hired only the best doctors whom I could trust explicitly. And then I hired mercenaries who valued money above all who extracted those non-humans and transported them to the lab. We were getting closer to our goal.

Juliet was still the missing link. I would have her back in my hands, I was certain. Sooner rather than later.

# Chapter 16

## Bronc

I shoved open the heavy door to our cabin and pulled Juliet inside like a man desperate for air. Her back hit the door with a low thud as I pushed her against it, burying my face in the curve of her neck sucking across my claiming mark. I worked the hooks of her overalls until they pooled at her feet, and she kicked them away. Her scent, a mix of her usual ginger and sugar mixed with lust and love, filled my senses. The damp silk of her panties was no match for my searching hand. The sound of our feet scuffed on the wooden floor, mingling with her startled gasps and the rhythm of my deliberate mouth. Each lick, each motion was a command, drawing out the raw urgency between us.

She trembled beneath me, panting as her head tilted back against the door. My tongue found a frantic rhythm, dragging along the column of her throat in swift, demanding strokes. Her hair came loose from its knot and spilled over my fingers, and I could smell the soft scent of her arousal as my fingers found her wet and wanting. The cabin echoed with the creaking of the wooden floorboards beneath our restless feet. With each shift, the door let out a groan, a counterpoint to the soft, fervent sounds escaping her lips. Her hands clawed at my back, nails biting into the fabric of my shirt beneath my cut as she pressed her hips closer.

Her cries rose to a fevered pitch as my fingers worked in insistent, knowing circles. It pulled an almost feral cry from her, high and breathless, and her legs quivered under the strain. I stepped closer, trapping her with the solid weight of my body. Her bare skin was hot to the touch, a heat that I swore burned hotter than the September sun. Her lashes fluttered like she couldn't decide if the weight of my stare or the pressure of my fingers was more intense. The sharp scent of sweat mixed with the smell of wood of the cabin rose as our movements continued in an urgent, frantic rhythm. She bucked against me with every stroke.

My voice rumbled against her neck, low and sure. My words measured, commanding. "Don't hold back from me, Juliet. Let go." Her cries turned to breathless pleas as her hands fisted my shirt, a sudden burst of wild energy as she arched toward me. My mouth never left her neck, the steady pace of my tongue keeping time with the movements of my hand. The entryway amplified her gasps, her voice raw and unrestrained as I continued my relentless, driving pace. I felt the vibrations of her moans run down my throat as I pressed harder against her, finally claiming her mouth with mine. Her lips opened instinctively to the insistent flick of my tongue, and her knees buckled as her body convulsed with the force of my demands.

The cabin wrapped around us, every sound magnified, each creak a note in the frantic symphony we created. I moved my mouth back to the claiming mark on her neck, relentless in my rhythm, insistent in my drive. Her skin tasted of salt and sugar; her voice nothing more than a collection of jagged gasps and breathy pleas. My name on her lips sounded like destiny. More than I deserved. I wanted to tell her everything in my heart. How much she made me feel. My words blended into the movement, the timbre of my voice drawing out her cries as my hand moved faster, sure of its path. "You are more than I ever dreamed of, mate." I growled my Alpha instincts filling her. The cabin closed in, holding us in a moment of sharp, dizzying clarity where the only thing that mattered was the insistent push of my fingers and the raw, desperate sounds that came from her. Her moans rose and fell in quick succession, her back arching, and her eyes locked on mine. The force of it took her voice, replaced by a low, guttural moan that was as full of satisfaction as it was of longing.

Every movement between us was frenzied. We let the raw urgency consume us. Her scent wrapped around my senses. I wanted to pull every ounce of pleasure from her as my fingers worked faster against the swell of her. Her hands slipped from my shirt and clawed at the door behind her as her body jerked forward with each insistent motion. Head thrown back, she exposed more of that beautiful, delicate skin to the push of my mouth. Her scream of release bounced off the walls of the entryway, ragged and uncontrolled, and I felt it everywhere. Her muscles tensed as the force of it ripped through her, as my fingers continued their assault, as I refused to stop until I had wrung every last shudder and every last desperate cry from her lips.

The air felt like it crackled with energy as I pulled her into my arms and up the narrow stairs. She wore only her shirt, bra, and panties by the time I set her down in our room; the dim light casting moving shadows across our skin.

"Strip Juliet." My command was steady. My words drove her forward as she tossed the overalls she had carried. Her urgency increased with each frantic movement as she fumbled with her boots. "Hurry." The single word cut through the thick air, sharpening her focus. She pulled them free, then quickly tore off her tank top and panties and threw them on the pile at her feet. Her bra followed with a quick snap, and I could see the sharp rise and fall of her chest as she stood before me, bare and exposed and beautiful.

I didn't waste time on admiration. My own shirt came off in a single motion, landing on top of hers with precise, calculated abandon. "Get on your knees." The sharp timbre of my voice left her no choice, no room to doubt or delay. Her wide eyes met mine as she dropped to her knees in front of me, the hallway's shadows playing across her bare skin in wild, unrestrained patterns.

"Remove my boots, then unbutton and unzip my jeans, then pull them down." Her little pink tongue licked her bottom lip as she worked my boots free. She then leaned up on her knees and reached for the button of my jeans. Her face was adorable as she concentrated on the job. After a minute, she worked the button free and unzipped my jeans and maneuvered them down my legs. Her face was full of admiration as I stepped out of them. God, my cock was straining against my boxer briefs, wanting to bust free. "Now, free my cock. And I'm gonna need you to be quick about it. I'm dying for it to be wrapped in your sweet lips."

She quickly got back up on her knees and pulled the elastic of my briefs towards her face so she could ease them down. My cock stood directly at attention. While she freed them from my feet; I stroked my erection in anticipation.

My stare pinned her there, drinking in the sight of her flushed cheeks and parted lips. Her hair spilled over her shoulders, a tangled mess that added to the reckless beauty of the moment. I could hear the wild thump of my pulse, the loud rush of blood in my ears as her hands found my hips. Her breath came hot and fast against my skin. The weight of my stare was a tangible thing, demanding, pulling, ensuring her actions were exactly what I intended. She didn't break eye contact, even as she leaned forward, even as she gasped my name and the room echoed with the raw urgency between us.

The air felt charged, heavy with the tension that sizzled like a live wire. Her hands moved with confident precision, tracing paths along the lines of my hips. I couldn't help the low growl that rose in my throat, couldn't help the way my fingers tangled in her hair, urging her closer, deeper, more. My control felt as if it might snap. The ragged edge of restraint sharpened by the sight of her and the sound of her, the reality of her on her knees. My voice was a guttural rumble, pushing her to give me everything she had, everything she was, every single piece until she was bare and helpless in the face of my demands.

"Put your mouth on me, Juliet." Her tiny hands grasped me as she led with her tongue, licking the pre-cum off the tip of my dick before taking the whole of me into her mouth. The growl that left my chest folded her ever so much, bringing out her own hum that zapped my chest. "Take me as deep as you can, sweetheart." And I'll be damned if she didn't take me to the back of her throat. My hips surged forward as I gripped her head in my hands. I swear I saw the bulge of my cock in her throat. Her hands kept me there as her tongue moved along the underside, massaging the vein that ran its length as she sucked. Her saliva bathed my shaft as her hands reached for my balls, stroking them with feather-light touches. I felt like a teenage pup about to fucking lose my load within the first five minutes. I quickly pulled her off of me before I came down her throat. The look of bewilderment on her face was so sweet. I pulled her up and consumed her mouth, caging her face with my hands with my searing kiss. She reached for me, wrapping her legs around my waist.

The spacious room filled with the scent of us. The mix of our arousal perfumed the air in a heady mix that was intoxicating. I threw Juliet onto her stomach, and the bed caught her with a bounce. She landed with a giggle, a quick, beautiful sound that filled the room. She moved around and presented herself to me, ass high. My fucking obedient omega, on her knees, ready for her alpha. She looked over her shoulder at me, waiting for the praise she so unquestionably deserved.

"Look at my exquisite Omega, my Luna." I spoke while caressing the orbs of her rounded ass. "Never have I seen anything to rival you, Juliet. Now, take what your Alpha gives you." My hands found her waist and pulled her back, spreading her legs with rough insistence as I leaned over her. Her skin was soft and warm, the curve of her back begging to be touched, kissed, licked.

My fingers found her nipples and pulled sharp and deliberate my chest across her back. Her cries turned to a higher pitch, a perfect, ragged harmony with the low rumble of my voice. Her body arched toward me as my hands worked her over, each motion exact and insistent. I could feel the pounding of my pulse as I took her skin between my fingers, relentless in my drive to hear more, feel more, pull more from her. Her breath came fast and unrestrained; every exhale pushing us toward a frantic edge that was as inevitable as it was consuming.

I kissed the line of her back, wet, claiming drags of my tongue that left her shivering in response. Her taste was vivid, alluring, driving me forward as my mouth moved lower, as I refused to stop until she was nothing but the sounds of her own gasping moans and the slick press of my lips against her skin. She moved against me, desperate in her motions, urgent in her need. The cabin's silence shattered around us as the bed creaked with every motion. Her soft cries of my name turned to the ragged sounds of her moans.

I licked between her ass cheeks, slow and sure, my tongue dragging along her skin in wet, claiming strokes. She trembled beneath me, and the sound of her voice filled the room in quick, impulsive gasps. Each lick pulled a new reaction from her, a new plea that rang against the bare walls and shot straight through my body. Her hands fisted the bedding, white-knuckled and urgent, as she drove herself backward to meet my mouth. Then I lapped her dripping pussy, my grip on her hips holding her still as my tongue drove into her over and over. She tried to writhe the closer she came to her release. I knew the exact second she was ready to break. I drew back and delivered a sharp, echoing slap to her ass, and the effect was immediate.

Laughter filled the air, and she was beautiful in the way that her wild cries delighted in it. How her body moved in sync with my demands. "You are a fucking goddess, Juliet," I whispered against her skin, and she shuddered in response, her muscles clenched as I gripped her tighter. "My Little Wolf. So beautiful." The words were more than just expressions. They were a claiming, a binding, a reminder of what she was to me. They hung in the air between us. I was hard as stone as I entered her in one swift thrust. Her voice came in a ragged cry, her cry of 'Alpha' rising to the ceiling in wild, unrestrained succession.

My thrusts were powerful, unrelenting, each one more sure and forceful than the last. Her groans turned frantic, filling the bedroom in raw harmony with the sound of our bodies coming together. Her skin glistened with sweat, a slick sheen that caught the dim light, and the sight of it, the feel of it, the sound of it, pushed me further, drove me harder. My knot swelled, filling her, and I could see her muscles tense, her back arch, her fingers grip the sheets as her breath came in stuttering gasps. I reached around and found her clit, working it in circles that matched the fierce rhythm of the pistoning of my hips. Her voice broke, fierce and raw, as she screamed my name, as I felt her clamp down around me, as her release pulled me deeper inside and held me there.

The room reverberated with it all, every gasp and groan and plunge amplified by the walls and wooden floor. We moved together, and her body was a frenzy of beautiful, unrestrained motion, a perfect counterpoint to the measured strength of mine. The more my knot swelled the more she moaned my name and moved ever so slightly. She was close again, and I knew it. Could feel it. I wanted it. Gentling my hips as much as my knot would allow, I moved in slow, deliberate motions, getting closer to my own release until it hit me like a rush. I came in an avalanche of cum, filling her to overflowing. Her muscles convulsed around my knot, her head thrown back, eyes closed tight as I moved against her, unwilling to stop until she had nothing left to give. Her release came like a breaking wave, pulling me under, pulling me deeper, pulling us both into a blinding, desperate oblivion.

I cradled her in my arms as my knot softened. The room held onto the warmth of us like a secret. Moonlight seeped through the curtains, silvering the curve of Juliet's shoulder where she lay against me, her breath still uneven against my collarbone. I didn't move at first—couldn't—not while the weight of her trust settled into my bones like an anchor. But slowly, gently, I untangled myself, pressing a kiss to her temple as she murmured something drowsy and incoherent.

I fetched a cloth from the bathroom linen closet, ran it under warm water until it steamed faintly in my palm. Back beside her, I took my time tracing the lines we'd made together—the flush of her skin, the hitch in her ribs when she sighed under my touch. "Easy," I whispered as she stirred, cleaning her with a reverence that surprised even me. Her fingers brushed my wrist once, soft as a sigh, before she stilled again.

When I was done, I pulled the quilt over us both and settled her back against my chest, her hair spilling like silk across my arm. She felt smaller like this somehow; not fragile but *precious*, something carved from starlight I'd been clumsy enough to catch. My throat tightened as I pressed my lips to the crown of her head.

"You're..." The words jammed up; too much, always too much when it came to her. But she deserved them anyway. "You're every brave thing," I said finally, voice low against her ear. "Every damn time."

She hummed faintly, turning into me until her forehead met my sternum. "Bronc—"

"No," I cut in softly, thumb skimming the ridge of her cheekbone. "Let me say it." The fear of sounding foolish dissolved under the weight of needing her to know. "You fight like hellfire," I whispered. "Love like a storm." Her heartbeat answered mine beneath my palm—steady now, but still fierce. Alive. "And you're mine."

The declaration hung there a moment before she tilted her chin up to meet my gaze, raw and unguarded in the dark, and kissed me slow enough to steal time itself from around us. When she sank back down against me with a shiver that wasn't born from cold or fear but surrender instead. I recognized then and there that I would do everything in my power to keep this woman, my mate, safe from every evil that wanted to harm her. Kill any man or woman who sought to cause her pain. This was my vow.

# Chapter 17

## Juliet

After days of what I'd dubbed the "wolf flu," my muscles were useless. I barely managed to roll onto my side on the old leather couch, groaning at the flu-like ache that seemed to tangle into the marrow of my bones. With my legs curled under me and a soft throw pulled around me, I sank further into the soft pillow beneath my elbow. Pearl's soup simmered in the kitchen. Even in my exhausted haze, I could make out the distinct scent of rosemary and sage drifting through the cabin. Light filtered softly through the windows, turning golden against the warm woods. The low glow added a gentle haze to my already fevered state. Pearl drifted back into the room and traded my sketchbook for a cup of coffee and warm words. I gratefully took the mug from her and held it with both hands. She lightly patted my knee as she gave me one of her looks of encouragement I'd grown to love so much.

"Oh, darlin'. You're in a bad way, aren't you?" Her voice was a quiet melody as she sat. "But that hasn't stopped your wonderful gift has it?" She admired the sketch of the trees and the moon I'd been drawing as she set my sketchbook on the coffee table.

"I'm fine," I murmured, more out of habit than truth. The warmth of the coffee settled into my bones. "My fingers just itch to draw more sometimes than others."

Pearl's hands, gentle but insistent, pulled the throw further up over my lap. "You have a gift, sweet girl. Several of them, in fact." She smoothed back the hair that had fallen over my eyes. "Now, I know your shift symptoms have been kickin' your hiney, but we'll get some soup in you and it will help. Got to keep your strength up for tomorrow night."

The mention of the full moon sent a ripple of excitement and anxiety through me, though it was buried beneath the fatigue. "I've felt worse," I managed, though I couldn't remember when. My fever left my mind a bit fogged and my limbs heavy.

"First change is always hard," Pearl said, her hand rubbing across my bent leg. Her presence was a steady comfort in the midst of my unsteady state.

"I'm sure I'll be fine. I'm from New York, remember?"

She drew back slightly, her expression equal parts worry and warmth. "Now don't you give me any lip 'bout this. You're not the only girl in the family who had it rough with bein' different."

Her words reached through the haze, echoing things we'd spoken about before but never this directly. Pearl had shared stories with me, family lore really, about women who hadn't known they were shifters and had to face similar situations. They'd survived and thrived.

"Thank you, Pearl." It was all I could offer. I hated how weak my voice sounded. She kissed the top of my head like a mother to a child, a gesture so foreign it made my eyes sting. I couldn't remember a time when my mother had ever offered me any type of motherly gesture like this. It wasn't something I could hide. Pearl sensed it and asked me about my childhood. About my mother.

"My mother is a... difficult woman." I began. I was honest with Pearl, telling her about what it was like growing up as the daughter of Renda Bettencourt. How there was no room for less than perfection. It seemed like I was telling a fairytale. The poor little rich girl who had everything that money could buy except love and acceptance from the people who should have loved her most. Pearl was such a good listener. She let me tell my entire story all the way to where they basically sold me to Harrison, and I made my escape. I paused as a tear fell down my cheek before I spoke again.

"Thinking about things now, I don't know if she did the things she did because it's how she felt, or out of fear of my father."

"Juliet, we're your family now." She said it softly, but her words were steel strong. I felt a knot in my throat, too many emotions choking me at once.

My response, an attempt to voice what this meant, was lost to the roar of Bronc's Harley as it cut through the stillness outside.

He was a storm through the door, his expression a wild mix of fear and relief when he found me on the couch. "Damn, Juliet." The words tumbled out in a rush as he crossed the room. His leather cut was cool against my skin when he scooped me into his arms.

"Bronc—"

"You're burnin' up." He touched the back of his hand to my forehead, then pulled me closer, like he thought I might disappear into a puff of smoke. "Thought you said you were fine, woman."

It should have been a reprimand, but I heard the strain beneath his voice, the raw edge of worry. He had sensed my distress through our bond. His wolf could also feel it when something wasn't right. I'd known that, but this was the first time I saw it laid bare.

Pearl's gentle laughter cut through the tangle of our words. "Didn't think I'd let her suffer through this alone, did ya?" She went to the dining table, settling plates and bowls with quiet certainty.

"I was ten minutes out when I got the call." Bronc shifted me to sit up more on the couch, his eyes never leaving my face. They were the bluest things I'd ever seen. "Maddie brought you?"

Pearl nodded. "And stayed to help. You ain't the only one cares about this girl."

The cabin's front door creaked, and I turned to see Maddie with the last of the dishes. Her grin was wide and teasing as she spotted us. "If it isn't Bronc, the Overbearing."

"Glad you came to help, but I got this." His voice was brusque but not unkind. He set a firm hand on my shoulder, like he thought I might bolt for the door.

"Your growly ass needs more than one woman to look after it," Maddie said. Her voice was playful, but there was a deep affection behind it.

I watched, bleary-eyed, as they bickered in a way that only siblings can. Bronc's intense gaze cut back to me every few seconds, but when he was sure I wouldn't vanish into thin air, he went to the table, finally settling in.

He ran a hand through his hair, exhaled hard. "Alright, then."

Maddie joined Pearl, setting down a salad bowl with a flourish. "You can't hover forever. She's tougher than you think."

He leveled a look at her but didn't argue, the tension in his shoulders easing by a fraction.

I hadn't moved from the couch, and maybe it was that fact as much as anything that finally convinced him I wasn't at death's door. Not quite. I let out a slow breath as they continued setting the table, the scene so warm and familial that I felt like an intruder in my own body.

Pearl caught my eye and gestured to the open seat. "You comin' or not, girl?"

I pushed myself upright, glad that Bronc let me do this on my own. And despite the way my vision slightly spun, I made it to the table. Bronc had taken the chair closest to mine, a little surprised that I'd moved at all.

The clink of cutlery and the low murmur of voices filled the space. The soup, once I lifted the spoon, was hot and rich, slipping down my throat like liquid gold. It was comforting, like the warmth of the cabin and the glow of the people around me.

I couldn't quite believe I was here, watching myself sit at this table, as if I were a character in someone else's life.

Pearl ladled more soup with a mother's care. "Eat up, darlin'."

She filled Bronc's bowl with the same insistence, and I hid a smile as he obliged, though it was clear he had one eye on me, checking that I was eating as well.

We were halfway through the meal when Bronc's foot nudged mine under the table. "You hangin' in there?" His voice was low, meant for me alone.

"You bet." I felt the weight of everything all at once, my fatigue and the strange new world I'd been thrust into. I was a little anxious and grateful and dizzy with both.

He reached for my hand, giving it a squeeze that shot warmth up my arm. He leaned over and kissed my forehead. "You got this." The words were as much promise as encouragement.

I nodded, not trusting myself to speak without my voice breaking.

Pearl smiled softly at me, like she knew everything I couldn't say. "Always a tough night for first-timers. You'll not just make it through; you're gonna love it."

There were more voices then, rising and falling in the shared rhythm of an unexpected family. My family, whether or not I believed it. I felt the weight of their certainty as strong as I felt the exhaustion dragging me down.

Maddie winked at me, her laughter a light through my haze. "Yep, we'll keep you around. I'm happy I'm not the only girl around here besides Scar."

The minutes blurred like the light through the windows. It was too surreal to be real, yet there I was. A girl with shifter blood, facing the full moon with a pack by her side.

The light was dimmer still when the men arrived. They came in like giants, their presence expanding to fill the cabin with something dense and unyielding. I watched them from the dining table, where I sat like a tired ghost. Bridger was first, broad and sharp-eyed. Eli and Jess were with him, moving through the room like shadows through smoke. JT followed, smiling in his way that suggested everything would be alright. When Ryder appeared, closing the door behind them all, the room felt smaller but infinitely safer. Bronc hovered close, still vigilant even with his closest brothers surrounding us.

"Juliet." Bridger's voice was a low rumble, more than a greeting. It was reassurance wrapped in a single word. As Bronc's VP, he was the man he trusted the most. The others echoed it in their own ways, brief nods and tight grips as they took their places.

My senses had dulled and sharpened at once. The warmth from the earlier meal lingered in my bones, battling the fever that hadn't left. My head was clearer, enough to absorb the weight of what was happening around me.

I'd met them all before, but never like this. They stood or sat, towering over the space with a careful watchfulness that bordered on reverence. They weren't the Iron Valor men I'd known, hard-edged and battle-ready. They were brothers, every last one of them, and they had come for me, their Luna.

JT was closest, larger than life, leaning in to speak over the low hum of the room. "Full moon jitters, huh?" His smile was a beacon, cutting through the fatigue that threatened to pull me under. This man, the chaplain, would pray over me, and I know he'd protect me as well.

I nodded, unable to find words that didn't sound small and inadequate in the face of their concern.

"Got your back," Jess said from across the table. He didn't need to say more. It was all there in his stance, the solid presence of a man, their Seargent at Arms who had never let a brother fall.

Ryder was next to him, hazel eyes steady on mine. He had a calmness about him, the kind that came with years of mending wounds, and I felt it seep into my bones. "First night's always hardest," he said. "But you've got this."

The words mirrored Bronc's earlier, different in their calm surety, but just as powerful. I was at the center of something immense, a force I hadn't realized was possible until it gathered around me.

Eli's gaze held the weight of a dozen unspoken promises. "Ain't nothin' to it." He folded his arms over his chest, an intimidating posture if I hadn't known the compassion behind it. Bronc's enforcer. Wrecker. He'd take a bullet for everyone in this room.

The men exchanged brief words and quieter glances, a silent communication that flowed around me. Bronc was a steady presence at my side, but the fear I'd seen in him before had dulled and was tempered now by their shared certainty.

They moved like parts of a single organism, shifting to fill the space with the perfect blend of strength and warmth. I felt them envelop me in ways that were too big to grasp, too real to deny. Their expressions and gestures, simple and genuine, made my throat tighten.

"You guys gonna stare at her all night, or you gonna let her breathe?" Maddie's voice carried a teasing lilt as she entered from the kitchen, a reminder that this was as much a family gathering as anything else.

The men laughed, a sound that was deeper and more sincere than I'd ever heard it. They settled into seats and leaned against walls, all of them within reach, all of them ready.

Bronc's fingers grazed my shoulder, a subtle anchor as he took in the sight of his men around us. "You're a lucky woman, Juliet," he said, the gravel of his voice giving way to something almost like awe.

"I believe I am," I murmured. The room spun slowly, and I felt the warmth of the soft throw from before still wrapped around my shoulders.

"We've all been through it," Bridger said, speaking more to Bronc than to me. The weight of it landed softly. "We know what she's facing."

The men's confidence was like a wall, built with brick and mortar and something stronger than both. They were as solid as the moon was round, as bright as my fever in the dark Texas night.

Bridger, Eli, and Jess exchanged another set of brief nods, each offering the others a quick smile. I watched them, trying to reconcile what I saw with what I felt. How I could be at the center of it when I was still just Juliet, the outsider with strange blood and a stranger life.

JT's voice broke into my thoughts. "Y'all should hear yourselves. A man's never been so cared for. And here you are, coddlin' this one."

His laughter was a comfort, and it spread like wildfire around the room. Even Bronc's lips twitched at the corners, his intensity easing as the mood lightened.

I was drowning in their certainty, in the truth of how much they'd already made me theirs. I thought of my other life, the one before Pearl and Bronc and the men in front of me. It felt like a fever dream, more distant by the second.

"Juliet." Bronc's voice brought me back, pulled me from the tide of my own thoughts.

"Yeah?" I met his gaze, my heart quickening despite my exhaustion.

He searched my eyes, saw everything I was and everything I feared I wasn't. "Gonna get through this?" It was half statement, half question. The look in his eyes made it both a promise and a plea.

"With you all breathing down my neck, I might." My voice was steady, though the weight of the moment was not.

I saw something unguarded in him then, a flicker of hope that seemed to catch and spread like wildfire through the bond I'd felt all along. It anchored me, even as it threatened to undo me.

When he pulled back, his expression was a mask of the same fierce determination I'd seen earlier. The transformation made me shiver.

Maddie's hands were quick and efficient as she cleared the earlier dishes, and it was barely a breath before she returned with fresh ones, loaded with food that matched the bounty of support the men offered.

"Brought you boys somethin' to soak up all that hot air," she said with a grin.

More laughter, more warmth as they settled into easy familiarity. The table groaned under the weight of everything Pearl and Maddie had prepared. It reminded me of them, the way they carried so much and never seemed to bend beneath it.

The sound of forks on plates and the low voices was a backdrop to my thoughts. He was right, what he'd said about my luck.

But luck was only a piece of it. They'd given me something more, something that felt like a glimpse into the next day. It filled the spaces where fear and uncertainty had lived for so long. I felt it seep into me the way fever hadn't, all-consuming and fierce and relentless.

"Still think she'll bail?" Jess said with a chuckle, and I realized they were talking about me again. Talking like they already knew the answer, even if I didn't.

"Not this one," Ryder replied, a knowing grin tugging at his lips.

Bronc's eyes were a storm when they locked on mine, swirling with too many emotions to name. But love, real and sure and undeterred, was the clearest of them all.

I made eye contact with Jess. "Couldn't chase me away, mister. I'm here to stay. This is where my mate is. Why would I want to be anywhere else?"

Just then, the front door swung open and Tyler walked in. I don't know why, but I stood to face him. Things had thawed a little since he'd basically told me I wasn't good enough for his father or this pack. My pulse skittered, fingers twisting the hem of my sweater until the fabric bit into my skin. *Here it comes*, I thought, bracing for the sharp edge of his words, the same disdain he'd hurled at me weeks ago when he'd snarled about my "being human" sullying his father's legacy. Too young, what right did I have standing beside Bronc as his Luna? Tyler's glare had made that answer clear: none.

But this time, his boots didn't thud with aggression as he crossed the room. His shoulders sagged, that military-rigid posture folding like armor discarded. When he met my gaze, his eyes weren't ice anymore—they were ash after a fire, soft and spent. "Juliet," he said my name like an apology, low and rough. "I... I was wrong."

A tremor ran through me. Bronc stood silently by me. I felt his presence like sunlight at my back as Tyler dropped to one knee, head bowed. The gesture stole my breath. This warrior, who'd faced warlords and war zones, kneeling for *me*.

"You're my father's fated mate," he said, voice cracking. "Fate chose you. And I—" His throat bobbed. "I disrespected our pack's bond. Our *Luna*." He looked up then, raw reverence in his stare that made heat prickle behind my eyelids. "I may not understand it all yet... but I swear on my life, I'll stand by you now."

The room blurred as tears spilled over. My knees buckled, but powerful hands caught me—Bronc's steady grip on my waist, Tyler rising swiftly to hover close, like he feared I'd shatter if he touched me. The irony; *he* was the one trembling now.

"Tomorrow night," he murmured, "during your first shift... I'll be there." His jaw tightened, not with anger, but with resolve. "No matter what happens with your wolf coming through... you won't face it alone."

A sob tore loose from my chest then. Relief and gratitude tangled into something wild and keening. Bronc's thumb brushed my nape in quiet pride. Not just for me, I realized, but for Tyler too: the soldier who'd bent instead of broken when truth demanded it.

And when Tyler pressed a fist to his heart in a pack vow, "Always," the other men around the room who had risen when

he had walked in also repeated that vow, looking directly at me,
"Always."

# Chapter 18

## Bronc

I woke before sunrise and watched Juliet sleep, her golden hair fanning around her head like a halo. Tracing the warmth of her face with gentle fingertips, I admired her peaceful form before heading downstairs to prepare breakfast.

Methodically, I arranged a carton of eggs, bread, and all the fixings on the counter while coffee dripped steadily into the carafe. I'd just set the iron skillet on the stove as the sound of small, bare feet pattered behind me. Juliet appeared in the doorway, her oversized shirt hanging just low enough to stir the wolf in me. She wrapped her arms around my waist and leaned her head against my back.

"Morning, handsome."

"Morning, yourself," I replied, turning to face her, feeling the heat of her against me. In one swift motion, I lifted her onto the kitchen island, her legs draping naturally around my hips.

She pulled me closer, and we shared a long, tender kiss. I tasted her lips like a man deprived. Damn, it'd been too long.

"How's my girl feeling?" I asked, my voice rough with all the need I'd held back.

"Better than ever." She smiled with that fire lighting her eyes, no trace of the weakness or feverishness that had plagued her over the last few days. Her shifter blood was coming on stronger than I'd expected.

"That's fucking music to my ears." I couldn't hold back any longer, not when she was right there in front of me, looking like she was made of golden light.

Her shirt came off in a hurry, my hands tracing every inch of skin beneath it. We'd already baptized this island with her cum once. Nothing was gonna stop me from doing it again right now. Our kiss deepened, a sweet heat rising between us. I hadn't been intimate with her in days because of the effects of her oncoming shift. I remedied that with eager fingertips that dragged a steady path between her thighs.

She let out a breathless gasp as I slipped them inside her already wet warmth. "I've missed this," she whispered, and I could feel her pulse quicken.

"Missed you more," I spoke, the words against her neck, then licked my way down her collarbone. I took my time, savoring every inch of her skin with lips and tongue.

When I reached her breasts, her fingers tangled in my hair, willing me closer. She arched her back, pressing against me, and the sound of her moans wrapped around us like the steamy air of the kitchen. Her skin was flushed with heat, and I could feel the change in her; the strength, the untapped power that came with her shifter blood. It made her wilder, and I loved every bit of it.

Lowering myself to my knees, I took her with my mouth, the intensity of her response igniting me. I'd let her believe she was in charge, at least for now. But I wouldn't stop until she screamed my name.

Her hands were in my hair again, tugging with a fierceness that only made me hungrier for her. Her taste had become more smoky, more intoxicating, more everything Juliet. She shuddered, every muscle tense as I drove her higher. I added two fingers deep inside her as my tongue continued its assault on her swollen clit. She threw her head back, her body leaned on her hands so she could thrust her hips toward me, wanting everything I could give her. She cried out my name as her juices coated my tongue. The sweetest taste, the sweetest sounds. As I leaned back, I licked my way up her thighs and stomach, all the way up to her waiting mouth. She drank herself off my tongue, her arms wrapped tightly around my neck. I pulled her hips until she was seated fully around my aching erection, holding her still as I moved in and out of her.

She raised her head, exposing her beautiful neck to me. I'd eased her further off the island, so I had more leverage. My thrusts became harder as my knot expanded.

"Nothing feels so good as your pussy wrapped around me, Little Wolf." I growled into her neck as I nipped and licked.

Her moaned reply was the only answer offered.

My knot swelled and held her in place as my thrusts shortened, and her body quaked. "I need you to come for me now, Juliet."

I bit her on my claiming mark, feeling her blood splash across my tongue. I came with a roar as Juliet's hips bucked as much as they could, up from the island. Her entire body shook from the power of her release as I lapped the small amount of blood that trickled from her bite mark.

She looked up at me with such immense emotion and love that it almost buckled my knees. This woman—my mate—had changed everything.

I cleaned her, and the kitchen countertop once my knot softened. Then I settled her at the dining table while I finished making breakfast. It was vital that she had hearty meals today filled with lots of protein and calories to prepare for her shift tonight.

While we ate, we discussed tonight's ceremony one more time. I wanted to make certain I had answered any lingering questions she may have had concerning what to expect. There was no room for fear.

Her eyes shone with resolve. "I'm ready," she said, taking my hand in hers, sealing her confidence with the touch of her skin on mine.

After all she'd already faced in her life, I knew this woman could take on the world. In just a few hours, we'd see if the world was ready for her.

We spent the day as peacefully as possible. A few visitors popped in and out. Ma dropped off a bounty of food for lunch and dinner. The men had stopped by to offer more encouragement. But mostly Juliet and I rested and talked.

Night had fallen, and we'd prepared for the ceremony. I gave Juliet privacy as she showered and readied herself in the bathroom. I'd dressed in a pair of white satin pants with the red heart and silver wolf Iron Valor MC Pack emblem embroidered on the leg. Sitting in the lounge chair in our room, I watched the door, anticipating her entrance. Juliet emerged from the bathroom dressed in a white satin robe that fell gracefully to the floor. She looked like a fucking angel. The long sleeves had a soft ruffle at the wrists. A wide red belt, tied in a bow, cinched the robe at her small waist. The Iron Valor red heart and silver wolf emblem was embroidered on the left side of the robe over her heart. Her golden waves trailed down almost to her waist. Her face was free of makeup, full lips naturally pink, and those damn adorable little freckles dotted across her nose and cheeks. I rose to meet her, cupping her face in my hands.

"You are the most exquisite woman I've ever laid my eyes on, mate." I whispered, kissing her with reverence.

Her voice was small. "Thank you, Bronc, mate, love."

I guided us out of the cabin and onto the open plains, the grass soft beneath our bare feet.

This was as much a declaration as it was a celebration, marking Juliet's transformation and our first full moon as a mated couple. My pack stood in formation, rows and rows of pack members. The ancient songs of our people rose into the night sky, an unbroken chant of loyalty and strength.

We walked arm in arm into the front of the clearing, and as we faced our pack, the chants quieted. More than a hundred pairs of eyes looked to the ground as they gave us space.

I stood rooted in the damp grass as J.T. "Big Papa," our chaplain, moved to address us all, his ceremonial robes sweeping through moonlit clover. His gravelly deep voice rolled across our gathered pack like distant thunder—respectful yet impossible to ignore. We turned to face him. My pulse quickened when he turned those knowing eyes toward Juliet beside me.

"The Moon Goddess paints tonight's sky for more than ceremony," he rumbled, gesturing toward silver light that fractured through storm clouds. Every syllable carried generations of tradition. *Her first shift*, I thought fiercely, my mate's trembling fingers tightening around mine. "She blesses not just warriors' strength tonight." A warm huff left my chest as his beard lifted in a knowing smile directed at us both. "*Our* Luna's awakening."

Heat climbed my neck when murmurs of approval rippled through the wolf-kind ranks behind us. My gaze never left Juliet's profile—the determined set of her jaw beneath falling platinum and gold curls that suddenly seemed to glow with its own light. *Our light.*

J.T.'s tone gentled as fireflies began winking awake around us. "When stars crown midnight," his palm pressed over his heart, "Bronc will guide his Luna beyond watchful eyes." Pride swelled beneath my ribs even as anticipation coiled tighter. "Let sacred solitude cradle this becoming." His wink flashed white in the shadows when nervous laughter broke from Juliet, musical notes swallowed by cricket song.

The ancient blessing came then—Old Tongue words flowing over us like warm oil. I barely registered my own claws pricking palms until Juliet's scent sharpened, ginger and sugar cutting through pine resin. Her shoulder pressed harder against mine as JT's final syllables vibrated in shared marrow.

*Soon,* I promised wordlessly as our pack began howling approval. *Soon we'd disappear into black pines until moonlight carved beasts from our skin. Soon we'd return blazing twin trails through forest loam, our people running* thunderously *at our heels. But this next breath? This quicksilver moment before becoming?*

This was ours alone.

I held Juliet's gaze, the silent connection between us pulsing with intensity. She was everything I never knew I needed, and now she was mine in a way I never thought possible. As the blessing concluded, we began the short walk to the secluded area Ma and Maddie had prepared. They'd hung fairy lights and pretty ribbons, and the soft grass beneath our feet felt like it could give way to anything. Possibility hung in the air.

I took Juliet's robe from her shoulders, my hands lingering a moment too long as she let it fall away. She stood before me, unashamed and beautiful in the night air, the pale light tracing her form like a lover's hand. The sky above was clear; the moon so full and bright it was nearly blinding. I could feel its pull deep inside, an ancient rhythm quickening my blood. I looked at Juliet, watching the way her body seemed to glow beneath the sky. The men had gathered at a respectful distance, their backs to us. It was a silent testament to their understanding of what was to come.

"This is it," I told her, hearing the gruffness in my own voice. "On your hands and knees. Let it happen. Don't fight it."

She nodded, eyes wide with trust. I helped her to the ground, where the moon's light cut through the trees and lit on her skin like fire. Her heart rate accelerated, a wild beat echoing through the bond. I spoke gentle words of instruction, my voice soothing her through the tension.

She did as I told her, though I could see the uncertainty flash through her eyes. I felt it in her, a fierce resistance that burned like white flame. The pain of her struggle cut through the bond, nearly doubling me over.

I steadied myself and spoke with the full weight of my alpha voice, the command so strong the air around us seemed to hold its breath. "SHIFT."

The force of it drove her further to the ground, her body shaking with effort. She screamed at first, a sharp, wild sound that fractured the night. I stayed close, urging her with every ounce of power I had.

"Stop fighting!" I yelled my words, finding the core of her resistance. "Let it happen, Juliet. This is who you are. Don't fight your wolf."

Her cries turned to whimpers as the words reached her, sinking deep into the marrow of her being. Her body was white-hot under my touch, and I could feel the moment she surrendered, the shift in her like the breaking of a fever. She welcomed her wolf, a sound more howl than human ripping from her lungs.

Then silence, and in that stillness, her form began its breathtaking transformation. I'd seen it a hundred times before, but never like this. Her skin rippled with new purpose, and the change was almost too beautiful to bear. Fur sprouted along her back, a rich, glowing gold in the moonlight. Her limbs elongated, her face contorting until the struggle disappeared into a breathtaking clarity.

The light poured through the trees and caught in her wild new eyes, the dark brown as brilliant as polished onyx. I heard her breath come out in a shudder, a long and shaky sigh as her transformation completed. I waited, watching, barely breathing.

Then her wolf looked at me and stepped forward, a low whine turning into something like a laugh, and I knew she was ready. I was more than ready.

I quickly shifted and broke free from the ceremonial space with a newly shifted Juliet by my side, and we dashed across the open plain beneath the moonlit sky.

In our transformed states, we engaged in a spirited chase—our movements vivid and real as we playfully nipped at each other along the rugged ridges. The energy of the night surged through us, binding us in a shared pulse that was as physical as it was emotional. I felt her raw joy, her wild laughter, her disbelief that this new life was truly hers.

Our shadows merged with the natural landscape, blending into one as we raced further from the meadow. I heard the distant cheers and respectful calls from the pack behind us, their voices growing fainter with every bound. I recalled every rapid footfall, every quick glance exchanged, and every physical push that bordered on both tenderness and wild abandon.

The land was wide open before us, and there was nothing to stop the freedom of our run. The golden sheen of Juliet's coat gleamed in the moonlight, a blur of speed and strength as we tore across the hills. She led me now, a vibrant force guiding me over the rough terrain.

I reveled in the new pace Juliet set, faster than I'd anticipated, more confident than I'd hoped. She looked back at me with blazing dark eyes, eyes that held a new promise. Her acceptance of the change transformed everything between us, deepening our bond in ways I hadn't imagined.

We crossed a narrow stream, water spraying beneath our paws, laughter echoing in our steps. Her breath was strong and sure, the cadence of it matching mine as we pushed onward. I marveled at how quickly she adapted to this new form, the same natural ease with which she'd taken to everything since she arrived in my world.

She darted to the left, a playful move meant to challenge, and I followed with an exhilaration that came from feeling utterly, purely alive. The crisp night air whistled past, filled with the mingled scent of earth and sky.

Our play turned into something more intimate, more urgent as the pull of the moon reached its peak. The physicality of it ignited my senses, her scent mixing with mine in the night air. She lunged ahead, daring me to catch her, and I met the dare with a burst of energy, closing the distance between us.

It was the shift back that brought us together, entangled in each other. When the fever broke, we collapsed in a tangled heap on a dewy patch of grass near our back door. Our breaths came in quick succession, bodies slick with the night's promise. We tumbled onto the ground in human form, exhausted and ecstatic.

Our laughter echoed in the stillness, a shared intimacy that deepened the bond forged under the transformative power of the full moon. I wrapped my arms around her and pulled her to me, the heat of her skin matching my own. Her damp hair tangled between us, a mess of wild gold and tangled want.

"We did it," she whispered against my shoulder, the words half disbelief, half triumph.

I kissed her with everything I had; the answer a physical thing unbroken by language. It was more than a first shift; more than a ceremony. It was us, all of us, in the space between.

The world felt new; every sensation more alive, more intense. I could still taste the night on her lips, the raw promise of the earth on her skin. When I finally pulled back, just enough to see her face, she was smiling in a way that made the entire universe seem small and perfect.

"Bronc," she said, the name a breathless song. "It's—"

I covered her mouth with mine, stealing the word before she could say it, wanting nothing between us but this.

Eventually, our quiet laughter subsided, replaced by a stillness that held more life than any movement could. The moon hung low, sinking toward the horizon, a reminder that we had chased it through the night and come out the other side, untamed and unbroken.

She sighed, a sweet sound of contentment as she curled against me. The warmth of her breath on my chest sent a shiver through the parts of me still human. I could have stayed like that forever, but the pull of the world was too strong. We were creatures of night and day, and there was a lot of both left to catch.

I nudged her gently. "Think you've got enough left for another run?" I asked, a teasing challenge in my voice.

She laughed, low and beautiful, the kind of sound that made my insides hum. "You're the one who needs a breather, old man."

"Old man?" I pretended to sound offended, lifting her effortlessly into my arms.

She wrapped her arms around my neck and looked into my eyes. "But you're my old man."

I let the words settle between us like an anchor, rooting us in something solid and real. The real that lasted beyond a lifetime, the kind I thought I'd never find. With her cradled against me, I stood and took the first few steps back toward the cabin and the life that waited.

"Yes, I am, forever?" I asked, a smile pulling at my lips.

"Forever," she whispered, resting her head against my shoulder. Her breath came easy, her body already at home in its new skin.

The walk was short, and before we knew it, we were at the cabin door. Stars faded, overtaken by the first light of dawn. The world around us softened, the hard edges dissolving into a promise of morning.

Inside, I set her down gently, my hands reluctant to let her go. She pulled me into another kiss, the urgency of it leaving us breathless once again.

The surrounding air was rich with possibility, and for the first time in a long time, I felt a contentment as wide as the plains that surrounded us. It was more than the moon, more than the shift. It was the sure knowledge that whatever waited, we would face it together.

The agony of separation would be more than I could have ever anticipated.

# CHAPTER 19

## HARRISON

The iron clinked sharp in the air, magnifying each tap of my pen against the stark metal table. Restraint thinned my mouth as I paused, eyeing the stack of data pages with Dane beside me. His presence like a military drill sergeant. Cold. Unyielding. This particular attempt at synthesizing a serum had ended, yet again, in disaster. Full-blooded shifter DNA produced only further setbacks. My father's voice gnawed at me over the phone, demanding to know why the serum hadn't been finished months ago, why this girl, my fiancé, the one I'd lost, held so much damn importance. I'd finally hung up. "He doesn't understand the scientific process," I said to Dane, leaning back in my chair. "Failures happen more than successes." My knuckles whitened around the pen as the tension of dealing with my father forced a thick knot to the surface.

"The fucker acts like all of this," I waved my hands around the state-of-the-art lab, "just sprung up out of the jungle by magic. He has no idea *why* it took well over a year to make this part happen. And the setbacks in testing are to be expected. We're moving in the right direction."

Dane was silent beside me, taking in the pages without so much as a twitch. Even I couldn't tell what he was thinking sometimes. His certainty an infuriating and yet valuable quality. But I didn't doubt his willingness to go further than any of the others on this. A pulse of satisfaction settled as he nodded, acknowledging the results like the calculated setbacks they were.

"You'll work it out." His voice was smooth, confident.

I stilled at the optimism, my eyes going hard as I pushed back from the table. Stark chairs and bright fluorescents felt clinical and precise, like every motion Dane and I made in this room. "The girl's blood is the key. We know this."

"It's taking longer than you expected."

"Time is of no consequence if we succeed," I said, turning back to the data. My father was less patient, and he'd made his threats clear enough the last time we spoke. But Dane and I, we were strategists. The victory would be ours alone if it happened. "He can wait."

The white walls echoed my words back at me, sterile and unfeeling, and my father's complaints echoed in my mind. I shut them out, focusing on the next step. Dane stayed where he was, an anchor against the disappointment I refused to voice.

"We'll need to take another approach with Juliet's family," I said, sharp and firm. "The only other viable candidate is her mother. But the risk of involving Jules Bettencourt... he could betray us."

"He might have information."

I shook my head, conviction as rigid as steel. "He's more useful believing the girl's hiding from him. We can hold him off. Let him think she's run from her life with him, and her heartless mother rather than from me. And there's no way Juliet would be in contact with her parents any more than she'd contact me. They gave her to me without a thought about what she wanted. She understands their position in all of this."

"So we take the mother." Dane's voice was quick, knowing.

I met his steady eyes. It was a risk, but not the kind my father thought. My father believed in strong-arming to get what he wanted, not strategy. The longer Juliet remained out of his grasp, the more he would demand action over sense. I'd let him bark at shadows if it meant I could move without interference. That's why he'd not be privy to my plans. And why I'll claim ignorance when the news of Renda Bettencourt's disappearance hits.

Dane waited for my response, his calm like a lure for weakness. I let the silence stretch, not giving him what he hoped for. But his face remained impassive, knowing he'd touched a nerve. He was as loyal as they come, but even he couldn't predict how much pressure my father would apply when the time came.

"We will take the mother," I confirmed, my voice a calculated plan in itself. "She's the closest we have until we locate Juliet. We'll leave her disappearance just messy enough to flush the girl out. While we're waiting for Juliet, we use her mother's hybrid blood. It's possible it will work as well or better than Juliet's. It won't stop Juliet from paying for her sins, however."

Dane inclined his head, a silent approval. We worked like this, all intention, every move playing into the next.

The room pressed in around me, and I imagined it was not so different from the space Juliet would find herself in once I had her. I hadn't been ready to use her blood when she slipped away. But losing her was a failure, and I didn't do failure. I shoved the memory aside, letting it fall into place among the other recent fuck-ups. I needed her blood, yes, but I wanted to punish her more.

"Whatever happens with her mother, it's a chance we'll take," I said, fixing my eyes back on the data. "I'll not have any more delays."

"Understood," Dane said, taking his cue to fall silent once more.

I felt the heat of my resolve, the precision that drove every damn decision. Juliet Bettencourt was now an obsession. The one gamble that mattered. I'd let my father think she was just a piece in our strategy. Let him threaten and push from afar. But I knew what Bettencourt blood was worth. Her family's blood ran with dollar signs. No one truly knew the value except for me. Not yet.

"We know the driver they use in the city," I said. "Set the team to follow him. Keep it tight."

Dane gave a crisp nod, accepting the order. I'd made a mistake in thinking Juliet would never run. I'd thought she was too weak to try to leave. We hadn't expected how damn fast and far she could run. "And when we have the mother?"

"Straight to the lab. We'll work fast, get what we need and make it loud. The headlines will bring Juliet to us."

"And your father?"

My mouth tightened, but my voice remained controlled. "Fuck him. He's got no actual power. He's one voice on the board of directors and no more. He didn't think of the consequences when he stepped down and gave me power. When we succeed, it won't matter. He's waiting for results. We'll give him more than that. And so help me God, if he even tries to get in my way, he won't live to see those results."

Dane seemed satisfied with my response. He leaned back in his chair, watchful. Trustworthy. He was everything my father wasn't.

"Move quick," I added. "They'll have her in Costa Rica before morning."

Dane stood and turned to go. He stopped at the door, hand on the knob. "This is a sound plan, Harrison. Juliet will be in your hands soon."

The words weren't consolation. Not between us. We knew better than to soften the truth with hope. We worked with clarity, with precision, with ruthless demand. And yet, there was a weight to what he said. I kept my expression unflinching until he'd left the room; the door shut with a firm click behind him.

I looked back at the failed lab data, a reminder of what waited. Cold inevitability wound through me. Yes, I would have her in my hands. Her mother's blood would lead us to the serum. It would lead us to everything. Juliet would lead me to satisfaction.

Intercepting the car was easy after the driver picked up Renda Bettencourt from her private club. I waited in the shadows, timing the pulse of each second with steady breaths, watching. The sleek black van rounded the corner, headlights like slashes through the thick New York air. Every precaution taken. Every camera in the vicinity had been hacked. The team, all donned in Hollywood production-level masks, moved in, swift and clean, as they forced the car to a stop on the quiet side street. Within moments, they had the driver subdued. The rear van door opened with perfect timing, and the street seemed to exhale into silence. Empty. Unknowing. They reached for the elegant woman still unaware in the backseat, and I felt the slow coil of success. Each action deliberate. Renda barely managed to register surprise before the syringe slid into her arm, neat and clinical. Drugged. Secured. A faint smile crossed my lips as they lifted her into the van and disappeared down the street. Not a single movement wasted. I turned, and the shadows seemed to close in behind me as if I had never been there.

They followed a calculated route, one we'd gone over a dozen times. The van wove through the maze of New York City streets, places they might be remembered. Not that anyone would. The city didn't notice things that weren't flashy enough to demand attention, and our actions were all deliberate silence and shadows. We drove to the secluded private airfield where my jet was fueled and waiting.

Everything was as expected. Everything but the time it took us to reach this point. Even then, there was an order to it, a structure I'd expected even in its delays. I let out a controlled breath as the van halted near the small plane, and I could see Renda's inert form, head resting like she'd fallen into a faint. Elegant even in her captivity.

Another car waited at the hangar, ready to pick up the trailing operatives. I'd timed it to the second, ensured that nothing felt spontaneous or unplanned.

The side door of the jet opened as they pulled up. A metal staircase jutted to the pavement. Renda's dress shimmered in the hangar's overhead light as they moved her from the van to the plane, taking care not to mar the image she projected. I watched the tableau from the doorway, knowing the silent spectacle of it would make Dane's team nervous. But they wouldn't question my methods.

Another brief flash of movement. The team worked with machine-like precision, securing Renda's drugged form into the plush seat, as though they were kidnapping royalty. In some ways, I supposed, we were. Bettencourt's fortune could be considered vast by any standard.

The hum of the jet engines replaced the van's low rumble. Everything was swift, clinical. The crew's smooth motions were like punctuation, hard and clear, on the page of my design. They buckled Renda's limp form into her seat, knowing she wouldn't stir until they landed on the airstrip miles from the lab. By the time she realized where she was, it would be too late for anyone to find her.

I knew how fast they'd move. Jules Bettencourt was a shark when it came to the appearance of family devotion. He'd make statements, hold press conferences, wring his hands for the media, pretend he hadn't offered his daughter up like a sacrificial lamb for his business deals. And she, his prized jewel, his bet, his folly—she would see the reports, be lured into thinking she could save the woman who turned a blind eye to her own abuse. We'd underestimated her once, assumed she'd been too sheltered to know how to get far. But I understood her more now. She was a survivor. A runner. I'd use it against her.

The transfer to the jet was seamless. I felt the anticipation of inevitable results, of looming success, a heady thrill just beneath the cold precision. The only loose thread was Juliet herself, and that would be quickly tied off once she surfaced. Once I had her in my grip, she'd understand the depth of her mistakes.

I stepped back from the window where I watched, one last glance at the jet. The team was exiting, a last sweep through the hangar before they returned to New York City and resumed their watch. Even they didn't know everything that was at stake here. Not yet. I'd make sure it stayed that way until there was no room for error or questions.

I checked the app on my phone to see the interior of the jet's cabin. Renda's hair gleamed under the overhead light, and her head slumped to one side, helpless. I could see the steady rise and fall of her chest, the muted thrum of life. She was as vulnerable as I needed her to be.

The hangar fell silent once the doors shut, echoing emptiness where the team had just stood. I held the weight of it, felt it settle like a shroud. Juliet Bettencourt was about to make the biggest mistake of her life, coming out of hiding for a woman who'd given her away like an object to be bartered. I knew what family meant to them, which was to say nothing at all. She'd learn it soon enough, but by then it wouldn't matter.

The plane roared to life, a low growl that shuddered through the hangar and faded into the thick night as it pulled away. The headlines would follow by morning, I knew. We'd laid the ground-work for it. I let myself savor the inevitability, how every move I'd made since she ran would draw her in, pull her back to me. She wouldn't know the danger, wouldn't see it coming until it was too late.

They'd arrive at the lab in Costa Rica by morning. Her blood would give me the answer to the only question that had ever mattered, the question that haunted me, consumed me. I'd have the serum. And I'd have Juliet. It was all there, laid out, waiting.

I turned from the hangar, the hum of the departing jet already lost in the dense air. The night swelled up, closing around me, and the next chapter of Juliet's life would be mine to write.

# Chapter 20

## Juliet

"Looks like your wolf is gettin' sharper by the day," Bronc said. He was close now, hands resting on my shoulders. His voice was soft, but the sound filled up the shop, carved through the noise of tools and engines.

"Pretty sure those receipts were covered in barbecue sauce." I flipped through the pages, knocking out mysteries and making endless notes and discoveries.

He smiled a confident smile. "You amaze me. I know you're having to be creative with the system you're creating to keep up with the mess." His blue eyes went past me for a moment, narrowed in on Skeeter as he pushed a cart through the bay door and tried too hard not to look our way. Then they flicked back to mine. "Got the other things you found?"

"Three or four parts orders that don't add up, but it's like there are chunks missing. Here, look." I twisted the ledger so he could see the page and inched closer to him. Our shoulders brushed. "Maybe more, I don't know."

"I do," he said. His breath ruffled a loose strand of hair, left me wanting more, and then he moved back to his full height. "Same kind of shifty numbers we've seen a couple of times." His mouth quirked when he saw me catch the pun. "Whoever is running this show had been at it for a while. Any ideas who else we need to keep tabs on?"

"Not sure yet," I said. I wanted to be sure I got it right before I threw out an accusation. I shut the ledger. Its echo made me flinch. "Skeeter, definitely. I just... I've got this weird sense that something big is going on, and it's making my skin..." I tried not to squirm and didn't finish the sentence. We both knew this was going to turn out to be something bigger than he wanted to have to deal with.

His eyes stayed on me a beat too long, and the weight of it pushed a breath from my lungs. His fingers squeezed my shoulder, and the heat was electric. "Whatever comes, we'll handle it," he said. "Together. Take a minute. Then meet me in my office. Show me everything you've got." The way his gaze held mine was different from before—urgent and unwilling to let go. He knew what the shifting inside me meant. More than I did.

His steps echoed when he left. I spent the time reining in my racing pulse. The wolf's pulse. The strangeness of it tangled with my hair at the back of my neck and stayed until I felt myself slow again. Saw myself settle back to human, to paper and ink and numbers. Saw Skeeter sneaking another glance as I worked through the mess of lies he'd hoped we'd never catch. Saw Arsenal look his way, suspicious and unreadable as he stripped down the engine of a black Road Glide. No one looked at him for long.

I couldn't shake the feeling that every gaze was meant for me, whether furtive or concerned or sharp enough to slice through the knot of my tensing body. Even Bronc's, when I ducked through his office door and he looked up like he'd been listening to the pattern of my footsteps to know when I was close.

"Juliet," he said, and the way my name sounded was more serious than sweet. "Take a look at this." A list of the parts that should have been there and weren't took up the whole whiteboard. "Your findings confirm what we thought."

The irregularities were too big for someone who didn't understand to catch. And for some reason, they were too close for him to let go of. "Looks like they were trying to be careful for a while. Then they got careless."

He laughed and dragged a hand through his hair. Dark strands fell back in place, mingling with the silver, just the way I liked it. "Well, honey, they didn't expect you," he said. "You're way beyond run of the mill when it comes to lookin' at numbers. They could hide stuff before. Now you're uncovering all their misdeeds."

When he pulled me toward him, sat me on the edge of his desk like it was the most natural thing in the world, I felt the quick jolt of lust through our bond. It was thrilling and wonderful. I felt my wolf preen.

"Got a lot of ground to cover. So," he said, his hand on my bare knee under the hem of the sundress I'd worn today. "Where do you want to start?"

"Start anywhere. But you know how this ends, right? Somebody close to you is behind it."

We both knew it was going to end badly for someone in our pack. Someone he should have been able to trust.

"We're bringin' you in closer to the fire," he said, standing, breath hot on my cheek. "Sure you can handle it?"

I wanted to lie, but the truth caught me off guard. "I'm the Luna of this pack now, Bronc. It's my job to shoulder whatever comes along right beside you."

A flicker of warmth reached his eyes. "You amaze me, Little Wolf."

I love how connected we were. The bond pulled me closer to him. We were more one than two since his claiming bite. His emotions were mine; mine were his. It made life easier and more complicated all at once. I had to be so careful to shield what I didn't want him to carry. But I knew we were stronger together.

He went serious again. Serious and warm, the way he knew would keep me grounded. "I appreciate how hard you work. You will unravel the mystery surrounding who is doing this and how bad it is," he said. "I've got no doubt." The way I heard it, he meant more than the ledgers. "We'll bring in Wrecker to do more snooping, see what else he can turn up on Skeeter. Not goin' easy on that one. We know there's somethin' off, even if we don't know who's pullin' his strings. The guy has been pack for 20 years. Need to get to the bottom of that." He paused like he was studying me, as if I were the real puzzle here, like I'd finally give something away. "Too much for one day?"

The question was real, not rhetorical. I shook my head, and the whole room seemed to swirl with the energy I felt pooling in my chest. Energy I wasn't ready to give a name to.

Bronc nodded, accepting more than just my answer. Then his lips were on mine. He didn't even pretend to let me breathe before he pulled me deeper into the kiss. It ended as quick as it started, a last tangle of his voice and his touch. "Meet me out front in ten. Lunch at Ma's, then back at it. We won't stop till it's settled."

I didn't trust myself to say much more than, "Okay," as he straightened to his full height, and grabbed his cut then cast another long look back. A glance that stayed with me, even after he left.

I found Bronc outside, leaning against his bike, all confidence and cool and ready to take on the entire world if he had to. When he saw me with the stack of ledgers tucked under one arm, he gave the saddlebag an extra tug to be sure it was secure.

I looked back over my shoulder. Arsenal was watching Skeeter, Bronc was watching me, and I was watching it all unravel.

Pearl's Bar and Grill buzzed with life, music and banter and TVs fighting for dominance. I was lost in Bronc's steady plans for the pack and us, for the best ways to stay ahead and keep us safe. Then a familiar voice came crashing through it all. I looked up at the TV in time to see my father's panicked expression. My jaw dropped, along with my burger, as I read the closed caption plea for my mother's life. He wore a stricken look on his face. His words knocked the air from my lungs, and I went cold, shivering through the sweat on my skin.

"Bronc," I said, and I felt my voice collapse on itself, felt the shock register long before my hands caught up and went still.

He looked up from his burger, and the urgency he saw on the screen froze him in place.

"This was an organized kidnapping," the reporter said, and her words ricocheted around the room, then around my head. Bronc heard the entire story before I could catch my breath, before I could explain why every muscle in my body felt torn between panic and disbelief. "The kidnappers haven't yet made contact, but Mrs. Bettencourt is believed to be in serious danger," the voice continued. "Her family begs anyone with information to please come forward."

"Oh my God," I said. I didn't hear my own voice until I saw Bronc start to move closer. His whole body went protective, like he knew I was about to shatter. "Holy shit, holy shit."

I watched as my dad's plea streamed by in yellow letters on the screen, a closed caption confession that meant more to me than he thought it did. "Please, whoever has taken my precious wife Renda. Please return her to me. I'll pay you any amount of money. Just let me know what you want." I read it once, twice, again, and my body started shaking.

Bronc grabbed the remote from the nearest table and turned up the volume. His hands were on me an instant later, and the place went silent as he pulled me in.

"He took her," I said, my words spilling over each other, a jumbled panic. "He took her to get to me. I know he did. He'll kill her, Bronc. He'll kill her, and it's all because of me."

We were close enough to feel each other's heat, but I was cold. I wrapped my arms around myself and felt the tremors work through me. He kept his eyes on mine, the same as he'd done with the ledgers, and it scared me that they were more worried than calm this time. "Juliet," he said, and I'd never heard him speak so quietly. "Darlin', breathe. We'll figure it out."

"No," I said. "I know him. I know how this ends." My voice caught on the way I thought it would end, the way I couldn't let it end. "You heard it. He won't even make the call. He's putting it on me. Again."

He took in the fear, took in all of it, pulled me so close that my pulse thudded back to normal with his own heartbeat. He made the edges of my shock less sharp, held me still while my mind reeled. When the fear passed for a moment, when the anger took its place, he let go just enough for me to see that he was letting me in, not pushing me away.

"Harrison took her," I said, sure as I'd ever been of anything in my life. "I know he did. He took her to draw me out. I bet my life on it."

"Ma," he said, lifting his chin to her as she watched from the bar. "Need you to get Arsenal and the others to the compound. Now."

"I won't let anything happen," he said. His voice was sure, the kind that no one ever questioned, least of all me. He tilted my chin up to face him, and I saw the Alpha in his eyes. Saw the strength that everyone in the pack leaned on, and felt it settle back in my body, keeping me together. "We'll get her back, Juliet. Swear to you we will."

The room stopped spinning when he spoke. The world stopped crumbling. We both felt the shift. My breath caught on what it meant, on everything I couldn't quite say. I stared at him, half terrified and half relieved. "How?" I asked. It was a small word, smaller than I meant it to be, but it held the room in place; it kept us there together; it let me take in his certainty the same way I took in my next lungful of air. "This is my fault."

"Juliet. Stop that talk. There is nothing about this that is your fault." Bronc was fighting to keep his control now. "The one and only reason that Harrison Hastings is even in your life in the first place is because those people, your mother and father, sold you out to him. So as bad as I hate that this has happened, if he has your mother, the fault rests solely on the shoulders of your father and her. Not on you."

I stood there numb for a moment. Bronc was right. I knew he was right. Even so, I would not turn into them. "Sweetheart," I said as I looked up into his beautiful face. "You are right. She has in no way, been the kind of mother she should have been. But I am determined to be a better person than she ever was. And my heart is breaking for her because she is my mother, and because of my actions, however they came about, she is now in danger." My voice broke as I finished.

He pulled me into his arms. "And that, my precious mate, is one of the reasons I love you so very much. And it's also the only reason I called my team together to discuss how we can hopefully find her and bring her home safely."

Then I remembered the other Iron Valor business Bronc had told me about a couple of weeks ago. This is literally the kind of operations and missions they run. I had to give them the opportunity to try to find her. But I also knew that if they didn't find her quickly, I'd have to contact Harrison myself and offer to trade myself for her. He will kill her otherwise. I had no doubt about that.

# Chapter 21

## Bronc

A hazy afternoon light slanted through the compound's meeting room as we assembled around the long, scarred table, each officer wearing their frustration like armor. Wrecker hunched over his laptop, every muscle coiled. I kept my gaze fixed on him and hoped to hell we finally had a break. "Please tell me you've got something new," I said.

His jaw tightened, fingers stabbing keys with impatience. "I'm in the goddamn dark here, Bronc. Two days and we got jack shit on Harrison. But I'm workin' other angles." The scratch of pen against paper filled the silence as I took in the furrowed brows and clenched fists around the table. Nobody liked where this was heading.

"Wrecker," I pressed, my voice steady even as I felt the same gnawing dread. "Don't care how you get there, but we need something now."

He swore under his breath, as close to rattled as I'd ever seen him. "Give me a minute," he muttered. I watched him hunch further over the screen, fingers quick as his eyes darted with intensity. We were losing ground, and with it, any semblance of control.

I leaned back, crossing my arms as Wrecker continued his furious typing. "This stays quiet till we know more," I warned, feeling the weight of what needed doing if he didn't come through.

The room felt smaller by the second, our world closing in. Finally, Wrecker stopped. He ran a hand over his shaved head, meeting my gaze with grim satisfaction. "All right. Listen up." His voice cut through the room, every officer's attention snapping to him with the sharpness of men hungry for direction.

"We hit Harrison's board members' servers," he announced, dark eyes gleaming with both relief and alarm. Harrison Pharmaceutical is researching some big new drug. Got emails." He went on, his voice gaining strength with each new piece. "Talking about DNA manipulation, performance enhancing shit. Fuck me. They are trying to synthesize DNA. Fucker's got a research facility, making some kind of drug. Might be a serum. Who the hell knows? They're moving fast as possible. Something tells me he's aware of Juliet's blood, thus he took Renda instead."

"That son of a bitch," I growled, my words echoed by the grim looks of agreement around me. My pulse hammered in my neck, anger mingling with the dread. I had known it was bad, but this was the kind of poison that spread.

Wrecker's expression was pure bitterness as he closed the lid on his laptop. "Harrison was after Juliet's bloodline sometime after they got engaged it seems, because this all didn't start until that time."

Menace, calm and steady like the eye of a storm, interrupted the silence that followed. "There's more." His words dropped like stones, gathering weight. "Fuck me sideways. This all checks. Remember those reports of missing shifters? They were Midwest packs. This guy's targeting areas from where her ancestors came from. He must have researched her family tree same way we did. Only he started picking people up for their blood. Then maybe some of them sang about other packs to save their own?"

My hands clenched into fists, trying to squeeze the truth from the gaps between what we knew and what we didn't. "Her family kept their shifter heritage sealed up tight," I said, disbelief tinged with frustration. "You sure?"

He nodded once, the kind of confirmation that sealed the world into new and darker shapes. "Old lineage. Matches with some of what we pulled in her background check. Nebraska" His eyes swept the room, assessing the reactions.

The murmur of voices rose as we tried to fit the pieces together, but nothing looked right when they settled. My gaze cut through the din and landed on Wrecker. "We have to get into Harrison's systems. Full-court press," I ordered. "And now we got names, use 'em. We're finding that lab and what they're making."

Wrecker nodded, resolute as the rest of us. He'd been in impossible spots before. I knew he'd dig like hell.

Menace's voice cut in again, an edge of urgency where cool control used to be. "If we're right about the missing shifters, he might not even be in the States. Overseas connections are popping up." He left the worst of it unsaid, but we all knew. Once they slipped beyond the borders, the chase would be ten times harder.

"Then look in Central and South America for other legit Harrison Pharma labs. Stands to reason he'd have sway with authorities in those countries. Maybe he'd build an *illegitimate* lab there, too. Christ, what kind of monsters would be working on something like this?"

Doc looked at me, shaking his head. "The kinds who value money over ethics. And there are plenty of them in this business, brother, I'm sad to say."

I took the measure of each man in turn, reading fear where it lived behind determination. The boys didn't have to say it for me to hear them clear as day: this ran deeper than we thought, with tendrils that reached into every one of their lives. I thought of Juliet and what she'd run from, and how close this might come again.

Every man at this table might not be a tech wizard, but they damn sure knew how to do research. Arsenal looked me in the eye. "We got your back, Liam. Juliet's too. This is as much our fight as it is y'all's."

JT looked up from his laptop. "What he said."

Doc reached over with a fist. I touched mine to it. "Brothers." He said in a growl.

"Brothers." I returned.

"The second we hear anything, I want to know," I said, a command with nothing left to question.

They nodded, stiff and focused, needing what little assurance we could offer. Harrison and his operation had already taken too much. We wouldn't give up anything else. Not if I could help it.

As we started to wrap the meeting, our somber mood only deepened. Menace shot me a hard look, reading every bit of grit and fury I felt.

"That lab has her name all over it," Wrecker added, looking almost hopeful now that he had a plan to chew on. "I'm gonna bury the fuckers when I get in."

More voices joined, brief but fierce. Promises to watch their families, to stay close, to move fast. I felt the swell of resolve rise and watched it pass over me, carrying us from the paralysis of fear into the momentum of action.

"We keep moving," I said, letting my tone ground them the way they needed it to. My eyes didn't leave theirs until they knew I meant every word. "We'll find it."

The meeting closed with the resolve that only desperate men carry. I watched the officers file out, their silence as deliberate as their strides. Outside, the low sun cut the land into pieces, leaving sharp lines of shadow as we walked toward our bikes. Menace stayed close, reading the fight in my eyes.

"We'll know more soon," he said as the others started their engines. His confidence rang through the doubt that hung over us.

I nodded, sure of him and nothing else. "Won't rest till we do."

It wasn't a threat, or even a promise. Just the truth I planned to live by until it was done.

Night settled over the cabin like a weight, heavy and uncertain. I found Juliet hunched close to the TV, shadows thrown long across the floor as her eyes tracked news channels, the remote a tight fist in her grip. She didn't notice me at first. The air buzzed with voices as they filled the space with clipped, senseless words about the financial market back east.

Her tension drew tight around us both; her breath hitched and expectant. When I finally moved toward her, a sharp intake of breath let me know she'd registered I was there. "Bronc," she said, and the relief and anxiety wound together in her voice, thin threads holding her too-still body.

I dropped down beside her, gathering her in as she began to shake. "Shhh," I murmured against her hair. "Not gonna find her on there."

Juliet slumped into my chest, the remote dropping from her fingers and thudding against the hardwood. She smelled like despair and rain, soft notes cutting through the sharper stabs of panic. "She's my mother," she said, choked and careful. "I know she failed at so many things, but I still have to try."

I held her tighter, burying my nose against her skin and breathing her in until the calm I willed through our bond settled enough to take hold. Her warmth and her hurt, her presence at the center of my world. "No, you don't," I told her. "Just gotta trust me."

A quiet rippled through the room as she went still. Her pulse fluttered beneath my lips as I pressed a line of slow, reassuring kisses along her neck and shoulder. Finally, her muscles unlocked, and she shivered against me in surrender.

When her voice came, it was low and uncertain. "What if he's already—?"

"He hasn't," I interrupted, fierce and sure. She would be devastated if Harrison made a move before she could find her mother. "He won't."

I felt the fight slip from her as she met my gaze, wet eyes turning dark and wide with both belief and doubt. I took her hand, threading our fingers together. "Come on," I said, rising and pulling her with me. "Know what you need."

"Bronc?" she asked, but she followed.

We stepped into the cool night air, our shadows stitched close as I led her across the expansive backyard. The sparse lights around the pool lent a ghostly illumination, each delicate ripple in the water throwing pale reflections that danced beneath the moon.

Juliet trailed behind, silent now, watching me as I came to a stop beyond the deck and turned toward her. Her breath the only sound in the darkness as she crossed her arms, holding tight to the tension she hadn't yet let go. I didn't wait for her to ask more questions. Instead, I claimed her lips with mine and let the intent fill her through the long, demanding kiss.

My hands moved from her face to her collar, slowly unbuttoning her flannel shirt. "Shift," I urged.

Her eyes flashed with uncertainty, her gaze as hesitant as the tremors I felt against my chest as I kissed her again. "Out here?" She asked, so human and unsure. So small against the massive expanse of the night.

"Out here," I echoed. I shrugged the shirt from her shoulders, leaving it in a puddle around her bare feet. My hands moved to the waistband of her cutoffs, fingers tracing her skin with warmth that beckoned her to trust me more than her own fears. I peeled them from her, one deliberate tug at a time.

She trembled, the question heavy in her eyes and in the quiet night around us. I kissed her again, deeper this time, a promise that anchored as well as provoked. "Shift," I ordered once more, moving back and away so she had the room to.

For a moment, she looked like she'd break. For a moment, she didn't know if she could. Then I watched as she closed her eyes, an exhale escaping her like the beginning of a prayer.

Her body convulsed, folding in on itself and then back out as she arched toward the moon, slender arms stretching in defiance and in release. I saw the dark blonde of her fur first, bristling like rebellion from beneath her skin, and then she was on four unsteady legs. Her wolf trembled where Juliet had stood.

She was magnificent.

I let her see how much I wanted this for her, letting my change take me with speed and force. I was black and gray to her honeyed coat, the familiar shape and freedom overtaking my senses. I loped to her side, pressing our bodies together and feeling the sheer, wild energy that poured from her unrestrained.

My touch sent waves of new feeling through her, each nudge and caress charged and electric. She buckled against me at first, uncertain and new, and then—when she felt me there, understood me there—her limbs untangled, sure and strong and alive.

We broke into a run, side by side across the open compound land. Her hesitance turned to joy, and I watched as each step grew bolder and more confident. She was learning this. She was learning herself.

We kept close, the dark and the open space ours alone as we moved. The smells and sounds, the colors and lights—everything bled into a sensory palette unique to our wolves. It filled us with reckless, unapologetic wonder. It filled us with each other.

I pushed faster, testing her as the ground passed beneath us in streaks of bluegrass and blurred shadow. She surged ahead, taking my challenge and throwing it back, fierce and untamed and leaving the old fear behind. I knew how the thrill of it seized her because it seized me, too.

We slowed when the night became a physical weight on our backs, panting and exhausted, but full and renewed. I nipped her ear, sharp enough to spark and to tease, and we shifted together. The intimate freedom left us breathless and exposed and even closer than before.

I pulled her to me, more than human. Human again and stronger for the animalistic abandon we'd just shared. "How'd that feel?" I asked against her lips, already knowing and needing to hear it from her.

Her face was flushed, chest heaving as she caught the breath that the night had stolen. She let out a laugh, the sound halfway to disbelief and more than halfway to pure exhilaration. "Unbelievable."

Her expression grew tender, and her hands traced the length of my arms. Her damp hair fell across her face, and she was radiant, despite all of it, because of all of it.

"Better than searching the news channels, yeah?" I said, feeling her respond to the deliberate nearness.

She nodded, still in that wonder-drenched daze. "So much better."

Her release, the joy she felt in this strange additional part of herself—everything bled through our connection, everything washed over us, and everything was enough.

She shivered against the night air, so I drew her back inside. Breathless with her and with what we were and with what we'd been given.

The wild freedom still clung to our skin when we returned to the cabin, flushed and unsteady with the release and with each other. I shut the door behind us as Juliet sank into my chest, new joy and fierce love overwhelming her with unexpected relief. She grabbed the robe from the hook by the door, and I pulled on a pair of sweatpants.

Her breathing slowed and steadied against me, and I felt her fill with what I could only call contentment. It was the closest I'd seen her to relaxed since the night she showed up in Dairyville, shaking and too thin and on the edge of collapse.

"Didn't know you could run like that," she said, the sly tease in her voice softened by the genuine awe beneath it.

I tangled my fingers in her still-damp hair, letting the moment and the sensation settle over us both. "You were keeping up just fine."

She gave me a look that was equal parts challenge and affection, the look I wanted to pin down and hold so I'd never forget it. The sudden courage I saw in her knocked the breath from my chest.

The memory of her helplessness was almost gone. Replaced by the reality of us, like this, now.

We moved to the small dining area, drawn by the smell of Ma's handiwork. She'd left covered plates for us on the table. Fried chicken, mashed potatoes, enough calories to rebuild the weight she'd lost from worry and worse. I pulled out her chair and took the seat beside her.

"We'll find them," I said, letting the assurance linger as she uncovered her plate and picked up a fork.

Juliet hesitated, reading my eyes and searching for cracks that didn't exist. I felt her silent questions pushing against our connection. I wouldn't keep anything from her.

"They're out of the country?" She finally asked, careful and afraid.

"Maybe," I admitted. She needed the truth, even when it cut.

I saw the brief flicker of despair at the news, the way her shoulders slumped and her hands fell back to her lap. But I saw other things too—things she might not even know were there. The tiny, persistent lights of hope still burned brightly beneath the rest. I watched them and marveled, half at their strength, half at her.

"I'm hoping within a week," I said, my voice a command and a comfort. "We should know by then. Each thing we learn leads to something else."

She nodded, her gaze brightening a touch, like it was feeding from the certainty I was pouring into her. "And you're sure she's…?"

"She's safe," I finished for her, biting back any hint of the doubt that gnawed. The reminder of Harrison's ruthlessness chilled my spine, but I couldn't let it infect her. "He's not moving as fast as we are."

It was a gamble, but it was true. She was his bait.

Juliet nodded again and then ate in quiet bites, each one a silent affirmation of trust. Of belief. She finished almost absent-mindedly, leaving nothing on the plate.

I brushed a loose strand of hair from her face, tucking it gently behind her ear as we sat together in the soft lamplight. "The guys are working nonstop," I promised, and it hung between us like an unspoken gift. They vowed to do this for her.

When she was done, I rose and pulled her to me. The two of us moved upstairs with quiet, hurried steps.

I led her into the dim bathroom, filling the tub with hot, steaming water. It swirled in lazy curls that matched the promise of what came next. The deep clawfoot tub filled just high enough so it wouldn't overflow, hot and welcoming and perfect.

Her body relaxed further when she saw what I'd planned, a happy sigh escaping her parted lips. I felt the sound like a wave, riding on our connection, filling the room with anticipation. She trusted me. With everything. It was the knowledge that only made me hungrier to prove I was worthy of it.

I stripped off her robe with deliberate care, each movement a claim, each inch of exposed skin bringing us closer. I pulled her naked body tight to mine before helping her in. She sank into the steaming water, eyes half-lidded with new warmth and drowsy gratitude.

I stepped in behind her, the heat a welcome jolt to my already charged system. Her back pressed to my chest, and my hands moved in slow, thorough strokes across her body, chasing the stray drops of worry until they melted, liquid and harmless, into the rising steam.

My touch was patient, knowing, coaxing the last of her tension out from the shadows where it hid. My fingers slid over her stomach and made their way between her thighs, coaxing a quiet whimper from her. Even in the tub's warmth, I felt the slick wetness of her heat coating my fingers. She lifted her right hip ever so slightly as I entered her with two of my fingers. Her sweet moans filled my chest with the pride that comes from knowing I was fulfilling the needs of my mate. I placed kisses along her neck as I continued to move my fingers in and out of her pussy, loving the feel of her.

"You are the most captivating being I've ever known, Juliet. My love. My mate."

She leaned her head back and looked over her left shoulder, then reached back with her hand and grasped my head with her hand, pulling me down so she could devour my mouth while my fingers thrust inside her harder, her moans reaching a crescendo. I pulled my fingers free and circled her clit with pressure until her hips rose from my lap, reaching for my hand. Her release came with a shout, her tongue still lapping at my own as she continued to kiss me with everything she had. Even as her body quaked and shuddered against my body, my hand held her in place.

When she finally went still, it was the perfect quiet of exhaustion and bliss. I felt it envelop us both, a weightless wonder, soft and consuming as the fog around us.

I stood and exited the tub and dried myself off. Then I reached for her hand. I dried her with the same attention to detail as I had when I made her come undone. Wrapped in a thick towel and in my love, knowing that she was safe and she was mine I carried her into our adjoining bedroom.

I tucked her into bed, watching her long lashes flutter once before the depth of her weariness and the security of our bond closed them for the night.

The truth of it: she was safe, and she was mine.

The truth of it: I had to keep it that way.

I stood watchful, breathing slow and steady, letting my presence and my resolve wrap around her sleeping body. This woman was a part of my soul. I'd waited so long for fate to bring her to me, and I will destroy anyone who thought they'd take her from me.

# Chapter 22

## Harrison

I could see her through the small, barred window before I stepped in, waiting with all the composure of a woman who hadn't been dragged out of her world and into mine. This cell of hers wasn't just a gilded cage—it was the prize at the bottom of my greedy quest. Her wide eyes made contact with mine as soon as the door closed behind me. A thrill ran down my spine as I returned the gaze, a lizard and a lion momentarily facing off.

Her face was blank as a slate, one she expected me to fill in with my explanations. I gave her a slow, cat-that-ate-the-canary smile as I broke the silence. "Hello, Renda. It's lovely to see you again."

The silence took over for a moment. I let it.

"How interesting that I'd finally be invited to a business meeting," she said, her voice as soft as it was cutting. "However, I'd expect to be seated in a boardroom. Not to awaken in a trussed-up prison cell."

She wanted her poised demeanor to piss me off, but I saw the nervous way her mouth shook. I held on to my smile, not willing to show the satisfaction beneath it. I needed this to work. It had been a hard-won gamble, but now I was here to collect the winnings.

"You know it wasn't really abduction, Renda." I said. "It's more like...a long-term business trip. It needed to be top secret to ensure a competitive edge. Big Pharma. Everyone wants to steal everyone else's formulas."

I took in the details as I talked. No trace of dust anywhere. The elegant lines of the furniture—straight from some fancy showroom in Uptown New York. The shelves, the table, all in perfect order. She had kept everything neat in the two days since we'd dragged her here. Of course she had. Nothing less would be acceptable to a woman like her. The controlled, crisp details stood in stark contrast to the single iron door that let me in and out of the room. The plain slip dress she wore wasn't fancy, but it was Chanel. And her room, while it was a cell, I'd made it quite homey. I had also supplied her with cosmetics and salon-quality hair care supplies. But I wouldn't give her everything. She stood in slippers instead of leather pumps.

I decided to crack her composure further. "You'll be an essential part of creating a groundbreaking product, Renda. It will ensure you and Jules will be secure for the rest of your lives. It will also ensure you'll live far longer to enjoy that fortune than you may have expected."

Her eyebrows raised a fraction of an inch, but that was the only crack I saw. Her cool voice washed over me. "How interesting. It might have been nice for you to have asked for my permission to participate before you yanked me out of my car in the middle of the afternoon and shoved me into a waiting van. I'm assuming this is why you would settle for my chubby little daughter. And I'm also assuming that since you couldn't even hold on to that pathetic excuse for a fiancé, you resorted to felony."

"Well, I had to get Jules to sign off on it, of course. I'm sure he had a very difficult time not telling you in the weeks leading up to completing the plan." This was, of course a fucking lie. I just wanted to see the look on her face when she thought her own husband had been playing her.

Oh, the satisfaction of seeing that bitch's face fall. It was a look best described as devastation for her to think her husband of almost 30 years had sold her out. I wanted to laugh in her face, which was so plump with fillers it was hard for her to frown. But frown she did.

She lifted her eyes to mine. "Yes, I imagine it was quite difficult for him."

I gave her a measured look, schooling my face to hide the delight. "No hard feelings, I hope. You know I'd never do you any harm, being a partner of Jules and all. It's a precarious time right now. Everyone wants a piece of the new formula. We couldn't take any chances. Powerful families have to watch out for one another. They always get involved in these matters."

The arched brow again, this time more pronounced. "Indeed, they do."

I pressed on. "We needed you in a secure location until everything was in place. Once the new formula has been perfected, you'll be back in your loving husband's arms."

She was quick in her reply. "Do you know that many women don't like to be treated like a possession?"

I almost lost it again, her turning my own obsession against me in such a cool, cruel way. But I played my part and kept my grip.

"The transformative nature of our new drug is worth a brief time away from home, I assure you. No lasting damage." I paused for emphasis, pacing my words and my steps to give me time to steady myself. To enjoy the scene despite her controlled performance. "I'll have my assistant collect the first sample."

"Then you'll be free to gloat somewhere else?" she asked. Her expression stayed as chilly as her voice, but I could see the muscles of her face clench as I made my way to the door.

"If it's any consolation," I said as I pulled the door open, "you won't be locked up much longer. Think of this as your spa day. Before you know it, you'll have the benefits of your very own miracle serum. And more life to enjoy it than you ever dreamed possible." I sounded like a crazy cult leader. I sounded convincing enough to be one.

*Room D-4. Make sure everything is pristine. Sample will be the most important we've gotten yet.*

A text popped back before I could put the phone away. *No problem. We'll make sure it's 100% clean.*

I did a mental check of the remaining variables, clicking them off one by one. Renda, secure. Sample, imminent. Juliet likely steps away from being in my grasp.

We were set and ready to go. The observation room was a place that demanded composure. The bare surfaces of it. The sterile silence of it. But composure wasn't what I felt when Dane mentioned Juliet. When the absence of her became its own presence. I wanted to slam my fist through one of the glass panels. I wanted to throw Dane's taunt back in his face. Instead, I stood next to him in front of the glass, looking into the lab room as Chen readied everything.

"*If* Juliet comes to you," Dane said, not moving his eyes from the glass, "is *she* going to be a problem?" Nodding toward the doctor. Dr. Lila Chen wasn't only the lead doctor on this project. She was also my distraction. The cunt I'd used to get my dick wet in those moments when I needed relief. Hell, Dane joined us on more than one occasion.

His voice was casual, like he had any fucking idea of my obsession with Juliet Bettencourt. I stared at him as if he were the subject on the table, watching for the flicker of a muscle as I tried to read the full intention behind his question. Juliet was mine. Mine to fuck. To punish. To claim.

I took a deep breath. The glass seemed to close in around me, my own reflection crowding me on every surface. I let it out as laughter, low and menacing.

"If she knows what's good for her, she'll pretend she's never seen my dick."

"Alright, Dr. Chen," I said, more than a suggestion. "Let's get this show on the road."

Through the glass, I watched Chen position the needle at the IV line in the volunteer's arm. I watched Subject 23-B, Andrew Olson relax himself onto the table. He was lying there like a man who had no reason to fear his own transformation. The dark stubble on his chin was as rough as his posture was calm. I could almost believe he knew what he was in for.

"This is the one," I said. "The right formula. The right subject." I turned off the mic. "This better fucking work."

My voice was colder than the surface of the glass. Colder than the pale linoleum beneath my restless feet. I shouldn't have felt that sort of rage. Restless, the need to move, the need to touch. I shouldn't have felt the pressure building where my jeans tightened. That was a problem. And I wasn't about to let a problem impede my plans, not this close to the finish line.

Dr. Chen met my eye through the panel, gave a stiff nod, then pushed the plunger down. I watched the plunger empty its charge and send the compound through the needle into the line. I watched Olson tense as his pulse rate climbed and his temperature spiked. This was the closest we had come, the final round after more failures than any man would know what to do with. But I was not any man. Chen exited the room. We'd learned our lesson last time.

The monitors blared their steady rhythms as I stared through the observation glass, knuckles whitening around my clipboard. My breath fogged the reinforced pane when I leaned closer—mesmerized. Subject #23-B's veins pulsed cobalt beneath his skin as if lit from within by bioluminescent ink. His restraints creaked when he arched off the medical table, tendons snapping taut like bridge cables.

"Heart rate 180 BPM," I muttered into my headset recorder, though my thoughts raced faster. Renda's serum is catalyzing structural mutations in real time. The air tasted metallic with ozone and adrenaline—his or mine, I couldn't tell.

A guttural snarl tore from #23-B's throat as his biceps rippled, fabric shredding beneath sudden knots of muscle. Bone cracked like popcorn kernels—his fingers elongated into obsidian claws that left gashes in steel cuffs when he flexed them free.

"Phase two." My voice trembled as I punched codes into the intercom. "Inflict test laceration."

The robotic arm descended behind the glass, blade glinting cold under surgical lights. A shallow cut bloomed across #23-B's forearm... then vanished as we watched—skin weaving itself whole in under three seconds.

Accelerated regeneration confirmed. I scribbled frantically despite my shaking hand until the clipboard cracked under grip strength I didn't know I had.

He moved next—a blur of reconstructed sinew and feral grace. He was still a human male. But better. I could tell by the look on his face it was panic and not rage that contorted his features. He still reached up and smashed CCTV cameras before I registered him leaving frame. Static fizzed across half my screens.

"Son of a—"

The emergency exit alarm whooped as dented metal groaned overhead. I barely yanked my head back before five black claws punched through the observation glass like rifle rounds—stopped inches from my face by its armored polymer core.

Through spider-webbed cracks, #23-B's eyes locked onto mine: feral gold eclipsing human irises entirely now... but no fur erupted beneath his torn scrubs. No full shift triggered by rage or agony. Only vestigial weapons ripped from halfway down evolution's road.

"Partial manifestation matches Bettencourt gene markers," I whispered into my recorder even as primal fear iced my spine—even as part of me wanted to applaud. His new teeth gleamed like bone shards when he grinned at me through blood-flecked lips... and for one fractured second before sedation gas hissed into his lungs they retracted...

I saw him. After he passed out and was carried to his cell, I knew we'd done it. I also knew that in a matter of weeks, when Juliet came to me, oh and she sure as fuck *would* come to me, she would have more than a man holding her. She only *thought* I was a monster before.

# Chapter 23

## Juliet

For a week, I had worked out of the cabin while Bronc and his team searched for my mother. I had faith they'd be able to find her. I knew they were the best at what they did. Sitting alone perched at the dining table beneath dawn's thin light with a year's worth of invoices scattered around me, I poured over one discrepancy after another. The motorcycle shop's books had their own mysteries to solve.

The television over the fireplace gave off a soft glow, illuminating the dim living area. I'd gone to leaving it on a national news station hoping they might mention something about my mother's kidnapping. Her story had fallen out of the news cycle pretty quickly after the first couple of days. I guess I knew until they had any leads, there would be no other mention. She was beyond our grasp until Harrison decided to make a move. I don't care what anyone thought. He had her. My gut told me he did. I happened to glance up as I moved from one invoice to the next, and my eye caught on the familiar face of my father. The chryon beneath, an urgent banner: KIDNAPPERS MAKE CONTACT. My stomach twisted as I dove for the remote, hit the unmute, then the DVR button. The voice of the anchor filled the room. "Jules Bettencourt heard from his wife Renda's apparent kidnappers today." Then I heard his familiar voice, familiar but strained. "The people who took my wife sent me a message today. In it, they told me she was well, but that they were growing impatient. They sent a picture of her and told me they expect something in return. But I swear to you, I do not know what they want. I'm begging you, please tell me what you want and I will see that you get it." The television screen filled with the picture of my mother wearing a sleeveless powder blue Chanel dress with a ruffled neckline and straight skirt. I knew this dress well. It was Harrison's favorite. He bought one for me in three colors. I hated every one of them. The anchor's face was now back on the screen. "If you have information on the whereabouts of Renda Bettencourt, please contact the New York City Police Department."

I replayed the footage, feeling sicker with every press of the buttons. My father's emotions were unreadable to me. They seemed to fluctuate between fear and anger. Surely, he knew Harrison was holding her because of me. Of all the reasons for him to resent me, this one was the worst. The weak disappointment of a daughter caused him yet another reason to harbor animosity towards me.

Could I just ignore what was happening when I knew I could stop it? My mother was fully aware that Harrison had continually harmed me. She basically told me that love hurts. But could I return that same kind of cruelty? Stay hidden and safe while they tortured her in my place?

That question mark had lingered above every stack of books and ledgers I tried to work on as the days had passed before now. My eyes had filled with the familiar blur of numbers, and I couldn't keep still at the table for more than five minutes at a time.

A weak morning wind played through the grass as I stood by the window, still clutching the remote. I closed my eyes against the strain of my thoughts. I had to decide quickly what I was going to do. Harrison wasn't a patient man. This was his final warning. I knew it was.

I tossed the remote onto the couch and bent to gather a mess of papers strewn across the floor, my focus and sanity eroded in equal measure. Each receipt, the printed blurs of ink, turned as meaningless as the promise I made to stay put. My mother's face flashed through my mind. Her possible suffering hung in the air of the cabin and crushed the breath from my lungs. The broadcast looped in my mind on the verge of constant panic. The dress, the plea, the terrifying confirmation that she was a pawn in his effort to get to me. If I waited for Bronc, her captivity could last forever.

How could I let my mother pay for my inaction?

I had to find a way to contact him.

The biggest problem was going to be not tipping my hand to Bronc. Speaking of, I heard a motorcycle outside.

The door flew open, and I saw in his eyes he knew something had happened. I hadn't guarded the bond. But that's alright. I'd have to tell him about the newscast no matter what. Maybe he'd see the picture and pick up some kind of clue as to her whereabouts. That was my biggest dream. If he and his team could find her, I could stay safe. I had to give them one more chance.

The floorboards creaked under Bronc's boots as he stepped inside, sharp eyes scanning me like I was a map riddled with Xs. His silver in his beard caught the light from the wall sconce. My God, but he was the most beautiful man I'd ever seen. His gaze burned into me. He knew something had happened. His eyes, too knowing. I turned away, fingers crushing invoices in my hand.

"Team picked up a lead near the Honduras," he said, shrugging off his cut slowly, deliberately. Stalling. Testing. "Your mom's trail's still warm, Little Wolf."

I spun around quickly. This was great news. A sigh of relief left my lungs. "Oh my God. That's great!" I wrapped my arms around his waist. The feel of his hand stroking the hair down my back calmed my soul, if only for a moment. I stepped back and grabbed the remote control. "Your timing is perfect. You need to see this."

I clicked play on the DVR button and watched his jaw tighten as he looked on.

"Fuck. He's getting bolder. That's for sure." He shook his head as he pulled his phone from his pocket. "Menace. Motherfucker made contact with Bettencourt. Sent a picture. Check out Fox News. Got it? It's mostly just her, but try to pick up anything you can. Timeline's bumped up. Call Randall. We need to be airborne at twenty hundred hours. That gives us six hours' prep."

My head reeled. "Bronc? What's happening?"

He cupped my face in his large hands. "Once we determined Hasting's private jet had set down in Honduras, we started mission planning. We're moving our operation base to Honduras. Either that's where his lab is, or it's near there. We'll be better able to move on him quickly, the closer to him we are." He leaned in and gave me a tender kiss, as though that was going to make his leaving easier.

"So, I'm going with you, right?" I was indignant.

He scrubbed his hand through his hair. "As much as the thought of being away from you for even a day kills me, I can't have you there. You'd be too big of a distraction. My focus would constantly be on keeping you safe instead of finding and eliminating Hastings. I know if you're here, you're surrounded by an entire pack of people I trust who will keep you in their care."

I wanted to stomp my foot. Rage at him. But I understood what he was saying. I also understood that this would give me the opportunity to take matters into my own hands if they didn't locate my mother within a day or two. I couldn't let their search go on for days and days. My mother didn't have that kind of time. "Fine."

The sideways glance I got in return for my response told me Bronc was suspicious as hell. "Juliet, we will find your mother. Don't get any ideas about trying to interfere."

Bronc's hand lingered on my shoulder, warm and steady. "Once my team's boots hit the ground in Honduras, I'll check in daily," he said, his voice low but firm. "We will track that lab. Harrison can't keep hiding forever."

I nodded, forcing a smile that felt brittle. "I know you'll do everything you can."

And I *did* know he would.

Daily updates.

Progress reports.

Trust the plan.

He took me in his arms and led me to the large leather sofa.

Bronc's rough palms framed my face like sacred relics cradling cracked porcelain. His breath smelled of coffee and cinnamon from Pearl's kitchen. Comfort layered over danger, and for a heartbeat, I let myself drown in it. The wall sconces carved shadows across his stubbled jaw where tension pulsed, primal and electric, as if his wolf paced just beneath his skin.

"Look at me." His voice scraped low, alpha resonance thrumming through my bones despite its gentleness. My pulse hammered against his thumbs pressed to my throat—not restraint, but connection. "You think I'd let that bastard breathe near you again? After what he's done?"

The confession tore from him like claws unsheathed: "I'll burn cities for you, Little Wolf. Drain oceans. Tear every lab he's built stone from stone until I find your mother." His lips brushed my temple—promise and prayer fused into heat. "But I need you here. Anchored to me."

Outside, cicadas screamed in the cedars lining the compound grounds, a symphony of wilderness mirroring the chaos in my veins. Harrison's face flickered behind my eyelids: cold champagne eyes, knuckles glinting as he'd backhanded me last winter for burning his steak.

Bronc's growl rumbled against my collarbone as though he could scent the memory roiling in my blood. "He doesn't get to touch you." Calloused fingers slid beneath my shirt, branding my waist where bruises once bloomed purple-gold under Harrison's rage, now barely scarred skin singing under Bronc's possession. "Not your body." His mouth trailed fire up my neck, teeth grazing the claiming scar still tender from yesterday's moonlight frenzy between our wolves' teeth and claws. "Not your fear."

I arched into him instinctively—flames licking where terror had frosted my spine—but faltered when twin truths warred: His loyalty could get him killed. My love might be his slaughter.

The whimper tore free before I could cage it. Part plea, part shattered confession. And Bronc stilled like prey caught mid-hunt. When he pulled back, the light fractured in his blue irises into something feral, yet unbearably human.

"You doubt me?" No anger, just a raw ache lay bare between us.

"I doubt him," I whispered through salt-stung lips. "What he'll do when cornered."

His laugh was a dark hymn against my mouth. "Let him come." Fangs glinted faintly as he grinned—predator's grace threaded with devotion that scalded worse than any threat. "All the better if he does. Saves me tracking him through whatever hellhole he's infesting."

Wind howled suddenly through the canyon beyond our window—a phantom wail that raised gooseflesh along my arms. But Bronc's hands were heat incarnate, kneading the chill from my flesh as his words sank talons deep:

"Harrison dies screaming for what he took from you." A vow etched in blood and bone. "And when I bring your mother out safely?" His thumb swept the tear I hadn't felt fall. "You'll finally believe you were made for more than survival."

The kiss crashed through me then—wilderness given teeth and tongue—as if he could rewrite every lie Harrison branded into me with nothing but fear and need for acceptance:

Mine.

Worthy.

Unbroken.

I closed my eyes. And let him hold the shattered pieces together just a little longer.

"Now, sleep, my mate. I need for you to rest." He kissed my forehead and walked out the front door.

His words looped in my head, but all I could see was my mother's face. My dad read Harrison's demand. I knew Harrison. He was angry. Finished waiting.

Even though my eyelids were heavy, I still thought about the backpack I had stored upstairs in my closet. The envelope filled with cash from when I fled New York was still there. My getaway money I'd called it then. I'd held onto it just in case Dairyville didn't work out. But oh, how it worked out. I loved it here. I never had any intention of ever leaving.

Give them another two weeks, I decided, counting the bills in my mind. Two weeks of Bronc's optimism, his cables and codes and covert sweeps. If Mom wasn't blinking into a video feed by dawn on day fourteen, I'd vanish before breakfast. I'd take Bronc's King Ranch at 5 a.m. and stop at the closest truck stop. There, I'd purchase a burner phone and a Visa gift card and use it to order an Uber to Amarillo International. I'd board a plane to somewhere far away. Then I'd call Harrison.

"You want me?" I'd say when he answered, cool as winter steel. "Then let her go first." He'd have me, but wouldn't be close to the Iron Valor Pack.

# CHAPTER 24

## BRONC

"FUCK. How can there be no leads?" I bellowed from my spot at the head of the table, my eyes sweeping the room with hardened determination as my voice reverberated over the low hum of urgent conversation. My elite special forces team surrounded me, a tangle of muscle and ego and intense skill. Menace and Doc focused on an aerial map spread on the table's scarred metal surface, markers of every color dotting its worn and pockmarked face. Wrecker, Arsenal, and Papa sat with their laptops, keyboards tapping and entering commands into already overloaded systems. It had been days since I'd held Juliet. Our bond stretched and thinned by both time and miles.

I rubbed my hand over the stubble that lined my jaw, then checked my phone again. Nothing. We normally worked on time-lines of weeks, not days. This was pushing our limits.

"How he vanished after intel said he landed in Honduras is a mystery," Doc said, his voice low and edged with annoyance. "He has to have someone on his team with skills."

"Somebody who knew how to disappear them," Menace added, his tone sharp with frustration. "I don't get it."

My chest ached with every beat, the distance between Juliet and our bond taking a toll I'd never thought I'd experience. I clenched my hand to still the dull, relentless throb and willed myself to focus on the task at hand. I had to get this shit handled so I could get back to her and make sure she wasn't suffering. We were going on almost a month. I never expected it to take this long.

Wrecker leaned back in his chair and regarded the rest of us with calculating eyes. "We got nothin' right now," he said, his deep, commanding voice cutting through the din of activity. "I've gone through every fucking file the DOD and CIA have. The only fucking way we even *knew* he'd landed in Central America was through tapping into the vampire mafia network. Koslov manages to have his lifeless fingers in everybody's pie."

My head snapped up. "What the fuck, Wrecker? You didn't think it was important to mention who your contact was?" My voice was little more than a growl, thinking that we were on a wild goose chase and had wasted our time here.

The tension in the room ratcheted up about 10 notches. Wrecker stood his ground. Every man in this room was an alpha in his own right. They all chose to bow the knee to me out of loyalty. But when it got like this, it was difficult to breathe.

"Kozlov's daughter is a friend of Juliet's no?" Wrecker asked. Looking me straight in the eyes.

Took me a minute to regain my composure enough to think straight. "Yeah. That's where Juliet got her fake papers. Why they were so legit looking."

"Kazimir is aware that Lucia takes her relationship with Juliet very seriously. He wants Harrison dead. His intel is good. He gave me all he had."

That information was good enough for me. It still didn't sit right with me, and I let him know it.

"Wrecker. You *ever* speak to another Supernatural Supreme Leader, especially if it's a king, without my knowledge, we're gonna have a problem. Understood?"

He pounded his fist over his heart. "Yes, Alpha."

I knew he had gotten the message.

"Okay, continue."

"I've found no trace of any offshore holdings. At least none connected to Hastings Labs. This fucker is a ghost."

Menace muttered a string of curses that put even my choice of words to shame.

"How in the hell does he have that kind of power?" I said. "And how's he keeping a base of operations the size of a lab so hidden?"

Doc didn't look up from his screen as he answered, the deliberate weight of his words silencing everyone else in the room. "Money," he said. "And probably some damn expert help. This part of the world? You can keep mouths shut with enough cash."

"He shouldn't be able to just ghost like this." My voice came out tight and sharp. "We're missing something."

"Maybe your little lady scarred him more than we figured," Menace said, a knowing edge to his words.

"She's not my little fuckin' lady," I said, trying to keep my frustration in check. "She's your fuckin' Luna."

A low rumble of laughter rolled through the group, and I couldn't help but crack a small, reluctant smile at their refusal to let me brood.

I picked up the list of countries we'd been considering; the paper worn and marked with pen and frustration. Harrison could have a lab in any of a half dozen Central American countries, and Juliet's mother, Renda—was as gone as he was. I tossed the sheet back onto the table and swore under my breath as it floated down like a taunt.

"Arsenal?" I asked.

He straightened and gave me a precise, clipped nod. "Our perimeter is clear. We're ready to roll on your word, Prez."

My chest squeezed at his use of the title, and I resisted the urge to check my phone again. Instead, I caught sight of the photo I'd taped next to my monitor. Juliet's wildfire eyes stared back at me like they were daring me to finish the mission and haul my ass home. I forced my attention back to the team.

"Should we give up on Guatemala?" I asked, my voice rough with reluctance.

"Negative," Doc said, leaning back in his chair and tilting it onto two legs. "It's a solid lead, Bronc. We have to check it out."

"I want to be damn sure we don't lose another week for nothing," I said.

"Look," Arsenal said. "We hit El Salvador. It could already be abandoned by the time we hit boots down. Same with Belize."

"Juliet is good at home," Papa said, cutting straight to my concerns with an unsettling clarity. "You're gonna be no good to her if you don't see this through."

I nodded once, acknowledging his truth, though it pained me more than I wanted to admit. We had to be meticulous.

"Fuck," I said finally, dragging my hand through my hair. "Alright, fine. We hit Guatemala. Doc, Arsenal, I want both of you ready to mobilize the second Wrecker gets a lock."

They exchanged looks, and Doc gave me a tight-lipped smile. "Roger that."

I shot him a hard stare.

My eyes wandered back to Juliet's photo, and I had to suppress the gnawing urge to abandon the mission and go back to Texas to find her and make sure she was okay. I knew her heart was breaking, and that was breaking my heart.

"Any ideas on what we're dealing with?" I asked.

Arsenal folded his arms across his chest, his movements precise and methodical. "Assuming we find the lab, count on heavy local coverage," he said. "There will be private guards, too. Wouldn't be surprised if some are local military."

"Or ex," Wrecker added. "He'll have every merc with a passport ready to protect those facilities."

"And they'll all be after our heads if we don't move fast," Menace said.

"If it even *is* Guatemala," Doc said with a touch of doubt.

"Wrecker," I barked, pushing aside my personal angst. "Get back to hacking again. We need any location you can grab."

"I told you I've got nothing."

"Then get us something."

Wrecker nodded once, then bent back to his computer, fingers flying across the keyboard in what seemed to be an impossible blur of motion. I was surrounded by the best of the best. All of us had spent enough time in the field to know just how badly a mission like this could play out.

Papa leaned back in his chair, stretching his arms over his head as if he didn't have a care in the world, and then studied me with calm, level eyes. "Still holding my bet on Costa Rica, but Guatemala's worth the shot."

"Our best hope is that he gets careless," Arsenal said. "We need to get rid of every piece of shifter evidence we can find."

"Ten-four to that." I agreed. Keeping supernaturals off the radar is part of our mission.

"And if we find her?" Papa asked. "What's the play?"

"Smash and grab," I said. "We'll get her out and scuttle any and everything else. Including personnel."

The unspoken *if* hung heavy in the air. If we find anything. If the site isn't cleared. If there's even a site at all.

"Let's hope we'll be stateside in three days," Doc said, answering my unspoken concerns with casual confidence.

"And you can go all Romeo on your Juliet," Menace added.

"Fuck you," I grumbled, unable to keep the edge from my voice. They didn't seem to mind.

The oppressive Central American heat bore down on us, and the humid air hung so thick it felt like it could be cut with a knife. It added to the sense of urgency, the desire to wrap up and head out.

I took a breath to settle myself and gave them all a determined nod. "Wrecker?"

He kept typing, kept searching, kept his focus even as I paced the narrow, utilitarian space, my energy nearly spent from the distance between me and Juliet.

"Almost in."

"See what you can find about his merc team while you're at it," I added.

Wrecker paused his frantic typing and looked at me, his stare as serious and menacing as I'd ever seen. "You know what it'll be like if they're as good as the crew you've put together."

"Just find us what we need."

I'd lost track of how many times I checked my phone since we'd taken up camp in this temporary location. There had been a text from Ma in the early morning hours letting me know Juliet was safe but withdrawn, a single line from Maddie a few days later telling me to keep the faith, but nothing from Juliet herself since I left. Her silence was louder than any response I might have received, and I hoped it meant she was as torn up about our separation as I was.

"There," Wrecker said, a sudden light of triumph flickering in his eyes. "Intercepted satellite comms, then patched a bug through. Lot of chatter between Guatemala City and here."

"Your lead's heating up," Arsenal said, confidence lacing his words.

I tried to ignore the small wave of relief that rushed over me, tried not to focus on what was waiting back home. Tried to be the leader they needed me to be.

"We don't move until Wrecker has vicinity," I said, struggling to keep my priorities straight. The conflict within me was brutal and barely controlled.

Doc shot me a knowing look. "It's go time, Bronc."

"Pack it up, people!" I called out, already halfway to the door.

"You heard the man!" Arsenal said, adding a sharp military tone to his words as he corralled the rest of the team.

I grabbed my phone off the table and gave Juliet's photo one last, lingering glance before shoving it into my pocket. The stark fear of losing her to time and distance consumed my thoughts. I couldn't shake the feeling that my hesitation had cost us too much already.

We geared up and hauled out to the landing zone, knowing our best chance of finding anything was to hit hard and fast. There wasn't a moment to spare, and if this lead was solid, it would get us back home in time to hold Juliet and bring her even closer to us than she had been before.

We hoped.

That night I finally heard from Juliet. A brief Facetime. I almost melted at seeing her beautiful face. She'd just gotten out of the bath and was settled into bed for the night.

"Hi baby." Her voice was so small.

"Hi there beautiful. Miss the hell outa you." I gave her a smile.

"Miss you more. Wish you were home. I'm guessing you've had no luck?"

"No precious. We're heading to Guatemala tomorrow. There's chatter. Gonna check it out. Finger crossed." I saw her face fall.

"Oh, okay. I'm hoping extra hard that'll be it. Tomorrow will be the day. Well, hey honey, I'm super tired. Think I'm gonna turn in. I love you so much. You're the best thing that ever happened to me. I don't know if I ever told you that."

"Sweetheart. You are everything to me. You know that. I cannot wait to see you. We're doing our best so I can get back to you. I love you."

The line went dead. Faint feelings of love and something else I couldn't name poured through the bond.

# Chapter 25

## Juliet

Harsh fluorescence pierced the early morning dim of the Amarillo truck stop. I'd never been there before. The checkered tiles and endless steel shelving could have been any such place, but they were foreign enough to be unnerving, bleak enough to set my nerves on edge. It was too easy to imagine someone watching from the shadowy parking lot outside. But I knew it was just me and any number of other desperate people making their way to who knows where in the early morning Texas hours.

I moved quickly and deliberately past display after display, the ache of dread a dull and constant throb in my chest. My legs were wobbly with nerves and exhaustion. I was being careful to keep the bond quiet, so Bronc wouldn't feel my anxiety. The few truckers inside barely glanced my way as I snagged a burner phone from a rotating rack, the plastic encasing slick beneath my fingers. It would be safer than the one I'd brought, less traceable. My pulse hammered faster than the heels of my boots on the tile. I could have sworn the glances grew longer, more curious, suspicious even. My imagination was running away with me.

I bought two prepaid Visa cards and a bottle of water. There's no way I was the first person the clerk had ever seen make these types of purchases. Any number of people have reasons for moving from place to place, needing to keep off the radar.

"Uh, miss," he said. He sounded uneasy. "Do you want a bag for that?"

The silence after the words stretched out far too long. I forced a smile, shaky and grateful to be dealing with strangers who didn't know I was a breath away from screaming.

"Yeah. Sure."

I snatched the phone out first. Already I was checking flights on it before I stepped foot inside the small diner inside the stop. I couldn't bear to head outside to do this clandestine business in the late September chill. It was before dawn, and you could feel the crispness in the air. Checking flights, Nashville seemed like my best bet. Seemed, because I was flying blind and desperate. But desperation was better than sitting still and waiting for something awful to happen to my mother. Because of me. Once he took me, I'd contact Bronc through the bond. He'd find me. I knew he would. And this would all be over.

I looked out the window. The blacktop was wide open, except for the looming shadows of eighteen-wheelers and the row of cars with men asleep in them, slumped and still. I hurried past, keeping my eyes on the thin streaks of early light over the faraway canyon walls, hoping they'd be a good enough guide to get me out.

I should have packed lighter. Or heavier. Or differently. The metal bench on the curb bit into my legs as I fumbled through my backpack. No time to dwell on it. The flight was more important than clean clothes or even the fake ID stashed in a leather wallet. I tried to convince myself of that as I booked the 6:15 a.m. flight and slipped the backpack over my shoulders. My palms were wet and shaky around my phone.

It was the same way when I got the Uber called and confirmed. The way the confirmation arrived in an instant, a buzzing satisfaction from the other side of the country, left me raw and wary. I set the cards and phone up in a rush and managed to book an urgent flight with sweaty hands. I worked the way I always did when I was on edge, fast and efficient, the way I had to before someone could get ahead of me. My mind went to Bronc just for a moment. I'd left my phone at home. It would be a while before Pearl would notice I was gone. She normally didn't check on me until lunchtime.

I ordered the Uber and finished everything before 5:15 am, with half an hour to spare and fear wrapped like an iron fist around my gut.

There was something strangely reassuring about the vehicle that arrived, about the female driver's warm smile and chatty nature. It almost made me forget for a moment that I was going headlong into the arms of a monster.

"You headin' far, honey?"

She probably would have been just as pleasant if I had told her the truth, if I said I didn't have a clue. I glanced out the window instead, letting the quiet of an almost deserted main road sink into me.

"Just the airport," I said. "Thanks."

Just back to the man who used to break my bones for fun.

The street signs we passed were unfamiliar and surreal, and I closed my eyes as the car sped along, cutting through more nameless terrain. It had to be enough. I'd tried to plan everything as perfectly as I could, account for every possibility. But each turn the car took felt like it would lead me straight back to where I started, and a chill settled deep in my bones, unwavering.

I held my breath as we pulled into the terminal, tension vibrating through me like a tuning fork as I jumped out. I strolled up to the TSA agent just like I was heading out on vacation. *Nothing to see here, folks. Just heading to confront a kidnapper. You know. The usual.*

I tried not to look back as I boarded, rushing past the security checkpoint and to my gate in a blur of nerves and gut-twisting apprehension. I hated having to face Harrison. I hated him.

I found my seat and forced myself to breathe deeply and slowly.

The tears surprised me. They were there as the flight took off, unstoppable and hot, and I wiped at them with the heels of my palms, thankful that I had the row to myself. Bronc. My refuge. The only good thing I'd ever known in my short life was going to be so angry or hurt.

The sleepless night and endless worries left me heavier than I thought. They worked into my bones, pushing down until exhaustion finally overwhelmed every other feeling.

I dreamed of Bronc. His smile was a broad and familiar comfort, and my own widened in return. We walked toward each other, through open space, his stride steady and easy and reassuring. Nothing like mine. Nothing frantic or broken. There were no worries that lingered over him like they did me, no anxiety. He called my name as he neared.

"Juliet."

I started to run.

The rest was foggy. Hazy and uncertain. Memories and worry tangled, bleeding into each other until I couldn't tell which was which. It felt like an eternity before the wheels finally touched down.

I left the airport in Nashville with just my backpack, a half-formed plan, and the gnawing unease that I was already steps behind. There was no way of knowing whether this was safe. Only Harrison's promise that he'd find me. That my mother would be safe.

I wanted to believe him.

With the way my heart was pounding, with the way my blood ran cold, with the way that I knew him, I didn't.

The cavernous interior of the terminal loomed around me as I walked toward the baggage claim, keeping my head down. There were too many people, too many possibilities. I hugged the walls and stayed close to the main thoroughfares, sure I could slip away in the crowds if I had to.

As soon as I thought I was out of sight, I dug my phone out, sending a quick message to the number Harrison had given me.

*I'm here like we agreed.*

A quick reply, then silence.

*Good. My man is waiting. You did the right thing, Juliet. As soon as you are in the limo, your mother will be returned safely.*

That was as much as I could have hoped for. The word of a criminal.

I swallowed hard and ignored it, the familiar burn of tears returning to my eyes. I needed to keep myself together. Keep my feelings from flowing through the bond.

The next text to Harrison was even shorter.

*My man is almost to where you are.*

They must have hacked into the airport's security cameras. He could see me. I was certain. My eyes remained focused on the ground curb of the passenger pickup area. Until a deep voice interrupted my thoughts.

"Let's go, Juliet."

A giant of a man stood beside me dressed in full chauffer's gear, complete with hat. He wore what had to be a mask. There's no way he'd risk showing his face so blatantly in front of the cameras that were everywhere.

He took my bag and opened the back door of the luxurious limo and helped me inside. Before I turned my head to look at him again, a sharp sting entered my neck. Within seconds, my world went black.

I woke in a room that felt unsettling and stark. It looked nothing like the one in the photo of my mother that had been splattered on newscasts. A distinct lack of windows on the four gray walls told me this was more a cell than a room meant to provide comfort. The only luxury was the soft sheets I lay upon. I sat up quickly, dizzy, trying to orient myself to my surroundings. My clothing had been changed. I was dressed in a short satin nightie, no panties. My body flared with pain, heat radiating from every tender muscle. I reached instinctively for my bond with Bronc, my lifeline in the darkness, but only a sickening absence responded. In its place, a new feeling. Chills and nausea swept over me; the foreignness of the sensation was nearly suffocating. My pulse raced, frantic at the feeling of this unfamiliar presence. Then came a stabbing, a brutal cramp that knotted low in my abdomen. My neck seemed to tingle with a piercing throb of pain. I assumed it was the sting from that injection still lingered. I reached out once more, desperate to feel the familiar pulse of my bond with Bronc. My entire plan hinged on connecting with him through our bond to guide him to me. Again, nothing. The connection was nonexistent. It hurt more than I could bear. It had to be some horrific nightmare. I blinked hard, forcing myself to look around the room with desperate hope. I staggered to my feet, unsteady and gasping for breath.

Panic surged as I rushed into the adjoining bathroom, where, in the mirror, I found a bloody bandage covering Bronc's unmistakable claiming mark. With trembling hands, I peeled back the tape to reveal it mangled by another set of teeth. Horrified, I sank to the floor in uncontrollable sobs. I buried my head against my knees, a little girl abandoned and bleeding. "No, no, no..." My voice was a trembling echo, breaking the room's horrible silence. "Bronc." His name was a broken whisper. Despair wracked my body, helpless and consuming. I curled tighter, knowing I needed to move but unable to muster the will. Agony replaced panic. It swept over me in a cold, brutal wave, and I wanted to drown in it. I touched the mangled mark. Each inch of torn skin told a nightmare. The bite wound mangled and cruel.

Oh God. Oh God.

I slumped back; the walls closing in, smothering me like a vise on my heart. Every emotion was a knife twisting in a place I didn't know could hurt so much. I wrapped my arms around my legs again and let the devastation come, choking on my own raw sounds. Sobs racked me until my throat was too tight to breathe, the space too small to hold the enormity of my anguish.

My mind was a mass of jumbled thoughts. Disoriented, I hadn't heard the bedroom door open. Suddenly, a shadow fell across the floor where I lay in a crumbled heap.

I glanced up in fear, disbelieving, knowing. A hulking figure stood in the doorway, a monster come to life. A nightmare with the exacting touch of designer clothing. The navy blue shirt clung to rippling muscles, straining against the impossible, the unreal. This was not Harrison. Not any Harrison I'd ever known.

The predatory eyes, the claws emerging like they had always been there. The flawless face transformed and other-worldly, savage beauty twisting in his gaze. My heart constricted, then pounded, panic-driven and wild.

His lips parted in a sneer, the amber eyes, now lupine, narrowing as he regarded me.

"Hello, mate," the creature said, the voice as perfect and cutting as I remembered, but now somehow twisting in my gut. "You shouldn't have kept me waiting."

No air, no room, no comprehension. I blinked, staring, trying to force the vision into something that made sense. Something I could understand.

It was real. It was all horribly real.

I backed into the counter, my arms instinctively shielding what they could, though I knew how futile that was. He loomed over me, expression coolly amused. I was prey and possession, and my soul ached with knowing it. My whimpers fueled his amusement.

Harrison. He had changed, had become like us, one of Bronc's worst suspicions. The man I had once thought so carefully groomed was not quite a wolf, but very much not a man either.

My head shook without conscious effort, back and forth and back, the floor slipping away beneath me.

"What—what did you do?" The question escaped me, helpless and unbidden.

"What I had to," he said, the calculating tones too smooth, too familiar. "It took time, resources. Thanks to your ancestors. Your family, in fact, darling. They are the reason we are now bound forever. Isn't that wonderful? I am grateful."

I didn't want to listen. Didn't want to hear the confirmation of everything that the marked skin screamed. But I couldn't stop.

"What do you...?" Words choked to silence.

His smile widened. Ice and control. "Nothing you should be surprised by. You should have known I'd never let you go, not so easily. There's no one to save you now."

He advanced a step, letting the nightmare draw closer, every movement reminding me of how powerless I was, how alone.

"The bite. The bond." My voice cracked beneath the impossible truth. "It can't work, Harrison. Never. You're sick if you think it will."

"Sick?" he repeated, his eyes darkening, something ominous lurking behind them. "Oh, Juliet. You have no idea."

This was his plan. All along. And now—my mind refused to process, refused to cope. Now he was capable of it. Harrison crouched beside me, his presence overwhelming, the proximity of his body terrifying in its raw, brutal strength. He let me absorb the threat, absorb the presence, absorb the cost. Absorb the damning presence of this bond.

His hand reached out to brush my cheek, and I wanted to jerk away. Instead, I leaned into his touch. Another whimper came from my throat as my body answered the bond against my will.

A feral grin told me he knew I didn't want it. "*There's* my mate", he crooned. And my body lit up for him. My God. I cannot do this. I searched for my wolf. She didn't answer. I was alone.

"Yes." He pulled back and stood. "I'm your alpha now, Jules. We're going to have such a good time. Now, get up and shower. I've left clothing on your bed. I expect you to wear it when you are done. We'll have brunch after. Disobey me, and you'll be punished. I expect it. I look forward to it. It's your choice. You're not leaving here mate. Make it easy on yourself, or don't. Makes no difference to me."

I couldn't see through the blur of tears. I couldn't hear above the chaos in my head. A soundless scream formed somewhere deep inside me, like it knew what I couldn't bear to say.

Bronc, *I'm sorry*.

# CHAPTER 26

## BRONC

The Guatemalan jungle clung to my skin like a second layer—thick, suffocating, alive with sweat and despair. I checked my watch out of habit: 7:14 p.m. The exact moment our bond snapped.

It felt like a bone breaking inside me. A jagged fracture tearing through marrow and muscle until all I tasted was blood and absence. She was gone. Not just out of reach, but severed clean from my soul. My knees hit damp earth as I braced myself against a tree trunk slick with moss, its ridges biting into my palm like a mockery of Juliet's teeth sinking into my shoulder during her heat.

Apparently, she'd left sometime this morning.

Ma's voice from earlier looped in my head through the static of our unstable connection. She'd called after noon to let me know Juliet wasn't at home when she'd stopped by to bring her lunch. It had become a routine. She'd been skipping meals since I'd been gone, and I'd asked Ma to try to make her eat. The best way to do that was to bring her food. She'd stopped by our house around 12:15 p.m. and discovered the place was empty. I'd called Juliet's phone, and Ma answered it.

"It's me, son. She left the phone. It looks like she may have packed a bag. She couldn't have taken much. Looks like all of her clothes are here. Let me check out back for your truck." I knew she wouldn't find it. Knew she'd taken it. To where exactly, I wasn't certain, but I'd goddamn sure find out. I sure as shit knew her ultimate destination. I hung up after Ma verified what I knew was true. I opened my tracking software and found my truck at an Amarillo Flying J. Made a call to T-Bone and had him pick the truck up and grill the truck stop employees on when Juliet had been there. Five in the morning. She had a seven-hour head start. She was fucking long gone.

But she hadn't run *from* me—she'd run *for* someone else. Her mother's face flashed behind my eyelids—Renda's cold eyes staring back from that news broadcast days ago—and I knew. Juliet had bartered herself in some sacrificial swap. For a fucking woman who never gave two shits about her. Stupid fucking bravery twisted into a suicide mission by Harrison's puppeteering hands. My beautiful brave mate didn't trust me enough to tell me what she was planning, and now our bond was severed, and I didn't know if she still lived.

The jungle roared around me—howler monkeys screaming while my wolf clawed at my ribs from within. I wanted to shift so badly my gums ached where canines threatened to lengthen uninvited. But shifting here meant losing myself entirely, with no control beyond primal need. And if there was one thing left anchoring me to humanity, it was rage sharper than any blade ever forged by Menace or Arsenal.

He had her now. Harrison who ripped bonds like they were paper chains meant for kindergarten crafts instead of sacred threads stitched into our DNA over lifetimes of wolf-blood legacy... Did he hurt her badly? Did she scream when he tore through our mating mark? Or did she shut down like she had when we first met—frozen prey hiding behind CPA degrees and lie after lie until my wolf pried its way under those walls? Did he lose control until her heart stopped? I roared, losing my mind.

"Bronc!" Wrecker's voice cut through the mangrove haze as he emerged from our command tent thirty yards ahead, where

Menace paced inside under lamplight maps spread across crates serving as tables because nothing here stayed clean or neat or permanent.. Just chaos upon chaos... "Intel came through—"

I didn't let him finish before turning toward camp though every step felt wrong-footed without Juliet shifting beside me in sync like moonlight over prairie grass back home... Home where Pearl would scrub counters raw trying to not cry while Scar prayed over another empty dining table placemat... Home where Skeeter was probably smirking through another stolen payout because God forbid any problem stay simple long enough solve before another disaster imploded...

But none mattered next to this singular truth scorching nerve endings raw: Juliet thought sacrifice made martyrdom noble.

Not cowardice couched as courage... Not abandonment twisting knife-deep... Noble... And maybe part of me agreed even now—admired that infuriating spark flaring bright enough to burn them both alive if needed because that was my mate—wildfire wrapped in soft curves.

But admiration wouldn't save her from cages built for corporate greed and revenge...

"Panama City airport," Wrecker rasped, handing satellite images showing black-site lab locations dotting the coastline like tumorous stars. But coordinates blurred red-laced vision already picturing Harrison standing over Juliet,, there smirking as monitors tracked heartbeat fading. My heartbeat. Our heartbeat. Gone silent at 7:14 sharp.

Menace slammed a fist onto the map where Costa Rica bled into Nicaragua. "He dragged us south intentionally—distraction while—"

"While she walked straight into his goddamn arms," I finished throat shredded raw quieter than midnight snowfall, knowing when I found him it wouldn't be a quick death. No, there would be claws tearing his throat slow enough to savor the terror. I'd see amber eyes widening, the same shade Juliet feared, the ones she'd faced as he tore our bond asunder. They'd reflect the fear of a beast facing his own death for his sins. He'd see vengeance was the only thing left for him.

I hit the command center like a man gone rogue, breaking and breaking away until my last shred of will brought me back. A shell of myself, no fucking actual body, but this broken one I couldn't feel anymore. A ghost of the wolf I was without Juliet to make me whole. The team gathered in the crowded room where we'd gathered what seemed like a hundred times, faces as rough as the plans we made. Maps, wires, desperation to find that bastard Harrison and make him pay. They shifted in their chairs, grew uneasy, never saw me come apart at the seams until now. Until my connection to Juliet snapped, and they felt the fury and the resolve to get her back. I slammed my fist on the table, guttural, barked orders or death threats. I couldn't say which, and I didn't care. We were going after the lab. Going after Juliet. I'd hunt her with or without them.

Papers scattered, sounds of boots and bodies jerking in shock as the table rattled under my fist. Desperation charged the cramped room, sparking between me and the men I ran this show with, static as sharp as the glances they shot my way. My wildness, my raw fucking need to find her. It pushed against their discipline and forced them to follow. They knew I was Alpha. They knew I'd keep moving until I brought her back, dead if not alive, but mine either way.

JT, big as a bear and just as watchful, shifted in his chair and ran a hand over his short, cropped hair. A lifetime of scars made him look old as hell when he was only thirty-seven, five years younger than me. A man of faith and never out of his element until right at this moment. "What's the plan, Bronc?"

His voice was slow and wary. The question shouldn't have needed asking. The answer was the same as always. Locate and destroy. But they could sense it in me now, my will on the verge of shattering just like my bond with Juliet had. A vein pulsed in my jaw as I gritted my teeth, let my breath and my rage and my promise of vengeance do the counting to ten before I replied.

My voice was low, barely human. "Juliet is gone."

Bridger raised an eyebrow and crossed his arms. He was built like a truck, left a presence even when he didn't speak. This time, he was quiet. Too fucking quiet, all of them watching me like they expected an explosion or a break. My wolf wanted both. My wolf wanted to rip through the jungle and never stop.

My fist came down on the table again, less a slam this time a more resolute, raw-edged command.

No fear. No fucking hesitation.

"Harrison took her," I continued, feeling my face go hard and unreadable as stone. "That's all we need to know."

Shuffling, bodies shifting. An awkward, uncertain sound from a crew I could always count on to have my back. To keep my head on straight when everything else spiraled.

Eli's sharp Southern drawl sliced through the mounting tension. "Hstraight,e's gotta show his face at some point. He's got a business to run.." A pause, a frown. "I frankly don't get how he's stayed hidden the last five weeks, Bronc. It's why we don't have a definitive trail this time."

J.T. nodded once, arms folded and face creased with a concern he never voiced. "He's communicating somehow. Whispers here and there. He's got too fucking much money to grease too many palms."

I could feel them looking at me, waiting for a decision or a meltdown. Waiting to see if I was still Bronc, if I was still Alpha, or if Juliet's absence left me less. "He can't run," I said, as much to myself as to them, determination spreading through my veins with all the comfort of venom. "He's got nowhere to go now. He's got what he wanted. I'm assuming he's made progress on whatever super-drug he's been working on. Juliet will be a distraction. But he does have to answer to a board of directors. We need to focus there. It could give us a clue sooner than later."

The mess of papers littered the room, caught my eye. They needed more than information. They needed me to lead, even when my mind was already halfway back to Texas and a fucking broken bond.

"Wrecker," I barked. "You know he's in Central America. You said he can't move the operation, and I don't give a damn what trail you think we're on, but I know you wouldn't fuck it up." My words came fierce, harsh. I trusted little outside the circle I'd built, but Wrecker had always been solid. And he wasn't the one who failed Juliet. "Keep at it. Any update at all?"

The room held its breath as his fingers flew across his keyboard. Then he finally spoke, all quiet calculation behind his glasses and the stubble he always let grow too long. "Panama City. Chatter says his plane was there yesterday."

My eyes narrowed, seeing only what mattered, blind to everything else. My voice rose to a snarl. "That means he's gotta be close to there."

A low murmur from the group, passing in looks and not words. A reluctant acceptance. They knew I wouldn't let this rest until it rested in Harrison's grave. "Wrecker. Arsenal. Papa. Doc. Anyone got a problem stayin' the course?"

Arsenal, quiet and easy, locked eyes with me. "You good to do this, Bronc? 'Cause we'd follow you straight into the pits of hell."

They looked at me again, measuring. I felt their strength filling me, lifting me.

Menace was next to me first, his scarred hand gripping my shoulder hard enough to bruise a human. "Alpha," he said quietly—not Bronc, not Liam—using the title like an anchor thrown into stormwater. "Talk."

"It's gone," I rasped, staring at my splayed fingers as if they might hold answers. "The bond."

Silence pooled thick as jungle humidity around us until Doc swore under his breath and kicked a chair aside to kneel before me. His medic's gaze flickered over my face like he was assessing battle damage. "Severed or suppressed?"

"Does it matter?" I snarled with a growl that vibrated in my throat. Juliet was gone—her light snuffed out or stolen away, and every instinct screamed that it was Hastings' doing. That bastard had carved his claim over her like rot sinking into wood...

Arsenal stepped forward then, his boots crunching gravel as he blocked the tent flap against prying eyes outside. "It matters because we need intel," he said evenly, though his jaw flexed like he was biting back fury of his own. "If they hid her somehow—"

"They didn't hide her." Wrecker slammed a satellite image onto the table—blurry shots of the Costa Rican coastline taken three days prior. "They broke her."

The words hung there for half a heartbeat before Menace wheeled on him with claws out and fangs bared—only to freeze when Big Papa stepped between them effortlessly, all 6'5" of muscle wrapped in calm authority that even other Alphas couldn't ignore. "Enough." His gaze swept over us all like rainwater rinsing ash from stone. "Battling each other won't bring our Luna home."

*Our* Luna. Theirs, not just mine. Always theirs. The pack bond shivered around me then—not Juliet's delicate thread, but dozens of others entwined with mine: rage and worry and resolve pumping through every connection until my teeth ached with it. Their faith, their strength flooded into the hollow space she left behind.

Wrecker exhaled sharply through his nose and stabbed a finger at the map. "Heads-up came from Fort Meade an hour ago: encrypted chatter on Hastings Pharma servers flagged keywords tied to shifter bloodwork trials. Lab location still unconfirmed, but—"

"But we track it," Arsenal finished for him, thumb brushing his sidearm holster reflexively. "Same way we tracked Al-Qaeda supply routes. Grid sectors, sat sweeps, local bribes. Sooner or later, they slip."

Doc snorted, pulling a flask from his vest to toss at me. "Hastings isn't insurgent-grade smart. Rich boys cut corners everywhere."

The bourbon burned going down, but I welcomed it. Let it fuel the fire spreading through my chest as I stood, the Alpha voice rumbling low: "Then we make him bleed for those cuts."

Menace crossed arms over his chest, mirroring my stance. "Pack moves as one. Your orders?"

Orders. Not pleas, not doubts—just pure certainty radiating from every man in that tent: They believed. In me. In her. In bonds, no knife could truly sever.

I met each of their stares: Wrecker with his tech-filed glare, Arsenal sharp as sniper focus, Doc steady-handed even now, Big Papa grounding us all like bedrock... and finally Menace: my brother, riding shotgun through hell since Kandahar days.

"We head out," I said at last, palming Wrecker's satellite images. "Shadow teams comb grid sectors here, to Panama City."

I shrugged, already striding toward the exit. "Let them bitch. We collect debts tonight. Move out in twelve."

As they dispersed, Big Papa lingered by my side, voice dropping below human hearing range: "She's alive, Alpha. You know that." Not a question-a statement woven with faith deeper than marrow.

*I do* I thought, watching dawn bleed gold over mist-choked treetops ahead. Because Juliet wasn't just mine now, she was pack. And Hastings had no idea what hell looked like when you stole from wolves.

# CHAPTER 27

## HARRISON

I found her perched on the edge of the bed like a wounded bird, wrapped in a towel. "JULIET." My voice cracked through the room like a whip as I loomed over her trembling form. She'd deliberately ignored my instructions, left her hair dripping wet after her shower, no makeup staining that blank canvas of a face. Her defiance tasted bitter on my tongue, but oh, how I'd savor crushing it.

"I gave you instructions for when you exited the shower."

When she muttered, "I didn't want to follow them," with that infuriating spark in her eyes, I moved faster than humanly possible. My fingers dug into the swollen flesh around the mangled claiming bite as I pinned her against the wall, relishing her gasp of pain. The towel fell away easily beneath my claws, exposing raw skin.

My violent temper, I knew, was what she feared most, and her pathetic defiance only intensified my resolve. "First rule," I snarled against her ear as my claws pricked blood from her throat. "When I enter a room, you beg to serve me. And you will address me as your lord, because I truly fucking am your lord now." Her rabbit-quick pulse hammered against my palm where *my* mate mark now thrummed with her confused feelings for me. Where it once beat for another, now it beats only for me. "Say it."

Her breath hitched, that delicious hesitation before submission, then came out in a whimper: "H-how may I serve you...my lord?"

She cowered as I barked commands. I told her to fix her rat's nest of hair, to dry it properly this time, to put on the expensive makeup I'd been so gracious to provide. My words hit her like blows, and I loved how she flinched at each one. The little whore wasn't nearly as strong as she pretended to be, and I was going to enjoy breaking her again.

"Now, get your fucking naked ass in that bathroom," I growled, watching her wilt as the command thundered through the room. My alpha growl bent her more with each word.

I dropped her to the floor with a harsh "MOVE." The starkness of the room only amplified her shame, leaving her raw and vulnerable as I kept my gaze fixed on her. The air crackled with her discomfort, which only fueled my triumph. She shuffled across the space with the fragility of a bird, her body wrapped in defeat as she followed my orders.

I was walking a tightrope. My research was paramount. The serum had been circulating through my veins for over a week. So far, so good. Dr. Chen had been monitoring my vitals very closely. Hovering like a mother hen, actually. I knew she was in love with me. I've had to tread carefully in bringing in Juliet. Lila Chen is the last woman on Earth I want in my bed now. She's no longer necessary to fill those needs. My transformation had been the perfect excuse to end that part of our relationship. But my sadistic side loved the idea of flaunting all the dirty things Chen would be forced to track in the name of science. We have to know exactly every physiological change I will experience as a newly created alpha taking on an omega. And the idea of Juliet being humiliated by being watched while I take her added to my sadistic delight.

The clash of the door behind her echoed my anger, and I quickly summoned Jenna to wheel in a cart loaded with the brunch I'd had guards pick up on their food run. Fluffy eggs, bacon, creamy soup, fresh bread, and jam—luxuries I knew she wouldn't appreciate, but they made her pathetic attempts to resist all the more entertaining.

With the tray in front of me, I was in complete control of her entire fucking world.

She emerged from the bathroom, trembling and exposed, and the pleasure I took in her fragile state was immeasurable.

"May I dress, my lord?" she asked, and the pathetic quality in her voice almost made me fucking hard.

I nodded at the tiny satin dress on the bed. She clearly didn't want to wear the revealing garment I'd chosen for her. "Put. It. On. Juliet," I said, my tone dripping with icy disdain. Her weakness was intoxicating, a sweet nectar that fueled my dominance. "If you know what's good for you."

"There are no panties." Her voice was small.

"That's by design. Your cunt is to be available to me at all times."

The way her head jerked up to meet my eyes gave me such satisfaction. Watching her struggle to follow my instructions was almost too delicious to bear. She had the garment on, such as it was, in record time and stood trembling as she faced me, wanting to speak but unable to find the courage. Her breasts were almost entirely exposed in the low-cut garment.

"Now what?" I asked, sneering as she recoiled from the steel in my voice.

"Thank you for breakfast," she whispered.

I watched her closely, letting the silence grow between us, letting her hope grow too.

"That's all?" I asked, feigning disappointment.

The change in her was instantaneous.

"What else do you want from me?" Her indignation was delightful. In just a few weeks away from me, she'd discovered a backbone. I'd be removing that with haste.

I stood and gripped her throat once again, lifting her until she stood on the tips of her toes. Allowing my claws to grow until she felt them prick her skin, I growled, my breath in her face. "I demand your respect, Juliet. I am your Alpha. You seem to keep forgetting. You said, 'Thank you for breakfast.' I asked if that was all. You forgot how to address me. It's all I was asking. And yet, you came at me with hostility. Now, use that beautiful brain of yours, Juliet. What was I looking for?"

She looked at me with those deep brown eyes and breathed, "My lord."

I retracted my claws and rubbed my thumb across my claiming mark that had healed over. She shivered at my touch. Then I brushed my lips across hers and couldn't hide the smile when she leaned toward me when I pulled back.

She watched my every move as I took a seat. I motioned to the floor in front of me.

The full weight of my authority crashed down on her. "On your knees, Juliet. Dogs don't sit in chairs." She hit her knees.

She shook as I began to eat, and I relished the shudder that rolled through her body. Every bite I took reminded her of who she was, of her place, and I let her feel it. The way she couldn't meet my eyes told me everything I needed to know. The longer we sat in silence the meekness I had hoped to see seemed to fade. Her mind was running away with her. I could feel through the bond a feeling of chaos and anger. I needed to take her down a few notches before she got out of hand.

"Juliet. I have much in store for you. Our relationship is not be what it was before." Her glare told me she hated the idea of anything I wanted from her. I cut a piece of breakfast sausage and lowered it to her mouth. She just looked at me. "I told you I expected you to eat. You will need your strength for what I have in mind for you." She opened and took the morsel from me. I smirked as she chewed. I continued in this manner for several bites, instructing her on how her life would be from now on.

I took a spoonful of soup and offered to her. She lifted her hand to push it away, causing it to splatter on my shoe. I calmly put the spoon back on the table, then made eye contact with her. My temper had risen like a rocket. "Lick that off of my shoe, Juliet."

Her mouth was in a straight line as she defiantly shook her head.

I reached out and grabbed a handful of her hair right at the root and yanked her head down to my feet. As she yelped, I repeated my instruction with an additional clarification. "Put your hands behind your back and Lick. My. Shoe. Fucking. Clean, Juliet. NOW." She gave a small cry, but her pretty little pink tongue slipped out and licked the drops of soup clean from my leather shoe. When she was done, she sat up on her knees with her hands in her lap and looked into my eyes. The satin dress I'd had her wear had shifted down until her breasts were almost fully on display. Her dusky nipples were taut. I swear I wanted to sink my teeth into them. And I would. But she was waiting for instruction.

"Good little slut." Don't ever hesitate when I tell you to do something, and you won't give me cause to harm you. Do you understand?

"Yes, my lord."

"Lovely, but your initiation into your new life here, Juliet, has just begun. First things first, and all that. You need to know that you have become a part of my company's most exciting medical breakthrough. The serum we're developing will change human history. Clearly, I've taken a dose. We will certainly modify it for everyday use, but I wanted to achieve this particular result so I could be what my wife needed. To be Alpha to my mate. As such, we will need to continue the research, which requires further monitoring." I walked over to the entry door wall and pulled back the curtain that ran its length to reveal the thick plexiglass that divided the observation room from her cell. Dr. Chen, Kiran Markeson, and Dane all stood watching us. Her gasp was audible as she jumped up and tried to cover herself. "Don't bother my little fuck toy. Every inch of you will be on display for my team. Hell, it already has been." I laughed as I guided the curtain closed. "Your tears are making me hard, by the way."

I strolled over to her and yanked her hands down. "We're not done here my darling. There's the matter of your breaking our engagement. Did you think I would not punish you for that?" I growled into her face, my voice low and dripping with venom. Her wide, doe-like eyes flickered with a mix of fear and defiance, but she didn't speak. She knew better than to answer back. Her reckoning was at hand.

Her eyes followed me as I walked to the handle of a re-tractable wall on the opposite side of the room. It folded in on itself as I pulled, revealing a control panel. With the push of a but-ton, another panel opened and a custom metal St. Andrew's cross thrust into the room on smooth hydraulic rollers. Juliet backed away. "There is nowhere for you to hide from the punishment you are due." I calmly told her.

I grabbed her by the wrist, my fingers digging into her delicate skin, and yanked her toward the cross. Her bare feet stumbled over the tile as I dragged her along, her breathing ragged, her heart pounding so loud I could hear it. The scent of her fear was intoxicating, a heady mix of sweat and the faint, sweet undertone of her arousal. She hated me, but her body betrayed her. The claiming bite assured it.

"You thought you could just run from me?" I snarled, shoving her. I took a claw and shredded the dress she was wearing. Her breath was coming in short pants. I picked her up and placed her on the raised platform of the cross, my hand around her throat yet again. "You thought you could leave me at the altar and disappear into the fucking wind? Do you have any idea what you cost me? How that made me look to my father?"

She opened her mouth to speak, but my hands gripped her face before she could make a sound, forcing her to look at me. Her lips trembled, and for a moment, I thought she might cry. But she didn't. Instead, she glared at me, her amber-flecked espresso eyes burning with a fire that only made me want to break her more.

"You're mine now, Juliet. My fuck toy to use any way I want." I hissed, leaning in so close our noses almost touched. "You may have escaped me once, but you never will again. And right now, you're going to learn what happens when you disobey your Alpha."

Her eyes widened, and I saw the flicker of understanding—and terror—in them. She knew what I was capable of. She'd felt it before. But this time, it was different. This time, I wasn't just going to hurt her. I was going to destroy her.

I turned her to where she faced the cross, then bound her wrists and ankles. She was spread open for me.

I growled, my mouth against her ear. "I'm going to fuck you, to hurt you, to make you scream. And you're going to thank me for it."

She said nothing. Good. She was learning.

I walked back to the wall that held the cross. A variety of implements hung there. I let my fingers fall across supple leather floggers, whips, and riding crops. Having made my choice, I slowly walked back to where she was bound.

Her back was to me, stretched taut against the cold, unyielding metal of the X. Her wrists and ankles were bound with thick leather cuffs; her body arched in a perfect display of submission. The soft, pale skin of her back gleamed under the dim light of her room, and I could see the faintest tremble running through her—fear, or perhaps anticipation. It didn't matter. She was mine now, and she would learn what it meant to belong to me.

I ran the tip of the whip along the curve of her spine, feeling her flinch as the leather kissed her skin. "You thought you could run from me, Juliet? You thought you could leave me at the altar, humiliate me, and just walk away?" My voice began to rise.

Her breath hitched, anticipating the blow. I let the whip fall with a sharp *crack*; the sound echoing through the room as her body jerked against the restraints. A red welt bloomed across her shoulder blades, and she gasped, her nails digging into her palms.

"Speak," I growled, my voice low and commanding. "Tell me why you're here."

"Because you're my Alpha," she whispered, her voice trembling but obedient. The words sent a thrill of satisfaction through me. She was damaged, but not shattered. Not yet.

"*Louder*," I demanded, circling her like a predator stalking its prey. My hand trailed down her side, feeling the way her muscles tensed under my touch. She was so responsive, so gloriously reactive. It was intoxicating.

"Because you're my Alpha," she repeated, louder this time, though her voice still wavered.

I brought the whip down again, this time across the small of her back. She cried out, her body arching as if trying to escape the pain, but there was no escape. Not from me. "*Again.*"

"Because you're my Alpha!" she shouted, her voice breaking on the last word. I could see the tears streaming down her face, but I didn't care. Tears were good. They meant she was learning.

"Good slut," I purred.

"Now, tell me why I am punishing you, my little disgusting tramp?" I asked her as I brought the whip down one final time across both of her ass cheeks, leaving a raised welt that was sure to burn.

"Because I caused you trouble when I ran away!" She screamed. Breaking down in sobs as tears poured from her eyes.

I took the handle of the whip and ran it through the folds of her sopping wet pussy. Her body jerked against it as I dragged it back and forth. "Look at this." I held the handle up to her face. "Dripping with your arousal. What a delightful little whore you've turned out to be, Juliet." Tossing the whip aside. I stepped closer, my chest pressing against her back as I leaned down to whisper in her ear. "Now, let me show you what happens to naughty little fuck toys who think they can defy their Alpha."

I reached around to cup her breast, squeezing hard enough to make her whimper. Her nipple pebbled under my touch, and I pinched it sharply, reveling in the way her body writhed against mine. "You feel that? That's your body betraying you yet again, Juliet. It knows who its master is, even if you don't."

She moaned, a sound that was equal parts pain and pleasure, and I felt my cock harden in response. Fuck, she was perfect. I released her breast and trailed my hand down her stomach, feeling the muscles quiver under my touch. I slipped my fingers between her legs, groaning at how wet she was.

"Listen to that," I sneered, rubbing circles over her clit. "So fucking wet for me." I pinched her clit. "You *are* a slut, Juliet. My dirty slut."

Her hips bucked against my hand, and I slapped her ass hard, leaving a red handprint on top of the welt from the whip. "Stay still," I commanded, and she froze, though I could see the effort it took for her to obey.

I pushed two fingers inside her, curling them just right to make her cry out. Her cunt was tight and wet, clenching around my fingers as I fucked her with them. I leaned in closer, my breath hot against her ear. "You're going to take my cock now, Juliet. And remember to thank me for it."

She whimpered, but I didn't give her a chance to respond. I unbuckled my belt and freed my cock, already hard and throbbing with need. I positioned myself at her entrance and pushed in slowly, savoring the way her body resisted before giving way to me.

"Fuck," I groaned as her tight pussy enveloped me. I grabbed her hips and began to thrust, each movement deliberate and punishing. Her cries filled the room, a symphony of pain and pleasure that drove me wild.

"Say it," I demanded, slamming into her harder. "Say you're mine."

"I'm yours," she sobbed, her body trembling with the force of my thrusts.

"Again."

"I'm yours!"

I continued to fuck her with brutal precision, my hands leaving bruises on her hips as I claimed her completely. Her moans grew louder, more desperate, and I knew she was close.

"Come for me, Juliet," I growled, reaching around to rub her clit. "Come for your Alpha."

Her body stiffened, and she let out a strangled cry as she came, her cunt clenching around me like a vice. I didn't stop fucking her through her orgasm until I felt my own release building.

With a roar, I buried myself deep inside her and came, filling her with my release. I stayed there for a moment, my forehead resting against her back as I caught my breath. Then I pulled out and stepped back, admiring the sight of her trembling form still bound to the cross, my cum trailing down her legs. I wiped myself off and pulled my pants up. Then I released her feet and wrists and caught her as she sagged. I carried her over to her bed and sat her down, and walked away.

"Clean yourself up," I ordered, tossing a towel at her feet. "And remember *this*, Juliet. You belong to me now. Forever. Oh, and thank your Alpha."

She nodded weakly, her body still shaking as she tried to recover from what I'd done to her. Quietly, the words came out of her mouth. "Thank you, Alpha."

I sent the cross back into the wall and shut and locked the door. A crew would perform equipment sanitization from the other side of the wall. Then I turned and walked away, leaving her alone in her cell to think about her place in my world.

But as I closed the door behind me, I couldn't help but smile. She was mine now, body and soul. And I was going to enjoy every moment of breaking her completely.

# Chapter 28

## Juliet

It had been several days that I'd been here, and I was no closer to finding my wolf. The shower had become a sanctuary and a torment, droplets striking like hot needles over the angry red marks left by Harrison's torture. I winced, each stinging touch blurring the lines between pain and a confusing, shameful arousal. My hands had trembled as I traced the welts, caught in a whirlwind of hatred for him and desperate longing for Bronc. Pressing my forehead to the cool, unforgiving tiles, I had let my tears merge with the water, a silent acknowledgment of how utterly overwhelmed and trapped I felt. The mate bite on my neck had throbbed with a dull ache, echoing the inner turmoil that left me shaking on the floor, sobbing and clutching my knees in a storm of emotions I couldn't escape.

The initial sting of leather on flesh, Harrison's face hovering above mine with a sick pleasure, had ignited an immediate outrage—a defiant heat that pulsed within me as I'd reeled from the shock of his attack. I'd fought him, not only with the flailing of my body, but with the burning anger in my eyes. And then, damn him, he had me right where he wanted—bound to him, in more ways than one, the throb of his claim binding me tighter than any rope. The physical pain lingered, refusing to fade, and worse than that, the maddening thrill that simmered beneath my anger had left me feeling guilty and torn apart. My mind swung wildly between the violation and the twisted desire he forced upon me, his power infuriating yet confoundingly, revoltingly compelling.

I'd touched each welt as if the motion could absolve me, my fingers trembling over the skin where the bruises met and overlapped, a vivid map of my confusion and shame. How much longer could I take it? His cruelty had burrowed under my skin, into my soul. And still, against my will, some awful piece of me longed for the danger he embodied. Was it the mark he left on my neck that kept me shackled to this impossible need? The bond? Or something more damaged and desperate within me? Something that reached out for connection no matter how it was given? I longed for release from the suffocating web that he spun, one that left me breathless and sobbing, yet craving and clinging.

What made it worse was how fiercely I had loved Bronc before any of this happened. I'd shown up in Dairyville, looking for nothing but space, and found so much more. He'd been like the clearest Texas sky, wide and limitless and full of possibilities I'd never imagined. The heat of our connection, wild and raw and right, had flared the moment we touched, a wildfire of mutual want that blazed hotter than anything I'd known. It was more than attraction. More than lust. It had been an anchor for a heart like mine, one that never knew where it belonged. When he offered his home, his pack, his bed, I thought the struggle was over.

But here I was. On a shower floor that wasn't mine, in a life that I didn't want. The walls of my cell closed in around me, each passing day growing tighter and more inescapable. When I left the compound, I truly thought I was doing the right thing. I'd free my mother and lead Bronc to Harrison. It seemed so easy. But I should have trusted him and his team to do the job. Why did I think I could do what they couldn't? I always had only myself. But I knew better this time. I'm sorry, Bronc. So fucking sorry.

The reminder of my new mate bite pulsed relentlessly, a maddening echo that tied me to Harrison, even now. It forced my desire, like chains on my spirit. Was it the bond drawing out some darker part of me that I never knew was there? Would my relationship with Bronc ever have awakened that part of me too, or would he always have seen me as too young or too fragile? I sure hoped we'd get the chance to find out. His arms were the ones I longed for. His eyes were the ones I wanted to look into.

In the searing hot water and steam, Bronc's words echoed back from before I left. "Little Wolf, we'll find your mom. Please give us more time. Get some sleep my love. Be sure and eat enough." He loved me. Maybe this was what I deserved. I couldn't even look at myself in the mirror to see the mess that I'd become, to acknowledge the turmoil written across my features. The chaos that was Juliet, broken and desperate. Bound and brutalized. Falling apart.

In spite of it all, I clung to the hope of release, the hope of rescue, the hope of Bronc. I rocked and cried and hated myself. But at that moment, on the shower floor with water washing me away, it was the only thing I could do.

I stayed there on the shower floor, hugging my knees, my body racked with sobs that I could no longer hold back. Bronc's face wavered in my memory, a cruel reminder of everything I'd lost, and of the strong arms I ached for as the hot water mingled with my tears. The memory had brought a bitter smile to my lips, and I let out a shuddering breath as a fresh wave of grief crashed over me. The mate bite tied me to Harrison. It ensured my compliance. It left me helpless, filled with a maddening guilt for the desire that kept my spirit in chains. I looked up at the ceiling, whispering a desperate prayer for a way out.

How was I ever going to escape him? The shame of wanting someone who hurt me, even when my body and mind screamed to run, knotted like a heavy chain around my neck. I couldn't fight this. Couldn't fight him. Even if Bronc tried to save me, would it matter? Was the bond Harrison forced upon me unbreakable? The questions ripped through me, tearing my soul into shreds as I sat there, the steam curling around like a thick fog, and the spray now turning lukewarm. There was no easy way out, no simple solution to this mess. It wasn't only a physical prison, but an emotional one that held me tighter than any bindings ever could.

I wanted to believe in rescue, to believe that Bronc wouldn't let this stand, but how much longer could I endure? My own thoughts circled like vultures, consuming what little hope remained. Even if I wanted Bronc more than my next breath, did he still want me after I messed things up by trying to rescue my mom on my own? Would he understand why I had to go?

"Please," I whispered to the water, to the walls, to whatever higher power might listen. "Please get me out of this." My words were lost in the steam, a final plea from a spirit stretched so thin it felt like it would snap. A silent cry as I looked up to the ceiling, the spray hitting me in uneven bursts, cooling along with my hope.

That's when the bathroom door crashed open, and the specter of my tormentor filled the space. Harrison, unyielding as the bond itself, stared at me with eyes that reflected nothing but a cruel satisfaction. The moment stretched, filled with a tension so thick I thought it might strangle me.

"Get up," he said, a command wrapped in velvet and steel. The harshest whisper.

The sound of his voice sliced through me, cutting deeper than any lash, any blow. I scrambled to my feet, unsteady, trembling, wrapping a towel around myself as the final shreds of warmth slipped away. His eyes never left mine, pinning me in place, making it clear that escape was futile. That I was bound to him in every sense, and that resistance was nothing but a fantasy.

"Follow me," he ordered, turning with the confidence of someone who knew they wouldn't be refused.

I went. Dragged one foot in front of the other, my soul screaming against it, my body obeying the cruel reality that Harrison had locked me into. The walls closed in around us as I followed him, as the fear wrapped tighter and tighter until I could barely breathe. What did he have planned this time? How far would he go to break me? Did he even know, did he even care, that the further he pushed, the more desperately I longed for release from him? For release from everything? That this was as much torture as anything he could inflict?

Even as terror settled like lead in my stomach, I realized with growing dread where he was taking me. To the wall. The wall in my cell that held every implement of torment imaginable. Items rolled out on hydraulic arms, benches folded out of nowhere that held me down as he administered his brand of punishment and humiliation. It happened sometimes once a day, sometimes more often. The most frightening part? I found myself giving in to all of them. Hating and loving them in equal measure. If Bronc ever found me, he would surely cast me aside. I was broken. Unloveable. Could I survive it? Would I be Juliet at the end of this nightmare, or just another possession of Harrison Hastings?

The answer, the only answer, was to endure. To last. To hold on to the slimmest hope that Bronc was coming, even if it was foolish. Even if it was a lie, I told myself to stay sane. To stay alive. I clung to that lie with all I had, my knuckles white around the edges of the towel. No matter what, I wouldn't let this break me.

Not yet. Not ever.

Harrison led me to the wall, a space designed for cruelty and submission, and I was drowning in the metallic scent of leather and the terrifying sight of the equipment it contained. My heart raced wildly, the sight filling me with a sense of dread that matched his gleeful eyes as he announced he had something special planned. His sadistic delight sent my fear crashing like tidal waves over my trembling body. What was he going to do? Would I survive it? As he approached with predator-like grace, my hope dwindled to a fragile thread. He touched the mate bite on my neck and whispered with breath hot in my ear, "You're mine, Juliet. And I'm going to make sure you never forget it."

The dim light threw shadows across the room, and the chains and straps and darkly gleaming tools loomed over me, each one whispering of the torment they were made to inflict. I was trapped. Caught in this twisted den with no way out, each tool moved in closer as my heartbeat thundered in my ears. Harrison reveled in it, the predator who'd caught his prey, and there was nowhere to hide from the reality that he could do anything. That I was helpless. That every shred of safety I'd ever known was lost the moment he closed the door behind us.

He approached slowly, drinking in my terror like fine wine. It filled him. Made him bolder. My mind raced with all the terrible things he might do, all the pain and the darkness waiting. Panic bubbled up, a visceral thing clawing at my insides as his predatory grace closed the distance. What would be left of me after tonight? How could I possibly endure? He'd set the stage perfectly, and as the realization of it all crashed down on me, I felt myself begin to unravel.

He walked over and pulled the curtain back so his "observers" had a full view of what he was doing. It only added to my shame. I locked eyes with the dark-haired doctor. I saw something flicker there. Jealousy?

The air seemed to grow thicker with the scent of leather, and something darker, something primal that made my skin prickle and my breath hitch. Harrison's hand clamped around my wrist like a vise, dragging me toward the wall where his tools of torment hung like twisted trophies. My heart hammered in my chest, a wild, erratic rhythm that matched the storm raging outside. But it wasn't fear that made my pulse race—it was something far more fucked up. Something I didn't want to admit.

"Oh no," I whispered, my voice trembling as he pressed a button on the control panel. A long metal rod stretched out over my head. Two chains with leather cuffs on the ends were attached to eyebolts. He reached up and knocked them loose. The loud *clang* made me jump. Calmly, he attached a cuff to each of my wrists. He pressed another button, and a metal platform slid from the bottom of the wall with two eyebolts attached to similar chains and cuffs. He tapped my ankles, so I stepped up. Within seconds, my legs were spread and cuffed to the platform that was flush with the floor. I then heard the sound of the wall's hydraulics as my arms were lifted above my head. I stood completely stretched and exposed to him, front and back sides.

His claws were extended as he ran them around my middle, walking a complete circle around me. "We're going to play extra hard tonight, Juliet," he growled, his voice low and dangerous, sending a shiver down my spine. "I'm going to hurt you tonight. And we're going to talk."

He grabbed a flexible cane from the wall, the polished wood gleaming in the dim light, and I swallowed hard, my breath coming in shallow gulps. The first strike landed with a sharp crack against my ass, and I cried out, my body jerking forward. The sting was instant, sharp and searing, followed by a rush of heat that spread through my veins like wildfire. My pussy clenched, wetness soaking my thighs as another strike came down, harder this time, leaving a red welt in its wake.

"That's it," he snarled, his voice dripping with malice and something else—something that made my knees weak. "Take it like the little whore you are."

I moaned, the sound torn from my throat as he brought the cane down again and again, each strike a mix of agony and ecstasy. My ass was on fire, the pain a living, breathing thing that pulsed through me with every heartbeat. He stopped and ran a finger through my wetness, and I cried out.

"I had no idea you were such a pain slut, Juliet. I've learned so many things about you." He crouched down and slid his tongue across my clit, causing me to jerk against my chains. "You'd like more of that wouldn't you?" He stood, his breath across my lips. His fingers rammed inside me while his thumb circled, bringing me closer to release.

"Please," I sobbed, tears streaming down my face as he abruptly pulled his fingers away.

A cruel smile split his monstrously handsome face. "I'm afraid you can't come yet, Juliet. You see, I need some information from you first."

I tried to still myself in the chains that bound me. "What do you want to know?" I asked.

I realized my mistake too late. In a flash, he had the cane in his hands.

The back of my thighs exploded in a flash of pain. Then he slapped my clit hard and painfully. "How are you to address me, Juliet? That's five swats. I'll give you ten next time."

I was sobbing. "M-m-my lord! I'm sorry!"

He started rubbing my clit again. I was right to the point of orgasm, moaning, crying. And he stopped.

"Alright, now. I have a few questions my little cum slut."

I could barely hold my head up to look at him. "Yes, my lord?"

"Better." He gave an evil grin. "I need to know the name of your former Alpha. His name, and where he lives."

Oh no, no. I was paralyzed with dread. "Please no, my lord." Oh god. He is furious.

He picked up the cane again. He hit up and down my back between every word. "JULIET. *crack!* TELL. *crack!* YOUR. *crack!* ALPHA. *crack!* THE. *crack!* NAME. *crack!* OF. *crack!* YOUR. *crack!* FORMER. *crack!* MATE."

I screamed in agony. I didn't want to say it. I tried not to tell him, but I hurt so much. His fingers rammed inside my pussy. His tongue ran across his mate mark.

I wailed, "Bronc Baucaum! Iron Valor MC! I HATE YOU!"

Harrison laughed again, the sound dark and triumphant. "Good little slut," he purred, dropping the cane and stepping closer. I could feel the heat of his body as he pressed against me, his erection pressing into my hip through the fabric of his pants. "Now let's see if you can take what comes next."

Before I could even think to protest, he was unbuckling his belt, the sound of leather sliding through the loops sending a fresh wave of heat straight to my core. He shoved his pants down just enough to free his cock—thick and hard and fucking massive—and I couldn't tear my eyes away.

He gripped himself with one hand, stroking slowly as he watched me squirm, his other hand gripping my hip tightly his claws extended, causing droplets of blood to form. "You're going to take every fucking inch of me," he growled, his voice rough with need. "And you're going to like it."

And then he was pushing inside me, stretching me open in one brutal thrust that had me screaming, my body arching against the restraints as he filled me completely. He was everywhere—his hands gripping my hips, his cock pounding into me with a punishing rhythm that left no room for gentleness or mercy.

I could feel every ridge, every vein as he fucked me, his hips slamming into mine with a force that drove me closer and closer to the edge. My pussy was soaked, clenching around him with every thrust, and I could feel the pressure building deep inside me, coiling tighter and tighter until I was sure I'd shatter.

"That's it, Juliet. There is only me," he growled, his hands moving to grip my ass as he angled himself deeper, hitting that sweet spot inside me that made me see stars. "Come for me, Juliet. Let me feel that tight little cunt grab my cock."

And I did. My orgasm hit me like a freight train, tearing through me with a force that left me gasping and shaking, my pussy clamping down on him as wave after wave of pleasure crashed over me. But Harrison didn't stop. He fucked me through it, his pace never faltering as he chased his own release.

When he finally came, it was with a guttural groan that sent shivers down my spine, his cum flooding my pussy as he thrust into me one last time. He stayed like that for a moment, buried deep inside me, before pulling out with a slick sound that made my cheeks burn.

He stepped back, tucking himself back into his pants as he regarded me with a smirk. "That wasn't so difficult now, was it?" he asked, his face held a smirk. "Just a few loose ends that need tidying up."

And as I hung there, every inch of my body in pain, I felt the sting of my betrayal more than the sting of the cane. I wanted to die.

# CHAPTER 29

## BRONC

Wrecker waved his arms frantically, trying to get my attention as I paced the Panama coastline. Once I saw the giant of a man who looked like he was trying to get airborne, I turned and trotted toward our makeshift command center.

"I'm here, brother. What's happening?"

The look on his face told me this was it. "Alpha, I believe we've finally gotten the break we've been waiting for. I just got off the phone with T-bone. He got a call from a woman looking for a Bronc Baucaum of Iron Valor MC. Said she had important information for him. Gave you 10 minutes to return the call. That was seven minutes ago." He thrust a piece of paper into my face. "Here's the number. Dial fast."

I dialed the number and hit 'speaker.' Sweat dripped down the bridge of my nose as my team and I crowded around the old table, waiting for our contact to answer.

"Bronc Baucaum?"

"I am."

Our informant was a doctor on the Harrison Pharma serum project who apparently had an attack of conscience. Her anxiety bled through every word as she delivered her message. I stood with my arms crossed, chin dipped in silent calculation as she told us what we'd suspected: the pharmaceutical lab was in Costa

Rica. A noisy, static-filled cell phone punctuated the dull murmur of the traffic outside of her location. Her nervous tone sharpened with conviction. It seemed clear she wanted these experiments stopped and wanted Juliet rescued. She stopped speaking after giving location details.

I cleared my throat. "Of course, I know this could be a trap you're setting for us. I can only go on faith that it's not. And in that spirit of faith, I'm asking, what defenses are we going to face when we arrive? How fortified is the location?"

"Dr. Hastings has grown complacent and overconfident." She spoke with the slightest tone of disdain. I got the feeling she had some sort of underlying beef with Hastings. "There are guards, of course. But only ten work on a rotating basis. Since the lab is underground, only three men guard the perimeter at the entrance." She went on to describe the interior hallways and holding cell locations.

There was one other woman, a shifter, besides Juliet being held at the facility. I asked her about the other shifters who were missing. She confirmed they had been used in experiments but had expired when those experiments failed. Her clinical attitude when discussing our brothers increased my fury. It was only Ryder's steady hand on my shoulder that kept me calm enough to stay civil with the monster on the other end of the phone.

She continued, "Any sensitive area is locked with key-coded locks." An email came through with a map of the facility that included the codes to the door locks. I couldn't help but be suspicious of this woman, but this was our best hope of getting Juliet back.

"Where is Renda Bettencourt?" I asked when she wasn't listed among those being held at the facility.

"Harrison pushed his experiments beyond her physical capacity. She did not survive." She replied, her voice carrying the first sign of her humanity.

My blood was boiling. Juliet put herself in unimaginable danger for nothing. We all felt the futility of her rescue attempt that had set this entire clusterfuck in motion.

"Tell me again why I should trust you." I asked her.

There was a long pause before she spoke again. "Harrison Hastings used to be a man I respected. I thought this serum could be a true miracle drug for humanity. Since he used it on himself, he's turned into a veritable monster. His body has transformed. He can change it to beastly proportions at will. Fangs, claws. I fear for your mate, Mr. Baucaum."

I felt my own fangs itch to break through my gums. My muscles tensed. Doc's hand on my shoulder calmed me only a little.

"Is there anything else we need to know?"

"There is another man who may soon be able to transform, like Harrison, at the location. A man who may have injected the serum I mean. He is Harrison's right-hand man. His name is Dane Garrison."

Danc Garrison.

The name burned, familiar and bitter, lighting up every memory of that snake. We all looked around at each other. I muted the phone. "That son of a bitch." It was Arsenal who spoke. "He'll finally get what he deserves."

Garrison was a member of his unit on his last deployment. His dishonorable was better than he should have gotten. Looked like he'd be on the receiving end of justice finally.

She continued. "The shifter woman is going to be on the receiving end of whatever Dane has in store if you don't act quickly."

"Roger that. We'll be on the move as soon as this call ends."

"Good luck, Mr. Baucaum. I won't be able to do much when you make entry. He'll kill me if he knows I'm the one who tipped you off. My name is Lila Chen." With that, she hung up.

Menace was up and moving. "This is it, Bronc. I have no fucking doubt." I let the words sink in and turned them over in my head, jaw set. The sharp certainty of them filled the air around us, alive in a way I hadn't expected. The sounds of rustling maps and gear came from my men, and I glanced up, ready to move.

"Lab was more hidden than I thought. Did *not* expect it to be below ground." His voice turned desperate as he tapped a finger on the table, almost manic with relief. "But we've got what we need now. We're gonna go get our Luna back."

My mouth was a hard line as I scanned the hand-drawn map, taking in every mark with the speed and precision of an ex-special forces operative. "Let's do this." I finally spoke, not wasting breath on the way my words lifted his panic into hope. My eyes went to Doc first, then moved across the others, letting each of them see the plan form as clearly as I did.

The room was dimly lit, a single bulb flickering above us, barely penetrating the humid air. We were sweating, not just from the stifling heat, but from the weight of what Chen had just handed over. The air felt like a living thing, coiling around us, alive with tension and possibility.

My mind churned over every detail. Our contact was no fucking fool. She'd confirmed it. Big Pharma was experimenting in Costa Rica. Harrison, the bastard, had thought it would be safe enough to do the unthinkable there. He couldn't fathom that anyone would betray him. I'd bet there was more to that story, but I didn't give one fuck.

His biggest mistake was taking his eyes off of his biggest endgame. Money. He let his dick get in the way. And I'd make sure he'd never use it again.

The weight of the words settled into the air, echoing against the bare walls, and my jaw clenched around the urgency of them. The distant traffic outside was a muffled throb against the stillness that followed, an odd counterpoint to the storm inside my head. I let the moment hang for a beat longer before the first scrape of a chair signaled our move.

"Doc." I nodded to him. He was already tucking a folded map into his jacket. J.T. was next, and I didn't miss the way his eyes found mine with an edge of dark determination. He understood. He always had. The risks, the stakes. How fucking far I was willing to go when my family was on the line.

The thought of family made my wolf stir, restless, and I pushed it back, concentrating on each decisive movement as the team packed up around me.

As I stepped out into the early evening air, the thick warmth hit me like a fist, a sharp reminder of the urgency now pushing us forward. I breathed it in, long and deep, feeling the tension wind tighter inside of me, and moved to where the others waited, my eyes scanning the street, my mind on fire.

Rain threatened the sky in muted bursts of electricity as we crossed to the next block, rounding a corner and heading toward the gritty shadows of a parking lot where a lone van stood. The space around us felt too open, exposed. I could sense the crackle of alertness in my men as we jogged the last stretch.

I swung the door open, motioning the others in with a quick jerk of my head. "Menace, Doc, Papa, Arsenal, J.T., Wrecker—let's go get our girl."

The interior of the van was stacked with bags and equipment. Our stateside cover a handy front for the mission ahead. Nobody hesitated, years of practice snapping into place as they climbed inside, heads bent over weapons and logistics.

JT, our Big Papa and spiritual leader, the youngest in the group but sharp as hell, slung a pack over one shoulder and gave me a wide-eyed grin. "It's going down, Bronc."

I met his gaze, felt the heat of shared commitment in the look we exchanged. "It's going down."

"Dane's gonna shit himself."

Doc cut in, his tone dry and precise. "Not if we take him out before he has the chance."

I grunted, allowing a small, humorless smile. My voice held the same steel that ran through each of us, binding us to the same end. "We will. Then after we extract Juliet, we're gonna burn that lab out of existence. Every scrap of evidence of shifters is gonna burn with it. Harrison and Dane aren't walking out. Nobody's walking out. Not even Dr. Chen. She may have helped us here. But she participated in the cruel torture all those abducted shifters went through. She's got knowledge of us. She's gotta pay for that."

The others didn't need more than that, a single-minded drive unifying our actions as they worked through the last of the supplies. I kept my focus on their efficiency, every fiber of my being tuned to the quick exchanges and sharp rustle of gear, but it didn't stop my thoughts from drifting to her.

Juliet.

Two fucking weeks. Two weeks in the hands of a monster who'd already proved he had no problem hurting her. Who'd use her to gain what he wanted. The absence of her scent, her warmth, the missing tether that linked us together, was a constant, pounding ache. At least now I had proof of life.

My wolf growled, a low, dangerous rumbling in my chest. The man I was, calculated risks and weighed possibilities, and this one had pushed me to a new edge.

"Watch the roads outside of San José. Word is they monitor traffic pretty closely." Menace's voice pulled me back to the van, his even gaze reminding me how close we were to taking Harrison down. We'd get the bastard. Get her back. Destroy that lab.

"We'll be in and out before they know what hit them." I slammed the van door, moving quickly around to the driver's side. Streets of Panama flickered by in the rearview mirror as we took off, their glistening shapes an echo of my thoughts. The team's quiet concentration was a pulse around me, an understanding that drove us all. The knowledge that this was the mission of a lifetime was at the forefront of our minds. It was more than just a job. It was family. It was her.

The lab turned out to be not too far inland, in an obscure province, the perfect place to hide an underground lab. We made it there in under three hours. I parked on a darkened, abandoned street. My mind reeled with everything we'd learned, the words growing harder to swallow with each cool drop of rain that hit my skin as we exited the van. I ran a hand over my face and felt the panic surging beneath my calm exterior. Doc's eyes were on me when we finally ducked under cover, a heavy pause before he spoke the fear I was trying not to face. "Bronc—you need to be prepared. Juliet may not be the same. It's been a couple of weeks with a monster. I guarantee she suffered."

His steady voice was a sharp contrast to the crackle of tension in the air, each word pushing my already-strained nerves closer to a breaking point. I met his gaze, felt the chill of his words settle into the space between us like an unwelcome ghost.

He didn't let me dodge it. "We both know what he's capable of."

My eyes drifted skyward. I hadn't even realized it was the night of the full moon. For a moment, I was back in our magical clearing, watching her first magical shift. My wolf was pacing, enraged and restless, barely leashed by the thin veneer of my control. I wanted to hit something hard, but I knew that wasn't what Juliet needed. "She's strong." I said it as much to myself as to Doc, trying to believe it.

"Just be prepared to help her. Don't let what you see shake you."

He didn't have to say more. He was right, and it hit me like the chilly rain that pelted the streets. I took a long breath, willing myself to focus on what had to be done before we could get her back. Before, I could see how she really was.

It felt like forever since we'd lost her trail, since my wolf and I had split into a hundred agonizing pieces, trying to decide which way to go. Seeing her safe had become an obsession, a singular focus that drove us harder than anything ever had. It was dangerous, the way I couldn't think straight when I pictured her in Harrison's hands.

"What if he knows we're coming?" Doc's voice interrupted the whirlwind of my thoughts.

I shook my head, dragging a hand through my damp hair. "It doesn't matter. We're ready."

I wanted it to be true. Wanted to believe that we'd trained for this exact scenario, that the weapons and skills and maps were enough to make sure we'd get in and out, get the job done. But there was no preparing for the way it would feel to find her broken, a shell of the fierce woman she'd been before he took her. I swallowed hard against the ache in my chest.

There was only one way to do this. Straight through.

I glanced at Doc, the clarity of his gaze cutting through my internal storm. "Let's take out a lab."

He nodded, his movements as measured as his words. He'd always been the calm in our chaos, the first one I trusted when everything went to hell.

"Arsenal." My voice was gravel, tight with an urgency I couldn't shake. "You with me?"

He didn't hesitate, an unwavering commitment in the look we shared. "All the way."

The decision was made. I let it fuel me, drive the fear out of my veins and replace it with the fierce determination to get Juliet back, no matter what.

The team met us as we turned back toward the van, their movements crisp and their resolve as unyielding as the concrete jungle surrounding us. Wrecker's eyes were lit with youthful adrenaline, his enthusiasm a reminder of my own reckless days when the stakes weren't quite so fucking personal.

As soon as we were close enough, I called a stop, the van's brakes protesting with a low whine. We spread out, scanning the perimeter, eyes sharp in the darkest night.

A corrugated iron structure marked the entrance, masked by overgrowth and plant life, the faint hum of a generator our first sign of life. Three guards, just as Chen said.

I set up the first recon position with a speed and efficiency that spoke to my desperation to move.

I motioned Doc over, my thoughts already five steps ahead, two beats past control. "I'm not fucking waiting. Let's go in."

He was right there with me, trusting my call, always knowing where I'd lead us next.

The hand signals came sharp and final: *Go.* We swarmed the compound entrance like shadows given teeth. Stealth only lasts until blood hits the air—and it did when Menace slit two throats in one fluid twist of his blade. Bodies dropped into blackberry thickets as Wrecker punched Chen's codes into the door panel. A breathless pause—then green light flared. *So far, so good.*

Inside reeked of antiseptic rot and copper—s*hifter blood.* Two more guards lurked beyond the foyer; their radios hissed static as we split into formation. Papa's silenced pistol thwipped twice—one crumpled mid-sentence. Arsenal snapped another's spine over his knee like kindling before shoving me toward the east wing: *"Go find her."*

Chaos erupted behind me, boots pounding steel floors, gunfire chewing through walls—as I sprinted deeper into hell's maze

Three white coats fled down Lab 6.

"Hostiles!" one screeched into his comms before my knife hilt cracked his temple. Another two scrambled for panic buttons; Wrecker's quick trigger ensured they never reached them—the shots shattered glass tanks full of... things. Twisted specimens floated in brine behind me as I ran.

Dane intercepted me at stairwell B.

Ex-team sniper turned traitor grinned beneath night vision goggles he didn't need anymore—Harrison had gifted him predator eyes that glowed sulfur-yellow now.

"Bronc." He lunged first.

Adrenaline burned through muscle memory: duck his swipe, elbow to ribs, stab upward. He twisted at impossible speed—my blade skated off tactical gear.

"She's already dead," he hissed.

Something primal snarled in my chest.

Gunfire exploded overhead—"Got company!" Menace barked in my earpiece before static drowned him out... then screaming... then metal tearing.

Dane struck again—claws snagged my vest strap just as Arsenal materialized behind him like vengeance incarnate: "Try me instead."

I didn't stay to watch their duel—but heard vertebrae crunch seconds later as I vaulted stairs three at a time.

Menace frantically searched the rooms around me.

I glimpsed him kicking open reinforced steel marked HOLD-ING further down the hall—a girl cowered inside wearing nothing but chains and fresh scars. Another experiment. Her green gaze met mine an instant before Menace snarled, "Cover us!" His bulk shielded her broken frame while smoke grenades choked pursuit.

Juliet was close.

My boots punched through Level 5 security doors into a corridor slick with bullet casings... then silence... then ragged breathing ahead.

The final door hung crooked on its hinges like an open wound.

Harrison stood silhouetted against flickering fluores-cents—talons dug into Juliet's throat as he yanked her flush against him like a trophy.

She was bare except for bruises and his bite mark sullying her shoulder—-still bleeding.

Her sob cracked in half when she saw me: "Bronc—"

Harrison licked her earlobe without breaking eye contact: "Kneel or watch her throat paint this pretty wall."

Wrong move.

Her knee jerked upward—too slow—he wrenched her head sideways hard enough to pop joints, but not before she spat crimson phlegm into his grin.

Roaring filled my skull.

# Chapter 30

## Juliet

Harrison's claws bit into my throat as he dragged me backward, using me as a shield. Blood from his latest bite slicked my chest; hot and accusing, as he snarled at Bronc across the room. "One step closer," he hissed, "and I'll carve her throat like a pig." His teeth grazed my ear, whiskey-sour breath thickening the air. *"Mine."*

Bronc froze in the doorway, muscles coiled like a spring. His eyes met mine—storm-dark rage colliding with my tear-blurred gaze. *Don't,* I wanted to scream. But Harrison's grip tightened, claws drawing fresh blood as he wrenched my head sideways with a sickening pop of tendons. Pain shot through me, white-hot and nauseating. My wolf stirred feebly beneath my ribs, but I felt her even if she was dulled by despair... or maybe shame. It's the first time I'd felt her since Harrison had destroyed Bronc's mate mark.

"Pathetic," Harrison spat at Bronc. "You think she *wanted* you? She begged for my mark." His laugh was jagged glass as he licked a stripe up my bleeding neck. My stomach roiled; my traitorous body shuddered anyway—omega instincts flaring at his touch like a poisoned kiss.

Bronc's snarl shook the walls. "Let. Her. *Go.*"

Harrison shifted me just as Bronc lunged, claws slashing air instead of flesh, as I choked on a scream. They circled like wolves now: Bronc's movements lethal precision; Harrison's brute savagery dragging me with him until my knees buckled under his weight... until I saw it: an opening when his grip slipped on my bloodied skin...

My wolf surged suddenly—a molten eruption in my veins—begging me to twist free...

But it was too late.

Harrison pivoted faster than thought, his claws raking across Bronc's chest with a wet *rip*. Crimson bloomed beneath the torn fabric of his vest; Bronc staggered but didn't fall... *No!* My heart seized as Harrison raised his hand for another strike—aiming straight for Bronc's throat this time.

The world narrowed to fire and fury.

I threw myself sideways with feral desperation, teeth bared even before fur split my skin...

The shift tore through me in seconds—bones snapping like dry twigs.. Claws erupted first; fur followed in a tsunami of vengeance.

Harrison turned too late...

I was already airborne... jaws wide... fangs sinking into his jugular...

He thrashed violently... claws shredding my flank... but I bit down harder.... tasted copper... *crunch.* He gurgled wetly. Then, he collapsed beneath me.... still twitching... still staring hate into my soul... until nothing... I'd all but detached his head from his body.

The silence hit louder than his death rattle.

My wolf vanished like smoke, leaving me human again. Naked. Shaking. Kneeling in a pool of his blood; my blood.

The bond snapped like a severed wire. Agony detonated in my chest. Bile rose as full-body tremors wracked me. *Mate.* The word echoed hollowly; *killer.*

Bronc rasped my name, hands hovering inches away like I might break. Maybe I already had.

"Juliet." His voice cracked, blood dripping down his chest, mingling with mine on the floor.

I scrambled backward. Every inch of skin burning under fluorescent lights. Under his gaze. How could he look at me? My thighs smeared red, hands trembling where they clutched shattered ribs. *Filthy. Unclean.* The mate-bond might be ash now, but its ghost clung like oil.

"I didn't—" The words shattered mid-sob. "My fault. All because that cursed bite made me crave his hands while hating him."

Bronc sank down beside me, slow as sunrise against hellscape shadows. "You survived," he whispered roughly. "That's all that matters."

But it wasn't true. Not when every ragged breath stank of Harrison. Not when half of me still screamed *WHY DID YOU MAKE ME KILL YOU?*

I gagged, retching bile onto concrete.

Bronc reached out again. This time I didn't flinch as his calloused palm cupped my cheek. So warm, so wrong. I shouldn't let him touch what Harrison ruined.

His thumb brushed away blood or tears as he leaned forward until our foreheads touched. "Little Wolf." Broken reverence. No disgust, only grief.

I wanted to collapse into him—but how? When guilt gnawed deeper than any claw mark? When even victory felt like chains?

In the silence between us, Harrison's corpse kept laughing.

The sound that broke from me was all anguish, no relief. It was never meant to be like this. I was supposed to just save my mother. Swift. I'd let him bring me here, then I'd call for Bronc and he'd save me. But Harrison was ruthless. A step ahead. The bite. He made me need him. Crave him. He broke me and made me something dirty. I killed my mate. Even now, he'd won.

I bit back the cries of pain. And now my wolf was gone again. She must hate me to have left me again. The thought swarmed like flies, filled the empty, rattling spaces of me. They all would hate me. I hated myself. My heart clenched, making every breath feel tight and perilous. I didn't even notice my nakedness, the way I lay bare and exposed, covered in blood under the white fluorescence, beneath Bronc's terror-stricken gaze.

I thought he might never speak. The man I hadn't trusted. The man I'd just killed for. The man who found me in the arms of another man. How could he touch me? How could he—

"Juliet." My name, ragged on his lips, broke through the staggering press of it all. He reached for me again. But I shook my head. I was too dirty for him. He deserved better than me.

"Bronc," I gasped, "I thought—I thought—" The words tangled between us like a snare, impossible to untangle.

He knelt next to me. Looking at me like I was a feral animal he was too afraid to touch. That's what I was. "I know Little Wolf. You wanted to fix things." There was no accusation in his voice, only sorrow. He closed his eyes for a moment before he turned to look at the ruin behind us. "I'm so glad he's dead. And you're not."

"I hate him. He only ever hurt me, and he made me want it. Now, I killed him, my mate, so I have to pay. I HATE HIM! I HATE HIM! IT HURTS!" I turned in on myself, leaving Bronc to kneel beside me, helpless.

A thousand unnamed emotions split through my chest.

The slam of the door was the only warning we got. Bronc reached for his gun before he saw who it was.

Doc had burst into the room, taking in the sight with a single sweep of his eyes. "Goddamn," he muttered, and then he was kneeling beside us, checking my vitals with one hand while the other rummaged through his medical bag. He was all focus, no panic, even in the blur of motion. "You're lucky she survived," he told Bronc. "You're healing?" Pointing to the gashes on his chest.

Bronc nodded, eyes still on me. "I'm alive thanks to *her*. She..." he nodded to Harrison's body, then he asked, "What do we need to do?"

"Get her cleaned up, stop the bleeding, and get her the hell out of here." Doc picked me up and took me to the bathroom. Then he worked in silence as he turned on the shower and helped me in. When I was clean, he helped me dry, then took care of my wounds. He pressed gauze to my side and wrapped a bandage around me like a belt. Bronc came in to help and had to catch me twice when I flinched from the pain.

Everything felt frayed, like a loose wire ready to snap. Harrison was dead. I was alive. This was supposed to be a victory, but all I could feel was the crushing absence where my mate should be Even a mate I hated..

I looked at Bronc with sorrow-filled eyes. My shame was overwhelming me.

"Would it be okay if Doc carried me?" I asked, looking down at my hands.

Bronc lifted my chin and looked into my eyes. "Juliet. Listen to me. I love you. Nothing that has happened could ever change that. You will always be my beautiful Little Wolf, who blew into my life one day and turned it upside down. And I never want to live in a world where it's right-side up again. I never want to live in a world where you're not in it." He kissed me lightly on my nose. "Do you have anything that is decent that you can put on?"

I started sobbing again. "No, he didn't allow it."

"Don't cry, sweetie. Hold on." He got on his comms and asked Menace to bring a shirt and sweatpants out of his bag. In a matter of minutes, I was dressed in his clothes and wrapped in a blanket, drifting off.

"Stay with us, Juliet," Doc murmured as he carried me. He was in my ear. We were in the stairwell now, Bronc leading the way with long, sure strides. "Just a little further."

Every word sounded like it was meant to soothe, but there was a heaviness to them that made my heart clench tighter, sharper.

"We almost there?" Doc called from a floor below. I could see the door at the bottom, flames licking out around the edges. My breath hitched. We were out of time.

"Almost," Bronc answered, voice low, urgent.

It was the first time I'm been outside in two weeks.

I looked back, watching as smoke rose in furious black columns from the building we'd left behind. I saw the outline of Harrison's empire burning.

Bronc was at our side in a flash, steady hands helping Doc load me into the van parked just beyond the shadows. "Jet's ready," he said. He spared a glance at the fire blazing behind us, then turned his attention to the blanket-wrapped mess of me in the backseat. "Let's go home."

I could feel Bronc's eyes on me through the rearview mirror as we sped toward the runway. He was in the moment, all instinct and urgency.

The soft, distant thrum of the private jet's engine drew closer. Every second between us and the plane was time I had to think about what had just happened. The full weight of it settled over me like a bruise. I shivered against the numbness that followed, pressed my cheek to the cool window as Doc worked silently to secure my bandages.

The hangar loomed ahead. Lights lit the asphalt beneath us as we screeched to a stop, and Doc was at my side again, and then Bronc, half-dragging, half-carrying me as we rushed up the jet's steps. The pilot shouted a quick, "Hang on tight," and we were airborne in less than ten minutes, the ground nothing but a distant smear of red and black beneath us.

My mind was an unsteady pulse, full of half-formed thoughts and hollow beats.

How could Bronc want me after this?

The unasked questions tore at me like a hundred unanswered wounds. My wolf was still silent through all of it, and Bronc's steady presence was the only thing that kept me from breaking into a thousand unsalvageable pieces.

We'd survived. I'd survived. But at what cost?

Harrison was dead.

The wheels hit gravel with a jolt that shuddered through my bones. Home. Or whatever this place was now. My hands clenched against the armrest as Bronc's plane taxied across Iron Valor's private airstrip. Pine trees blurred outside the window like smudged watercolor strokes. Safe ground didn't feel safe yet.

"Stay with me?" I asked before Bronc could unbuckle his seatbelt. My voice cracked like dry kindling. "In our cabin. Keep everyone else...away."

He didn't ask questions, just nodded, his calloused thumb tracing circles on my wrist until my pulse slowed to match his rhythm.

By dusk, whispers of pack life buzzed beyond our cabin walls, distant laughter, engines rumbling toward the lodge, but none of it touched us. The fire crackled as Bronc handed me the tea he'd brewed too strong. I let it scald my tongue, anyway.

"The shifter woman from Illinois," I finally said, staring into the mug's murky depths. "She won't go back?"

Bronc sank onto the couch beside me. "No." His thigh pressed warm against mine. "Menace offered her your old apartment. Ma was happy to have a new pup to dote on." A beat of silence thickened before he added carefully, "Penny thinks she should stay close."

Penny. The name scraped loose something brittle in my chest. "And you think I should talk to her too?" I asked flatly.

His exhale ruffled my hair as he leaned closer. "She gets it." No pity there—just a quiet certainty that made my throat burn hotter than the tea. "Survivors shouldn't heal alone."

I didn't look at him when I whispered okay, but his low growl of approval hummed under my skin like static before a storm.

Later, fingers tangled in his shirt as moonlight pooled on our bedspread, I pressed my lips to his collarbone and let myself say it aloud: "I want your bite over Harrison's scars." The words trembled like prey in a snare—weak, raw. But Bronc stilled beneath me like lightning had struck him before rolling us sideways in one fluid motion until our gazes locked.

"Whenever you're ready," he rasped, pupils blown black with hunger even as his palm cradled my jaw like something breakable. "But we go slow." A promise and a warning rolled into one breath that smelled of bourbon and cedar smoke. Beneath it all, steel resolve sharp enough to gut any ghost that tried clawing between us again... even mine.

He fell asleep first for once; exhaustion pinching those stubborn furrows between his brows soft again in shadow light while my fingertips hovered over his throat where no scar would ever tarnish what we claimed next time—and there *would* be a next time soon as Penny helped me carve room for him there without drowning in old blood.

# CHAPTER 31

## BRONC

I'd been worrying about Juliet for weeks—four weeks since she'd come home hollow-eyed and brittle as winter branches. The news about her mother hit like a sucker punch: all that desperate risk she'd taken to bring her home only to find out she'd never made it back alive took a toll. But we'd had several conversations about how it had all come about, and she finally realized that she did not bear the responsibility. Her parents truly set all of the events in motion by bringing Harrison into their lives in the first place. Tragic? Yes. But Juliet bore none of the blame. For anything. The only guilty party in the entire horrible situation is Harrison Hastings. And we were going to fight our way through it.

Every night, I caught her staring at the scar on her shoulder like it held answers. The guilt ate at her. It was all for nothing, she'd whisper in the dark. I hated how she said it: not angry, just resigned, as if surviving Harrison hadn't cost her enough already. I was ready to put my mark back where it belonged.

But then there were the sessions with our pack therapist three times a week. Small mercies. She came back softer some days, less shattered at the edges—started talking about "processing" instead of drowning in silence. It didn't fix everything (nothing could), but hell if I wasn't grateful for whatever kept her from crumbling entirely. We had started going as a couple last week and for the first time, I felt... hopeful.

Our session today got to the meat of it. The counseling room was softly lit. It was far from where Juliet should have had to be, but for now, it was exactly where she needed to be. I listened as I sat next to her on the large comfortable sofa. "I'll do everything I can to help," Penny said. "But, Juliet, it's up to *you* to make that final commitment."

She sat across from us, comfortable and easygoing. Then she addressed me. "Her assailant turned their bond into a power play." She leaned forward, then added, "She needs to explore that power safely."

Accepting what happened was a part of moving on. This room felt safe. Small touches of healing décor sat around us. Peace lilies and framed quotes about faith and hope. That's what Juliet had. Hope. The sort that drew her out of captivity and straight into my arms, even if her time away had unleashed a part of her I'd never expected. That I didn't know how to protect her from. That I had no business wanting.

I stayed quiet, giving her room.

The soft scent of lemongrass made my wolf skittish.

"Omegas are rare, but I've had extensive training," Penny said, confidence threading through the timbre of her voice as she looked at me. "I've worked through what her assailant's manipulation brought out in her. She's going to be fine." Her understanding of my protective instincts and my stubborn nature was almost as strong as my mate's.

I nodded once, acknowledging the weight of what she was saying and the risk of leaving my alpha control unchecked.

"His manipulation of the claiming bite brought out her desire," Penny continued. "His sadism was his way of satisfying his needs. Her being an omega coincidentally answered her call. If she needs that from you, can you do it?"

I looked lovingly at my mate. "I am her mate, and her Alpha. Her needs come before my own just as the needs of this pack come before my needs. You need never worry about whether or not her needs will be satisfied. It is the reason I exist. As an Alpha, I am also predisposed to specific needs. I can temper those needs if I must. But dominance and demanding submission is my way. Dealing a degree of pain with pleasure is also my way. Knowing I have a mate who also finds her release and pleasure in those things brings me a great sense of pride and satisfaction. I loathe the method by which the discovery was made, however." I pulled Juliet to my side. Her tiny hand reached over and squeezed my arm.

Penny's smile lit up her face. "I believe we have had what we like to lovingly call a breakthrough this evening. I believe y'all are on your way to many happy and successful years as Alpha and Luna of the Iron Valor Pack."

## *Juliet*

That morning I was eager when I woke, amber light sprawled over the cabin's rough-hewn walls, so bright it nearly smothered us in gold. Bronc's warmth, the weight of his arms, grounded me in a way I hadn't expected, like something pure and new was possible. The past, this murky shadow I could finally see beyond, didn't seem to matter for the first time in longer than I could remember. It felt like waking from a fever, the edges of reality just as surreal and soft-focused as they'd been in the strange rush of revelations after yesterday's couple's therapy. That ache of shame that once dug beneath my ribs now replaced by a tremor of anticipation. The simple fact that I no longer had to look over my shoulder in fear that Harrison might finally have found me gave me freedom to breathe.

There were words that needed saying, and they tumbled out of me like confessions as I curled into him. Words that had seemed impossible even a week ago but were as simple and honest as air. "I'm ready for you to mark me, Bronc. Like before." And his sharp, sky-bright eyes told me he understood exactly what it meant.

Our breaths seemed too loud in the stillness, mingling with the creak of settling wood and the sharp cry of a bluejay. I didn't know what kind of new world I'd wake to after yesterday, but it felt like it might finally be ours. He pulled me in tighter, and I melted into him, forgetting myself the way only he could make me. The sun was warmer than it had a right to be in late November, but I didn't complain. Instead, I focused on the rhythm of my Alpha's heart and the possibilities this day opened up.

We lingered over breakfast, the scent of fresh coffee filling the cabin like an invitation. His big hands had wrapped around mine earlier, anchoring me in his wordless way while I spilled everything I'd kept locked away. "You sure you're ready, Juliet?" he asked, setting a plate of eggs and bacon in front of me. His voice was low and steady, charged with the quiet intensity that made my pulse quicken.

"After yesterday?" I met his gaze, holding it with a certainty I hadn't felt before. "Yes."

Penny's office was small and dim, the leather sofa warm and intimate. She'd looked me in the eye and told me the truth: finding pleasure in pain wasn't wrong for an omega. It actually wasn't wrong for anyone, but it was intrinsically natural for omegas. Shame and desire tangled like vines around my ribs. My words came haltingly, as if letting them out might shatter me. Bronc had been quiet beside me. Steady. She'd asked me how I would feel if I knew my Alpha shared that need, and I'd frozen, the room tilting around me. "Relieved," I finally whispered.

And now, my words rushed out like they couldn't be stopped, "I needed to hear that I'm not broken. That it's okay for me to need what I need."

The mug was warm in my hands as I curled my fingers around it. We were still on this strange frontier, exploring and pushing past the limits I'd not known before. It was terrifying and exhilarating. I set the cup down, voice trembling with new resolve. "I needed to hear that what Harrison did wasn't so different from many omega's stories. But finding out that it was shifter blood—not something damaged—that made me want pain...it opened my eyes." I took a deep breath, holding his gaze as if it were a lifeline. "But make no mistake. I hated that it was his touch that my body responded to. I told him that. There was not enough scalding water to wash the shame away afterwards. No matter how hard I tried. Everything was confusion and sadness. I never stopped thinking of how much I loved you and wanted it to be your hands on me. But at least now I understand that beyond his awful bite, I know my response was an honest one. I don't have to be ashamed because of something that was done to me."

The world outside was obscenely bright, the sun hanging defiantly high and white. There was an impossible lightness to it, and it almost matched the feeling inside me. I'd left so much of the past behind in that dim office.

"Juliet," he said, his voice like a magnet pulling me back to him.

"I thought I *must* be broken for finding pleasure in what he did." The admission felt like stripping myself bare. "Sick and ashamed. But now... Now I know it's okay. And yesterday, when I realized that you're the kind of Alpha who finds pleasure in giving pain... *controlled* pain, and I can trust you not to take it too far..." My words faltered as the intensity in his eyes stopped them short.

He stood, came around the small wooden table, and pulled me to my feet. His touch was as electric as ever, a surge through my skin that left me dizzy and wanting.

"I cannot wait to mark you again. To feel you in my soul." His words were a low rumble that made my chest tighten in the best possible way. "Since our bond was severed, I have been like a ship without a rudder, drifting endlessly at sea. Lost. With no way to find true north. Only you can bring me back."

"I want that more than I can say."

A smile broke across his face, a warm, genuine thing that melted any resistance that might have clung to me. He took my hands again, pulling me closer, our foreheads touching as he breathed the most beautiful words I'd ever heard.

"You'll have it. Tonight."

The way he said it made my skin tingle with anticipation. A promise as vivid as the sky outside the large living room window. His words echoed through me, resonating deeper than anything had in weeks. Maybe years.

"I need to make you understand," I said, needing to tell him everything before we both went forward. "Losing you was the most devastating moment of my life. When I woke up in that bed and reached for you through our bond and felt nothing, I thought my life was over. I knew I'd made the single biggest mistake of my life. At that moment, I knew what hopelessness felt like. It was like losing a limb."

"Darlin'," he whispered, pulling back to look into my eyes. His thumb grazed my cheek with the same care he might have given a butterfly's wing. "I'm gonna make you mine. Completely. Exactly like before, but more."

I felt a passion that ignited fierce and wild in my chest. Gripping his arms, I felt the heat of his skin and the promise in his pulse. My own pulse raced as I told him I'd take everything he had to give me. His eyes held my gaze. "I'm desperate for your knot, Bronc. I want it. I want everything."

He groaned low in his throat, a sound that shot straight through me. Then he caught my mouth with his, a fierce claiming that spoke all the words we didn't need to say.

The kiss seemed to stretch the morning out, bending time until there was nothing but the pulse of our heartbeats and the warmth of his hands threading through my hair. When he finally let me go, I was trembling.

"Tonight," he said again, a vow that left me breathless.

His arms wrapped around me, lifting me from the floor in an embrace so fierce and tight it was like he was afraid I'd disappear. It filled me with a kind of liquid warmth that soaked into every part of me.

I buried my face in his neck, inhaling the familiar, grounding scent of him. "We're going to be the Alpha and Luna this pack deserves," I said, and I heard the conviction in my voice. The certainty.

He set me down, his eyes burning with something raw and open that mirrored my own. "The way fate ordained."

I nodded, unable to find words, but they didn't matter. I could feel his confidence and love in my heart, meeting the wild hope in my chest.

"You know how I hate waiting." I whined.

His low laugh was a rumble beneath my palms. "You're killin' me, Juliet. But I want everything to be perfect. I have some preparations to make. There is a room in this house you haven't seen. I was waiting for the right moment. It seems that moment will arrive this evening."

My mind raced as I tried to figure out where this hidden room could be. Honestly, I'd not explored the entire large cabin. There hadn't been time for that. But my anticipation was heightened, and I felt light as air, reckless with anticipation, as if daring the world to hold us back. "I need to work on my curiosity. I never thought of exploring while I was home alone."

"It's not even hidden, sweetheart. You just didn't pay attention to the door. You'll see soon enough."

The day was a shimmering promise that sealed itself around the edges of the world until there was no past and no shame.

There was only Bronc and me and the bright certainty that tonight I'd become his, wholly and completely.

# CHAPTER 32

## JULIET

Evening settled like a second skin, clinging close as I stood naked in the room that promised both pain and redemption. I waited by the door, wearing the satin robe from the night of my first shift and nothing else, as he'd instructed. My breath was loud in the hush, a stark contrast to the slow, insistent beat of my heart. Shadows leaped on the walls, dark specters in amber light, while a mirror flung my image back at me—stripped of pretense, as raw and vulnerable as I'd ever been. A low table held what was left unsaid, scattered tokens of surrender and trust in the form of leather cuffs and silent promises. The tension was thrilling and familiar. It coiled tight beneath my skin and sang a song of need so sharp I couldn't draw breath without feeling it. I savored it. Leaned into it. And then he was there, and the very air shifted with his presence.

His eyes, bluer and more electric than I'd ever seen, locked onto mine and set every nerve ending on fire. He closed the distance between us with the quiet assurance of a man who knew exactly what we both needed. His heat was a tangible thing, radiating through the room and melting the last of my restraint.

"Juliet," he murmured, the word a promise and a claim.

I trembled beneath his gaze, but the uncertainty of earlier weeks was gone. There was nothing left but raw, urgent want. "I'm ready," I breathed, and it was as much a plea as a declaration.

"Turn around, mate."

My breath caught as his fingers grazed my back as he gently braided my hair. He expertly added an elastic to tie it off. He then reached around and loosened my robe and slid it from my shoulders.

"Exquisite." His breath was on my neck.

Still standing at my back, he placed his rough hands on my shoulders. "I don't know your limits, Little Wolf, so we will use the traffic light system. Green if everything is fine. Yellow if you're feeling unsure but want to continue. Red is full stop. If you use the word red, I will stop what I'm doing and we will not go back to it. So, be sure you mean red and not yellow. Do you understand?"

I nodded.

Bronc swatted my rear, and not gently either. "Words, Juliet. Do you understand the traffic light system?"

"Yes."

Another thing he continued. "You will address me as Alpha in this room. Do you understand?"

I could feel moisture growing between my legs. "Yes, Alpha."

"Good Little Wolf."

His praise made my stomach give a little flip.

"Look around this room. You can see there are several pieces of equipment that I will use on you, Juliet. If we go toward something that causes hesitation, use your colors."

There was only one thing in this room I wanted to avoid. He had one of those cross things.

"May I speak, Alpha?"

He tipped my face to his and gently kissed my lips. "Yes, my love. You may speak."

I pointed to the big X. "That. I don't want to use that. I'd rather never see that. If you don't mind. Alpha."

He left my side and walked past me. I just noticed he was wearing only a pair of tattered jeans that sat low on his hips and nothing else. His broad muscular chest and arms covered in ink made me want to do unspeakable things to him. God that man.

He then took the X that had wheels, wheeled it into a large closet and closed the door. He came back to me and gave me another sweet kiss.

"You'll never have to see that again."

"Thank you, Alpha."

As no-nonsense as ever, he continued.

"Let's get started. Give me your hand, mate."

He led me to a long padded bench with four lower areas that were also padded.

"Climb onto the spanking bench on your stomach, Juliet." My knees and elbows settled on the lower padded areas. Bronc maneuvered me until my butt was just off the back edge. Then he secured my thighs and arms to the bench with leather straps.

"How does that feel, Little Wolf?"

"Green Alpha."

I shivered with anticipation as his hand ran up my back.

I could feel the bruises forming on my wrists from where he'd tied me down to the bench, leather biting into my skin like a lover's desperate grip. My heart was pounding like a war drum, my breath coming in shallow gasps as he stood behind me, his presence heavy and commanding.

"You've been such a good girl waiting all day for your Alpha," he growled, his voice low and gravelly, sending shivers down my spine. I could feel the heat of his body radiating against my naked skin, the air thick with the promise of punishment.

He chose the riding crop with deliberate precision. It was beautifully embossed. I was certain it was going to bite when it hit flesh.

The first strike came without warning, a sharp crack that echoed through the room like a gunshot. I gasped, my body jerking against the restraints as the pain bloomed across my lower back, hot and electric. He didn't let up. Over and over again, the crop lashed my skin, the heat of each strike filled my body with both pain and pleasure.

"That's it Little Wolf. Take what I give you," he commanded. His growl somehow made my pussy clench tighter with need. "You're doing so well, mate."

He left no area untouched as he made his way to my tender thighs. I knew there would be welts, but I didn't care. The feeling was too delicious. The burn curled deep, making me want more.

"Please," I needed him to touch me, to make me come. "Please, Alpha."

He teased me now as the crop grazed my clit, as he dragged it up and over my butt. I cried out as I tried to lift my hips from the bench.

Then he was on me, his hands spreading my ass cheeks wide as he buried his face between my legs. His tongue was rough and demanding, lapping at my pussy like a man starved. His tongue cooled the heat that had gathered. I was teetering on the edge. He flattened his tongue and pressed in, adding just the right amount of pressure I needed.

"Alpha!" My body jerked and shuddered in the wake of the seismic orgasm that he had pulled from me.

Suddenly, he pulled me from the spanking bench quickly, unclasping my restraints, like I was nothing more than a rag doll, his hands firm and unyielding. My backside throbbed from the welts he'd left with the crop. My body was still humming from the orgasm he'd wrung out of me with his tongue. But I wasn't done. Neither was he. His eyes burned with a heat that made my stomach clench as he carried me across the room to the large wrought iron bed in the corner of the room, his muscles flexing under my weight.

He laid me down on the soft sheets, his gaze never leaving mine, and I could see the hunger in those blue depths, the raw need that matched my own. "You're mine, Juliet," he growled, his voice low and rough. "Every inch of you."

Trying to catch my breath, I could only nod as he stripped off his jeans. His cock sprang free, hard and thick, the head glistening with pre-cum. I ached to taste him. I wanted every inch of him to fill my mouth, needing to feel him in every way possible.

That was clearly not Bronc's plan. He pinned my wrists above my head with one hand. "Stay still," he commanded. "Tonight's not about what you want. It's about what I'm going to give you."

I whimpered, my body trembling with anticipation as he reached for the leather cuffs that were draped over the bedpost. He secured my wrists in them, the leather soft against my skin but unyielding, as I tested them, feeling the bite of restraint. My heart pounded in my chest, and I could feel my pussy clenching, even more wet and ready for him.

Bronc stepped back, his eyes raking over my body like he was memorizing every curve, every mark he'd left on me. "You're so fucking beautiful like this," he murmured, running a hand down my side, his fingers brushing over the edges of the welts he'd left. "Laid out for me. Helpless. Mine."

I moaned, arching into his touch, but he just smirked and stepped away, leaving me wanting. He moved to the foot of the bed and grabbed my ankles, spreading my legs wide cuffing them to the bedposts as well. I was utterly at his mercy, and the thought sent a jolt of heat straight to my core.

He climbed onto the bed between my legs, his hands sliding up my thighs. His touch was electric, the pleasure of it every-thing. "You ready for me, mate?" he asked, his voice low.

"Yes, Alpha," I whispered, needing him to touch me already.

He leaned down, his breath hot against my neck as he licked the spot where his claiming mark had been destroyed. "Good girl," he murmured, his teeth grazing my skin, just hard enough to make me gasp. "Now let me remind you who you belong to."

His hands moved to my pussy, his fingers sliding through my wetness, teasing my clit until I was writhing beneath him, begging for more. "Please," I whimpered, my hips bucking as he circled my clit with slow, deliberate strokes. "Please, Alpha."

Bronc chuckled, the sound dark and possessive, and then he pushed two fingers inside me, stretching me, filling me just enough to make me cry out. "Fuck, you're so wet for me," he growled, his fingers curling inside me, hitting that sweet spot that made my vision blur. "You want my cock, don't you?"

"Yes," I gasped, my body shaking with need. "Please, Alpha. I need you."

"You'll get it," he promised, his voice rough with lust. "But not yet."

He pulled his fingers out of me, and I moaned at the loss, but then he was moving down my body, his hands spreading my thighs even wider as he buried his face between my legs. His tongue was relentless, licking and sucking at my clit until I was screaming his name, my body trembling on the edge of another orgasm.

But he wasn't done. He slid a moistened finger into my ass. The unexpected intrusion made me gasp as he pushed deeper, stretching me in a way that sent pleasure shooting through me. His tongue never stopped working my clit, and when he added a second finger, I shattered, my orgasm crashing over me like a tidal wave.

I was still coming down when he moved up my body, his cock pressing against my entrance. He leaned down, his lips brushing against mine as he whispered, "You ready for me now?"

"Yes, Alpha, yes," I breathed, my body still trembling with the aftershocks of my orgasm.

He entered me in one slow thrust, filling me completely, stretching me. I cried out, my nails digging into my palms as he buried himself balls deep.

He groaned, his head dropping to my shoulder as he bottomed out, his hips pressing against mine. "Fuck, you feel so good," he growled, his voice rough with lust. "Every time it's like coming home."

He pulled back and thrust into me again. He knew my body so well. His hands gripped my hips, holding me in place as he fucked me. His cock hit so deep I swear I could see stars.

"No one will ever take you from me again," he growled, his voice low and possessive. "You are my mate. My Luna. And I'll never let you go."

I felt his knot swelling at the base of his cock, stretching me even more as he pushed into me harder, faster. My body was on fire, every nerve ending alight with pleasure as I felt myself falling apart around him.

And then he bit me.

His teeth sank into the flesh of my neck, right over the spot where Harrison had destroyed his original bite. I screamed as pleasure and pain exploded through me. My orgasm hit me like a freight train, tearing through me with such intensity that I thought I might pass out.

Bronc's knot locked inside me as he came, his cock pulsing as he filled me with his cum. He groaned against my neck, his teeth still buried in my skin as he held me close. Our bodies joined in every way possible.

When he finally pulled back, his lips were stained with blood, and I could feel his claiming mark burning into my skin. He leaned down and kissed me hard, his tongue sliding into my mouth, and I tasted my blood on his lips.

"You're mine now, as it always should be," he growled against my lips. "Forever."

I could feel our bond snap into place, stronger than ever before, and then I felt her—my wolf. She stirred inside me, awake and alive for the first time in weeks, and I gasped as her presence filled me.

Bronc smiled down at me, his eyes soft with love as he brushed a strand of hair from my face. "Welcome back, Little Wolf," he murmured.

I could feel tears pricking at the corners of my eyes as I felt the throb of his claiming mark on my neck. "I'm yours," I whispered. "Always."

He kissed me again, slow and deep, and then pulled back to look at me with a smirk. "Now it's your turn," he said as he undid my restraints.

I sat up slowly, feeling the weight of his knot still inside me as he maneuvered me until I straddled him. My hands brushed over the smooth skin of his neck as I leaned down and sank my teeth into him, claiming him just as he had claimed me.

He groaned beneath me, his hands gripping my hips as I bit down harder, marking him as mine. Our bond flared to life again, stronger than ever before, and I could feel our wolves intertwining inside us.

When I finally pulled back, I could see the love and pride shining in his eyes as he reached up to touch the mark I'd left on him. "You're mine," he whispered.

"And you're mine," I replied.

Our lips met again in a kiss that was filled with promise and love, and as we lay there together, our bodies still joined by his knot.

The bond of Alpha and Luna flowed throughout the pack, and in the distance I could hear the song of wolves rise in the night air.

# CHAPTER 33

## BRONC

The pack barbecue raged bright and festive against the Texas sky, a wild feast of smoke and chatter as my mind spun miles from the celebration. Everything weighed heavily after Juliet's rescue—tangled shifter knowledge, threats from her past, fires we'd lit to keep our people safe. I needed to huddle with the officers, map out the dangers crowding us, so I jerked my head toward the compound where church met, and they followed me inside. Wrecker dove right into our latest intel. "Hastings Pharma lab data's gone. Wiped from every system after the accident," he said, the word slick with irony. We all knew it was no accident. My hands fisted, but my heart eased some. Harrison was dead, the rest of them as well. Juliet was free. Still, my gut churned remembering all that had happened.

Big Papa rose from the rolling chair and stepped over to the huge wood table where Wrecker sat. "That fire took out all of their shifter research?" His calm eyes found mine. "Everything?"

Wrecker nodded. "Lila Chen was their lead shifter researcher, and she bought it with the rest of them. So did their guards. We made sure there was nothing left to pick up. No trace of anything for anyone to find." The tightness in his gravelly voice showed the weight of what we'd done, how dangerous those few weeks in Central America had been.

But there was still a bigger danger waiting in the wings. "We didn't plan on Charles Hastings," I said. "Him bein' on his deathbed makes it more and less complicated, though."

"Couldn't risk a hit on him at this stage. We can make it look like natural causes," Wrecker said.

"If his ramblings ever turn into more, we may need to. Took us too long to find Harrison. He clearly had too much time to further his plans." Menace leaned back, tapping his fingers on the table. His face was unreadable, but I could tell he wanted this behind him. "We won't make the same mistake with the old man."

"Juliet's doing better?" Big Papa's voice had the soothing tone of a lullaby.

"She's tough," I said, my words more of a growl. "We all knew she could be feeling some PTSD, but fuck if that little wolf hasn't been more resilient than any man I ever knew. She's a fighter through and through, and she'll be damned if she lets that fucker stop her from thriving as Luna of this pack. I know she'll have some bad days, but she's not gonna let anything get in her way. And I'm gonna be right beside her, making sure she's okay."

Menace nodded. "You got yourself a good one there, Alpha. We're all lucky to have her as our Luna. And we've all got her back."

I cleared my throat and stood, my emotions raw. "I'd have never gotten her back if it weren't for every one of y'all. You are exactly what brotherhood is all about." I looked down and tapped my knuckles on the table, trying to keep myself in check.

Sitting back down, I got us back on to the business at hand. "So, there's still a goddamn mess we need to deal with before it comes to bite us all."

They all knew what I was talking about. They'd helped track the financial drain that had hit my business.

"I'm, of course, talking about the theft of funds from the motorcycle shop. What started out as small amounts seems to have grown to larger ones. This has been going on for well over a year. And until Juliet, it was happening without notice."

Wrecker moved his tablet aside and leaned forward, clasping his massive hands together. "Juliet's expertise is possibly going to draw out the mastermind of the entire operation. I honestly don't believe it's some lower level patched in guy."

Arsenal shot me a concerned look. "So this could be more dangerous than we think."

The stark truth of it carved itself into me. She'd walked right into another shitstorm. My chest tightened at the thought.

"We can handle this," Big Papa said. "We've handled threats from other packs and other clubs before. They aren't targeting Juliet. They're targeting us. She just happened to be the one to take the lid off the pot of shit they're stirring. We'll be meticulous as always and find out who's got beef with us, and then we'll take their fucking heads off."

The man had a way with words. I couldn't help laughing. "Easy enough."

"Then there's Sawyer." Menace's voice broke through the quiet that settled after Big Papa's statement.

My eyes shot to his. We'd pulled Sawyer out of the same hell as Juliet, but there was a nagging doubt in my mind, an uncertainty I couldn't shake. "Is she adapting?" I asked.

Menace took a deep breath. "She's doing okay. You know how these things are. Takes time."

"You keeping her warm at night?" I shot back. There was an edge of humor in my voice, trying to lighten the mood that threatened to drown us.

"Fuck you," Menace said, but there was a smile in it. "It's a process." He rubbed the back of his neck and leaned back in the chair.

Big Papa laughed. "More of a process for some than others." He fixed Menace with a look. "She planning on staying?"

"Hell if I know." Menace shook his head. "I didn't think I would care."

Damn, he doesn't want her to go. "Why isn't she reaching out to her pack?"

He looked at me, then down at the table. "She's a little like Juliet in that way. Might not be telling me everything."

It confirmed what I'd been afraid of. Her past could come back to bite us in the ass, and it could be as dangerous as what we were already facing. "That girl has secrets. Could be trouble."

"She's okay," Menace repeated, more to himself than to us.

"Juliet should befriend her. We need to know what's up," I said, watching for his reaction. "Last thing we need is trouble with renegade packs. I know you don't like it, but Wrecker's gonna need to do a full background."

"She's gonna stick around, so maybe you'll see how wrong you are." Menace looked annoyed by the prospect of us digging. "She's not a risk."

"That'd be a goddamn change," I replied. It was his turn to scowl, and I fought the grin that wanted to spread across my face.

The topic shifted again, this time back to business. Back to the gnawing concern that twisted my gut. "Let's focus on this mess at the motorcycle shop. We need a plan," I said, leaning over the table. "What if this hits us harder than we think?"

Wrecker's eyes met mine, cold and sharp. "We've got some theories. Leads to follow."

"I want more than theories," I said. My voice was sharper than I intended.

"We need time to figure it out." Menace was all business again, arms crossed over his chest.

"How much time?" I asked, knowing it was a dangerous question.

"Give me two weeks. We'll know more by then. We can give a full report when it's locked down," Wrecker said. "I'll keep on it. You know I will."

"Two weeks. Then we take action, whether we know or not." I needed this resolved, needed the weight off my shoulders, and Juliet safe again. I dismissed the others, gave them their assignments, my mind still running with the possibilities.

They left one by one, leaving me alone in the church room. I sat at the table for a long minute, my eyes staring at nothing, my thoughts lost in the chaos of it all. We'd survived so much, had so many successes, but this felt different.

My head was still spinning when Menace walked back in. I hadn't expected him to come back. "Sawyer really worth the trouble?" I asked, as he sat down again.

"She's worth more than you think," he said, his voice low, intense. "I'm not gonna screw it up."

"Never thought you would," I replied, and this time there was no bite in my words.

"She's stickin' with us," Menace murmured, almost to himself. His words told me he believed it, that maybe I should, too.

I sat in the silence, knowing we didn't have much of it left. "We need to get a handle on all this. Before it's too late."

"Gonna find out a lot in two weeks." He stood and moved toward the door. "Let's hope we're ready."

"Goddamn, let's hope." I felt a strange mix of relief and tension as I stood and followed him.

I stepped out of the quiet church meeting, leaving behind my whirling thoughts and a crisp agenda for the pack's survival. Returning to the backyard barbecue was like stepping into a Texas Indian summer, full of life and heat and something wild I'd tried to keep at bay. Juliet's laugh caught on the breeze before I saw her, burning away the doubts I'd fought with all week. This woman who chose me and our mad world—my reckless girl who'd seen too many dangers at her heels. I found her near the crowd, under strings of twinkling lights. She looked up at me, radiant, and all my defenses cracked like the sound of the first shot in a war. Her small wave and adorable smile shattered me. Pack women and children surrounded her, and she lovingly gave them her time.

She'd handled becoming a part of this world with amazing resilience. I'd explained to her that the supernatural world was vast well beyond shifters. Mapping out that the governing structure of the Supreme Council of Supernaturals consisted of representatives of Shifter Kings, Vampire Kings, Witch Queens, and even a Demon King and Angel King, almost knocked her for a loop. But yet again, she took it all in stride. I hadn't yet informed her that her best friend from college was a vampire princess, but I couldn't keep that from her much longer. I had a feeling Lucia would be on our doorstep any day now.

The aroma of grilled meat mingled with smoke floated under the deepening sky. I let it wash over me, trying to shove down the sense of doom that had followed me since we'd brought Juliet home from Costa Rica. She was my world, the wild heart I couldn't live without, but trouble stuck to her like glue. I knew better than to underestimate what we were dealing with. My jaw clenched as I moved across the lawn.

Everywhere I looked, pack members were wrapped up in the freedom we'd fought to protect. Groups stood in clusters with food and drinks, smiling and alive under the fall sun. Someone let out a whoop as a beer spilled, and I caught myself almost smiling at the sound. My gaze landed on Juliet again. Her golden hair fell like a halo around her shoulders in the light. She was the same storm that hit me the day we met at that bus station, and my soul burned to keep her even while I braced for the next gust of wind. I made my way over, determined to hold her like I could keep the whole damn world at bay.

Her eyes lifted as I neared, that untamed spirit blazing from her in waves.

"Was starting to think you weren't gonna make it back to the party," she said, hands resting on her hips like she'd been waiting just for me.

"Wouldn't miss it," I replied. I pulled her into me, drowning in the rightness of it. Her laugh spilled through the night again, and I drank it in like a man starved.

We swayed slow to the muted music, her warmth flooding through me. I held her like a lifeline, and she molded against me, fierce and mine in a way that still shocked me breathless. Her scent of ginger and sugar wrapped around me, drowning out everything else.

I knew there was a storm coming, but life was like that. We'd face the storms as they came, and we'd stand strong. "Juliet," I said, and there was a warning in it I didn't want to put there.

She looked up at me, all defiance and certainty. "What is it, Bronc? You've got that dark look in your eyes."

My words stuck in my throat. Couldn't bring myself to break her confidence. Not yet. "You an' me, we got this. No matter what's coming, yeah?"

Her laugh stopped short in her throat, and her eyes grew serious, deep like the Indian summer sky. She felt the weight of it as much as I did.

"What are you so afraid of?" she asked, words quiet between us, cutting through all the noise.

"Just thinking about what's ahead. Whatever trouble that's connected to the shop. I'm hopeful it will be a minor dust storm and not a tornado. Either way, I need you to be on your toes."

"I'll be ready."

I could feel the confidence of her words flow through our bond. She was trying to convince us both. Her fire had me wanting to believe it, too. My hand moved to her back, pulling her closer, like holding her tight enough would erase all the other threats from our world.

Our bodies kept time beneath the twinkling lights, moving as one, pushing the worst possibilities to the edges of my mind. Her confidence poured into me, and I let myself get lost in it for one fleeting moment. My gaze drifted over her shoulder, finding the rest of the pack caught up in their celebration.

Menace and Sawyer danced close together, lost in their own orbit. They looked young and damn near happy, and it gave me a sliver of hope that this could work. Maybe we could all make it through without anyone getting hurt. Sawyer's past haunted her the same way Juliet's had, and I wondered if Menace would hold on as tight when the rest of it caught up with them. I hoped she wasn't bringing more trouble to our doorstep.

Juliet caught my glance, followed it over to the two of them. "They look happy," she said, resting her head against my chest.

"For now. Wonder how long it'll last."

"You're awfully pessimistic tonight, Bronc." Her voice was teasing, but I could feel the worry behind it. She knew how these things could go. She'd lived it firsthand.

"They gonna be a pair?" I asked. My lips brushed her ear, voice low and rough.

"They are if Menace has anything to say about it." She gave a soft laugh, and I could feel her breath against my neck, could feel the certainty that she had in them.

"You like her?" I asked, knowing how much hung on that answer.

"I think she's more like me than we realize. She's stronger than you think."

Her words twisted in me, cutting with the sharp edge of truth.

"Y'all should have a girl's night or somethin'." I wanted her to agree, wanted her to see the possibility of danger the same way I did.

She stilled, and for a moment, I thought I'd gone too far. But then she looked up at me again, eyes sparkling in the light. "Maybe we will," she said. Her hand traced a path across my shoulder.

We were caught up in each other, our dance lost in the noise of the celebration, but the weight of it never really left me. My eyes found Skeeter standing off to the side, his phone to his ear.

He talked in low, urgent tones, and I wondered who was on the other end. Sounded like he was talking financials. He'd have to be watched more closely.

Juliet watched the line of my gaze, knew the thoughts churning in me. Her voice broke through the thick silence I couldn't shake. "We've dealt with worse," she said. "We'll deal with this too."

It pulled me back to her, to the moment, to the wild hope I tried to keep from slipping away.

"Couldn't do it without you, girl," I said. And I meant it, every goddamn word. She kept me sane and insane all at once.

The evening was turning dark, the stars out bright and fierce against the night. She was in my arms, everything I never knew I needed, everything that terrified me to my core. I pulled back slightly, just enough to look her in the eyes again, to tell her the thing I needed her to hear.

"Brace yourself," I said, my voice rough with the gravity of it all. "I love you, Juliet. Don't forget it."

Her hands were in my hair, and she was fierce and alive and mine. "I'm never forgetting that."

She drew me back into her, and we moved in a slow circle, the music and lights spinning around. I didn't know what the future would bring, but this moment, this connection—it made everything else worth it.

And for now, that was enough.

She gave me a little wink as she stepped away, pulling me along. "Hey, my wolf wants to come out and play." Then she started to run as she tossed over her shoulder laughing, "Catch me if you can old man."

"Just wait, Little Wolf. Your Alpha is hot on your heels."

# EPILOGUE

## SAWYER

"So then Lily says, 'Just because you're the Alpha, doesn't mean you can leave your dirty clothes everywhere!'" Juliet's laughter mixed with Maddie's in the soft, inviting space of the living room. I perched on the edge of the sofa, nursing a glass of wine and the loneliness of my secrets. They were trying to make me feel welcome, like I belonged. But I'd been here before, letting my guard down only to have it slice me open when I least expected it. The cabin was so different from the sterile hell Dane had locked me in. Warm lighting played off hardwood floors. Furnishings that looked like they were out of a magazine surrounded us. This should have been comforting. But every gentle question Juliet asked about my past brought my shoulders tighter. Every time Maddie switched the conversation away, I saw the worry in Juliet's eyes. They were so kind to me, and I was lying to them about who I was and what I'd run from.

I forced a smile as Juliet handed me a fresh glass of wine, the dark red reflecting against the plush pillows like drops of blood. "Thanks," I said, trying to sound grateful. "This is really nice. I'm not used to... nights like this." My voice felt foreign in my throat, words I should have said but never could. I took a sip to mask the hesitation.

"Well, Sawyer," Maddie chimed in, a teasing lilt to her voice, "you better get used to it if you're going to stick around here." Her eyes sparkled, her short dark hair catching the light like a halo.

Juliet nodded, her expression softening. "We want you to feel at home. Like you're part of the family."

Home. Family. Things I'd only known in name, but not in heart. "I really appreciate it," I said, not trusting myself to say more without my voice cracking under the weight of falsehoods.

Juliet sat next to me, her sincerity palpable. "So, what's your story, Sawyer? Where are you from?"

The question hung in the air like a sniper's bullet. I had my answers prepared, the same evasive maneuvers I'd used on Pearl and anyone else who got too close. "Up north," I said vaguely, studying the glass in my hand as if it held some revelation.

"And you decided to stay in Texas?" Maddie pressed her curiosity in earnest.

I shrugged, my shoulders tensing. "I needed a change," I said, keeping my tone light, my insides a churning mass of fear and memory. I could still feel the cold steel of the lab, the clinical detachment of Dane's voice as he charted my responses, the gnawing realization that I was little more than a tool to be wielded by my father's ambitions. Distance, I reminded myself. Distance is your friend.

Juliet must have sensed my discomfort, because she shot Maddie a look. "It's okay," she gentled. "We don't mean to pry."

"It's fine," I lied, hating how easy it was becoming.

Maddie leaned back, changing gears. "So... Bridger, huh? He's kind of a big deal around here."

At the mention of Bridger, something flickered inside me. It was the same flutter I'd felt when his hazel eyes first met mine, like he could see past the lies and straight into the truth I'd hidden even from myself. "Yeah," I said, the word laced with more meaning than I intended.

Maddie raised an eyebrow, catching the subtle shift in my voice. "He's a good one."

I felt heat rise to my cheeks and hid behind my glass. "He's been so great. Since he broke those chains off of me..." my voice trailed off.

"Oh, shit!" Maddie just remembered he is who brought me out of the lab. "I'm so sorry, Sawyer. I'm such a dumb bitch. Forgive me for reminding you of that."

"Maddie, it's okay, truly." I gave her a genuine smile. "Bridger was the light in the midst of that awful darkness."

Juliet seemed pleased with my admission. "He's a good guy," she agreed. "Loyal. Like all the pack." There was an emphasis in her words, a hint that she knew more than she was letting on.

They continued to chat about Bridger and the other pack members, the rhythm of their voices soothing despite my anxiety. My mind was a battlefield of thoughts, each more volatile than the last. How long could I keep this up before they discovered the truth? The guilt of deception was heavy, a weight I didn't know how much longer I could bear.

I should have left it at that. Let them carry the conversation without me. But some reckless part of me wanted to hold on to this fragile sense of belonging, even if it was built on lies. "I heard Bridger used to be in the military," I said, testing the waters.

Maddie nodded, jumping at the chance to share. "Yeah, Delta Force. A lot of the guys in the club are former special ops. And now they run Dairyville. It's pretty amazing."

I absorbed this, realizing just how far outside their world I was. Not only did I lack their camaraderie, I was a shifter of unknown blood. An outsider among outsiders.

"Don't worry, Sawyer," Juliet smiled. "You're one of us now."

The knock at the door cracked through Juliet's laughter like a gunshot. My spine stiffened before I even registered why. Must have been some primal instinct honed by a year of running flaring to life. Juliet sprang up with a squeal, nearly tripping over the wine bottle Maddie had cracked open an hour earlier. "You have no idea who this is," she gushed, eyes bright as she flung the door wide.

The woman standing there wore danger like perfume. Dark curls framed a face sharp enough to draw blood. A Russian accent dripped from her lips as she said, "Hello, kotyonok." Juliet threw herself into the woman's arms, babbling about missed calls and chaotic months while my pulse thrummed in my ears. Lucia Kozlov. The name slithered through my memories whispering of Bratva dealings at college parties, Juliet oblivious to the blood running colder than ice in her friend's veins.

"Maddie, Sawyer—this is Lucia!" Juliet beamed, none the wiser that she'd invited a predator into their midst. Maddie offered a polite nod, but Lucia's crimson-lined gaze snagged on me like claws. "Sawyer?" She repeated slowly, head tilting in a way that made my ribs cage my pounding heart. "How... interesting."

The room suddenly felt airless. "Bathroom," I blurted, chair screeching as I stood. I didn't look back as I fled down the hallway. Her stiletto heels clicked behind me in a languid staccato.

She let me yank her into the shadowed corridor by her designer sleeve, amusement playing on her lips as I hissed, "Don't."

"Savannah," she purred my actual name like a curse. My knees locked to keep from buckling as she leaned in close enough for me to smell lies and bergamot tea. "Your father has bounty hunters crawling through every territory." Her nail traced the frantic jump of my pulse. "Poor Dominic must feel so... jilted."

Ice flooded my veins. She knew everything.

"I'm not going back," I choked out, clinging to fraying resolve as Bridger's face flashed behind my eyes—his laugh against my hair last week when he thought I was just another rogue wolf needing shelter. Not a crown princess in hiding. Not collateral in an alliance binding the Eastern wolves to Dominic's Midwestern throne.

Lucia clicked her tongue. "Running from an arranged marriage? How delightfully human of you." But something flickered in her glacial stare; a sliver of old camaraderie from winters when we'd built snow forts while our fathers carved up cities between sips of vodka.

Juliet's voice trilled down the hall—"You guys okay?"

I didn't breathe until Lucia stepped back with a smirk sharp enough to flay skin from bone. "Enjoy your little rebellion while it lasts, volchitsa," she murmured silkily over my trembling silence—a promise and a warning tangled together.

The crown felt heavier than ever as I followed her back toward wavering laughter and flickering trust, toward Bridger who couldn't know his stray smelled of autumn forests and king's blood.

But when Lucia glanced at me over one shoulder? For half a heartbeat...

She winked.

# ALSO BY DEX

Kazimir made his first appearance in the bestselling Wolves of Iron Valor MC series. If you have somehow missed any of the books in the Wolves of Iron Valor MC series, you need to read them all!

Bronc- Book 1, Menace- Book 2, Wrecker- Book 3, Big Papa- Book 4, Arsenal- Book 5, Gunner- Book 6 and Doc- Book 7

Be on the lookout for the Nickolay: Kozlov Family Vampires Book 2 SOON!